Praise for
JUDY COLLINS'

Shameless

"A wonderful book, a compelling inside look at the music business by one of its most enduring (and endearing) heroines."

—Erica Jong

"Writing that is reminiscent of the songs and ballads Judy Collins has composed, literate and poignant. . . ."

—M. R. Aig, Newark *Star-Ledger*

"I felt as though I knew all of these characters. Talk about déjà vu! Sweet Judy has another kind of hit on her hands."

—Graham Nash

"SHAMELESS is a tale of survival, of one woman's emotional and spiritual odyssey through the music industry."

—Sue McClure, *Nashville Banner*

"I almost missed my flight because I got so engrossed in reading SHAMELESS at the airport."

—Susan Cheever

"Rock with a mystery beat. . . . Judy Collins' glimpses into the workings of the rock-'n'-roll scene—the drugs, the groupies, the sudden fame—have the ring of truth."

—Sandra Dallas, *Denver Post*

"Steamy. . . . SHAMELESS exposes rock's underbelly."

—Naomi Freedman Serviss, New York *Newsday*

"Judy sparkles as a Renaissance woman. Now she turns to fiction—and with a vengeance. SHAMELESS has lots of plot, character study, unearthly fantasy, and earthy sex. Judy comes across!"

—Ned Rorem

JUDY COLLINS

SHAMELESS

POCKET STAR BOOKS
New York London Toronto Sydney Tokyo Singapore

This book is a work of fiction. Names, characters, places and incidents are products of the author's imagination or are used fictitiously. Any resemblance to actual events or locales or persons, living or dead, is entirely coincidental.

A Pocket Star Book published by
POCKET BOOKS, a division of Simon & Schuster Inc.
1230 Avenue of the Americas, New York, NY 10020

ISBN: 0-671-89234-7

First Pocket Books paperback printing June 1996

10 9 8 7 6 5 4 3 2 1

POCKET STAR BOOKS and colophon are registered trademarks of Simon & Schuster Inc.

Front cover photo by James McLoughlin

Printed in the U.S.A.

For Clark,
forever

Acknowledgments

My gratitude goes to the following people: Lynn Nesbit, a great friend and a great agent; Tom Miller, my editor at Pocket Books, with love, for your patience, good humor, and sensitivity; Louis Nelson, my life partner, for his support during the long haul; Max Margulis, for the thoughts on voice that appear during the singing-lesson scene; Beverly Camhe, for her encouragement; Jack Romanos, for his enthusiasm; Joanna Schwartz, my wonderful assistant, for her insights and for being there.

"Was it a vision, or a waking dream?"

—*John Keats*
Ode to a Nightingale

1

"The nude—that's the one," I said. It was the fifteenth of March, the day before the trouble started. I stood at the window watching the rain outside pour like a waterfall of tears.

"Maybe you should make it a head shot," my friend Julia said. "Crop the nipples."

Sixteen stories below, the headlights of taxis shone their golden bars of light down the sparkling, drenched length of Central Park West. The street was a river. "I like it the way it is," I said.

Julia frowned at me from under her black, elegant eyebrows. It was a look I had photographed many times. "It's sort of like the Venus de Milo, with arms," she said. "Or Venus on the seashell, without the hair." She smiled and fingered the edges of the C-print.

"If I ever lose my faith in you," sang Sting. The walls of my office were covered with framed platinum albums—Sting, Paul Simon, Madonna, U2, and Julia Clearwater, among others. Julia was a legend, one of the great singers of our time. She was also my best friend.

Julia was barely five feet tall but I knew she was as strong as an ox. She was dressed this afternoon in a white satin blouse and black cashmere pants and sweater, and her body beneath the satin spoke of a lifetime of discipline and good nutrition. Julia wasn't a smoker; I was. Her mouth was a red rose, her hair a tight black cap. She was beautiful and delicate, if you consider a Rodin bronze delicate.

"The nude feels *outrageous* to me," Julia said, her voice soaring an octave easily, to emphasize her point. Sting's voice faded and strains of a Brandenburg Concerto came over the speakers. Clean orchestral music flooded the room with trills and arpeggios that seemed to match the falling rain, running to keep up with the drops gliding down the windowpanes, sliding down the walls in reflections.

I moved to the worktable and put my arm around Julia's slender shoulders. "You're the queen of rock and roll," I said. "You can be as outrageous as you want."

Her white satin blouse reflected light onto her high cheekbones and into her big brown eyes. The lightning flashed.

"This may be the last image of my career," Julia said. "Do you think my audience should be encouraged to remember me without my clothes on?" she asked.

"Why not?" I said. I was sure Julia would change her mind about retirement.

The wind howled suddenly, like a terrified soul. A clap of thunder boomed and Julia joined me again at the window. The trees in the park below danced like thin puppets in the wind and dark clouds hunkered close against the skyline. All of a sudden I thought of Dr. Ernest Wheeling, my horrible old shrink. Then I remembered I was having dinner with my lover, Edward, and life wasn't so bad.

"It's a great picture," Julia admitted, chewing her lip.

"Thanks," I said, coming back to the present. "I know you won't be sorry."

Julia's nude picture would be a wonderful addition to the new collection of my photographs—*Catherine Saint: Portraits*. Lately my work often appeared in *Life, People,* and *The New Yorker,* vivid color pictures and severely edited versions of stories of rock-and-roll events around the world along with interviews with Whitney Houston and Madonna, Cher and Natalie Cole, Sting, Bruce Springsteen, Garth Brooks, k.d. lang, and Paul Simon. My articles and pictures also appeared in *Vanity Fair, Rolling Stone, Esquire,* and the music industry magazines like *Spin* and *Billboard* along with the work of Duane Michaels, Annie Leibovitz, Linda McCartney, Bruce Weber, and Francesco Scavullo.

Most of the photographs for the book were finished—Sting, Elton, Cher, Barbra Streisand. Some would be added, like the pictures of the Newborns, the hot new rock-and-roll band I was scheduled to photograph in the coming week. The deadline for *Portraits* was a few weeks away, so Julia's picture would be ready just in time.

I began collecting prints, stacking rejects in a pile on the worktable. Blue, my Himalayan cat, frightened by the loud noise of the thunder as it roared through the room again, leapt up on the worktable, meowing as he looked at me for an explanation of the tumult, then settled down on a cleared space. Just like me, I thought, to have cat hairs on my prints and piles of work in my office, waiting for someone to help me get through it.

My friend smiled, slipping into a purple raincoat and tucking her short black hair into a little hat that hid her shining helmet of hair. "I suppose I will be known from now on as the *naked* queen of rock and roll," she said, giving me a hug. "See you tomorrow? Same time, same place?"

Julia and I had a regular Wednesday date for tea

at the Mayfair Regent. "Right," I said. "That is, if both of us haven't drowned."

More thunder sounded, shaking the windows as if to tear them out of their white wooden frames. Julia gave me a hug and I returned it, feeling her whole body, slender, familiar. I saw her to the door, Blue padding behind me, glad to leave the noise of the storm behind as I punched the alarm to seal out strangers and other rainy-night apparitions.

Back in my office I gazed once more out at the rain. It gave no signs of letting up. I pulled out a Pall Mall from a crumpled package on the desk, lit it, and blew smoke rings into the raindrops on the wall, trying to catch the falling, silky patterns in my fingers as I listened to the Brandenburg Concerto play. The weather made me somehow sad, nostalgic. My thoughts moved from the beautiful nude portrait of Julia to the famous and infamous people immortalized in my pictures—and then, to the past.

I have had highly vivid dreams all my life, but lately they have seemed to take on a life of their own. Dreams of shame mingled with dreams of ecstasy and joy. I thought about where my rocky path had begun and how far it had taken me—to an amazing place, a good place.

Or so I imagined.

2

I dream of an infinite sky, a universe devoid of stars and yet sparkling with a savage darkness. In the middle of this bright blackness stand two huge figures, out of proportion, tossing a blue-and-white ball between their upraised arms, like figures playing at volleyball, laughing. I can see that the thing they toss between their arms is the world, oceans blue and mountains white.

But upon its round surface a black death covers the earth. Wind, water, fire and stone, storms of sand; the rivers are dying and the whales have no song. The planet spins through space, battered like a woman who can't recall her face, but who remembers the way she used to shine, rivers in the sun, herons on the wing, crickets singing, a million forest birds, the sea a mantle green like a banner of hair around her shoulders.

As though in a trance upon a verdant road, I meet a man who says he's seen a flock of nightingales; the child beside him speaks of the sound of rain like silver angels' wings. I hear my own voice singing, "You can't sink a rainbow in a world that is green . . . you can't sink a rainbow."

5

3

MY JOURNEY FROM KANSAS BEGAN WITH A PASSION for singers and hard country rock and roll when it was clean and squeaky and full of nothing more sinister than marijuana and left-wing politics.

I was born and raised on a ranch a hundred miles from the nearest big town. Topeka was a mirage of intersecting streets, twists of trees in sudden gulches, and an occasional cluster of cottonwoods by the shining thread of a stream. I remembered—even at fortysomething—the taste of green rivers and cherry Cokes on rare visits to the pharmacy on Main Street in Topeka.

At night my brother, Ben, and I listened to Elvis and the Beatles on the radio from New York, coming through on the clear midnight air via the shortwave radio I had pestered my father to buy me for my sixteenth birthday. Ben was two years younger than I was and loved to play guitar. Ben and I spent a lot of time with our cousin Marty, Aunt Cheryl's son. Gene was my father's brother, and his ranch was the next over from ours. We kids spent lots of time together; we were like children in the same family. Gene had been killed when I was twelve.

On Friday nights, when school was over for the week, we would sit around my brother's room and sing all the songs together that we learned off the radio. Marty always knew all the words to the songs, and my brother Ben could play the chords.

Ben was a good artist. He drew portraits of Elvis and Mick Jagger on the back of his old, beat-up National guitar in bright, vivid colors. He tried to teach me to draw and to play the guitar, and although I couldn't get the hang of either, at eighteen I developed a passion for choral singing, inspired by my high school music teacher. He arranged a voice scholarship for me at a small college in Missouri, where I quickly discovered that, in the absence of my teacher's faith in me, I had no real talent for music.

When Jim Morrison came to sing at the local music club, I became first a devoted fan, then a groupie. To my father's horror, I quit school, left my cousin, Marty, and brother, Ben, and my mother and father behind, and followed the Doors to New York on what was left of my first-year scholarship money. I took a room in the Village and began haunting the music clubs till four in the morning every night of the week.

~

One cold December Saturday, as I watched the Doors at the Fillmore East, I knew I wanted more than anything in the world to write about them, to describe Jim Morrison's raw, haunting melodies and the syncopated, driving rhythms of the band. I knew the only way to do that was to get a newspaper to pay me to follow them around. I contacted *Thunder and Lightning,* a newly formed national music weekly out of New York, and talked them into paying me bus money, hotel costs, and a little loose change. In a dozen cities between New York and Hollywood, where the Doors wound up their first major club date at the Whiskey-A-Go-Go, I wrote about life on the road with a rock-and-roll band. By the end of the summer, with a dozen articles in print in a New York paper, I was a music journalist.

That fall I took a Greyhound bus back to New York and rented a one-bedroom apartment on Bleecker Street where I put my suitcases and my typewriter. In a week I was working part-time for *Thunder and Lightning* and doing freelance for every other music newspaper that would print my articles. I spent my nights at the Fillmore East, listening to Janis and Jimi; by day I roamed the Village, with its winding alleys, tree-lined streets, antiques vendors, record stores and bookstores, flower children and slices of the Hudson River glimpsed between warehouses, the river's light reflected in the cobblestones near the docks, oceangoing liners pulling in from ports in every part of the world. I knew I had hungered for those streets, those views, all my life on the plains of Kansas. I sat in front of my ancient Olympia typewriter, doing testy little articles for *Crawdaddy* and *Rolling Stone* about the music I couldn't really admit in print that I adored. I wanted to sound jaded, uptown (as though I were slumming from Fifty-seventh and Fifth). I wrote sharp reviews, smart reviews, cutting-edge reviews. "Crucify it even if you love it, just make yourself a reputation," was my motto.

But rock and roll fed me. It kept me from thinking about the rent I hardly made, and the fact that I was not fulfilling the dreams my Kansas parents had for me.

I bought leather bags for cheap from Braun's village shop, purses tooled with flowers and birds; I filled the one shelf in my tiny kitchen with blue-rimmed Mexican glasses from Fred Leighton's storefront and added his imported white wedding dresses to my meager wardrobe. I swore off the rough-out boots and sweater sets from my Kansas wardrobe and gave them away to a thrift shop that raised money for St. Vincent's Hospital.

The Village, alive and Bohemian, was a good place to live in the mid-sixties. It was human-scale and human-oriented. Nobody had much money. Everybody shared a love of things unsuburban and lived in an arty, friendly way. I hung out in a funny little pastry shop on the corner of Greenwich and West Tenth that smelled of almonds. Allen Ginsberg, Bob Dylan, Peter Yarrow, Marianne Faithfull, Anaïs Nin, Judy Collins, and the Kingston Trio all stopped in occasionally for croissants and good dark coffee. The *Village Voice*, housed in an elegant building facing Sheridan Square, was open to the public. You could walk in the front door and talk to the editor of the music section just as if he were your neighbor.

The Village was a good home for a girl from Kansas with stardust and rock and roll in her eyes.

* * *

For a few years I scuffled to become a professional. There were the weird, lonely trips to Europe where I stayed in fleabag hotels and chased Eric Clapton and the Cream and Mick Jagger around on tour, trying to get them off in a corner for a word or two for a private "interview" about anything in the world they might like to say, then either print it in the current magazine I was working for or sell it to one of the big ones. A big break came when I got to Altamont and interviewed a dozen Hell's Angels, as well as the crazy who committed the murder. *Time* magazine published the piece. I listened to every retro band from here to Seattle and back, heard them play in funky basements and smoke-filled theaters, poked tape recorders in their faces, more and more depressed that as the years went by, kids in rock and roll knew less and less about the English language and what was going on in the world. That was what did it.

My father had taught me to appreciate language. Needing a change, I bought a good Nikon with all the fancy attachments. I read books on photography, signed up for a course at the New School, and began to get the hang of taking pictures. Pictures, I found out, did speak louder than words.

Then my grandfather died, leaving me the money nobody knew he had. It turned out Grandpa Wilson had seven acres of land he had kept after he sold the rest of his little ranch, and they found oil on it. He sold the land for an ungodly amount of money to Shell Oil, and then died, leaving me, his favorite granddaughter and primary heiress, a small fortune.

I didn't have to work anymore, and that was when I started to make it as a photographer. Them that has, gets, my father always said, and I learned it was true. My family was well enough off on the ranch in Kansas, but now I could give them back some of what they had given me, and I made them a gift of a four-wheel-drive truck, bought my brother Ben a round-trip ticket to Florence to study sculpture in the Renaissance tradition, as well as a new Martin guitar and a pair of genuine hand-tooled boots from a special place in Santa Fe.

After all those years of struggle, I had to work harder than I ever had in my life—but I was officially a photojournalist.

4

Wednesday dawned clear and bright, the rain and wind of the previous night having scoured the sky into a polished jewel in the clean air. I felt good about the big story on my work that had come out in *Rolling Stone* that month. There were articles in every major magazine and paper; my career was booming.

The music scene had changed from my early years writing about the Doors. Now it was often mean-spirited, not the lighthearted enterprise in which I wrote my old zinger-stinger reviews. Now big money, even the Mafia, replaced the little club owners and the innocence of the rock-and-roll flower children I once knew. Spikes had replaced buttery-soft finishes on guitars, the metal ring of electronics replaced the sound of unamplified instruments.

I stayed above the tide, thinking kind thoughts amid the hard rain, riding on a wave of self-improvement, getting to the gym where I worked on my thighs by lifting weights and swimming laps in the pool between afternoon video shoots and long evenings at the Hard Rock Cafe and the rock-and-roll clubs.

The business of music was good to me in my late thirties, in the midst of the youngsters dressed in safety pins and leather thongs, I outfitted my well-trained muscles in contemporary-looking clothes, bought on sale from stores on the Upper West Side with names like Charivari, To Boot, and Handsome Is Unisex. (Charivari means headache in Italian!)

My eyes teared up from cigarette smoke and my voice was often hoarse from shouting at record executives over the roar of the currently popular rock-and-roll pretenders to various thrones. I shot pictures of stars and would-be stars and drank Diet Coke. At the health club, I sat in the steam and sauna to detox from NutraSweet.

A girl from Kansas, with blond-streaked hair and lungs scarred from twenty-five years of cigarette smoke, a little too old for the parties at Tatou and the Ballroom, I supposed I had made it to the big time. After all these years I was a pro, although I had a lingering feeling that the music business had become my gigolo, the lover I hadn't yet had.

The day Julia and I selected her nude photograph for my book I knew nothing of Renaldo Pierce. The mysteries of his personality and the synchronicities of our mutual pasts were hidden to me.

Feeling successful but overwhelmed, I finally realized I needed an assistant. I called Ellen Carney, the wife of my friend Stan Shultz, the entertainment agent and lawyer. I had known Stan and Ellen for years—I had introduced them, in fact.

Ellen was a self-motivated woman who ran an employment agency placing production assistants in the music business. Although she was not a particularly beautiful woman, Ellen knew how to dress, how to emphasize her looks. She was naturally dark-haired, but often got her hair frosted at the most exclusive salons. She loved what she did and was very good at it.

Twenty years before, Ellen and I had gone off together on a wild vacation to the Bahamas on which we drank rum punch, basked in the sun, went scuba diving and sail fishing, played tennis—and hunted for men. I remembered the vacation with Ellen so long ago, before she had married Stan . . . long nights and rum drinks, lethal in spite of little pink umbrellas poking out of their innocent-looking surfaces—days of sailing, laughing, burning in the sun, Ellen seducing men she had picked up and me reading novels and spreading sunscreen on my body. At that point I already knew Stan, but I hadn't yet introduced him to my friend Ellen. I had been seeing a few men then, none of them long-term material, in fact hardly even short-term. I was working hard on the business of becoming a photographer and writer, and Ellen was engrossed by her new business.

We had shared a wonderful adventure; it still made me feel giddy when I remembered it. Even on vacation Ellen managed to look as though she had stepped out of a high-gloss printed guide to the Bahamas, while I appeared to have been rolled, fully dressed, in the sand.

Over the years, Ellen and I had drifted apart as I had gotten closer to Stan, and especially to Julia, who never really liked Ellen.

"I need somebody who will pay my bills," I had told Ellen yesterday. "They also have to answer phones, manage the office, help me in the darkroom, and maybe feed my cat if I'm out."

"It sounds as if what you need is a wife," Ellen had said, laughing. "I think I've got someone you'll like. I'll send him over tomorrow. His name is Renaldo Pierce. He's English, but he's a U.S. citizen. He'll be perfect." She paused. "By the way, are you coming to dinner next week?"

Ellen and Stan were hosting a Grammy party for Stan's new clients, the Newborns, who were probably going to walk away with a dozen Grammys this year. My boyfriend Edward's daughter, Malinda, was in the group. I told Ellen I would be there and that I was going to shoot pictures of the band the next day at Stan's request.

"Say hello to my husband for me, will you?" Ellen said. "We hardly see each other lately." I knew Ellen was being only partly sarcastic.

Renaldo was scheduled to arrive at ten, so I worked in the darkroom for an hour, printing pictures of Paul McCartney, Randy Newman, and Cher for articles that were due. I felt incredibly disorganized.

My housekeeper, Flora Irving, brought me a cup of fresh coffee at ten o'clock, telling me a young man was on his way upstairs. Flora is the steady, kind woman who looks after me, telling me every so often I should get married. Flora also cooks, which I do not, and Flora knows where all my stray clothes have vanished. Without Flora I could not boil water or find my house keys. I was sure she was sent by some generous goddess. Today she was dressed in a periwinkle blue skirt, a white cotton blouse, and black, low-heeled shoes. The sides of her shoes poked out from large bunions on both her feet.

In a few minutes, Flora ushered in a good-looking man in his twenties who introduced himself and settled into one of a pair of antique, purple-velvet-covered wing chairs. He looked toward me brightly as I sipped coffee and studied his face. We talked for a few moments and then I studied the brief history of his life contained in his résumé.

It was quite a story: London to New York at fifteen, part-time work while going to school, gofer, do-everything jobs; then he became an American citizen. NYU for his bachelor's degree; some time in retail, business management for one of the big lingerie companies on Seventh Avenue, clerk at a major firm specializing in entertainment law.

I glanced up from my reading occasionally to scrutinize Renaldo's face. He was calm under my gaze, good-looking to the point of gorgeous, young enough to blush, and probably straight. He had bright blue eyes, light brown hair, wore polished cordovans, a beige suit, a white shirt, a Windsor knotted tie of dark blue silk that had tiny white whales in an all over pattern, and a pair of Elton John glasses, their frames sprouting wings that tipped over his coffee cup when he drank.

I liked what I had read and who I was looking at. Renaldo appeared to be the kind of an individual you would trust with your dog, your keys, your china, your checkbook, your secrets, and your husband.

I didn't have a husband. I was married to my work. I just had a boyfriend, whom I sometimes called the sex machine—Edward Valarian.

Blue jumped up on Renaldo's lap with a meow of what I suspected was approval.

"Get down, kitty," I said, but Renaldo shook his head. "I like cats," he said, "it's all right." Blue purred and rubbed. Renaldo's suit would look Himalayan by the time he left. "You know," he said, looking at me intently, "I really want to work in the music business." In my office, with the view of the park and the reservoir out the window, Swedish ivy trailing out of hanging pots, the sun painting the Chinese rug lemon yellow, photographs of a crowd of stars, and a desk piled with papers and contact sheets, Renaldo had indeed fallen straight into the center of the music business.

I continued reading. In the middle of the second page was a name that took my breath away.

My God, I thought with a shiver. Listed as a reference on Renaldo's résumé was the name of Dr. Ernest Wheeling—the shrink I had seen for over a year. This was the Ernest Wheeling whose power had invaded my life. Our parting two years earlier had been bitter and unprofessional. Except for an appearance in front of a cold-faced judge in court, I hadn't seen Wheeling since. I shook myself, as though I had seen a ghost in the sunny room. "How do you know Dr. Wheeling?" I asked slowly.

"Well," he said, seeming embarrassed, "I was having some personal trouble."

"I don't mean to pry—" I started to say, but Renaldo continued speaking.

"No, it's all right. I don't mind telling you," he said. "I went to see Wheeling for counseling a few times, about my having trouble with relationships. He said I should get married."

That was a switch, I thought. Wheeling had considered all families toxic and marriage a decadent institution, best left in the past. He said, "The family that stays together, decays together."

"And did you get married?" I asked. Was I trespassing? Surely I should tell him what this doctor had done, how dangerous I thought he was.

"Oh, no, I decided not to." He smiled wanly. "I broke up with that girlfriend," the young man explained. "Dr. Wheeling was one of the psychiatrists on my health-care plan," he said, sensing my next question. "The insurance paid for my sessions."

I relaxed. This was only a strange coincidence. "Are you still seeing Dr. Wheeling?" I asked.

"Oh, no," Renaldo replied. "But after my therapy I worked for him a couple of weeks. That's all."

I excused myself and stepped from the office into the hallway. Julia always calls this particular corridor "the separation of church and state." There was a small Prince Albert table under a mirror in the foyer, and I removed a pack of Pall Malls from its wooden-sided drawer, pulled out a cigarette, lit up, drew smoke into my lungs, and stood by the open front door, blowing smoke into the hall. Thinking. A fresh scent lingered in the air, some traditional aftershave, like the one my dad used.

I felt a tenderness for Renaldo's youth and his soft English accent, an older-sisterly feeling toward him. I let out the smoke, gazing at the prints on my walls—

a dazzling Frankenthaler with brilliant reds and oranges; a Ken Noland, bars of rainbow light; a black, etched woodcut by a South American artist. I took a couple more quick drags on the cigarette and stubbed it out in the ashtray I kept in the hall.

I wondered if Ellen knew about Dr. Ernest Wheeling. After the suit, I had begged Stan not to tell Ellen anything about my troubles with Wheeling. I felt an irrational shame about what had happened, although it had not been my fault; and my suit, after all, had been successful. If Renaldo wasn't seeing Wheeling at the moment, surely there was no reason to cloud Renaldo's happy mind with darkness. I decided I would keep my knowledge about Wheeling to myself.

Shutting the front door behind me, I moved back through my apartment into the office and gave Renaldo a quick smile as I picked up his résumé. Blue was still sitting in the young man's lap and Renaldo was petting him, clumps of gray-blue fur between his fingers. I excused myself and stepped into the den next to the office, where I shut the connecting door and dialed the phone number of Renaldo's second reference, a lawyer named Ellis. We discussed Renaldo's credentials. Ellis told me he was sorry to lose Renaldo and would take him back in a minute at a higher salary if he ever changed his mind about the legal business.

I would hire him. This guy seemed great. I went back into my office and named a salary, to which Renaldo nodded enthusiastically. "You're hired, then," I said, "that is, unless you have a dinosaur living with you or something." He smiled. "I'd like you to start tomorrow."

"I'll do a great job for you. I promise." We shook hands and I felt as though a burden had slid off my shoulders. I walked Renaldo to the door and waited while the elevator hissed open. When he stepped in, he looked right at home in the glass and wood-inlaid interior of the elevator, just as he had in my office.

5

I dream of Edward. We are making love high above
the sea; below us the waves crash, battering up
against the tall cliffs of stone that lead from the sea
up to the lush, long, waving emerald-green grass
in which we lie, our bodies naked in the sun, our
faces turned to each other. My head is thrown
back and I feel the thrust of Edward's body in mine,
the point of flesh against my bones, against my
center, till my completion, like a wave of salt water—
reaches my cheeks, flushing my face.

Edward stays in me even as I moan and arch my
head back, his hands roaming my body as my
pleasure spills over us, crashing on the rocks below;
he rolls me over so that my body is on top of his,
my hair brushing his face.

The feel of his body in mine is full and pointed.
Suddenly thrusting himself out of me, he pulls my
lips down to his chest, so that my lips are moving
on him as he strokes my hair and begins to rock
me back and forth across his body. I feel him flow
into my center as our voices call together, the sea
pounding beneath us, our bliss a total and fulfilling
ecstasy.

6

I punched number 1 on the telephone key pad and waited expectantly.

"Hello," Edward said, picking up his direct line almost before it rang. Bella, his secretary, must have taken an early lunch.

I wondered, not for the first time, how Edward could put so much sex and warmth into "Hello." "Were you expecting me or some other beautiful woman?" I asked.

Edward was one of the most successful financial managers in the business, a founding partner at Winter, Valarian and Marshand. He had been handling my money for the years we had been together. Edward took care of me in physical as well as financial ways, but despite the loneliness I sometimes felt on nights when we were apart because of our work, we had decided not to live together, both being independent. Yet I was committed to Edward and I assumed he felt the same way about me. He was a terribly attractive man and I knew he must have his choice of delectable women. I was thrilled he had chosen me.

Now he reassured me, laughing a deep, provocative laugh. "For me, there is no other beautiful woman, you know that."

Edward was handsome all right, with curly black

hair and a wicked, twinkling smile. I heard the lust in his voice even over the phone and knew my lover could turn me on with just one lewd suggestion. I imagined him now, sitting in his office, looking out the windows at the magnificent view of Central Park that spread beneath his desk, his trim body, five foot eleven, and his charismatic looks reminiscent of Jack Kennedy or Richard Burton.

Edward's voice purred when he spoke to me. He aroused me skillfully and often.

Since first meeting Edward, three years before at a party at Julia's, I hadn't looked at anyone else. On our first date, he confided that his only marriage—to his high school sweetheart—had ended after she got a face lift, a tit job, liposuction, and left him for her yoga instructor. I assured him I already knew yoga.

Edward was also the father of a twenty-year-old daughter, Malinda. Malinda had recently joined the Newborns, the hottest band to hit the scene since Nirvana—the next step after grunge. I had already photographed them and would again soon. I told Edward I was about to shoot the Newborns for *Vanity Fair*.

"Tell her to call me, okay?" Edward spoke in the wounded tone of a parent whose child only calls when she needs money. Malinda did not need money. She was rolling in clover.

I was close to Edward's daughter; closer, I thought, than her father in many ways. Malinda had come to me for help a few months after her father and I had met. She had dropped out of school in Vermont after an unwanted pregnancy and an abortion. She confided in me, she told me, because she didn't trust her father and her mother was running a health spa in Maine with the yoga instructor and wasn't around to talk to. She had looked awful, underweight, ill, and stressed. I sent her to Victoria Friedman, my internist, who told me she suspected clinical depression.

Malinda came to stay with me for a few weeks while I did everything I could think of to help her. I put her up in my guest room and we shopped and went to the movies and talked for hours on end when Edward wasn't around. When the three of us chanced to be together, Malinda barely spoke to her father. She explained her attitude by saying that at the moment she hated all men.

Hair may not be the most important thing in a woman's life, but it counts for a lot. I took Malinda to my salon for a trim for her wonderful lemon-blond hair. I treated her to some new clothes, buying things I knew would complement her tall, lanky figure. Malinda gained a little weight and began to look healthy, blooming, more like a nineteen-year-old than an old, worried woman. She went to self-help groups that I didn't ask about and she didn't tell me about. She alluded to troubles, but quickly began to look brighter and younger than she had.

Whenever Edward came over, Malinda would manage to be busy somewhere else.

I encouraged Malinda's talent and she began to sing in the clubs around New York City and get some local attention.

Although she never identified the father of her unwanted baby, we seemed to talk about everything else. At the end of the summer, I took my friend Stan, who is one of the best agents in the business, to hear Malinda in a little club in SoHo where she had started singing once a week. Stan and Edward knew each other and were friendly, too. We had dinner, Stan, Ellen, and I, and watched Malinda's show. Stan was bowled over and arranged for Edward's daughter to audition for a new band he was representing.

By now Malinda was splendid-looking and healthy, long-legged, blond, and beautiful. She got a job with the new group, which was called the Newborns, packed up her sorrows, and went on the road with the rock-and-roll band. There were four other kids in the band, all men; in a few months the Newborns were the hottest band in the business.

In spite of the odd distance between father and daughter, I assumed Edward was proud of his offspring.

"I'll say hello," I said. "And you should probably see her. They're staying at the Plaza, you know." He knew little about his daughter's new career, and I assumed he wanted it that way. Edward grunted. "You know they've been nominated for almost everything there is," I continued. Malinda and the rest of the Newborns would be big winners at the Grammys in a few weeks, with even a modest bit of luck.

"Of course I'm proud of her," Edward said, sounding defensive.

"Hasn't Stan retained you to do their taxes this year?" Stan usually told me everything, and had hinted there were problems he wanted Edward to sort out for the Newborns—problems having to do with their overseas touring and all the money they were suddenly making. There were always financial problems with rock-and-roll bands.

"That's right," Edward said, smiling. "You don't think it's a conflict of interest, do you?"

"Not if you don't," I said. "But I still think you ought to see Malinda while she is here." Edward's voice was sounding annoyed, and I went on. "I have some news," I said, "I need to talk to you."

"What is it, Catherine?" Edward said now, regaining the sexy voice that had never ceased to turn me on, with its slight New England accent—he was from Connecticut—its hint of pirates and briny blue seas, and I heard the lure of it now, felt the luster of the sex, the best I had ever known. Edward lowered his voice now to a deep molasses pitch. "I can't wait to get my hands on you," he said, almost murmuring.

I decided to tell him about Renaldo.

"Tell me again, I love to hear it," I laughed and went on in spite of the sudden wetness I felt between my legs.

"Are you going to come to my office and make love to me on the rug?" he asked. We had done that on our first date, with the moon pouring through the floor-to-ceiling windows that overlooked Central Park.

"How I wish," I said, yearning for it. "Later, perhaps." The sex with Edward was hot and steamy although I was painfully aware of my biological clock ticking away. I had always wanted children, but Edward had made it clear he was not the type to start a second family. I had decided to settle for great sex.

"Gotta go," Edward said suddenly, as though he had been interrupted by someone entering his office. "My next appointment's here."

We arranged to meet for dinner at eight at our favorite midtown Italian restaurant, Enrico's.

Content, feeling an anticipatory sexual glow, I searched the cluttered desk, looking for my house keys and pushing the cat gently out of the way. As I glanced at the pile of unopened mail, a letter caught my eye.

The envelope was manila, about seven by four, with no return address. *Catherine Saint,* it said. Apparently this one was hand delivered, as there was no stamp either. *Personal* was written in the bottom left corner.

I slit the innocent-looking letter open. Inside was a note scrawled in a hand I did not recognize.

"No matter where you are, don't think you can hide from me—I am going to find you and kill you, Catherine."

2

I dream I see the dark, tall figure of a man lurching out of the shadows along the edges of a dense woods. He is covered in heavy, black fabric soaked from the rain that falls steadily. He moves through the mist, gliding through the hovering fog, searching, pausing, moving on along a row of houses at the edge of the woods. The man's face is a white, masklike blur behind a dark hood. He smokes a cigarette, plucking the damp residue of paper from his lips; at his heel a dog follows, as dark and shadowed as his master, fangs bared and showing dull white in the half light. They hunt together, the dog of despair and the hooded stranger—the dog sniffing under doors, scratching at gate posts, the man gazing from the eyes set deeply in his haunted white face, past the fences, into darkened windows. Finally they come to an open, unprotected gate and slip stealthily across the wet grass to the narrow opening of an unguarded door, their figures disappearing in the darkness, leaving only the descending silence as the rain and fog enclose the house.

There is a deep quiet for moments while I hold

*my breath, and then, from the house, the sound
of screams, a scuffle of footsteps, panic in the faces
of those who reach the window, me among them,
looking out toward the woods as blood runs down
the side of the house, thick and black as oil in
the rain.*

8

My hands were shaking, my breath shallow when I redialed Edward's number. His private line was busy.

I hung up and dialed Stan's number. How did this letter get here? I wondered. Many of my friends—the famous ones—had received notes like this, but this was my first.

"Stan," I said, trying to keep the hysteria out of my voice, "I've received a threatening letter. It says somebody wants to kill me." I felt cold as ice.

"Call the police," he said immediately.

"Just for a letter?"

"Right. You haven't ever had a threatening letter, not since I've known you," he said. "Maybe it has to do with the *Rolling Stone* piece. Some nutty fan getting all excited."

I fingered the manila envelope. "Shit!" I said, dropping it on the desk. "I've smudged the fingerprints, if there were any."

"Call the police, okay?" Stan said. "Even though it's probably nothing, you'll feel better. And, Catherine, you'll be here in an hour, right? The band is looking forward to the session. You'll get to work, you'll forget all about this craziness."

I knew he was right. Lawyer and friend, Stan was always practical. That morning I had a date to take pictures of Malinda's band at Stan's high-rise office. "I won't leave town this time, that's for sure." The year before, after the incident with Wheeling, I had gone home to Kansas, afraid of staying in my apartment alone. There was no response from Stan, and I went on. "By the way," I said, "I just hired a new assistant Ellen found for me."

"Good," Stan said.

I detected what I thought was a note of sarcasm in Stan's voice. I knew he and Ellen had been having some trouble in their marriage. Stan hadn't said much and Ellen hadn't told me a thing, but I sensed unhappiness. Their kids, both at Harvard, had floated out of their lives.

"Catherine," Stan said, "why don't you have your new assistant screen your mail from now on? That way, if there is anything else that seems strange or unusual, she can send it to me. I *am* your lawyer!"

I told Stan my new assistant was a he. "By the way, Stan, Wheeling's name was on this guy's résumé," I said. "Did you ever tell Ellen what happened, what Wheeling did to me?"

Stan replied with concern in his voice. "Of course not, Catherine," he said with energy. "I promised you I wouldn't. Also, I would never divulge information about a client to my wife. Or anyone else, for that matter."

"Sorry," I said, "I thought not, but had to ask." Uncomfortable, I went on. "Anyway, there seems to be only a vague connection. And I hired Renaldo, anyway." I fingered the manila envelope.

"Maybe you're getting over the whole thing with Wheeling at last, Catherine," Stan said. "See you at GTO in an hour?"

GTO, Greater Talent Organization, was the agency where Stan presided over a prestigious stable of rock-and-roll artists. He booked concerts and oversaw the careers of new bands as well as established solo artists on the recording and concert circuit.

"Right," I replied, "thanks, Stan." I hung up the phone, feeling tension flow out of my body. I put the manila envelope on the desk and called information for the number of the nearest precinct, which was at Eighty-second and Columbus.

I spoke to a police officer who asked me some questions that I thought were a little personal—like "What does your husband do for a living?" And then, "Oh, you don't have a husband—do you live alone?" After a few exchanges with this somewhat annoying man, I said I would call him again if there were any further developments and hung up. I felt better, but it was mostly from hearing Stan's soothing voice. Yes, I would have Renaldo open all my mail. The police I could do without.

I grabbed my coat, camera bags, and purse, shouted over my shoulder to Flora that I would be back around six, and headed out the door for GTO, stopping only to pet Blue on the way out. The big Himalayan looked forlorn, his black and gray fur silky under my fingers as I leaned down to pet him. "I'll be back soon, precious," I said, shaking the thought of the threatening note out of my head.

I hopped a cab and told the driver to take the drive south through Central Park.

9

*I dream my cousin Marty stands on Main Street in
Topeka, his face thin, his eyes as big as saucers.
On his feet are shoes with holes in them, in his outstretched hand a tweed, worn, ragged hat in which
are three or four quarters and a dollar or two. His
clothes are ripped, his face is dirty, he is un-
shaven, scary.*

*I cross to the other side of the street, while other
pedestrians on the sidewalk turn to look at our
two figures. He is following me, crying my name out
as I pass the shiny windows lighted for the
holiday.*

*"Catherine, save me—Catherine, it's me, your
cousin! Catherine, help me!"*

*I know I can't help this poor soul. I have tried,
we have all tried. I know this gaunt figure is a
ghost, because two years before, Marty had died a
drug addict's death.*

*"Catherine, PLEASE," the figure pleads. I turn
to look again and then start to run, lengthening
the distance between us. I sob for breath, my feet
pounding on the pavement as he slows down and
finally stops, a pale, pathetic figure on the eve of
Christ's holy day, waving his empty arms in his
tattered coat.*

10

Inside his office at GTO, Stan pulled me into his arms for a bear hug. I returned the hug and Stan gestured toward a crowd of rock-and-roll musicians.

"Catherine," said Malinda, "I'm so glad to see you. How are you?" From a gangly waif, she had become a tall, beautiful, blond bombshell. She gave me a hug too.

"I'm good," I said. "And your dad's fine, he sends his love," I said, hugging her back.

"I'll call him later," Malinda said softly.

The assembled rock-and-rollers made a powerful image, with their long hair and torn clothes.

"Catherine," Stan said, "I don't think you know the rest of the group—Fred, Z-Train, Reed, and Sahid. This is Catherine Saint." Stan was right, I hadn't yet had the pleasure.

"Hi," I said with a smile. Four heads flopped back from where they were sitting on the couch, and eight eyes looked at me through lots of multicolored hair.

"And I don't think you've met Max Freestone," Stan said, gesturing to a huge black man standing by the door, "the Newborns' manager."

Max looked more like the group's bodyguard or a sumo wrestler. Three of the boys would have fitted into Max's custom gray flannel Armani suit. His shirt was Turnbull and Asser. The tie was Versace, the shoes were Bally—clearly the biggest size they made. He looked ominous, but when he smiled it was a beautiful day; you were glad to be on his side, glad he was on yours.

"Hi," I said, sticking out my hand. Anyone who could get designers to make clothes in those sizes was a force to be reckoned with. Nobody would mess with the group when Max was around.

I looked from Max to the Newborns. The stars had their chewing gum going and wore their hair wild. Their jeans were appropriately frayed at elbow and crotch. The male members of the Newborns looked like ragamuffins. They might have been auditioning for a movie of the week, or posing for a Benetton ad. Although they looked harmless today, in the show I had seen on television, the males in the Newborns had looked like four Draculas from an Anne Rice novel. Without their makeup they were not so scary. I assumed they all had eyes—although there were none to be seen behind the hair and glasses, except for Malinda's, which were blue and sparkling. Malinda was a gentle soul, but it was hard to tell whether the rest of the band members would be cretins or a pleasure off the stage, under the torn and chic fashions they wore on their emaciated limbs. On the other hand, I knew compliments could defang even a rock-and-roller of the most vicious type.

"The MTV special you did last month was wonderful," I told them sincerely. Five voices mumbled thank you and I thought it might really be shyness that kept their noses tucked into their various shirt collars, or what was left of them among the tatters.

I started pulling out lenses and rolls of color film, unzipped the pockets on my leather bag, tweaked knobs on my light meters, and snapped open my small portable umbrella, which I clipped onto the fold-out aluminum tripod. I pulled out the round golden light reflector and placed it on a chair under the group so that it softened the Newborns' lovely young faces, or what I could see of them. Almost at once, the kids began jockeying for position with the camera, even at this early stage of their stardom preening like peacocks. Young, but far from amateurs. As they moved, I began to get a better look at them.

Malinda was looking even more beautiful than when I had last seen her, with her angelic, dramatically beautiful face and body. She had apparently fully recovered from the troubles of the summer before. She had grown even more vibrantly female with her clear, sharp features, pale creamy skin, wavy waist-length lemon-blond hair, wide smile, and long lean legs. Malinda had become a total sexual turn-on.

Reed had tightly curled blond hair that waved wildly all around his handsome face. He exuded a sexual energy that was explicitly, powerfully male. On the MTV concert I had seen, Reed had come across as a powerhouse of energy. He had a raucous, golden voice and muscles that were shaped, toned, and shining under the torn denim of his clothes. I was sure he must travel with a personal trainer as well as his own NordicTrack, which I could envision in his room at the Plaza.

Although the posh Regency on Park Avenue was often the favorite of the entertainment industry, Reed had insisted that the group stay at the Plaza, a swanky establishment in the middle of Manhattan overlooking Central Park, because it had been the hotel Brian Epstein chose for the Beatles when they did their first American tour. Donald Trump was a fan of the Newborns and had given them the better part of an entire floor overlooking Central Park for their three-week stay in New York.

Sahid had a dark complexion, and his long, curling

halo of black hair could not disguise the face amidst its tangles; he had big, liquid gold eyes swimming in very white orbs, framed by incredibly long, thick lashes. He had a classic face of pure beauty. I wondered if just this once I would break my rule of never sleeping with the talent.

Z-Train was an ebony-black African-American. His dreadlocked hair was studded with blue beads and bits of red stone that sparkled around his face, hiding most of his high cheekbones and wide eyes. Around his neck he wore silver and gold necklaces braided with crosses, amulets, totems, fetishes of bone in the shape of every animal from the forest, as though he were American Indian as well as African-American. If he thought he needed luck, it looked as though Z-Train wasn't taking any chances.

All of the group seemed young and healthy—except Fred, who appeared to be vibrating slightly. With dyed silver hair and a wired, shaky leanness, Fred looked terrible. When I got a good look at the face behind the wild mop of hair, I hoped the problem he was having was hunger.

And doubted it.

These kids had experienced gigantic success. Shortly after Malinda joined the group, Stan had urged them to make a "garage" album—cheap and brilliant. It had become an overnight, platinum smash, released by Vertigo Records. They had just finished a sold-out world concert tour. Each of these shaggy-looking children was making a fortune.

"Sahid," I said, starting to snap pictures informally, "where are you from?"

"I'm Turkish, actually," Sahid replied in a mellifluous voice. Under the clouds of hair his eyes did not leave my face. I let the shutter roll, trying to avoid staring at Sahid's open invitation. I limited the sex to my lens. Sahid was now making love to my camera.

"I saw you on *20/20*," he said, smiling. "You were great." The interview with Barbara Walters two weeks before had changed things for me. I saw people noticing me even in the streets of New York. I knew I had arrived.

I thanked him and concentrated on getting good pictures of the group.

"The Newborns have what it takes," Stan had said when Malinda joined the group. "I'm going to make sure they are as famous, and as well-paid, as they deserve to be." Stan had been as good as his word. Four unknown scruffy guys plus a beautiful woman, all with hair where their faces should be, had hit the big time almost overnight. Now they were up for ten Grammys, including best new group. Julia was also up for one— for a single from her final album.

The Newborns. A strange name, but not as strange as many. Recording groups and artists nowadays always have odd names, I've found—Trash, Flash & Money, Liquid Jesus, Screaming Broccoli, Heavy D, the Dream Warriors, Nirvana, Hipno Love Wheel, U2, the Rembrandts, Flat Duo Jazz, the Swans, Pilon, Guns N' Roses, the Dream Syndicate, Color Me Badd, Ice Cube, HuduGurus, the Cranberries, Smashing Pumpkins, the Lemonheads, Dead Can Dance, My Little Funhouse, Nikita, Thrill Car, Vertical Hold, Sheep on Drugs, Alice in Chains, Violent Femmes, Fahrenheit 451, Junk Monkeys, Twister Alley, Quicksand, Laura John, Sacred Warrior, Broken Arrow, 10,000 Maniacs, the Halos, the Lakes Progress, Too Much Joy, the Vipers, Flaming Lips, Mind Bomb, the Scubas, Rage Against the Machine, Stone Temple Pilots, Snow, Silk, White Zombie, the Hit Factory, Green on Red, Dangerous Toys . . .

Amazing names. Not at all like Bing Crosby, Barbra Streisand, or Neil Diamond—not even like Madonna. *Definitely* not.

But it was seldom the music or the weird names that made any difference at all. The difference lay in whether these groups had the drive—something that pushed them. They had to love the life, the music, and want it more than home, more than family, more than love, peace, breath, or even money. If they wanted success more than life itself they might possibly win it. In a year or two, many of the members of these groups would be dead of drugs. Some would fade away like the morning dew, some would move back to Detroit or New Jersey or Bakersfield or Georgia, go to work for a steel mill or a bank. Some would go into the stock market, and some would end up on the street. For the rest of their lives most of them would continue to dream of the New York, London, and L.A. rock-and-roll machine and watch the televised music awards with misty-eyed envy. Some would become huge, like U2 or Nirvana, giant stars; some would go to the Grammys, like the Newborns. It was luck and timing, and good producers, and a team of people at the record company who wanted to make them great. I wondered if the children in front of me had that steel, and if they really made it to the very top, whether they would stay there.

There was one more thing that helped, and that was having someone who believed in you more than you believed in yourself, who believed in you when you had your doubts, believed in you when the press hated you, believed in you when you had laryngitis, when your lover tore your life apart, believed in you without your makeup on, when you stumbled and fell, when you rose to the stars, when you lurched out of the spotlight. Someone to help you stay alive against the odds, surviving drug addiction, drinking problems, car wrecks, broken marriages, busted bank accounts.

These kids had such a champion in my old friend, Stan Shultz. Stan's experience was vast. He used to say he had learned to get what he wanted. He was at ease in the world of rock and roll. I knew he wanted success for the Newborns.

I thought of Edward, my lover. I wondered if Edward believed in his daughter that much.

Sometimes I wondered if Edward believed in me that much.

I had liked the Newborns' music from the first time I heard it. They had everything the industry wanted. They sounded a bit like a quintet of buzz saws; they sang slightly off key, they looked like unmade beds with their wild manes of silver, black, gold and brown curls and dreadlocks surrounding their faces. But their music had great charm, a peculiar, exotic rhythm, almost like the South African drum sounds of Paul Simon's *Graceland,* and a sweet, distinctive bluesy overtone.

The Grammy nomination committees liked it too.

Stan led us into the conference room where a side cabinet was stocked with Cokes, ice, and glasses. While we served ourselves, Stan clasped and unclasped his hands, a sign of nervousness I recognized. Max took off his jacket and hung it over a chair, where it looked like a tapestry from the Museum of Modern Art. Across his shirt Max wore a holster and in the holster was a black and blue steel handgun. I had to assume it was loaded. I took a step away from Max and tried to concentrate on rearranging my setup, fiddling with lights and film.

"Stand over there, everybody," I said. I posed Malinda with Z-Train, both looking studious under the shiny poster for their new album, *Birth Canal.* I shot the Newborns together, then individually. To put them in the mood, I put on their new CD. Rock and roll boomed and sparkled through the room and the boys and Malinda loosened up. All of the group put together probably weighed only a few hundred pounds, and they already knew that part of the price of fame is working every pound of flesh for all it was worth.

They needed me, and I needed them. I moved my tripod, light setups, and cameras around the room, and soon they were dancing while I shot a dozen rolls of black-and-white and color film. Max moved as well now, every inch a fan.

Everything was fine.

Except Fred. Fred was giving me a problem. Every time I shot a picture, I found he was just to the right, or just to the left, and I would need to redo the shot. He would stand tall and straight then suddenly stagger, wobble, and be out of control. Z-Train would grab him, steady him, then he would be okay. He leaned up against Sahid between shots, sniffing; he would mumble unintelligibly, singing along with the tracks—screaming, really, not singing, and getting worse all the time. Everyone in the group, including Max, looked embarrassed.

Then Fred grabbed Malinda and tried to kiss her and she threw him a punch and began pulling at his hair, shouting.

"Fred, get out of my face!" Malinda shrieked at him and grabbed for his skinny neck as though to break it. He laughed and, throwing his hands up, broke her grip, sending her arms flying. One of Fred's elbows caught a glass of Coke on a side table and it went flying across the room, scattering ice cubes and broken glass on the carpet. Malinda stooped to pick up the glass and gave me a dark scowl.

"Malinda, back off," Reed said, "you could get hurt." Reed unruffled everybody's feathers. To Fred he said, "Cool it, time out. Just take it easy."

Fred laughed at him and headed for the john. In his absence an uncomfortable silence hung over the room during which I kept the cameras going. Fred was gone a long time for a pee and when he came back he had a handkerchief to his nose and was sniffing.

It didn't take a brain surgeon to figure out that Fred was coked to his eyeballs. The realization made my stomach jump, my breath stop. I knew cocaine could break your heart and kill your soul.

My cousin Marty, beloved childhood friend, confidant, playmate, soulmate, and partner of Ben's and my childhood on the ranch, had died of drugs two years before, overdosing in his shit-filled, filthy apartment in Kansas City. In therapy with Wheeling at that time, I had tried to help, and learned that all my love, my family's love, our mutual attempts to help my cousin find his way out of the nightmare had failed. I blamed myself.

Denzel Keating was a tall, attractive cameraman who had been my friend since we met years before. During a time when his wife was drinking heavily and going on one week-long bender after another, Denzel had found Al-Anon and changed from a crazed, unhappy, suicidal man, shivering in apprehension about how he was going to handle his wife's next blackout, to someone with poise, grace, and serenity. After Marty's death, Denzel had taken me to meetings of Al-Anon. He said I hadn't caused it, couldn't control it, and couldn't cure it. Denzel and I became much closer after Marty died. We often worked together, shooting the same groups, I for print, Denzel for television and the movies. He had helped me understand Marty's death. Understand it, but never accept it.

Alcohol and drug addiction were often par for the course in rock and roll. I knew that, but for the Newborns to be messing with cocaine this early in the game could bring them crashing down.

This is not your business, Catherine, I thought. Just get the pictures. I tried to let it go and just do my work. Trouble was, I already had a fondness for these five crazy kids. Fondness, I knew, could be dangerous.

Everybody had worked up a sweat by then. Fred sank onto the couch, slumping into a knot. I took pictures of his bent figure with the last frames of a roll and changed cameras. Reed began to sing a melody that sounded strangely familiar, as though he wanted to take my mind off the subject of Fred. The song he began to sing was so beautiful, so haunting, that for the moment he succeeded in diverting my attention.

"What is that?" I asked.

"That's one of the songs we used to sing in church in Macon. 'Bright Morning Star,' it's called." It was a lyrical song. Sweet. Different for a mop-headed hard rocker. Reed sang it as sort of a lullaby to Fred, who had stopped shaking and just looked sleepy. Sahid joined in and sang a harmony, then the two other boys added their voices—even Fred perked up from his doze on the couch. They sounded good: Z-Train gave it sizzle, snapping his fingers, moving his feet. Pretty soon the melody rose and fell, counterpointing the rock-and-roll music that had filled the room minutes before.

> *Bright morning stars are rising,*
> *bright morning stars are rising,*
> *bright morning stars are rising,*
> *dawn is breaking in my soul.*

When the song ended in that mysterious, complete silence that follows a familiar hymn sung a cappella, I could almost hear the crickets begin to chirp again, the grass blow in the wind outside the country church in Kansas, nature taking up where the singing had left off.

"Why don't you sing that in your show, between

the rock and roll?" I asked, putting a new roll of color film in the Leica, winding it to the start point, clicking off the first picture. I was sorry the song was over. "People would love it."

The Newborns looked at me like I was crazy. "People would walk out," Reed said. "And what would the record company say?"

I suggested we try another location, go out into the street. Max agreed eagerly, hoping, I thought, to diffuse the situation with Fred. We said goodbye to Stan and I shouldered my bags. Max and I herded the Newborns into the elevator and out onto Fifty-seventh Street, where a long sleek black limousine was waiting. For the next half-hour, the car, like some great black shark, shadowed us down Fifty-seventh as I took pictures, first in front of a poster of Yo-Yo Ma at Carnegie Hall, then strolling toward Sixth Avenue. I got the kids to stop in delis and pose with bunches of flowers and grapes, wander into a shoe store and pose with the owner, and climb on the sculpture in front of a modern office building in the bright sunshine of the March day. I posed my lover's daughter in a horse-drawn carriage in front of the Plaza, lining the boys up around her, Reed sitting on the driver's box, the rest climbing over the coach.

Suddenly Fred climbed down off the carriage and sprinted into the middle of the street.

"I'll never get hit, they wouldn't dare," he screamed, laughing hysterically, planting both feet on the yellow line in the center of Fifty-ninth and Fifth.

Traffic screeched, brakes squealed, a chorus of taxi drivers shouted obscenities. Max dodged elegantly among the honking horns and waving fists and put his arms around Fred, hauling him back to the curb like he was a big fish. Reed and Max propped Fred against the wall of the Sherry Netherland Hotel. Malinda kept running her hands through her blond curls, chewing her gum and tapping her heel. Taxi drivers and cars on the street came to a virtual standstill at the sight of the quintet's wild halos of hair glowing in the afternoon light. People rubbernecked and shouted out of car windows.

I took Reed's arm and pulled him aside. "Will he be all right or should we stop?" I asked.

Reed shook his head. "He's fine, he can make it." Fred had regained some measure of composure, and we crossed to Central Park and walked down toward the golden statue across from the Plaza.

"Reed, if you need some help with this, I could put you in touch with someone," I said. "Denzel Keating has been to hell and back." I wrote Denzel's name and number on a card for Reed and he thanked me, putting the card in his pocket. Fred was docile now, his limbs seemingly under control.

"He's never been this bad," Reed confessed. "We got to get him straight for the Grammys."

Sahid and Z-Train sat Fred on the stone wall in front of the F.A.O. Schwarz toy store. There, Fred was soon busy talking to his shoes.

"Where do you think he's scoring?" I asked.

Reed gestured with his hands. "Beats me. He was okay when we got here last week. He made a commitment he wouldn't use on this trip, see."

"It's a disease, you know," I said.

"Of course," he said. "That doesn't make it any easier when it's your career . . . careers that are at stake," he said, his arms outstretched to include the rest of the quintet.

"This disease doesn't play favorites," I said, thinking of Marty.

"Fred was in treatment last year. We all went to family therapy for him. His adopted family didn't want to have anything to do with treatment, so we all stood in for his family. We *are* his family, you know." Reed's eyes followed Fred, who was now dancing in the street again. Horns were blowing and the traffic was tied up. "He was fine for a while. We were actually talking about breaking up because of him, then the record hit. He promised not to use, not ever again." Reed shook his head. Malinda joined us.

"Our counselor in Atlanta told us that after the Grammys maybe we need to do another intervention," Malinda said. "We hoped Fred could stay straight for a few weeks, maybe stay straight, period. I don't know what to do."

Suddenly Fred stood up a few feet away, cursing his partner. *"Fuck* you know about it, Sahid! Preachy son of a bitch."

"We're out of here," Max said, grabbing Fred and giving me a sad smile. He gathered the group together like a few small parcels and seemed to tie them in a bow with his big arms, heading for the sleek black limo.

I told them I would see them at the Meadowlands, the big New Jersey arena. The Newborns were scheduled to perform there on the weekend.

"Promise?" Fred pleaded.

It is unsettling to have to leave someone who has been concentrating on you exclusively for a period of hours, making you the center of their universe, even when you're stoned. Especially when you're stoned.

Stars. Rock and roll.

Drugs. They were too good, this group, for this trouble in waiting that was bound to backfire. I hoped someone would be there to help them when it all came tumbling down.

The group climbed into their limo and pulled away from the curb. The hotel was maybe a minute away, U-turn and all.

I could have afforded to hire a driver for my car, I thought to myself, lugging my bag of equipment that felt heavier with each step I took. I certainly had the money—the windfall from my grandfather had guaranteed that, and I made more than a good living from my photography. That, and the settlement in my suit against Ernest Wheeling . . . I brushed the thought of Wheeling from my mind.

But the habit of pinching pennies dies hard, I thought and decided, that as soon as Renaldo was functioning as my assistant, I would hire somebody to schlep me around town in the Daimler Princess I already owned. Then, like the rock-and-roll bands, I, too, wouldn't have to walk six feet if I didn't want to.

I hailed a cab and headed north on Park Avenue, looking forward to tea with Julia.

11

AT A SUMMER BE-IN IN WASHINGTON SQUARE PARK IN 1968, Jim McVee, a good songwriter who had become well known for his group the Frogs, introduced me to Sally Broomfield, another journalist who was writing about the New York music scene for *Esquire*. She was the hot writer of the moment.

Sally and I liked each other immediately. She had an apartment close to mine in the West Village and was the first woman friend I had in New York. I crawled Bleecker Street with her that summer, rode out to the Statue of Liberty, took the Staten Island Ferry, explored the upper Hudson River Valley by boat and car, and discovered that New York was more than the intersection of Sixth Avenue and Eighth Street.

One night we went to see a new group, Crime and Punishment, at their debut at the Bottom Line. We were both writing about them and afterward we went to a party at the home of their manager, Ted Zimmerman. At midnight we found ourselves off in a corner, talking, looking deep into each other's eyes until we fell silent and the smoky room disappeared. We left the party and made our way down Bleecker to Sally's apartment, saying nothing, our fingers touching.

Sally had had other women lovers but this was all new to me, an experience for which I was unprepared.

"No vice, novice," she said, holding me to her and laughing with pleasure on that first night as we plunged and rolled on the daybed in her pretty apartment on Christopher Street.

The next morning, I awoke as she fondled one of my breasts, bare under a loose diaphanous top, something I had borrowed from her closet of soft silk clothes to keep off the chill of the night air after our last orgasm.

"You are an amazing woman, Catherine," she said, as her hands sought between my legs again, running over my sensitive skin. "You don't drink, you don't take drugs, you don't smoke. How can I corrupt you?" The sun warmed the narrow bed, and as we lay together, our legs entwined, I felt her fingers rousing me as well as any roughneck in a pair of Levi's ever had. Her lips on my nipples, her breath coming in faster sighs—it was as normal as climbing the stairs to the hay in the barn, fondling the heaviness between a man's legs.

I lay back and let her corrupt me, again and again.

Soon, I did not hesitate to be her corrupter as well, and as often as possible.

Women had had nothing to do with my education in the art of love. At twenty-one I had learned much from the wiles of the ranch hands my father was so rightfully afraid would ruin my reputation before I was sixteen. In long summer nights on the seats of pickup trucks, under steering wheels, dashboard lights, and a western moon that lit up the world from the Rockies all the way to St. Louis, I had surrendered to pleasure from the roughest of the sweethearts of the rodeo, boys who were already men by the time we graduated from high school. They came from the ranches around ours, mostly, and smelled of horse manure and aftershave. They were named Wayne and Curt and Anderson; they taught me how to hear their voices call into the prairie, like wild creatures, and led me to my own calling voice; they had schooled me in the art of love with half your clothes off under a four-wheel gear shift, with one foot on the floor and the other holding back from knocking the truck windows out with your rawhide boots.

But now, the sex with Sally Broomfield was sweet as honey, true as truth, hot as fire, deep as the deepest well, satisfying as nothing I had ever known, and at times I could come to completion as she just hovered over me, her eyes looking deeply into mine, her hands not even touching me. It was good to be out from under the steering wheels and I knew by the end of that first summer I felt something that had been missing in the pickup trucks and beneath the wide Kansas sky. I wasn't sure quite what it was, but it felt extraordinary.

One night that winter, Sally was driving with a new band out to a gig on Long Island. The weather was bad, snow and sleet covered the highway. On the return trip at one in the morning, the road manager was driving the big, cumbersome van in which Sally as well as the lead singer and the lead guitarist of the band were riding. The roadie must have been drinking—he was certainly speeding—and in the bad weather, the fog and the sleet, he hit a bad patch of road, skidded, slammed into the embankment near the exit to Glen Cove, and killed everyone in the van except Sally, who had been sitting in the passenger seat. Her seatbelt was on, but on impact the buckle tore through her liver and into her backbone.

Half of the bones in her body were broken, but she lived long enough to be taken to Long Island Hospital. I was listed in her wallet as the person to call in case of an emergency, and the hospital telephoned me in time for me to get to her bedside. The doctors knew she was dying and let me hold her hand. Her lips were blue, her face was white, the body under the sheet was smashed to pieces, but she was conscious for an hour. Though she couldn't talk, she looked at me for what seemed like a week, and then she closed her eyes and died.

I reached the one relative I knew she had, her brother Ralph, who lived in Melbourne. I told him she was dead and asked him what I should do with the body. His voice was distant, but I heard the words clearly enough.

"I don't care. Do whatever you want, it's all the same to me," he said in a strong Aussie accent and hung up.

I called a funeral home and arranged her cremation;

I invited a few Village friends and some of the people we knew together for a brief private ceremony and then called a powerful man in the music business who was a close friend of Sally's and asked if he would pay for the wake, which he did. He also helped me invite the famous and infamous from her little black book.

The moguls of the music industry, crumpling Kleenex, wearing dark glasses and gold chains, were there: David Geffen, Ahmet Ertegun, Clive Davis. And artists, their faces grim: Bob Dylan, Mick Jagger, Jim Morrison, the Jefferson Airplane, Joni Mitchell. The wake was a Who's Who of the music industry of New York, Los Angeles, and Montreal. Many of the artists and music business managers had looked to Sally to immortalize their clients in print, and they showed up to preside over her immortality, to witness the making of Sally into a dead legend. After it was all over, I went to Sally's apartment, packed her things up, and sent them to the St. Vincent's thrift shop. I didn't even keep the silk shirts and robes; I couldn't bear the thought of wearing them. I slipped her book of music and press contacts into my pocket and struck out, armed with what I knew were Sally's blessings.

I soon began to conquer Sally's rock-and-roll world. I had the names, I had the Rolodex.

I have missed Sally Broomfield every day since she died. Her death left me shattered; it eventually sent me, still in mourning some years later, to seek the professional services of Ernest Wheeling. I was grieving—and wondering why it took a woman to give me the love I needed.

12

At the Mayfair Regent, Julia was sitting at a corner table under the light from a pink, flower-print-covered lamp, her face reflected in the giant mirror that covered the wall. Denzel Keating was sitting across from her.

"You two know each other, don't you?" Julia said.

"Of course," I said, smiling at my friend. It was like him—to appear just after I had been telling Reed about him. Denzel always seemed to be around when I needed him.

Julia put an arm around his shoulders and smiled at him. "I'm going to think about what you said, Denzel. But first I'm going to have tea with Catherine." She gestured for me to take the seat he had vacated. "Denzel was just leaving."

Denzel stood up awkwardly, and, sliding out from behind the delicate table, got to his feet, all six feet two of him. He kissed her on the cheek.

Julia put out her hand to me as Denzel made his way out of the tearoom. "He's such an angel, Catherine," she said. "Why is he married?"

"Because he's an angel," I replied. "They're all married." I thought of Edward and wondered why we weren't. "What were you two cooking up?"

"He wants me to let him do a retrospective, a sort

of film of my life, for Fox," she said. "You know, Atlantic Records has just released my version of 'Melody' again." Denzel had produced a lot of Julia's videos when she was making records.

Julia had had a platinum single of the beautiful song from her last album, *Body of Light*. It was climbing the charts once again, going into the top ten, and it had been nominated for a Grammy.

I looked at her, taking in her beauty, relishing her friendship. Julia looked every inch a star this afternoon, her eyes sparkling, her mouth a sensuous smile, her face almost as familiar to me as my mother's. She had put Andrew Lloyd Webber's name on the map. She had had top-ten hits with the most beautiful songs written in the mid- to late seventies, eighties, and early nineties. This afternoon Julia's face was pale and pink, like a fresh rose. Her black hair was cut as snug as a cap—Madonna had borrowed this look recently. Julia wore a mauve suit with a long skirt and black boots that came up to her knees. She looked as though she had stepped out of *Vogue*. She always had.

My photographs of her taken over the last fifteen years of her career portrayed a stunning woman, happy in the limelight. Two years before, at the age of thirty-six, Julia had done something that seemed on the surface totally out of character. After all the platinum records and the concert tours, all the television appearances and traveling, she had decided to change her life. Completely. This way, she said, she wouldn't have to die to become a legend.

"I have all the money I need," she had said. "I don't have to continue this life. I want a change. I've had enough of singing." Her decision had shocked me. Her decision shocked a lot of people in the industry as well. They thought she had gone around the bend, or worse, that she was ill and didn't want anyone to know how ill. My friend pursued her course.

"I want to spend more time with Jim and Jenny," she had said.

Julia changed her life and focused more on her husband and her daughter. She stopped recording and doing concerts. Something in Julia longed for a quieter, saner, calmer existence than the one she had been leading for so many years. She announced she would start a new career—painting.

"Let them write all they want about health problems. I've never felt better in my life." At first the press had speculated that Julia had gone berserk, that she had had a nervous breakdown. Then they wrote for a few weeks about absurd reasons for her absence from the talk shows and the fund-raisers, from the political rallies and the social skirmishes that had been her stock in trade. They speculated she was suing her record company, that she had AIDS, that she was lesbian, that she was bankrupt. None of this was true. Then her husband, Jim, left her for a younger woman, and the tabloids, even the *New York Times,* had a field day.

There was one thing the press didn't know. At nineteen, Julia had given a baby boy up for adoption. That was the year we met, when both of us were just starting out in New York. I knew the loss of this child haunted my friend. Julia gave the child up because she felt she was too young to raise him; and the father, as young as Julia, quickly evaporated from the scene. She began to search for her son after she started to get some fame, but all roads to his whereabouts were dead ends. The hospital where the baby was born, in a small upstate New York town, had no records of the adoption. She couldn't even find the doctor who had delivered her baby. The agency that had handled the adoption had gone out of business. At the time of her "retirement," I knew that Julia had hired another agency whose sole purpose was to unite adopted children with their birth parents. It was already two years that they had been hunting for Julia's child, who would be a young man by now. Julia referred to him as "the kid."

And, while the media kept digging for reasons why Julia would want to do a Garbo, Julia survived.

I understood by now that my friend had rare powers. She started painting—all day, every day. Soon she decided she needed figure drawing classes and more structure in her schedule. She had always wanted to get her college degree and she went back to school, to the School of Visual Arts. She wore a brown wig and nerdy tortoiseshell glasses to class, but people recognized her anyway. But by then she didn't care. She started taking an odd course or two in addition to the painting classes. Since she had decided to paint the nude body, she said, she wanted the information about the human animal that courses in anatomy, psychology, gender studies, and religion would give her.

"I know a lot about singing and a lot about painting, a lot about religion and a lot about sex," she told me. "I think for now I'll major in painting and sex." She began to paint enormous nudes, huge figures, colorful, exotic, big-breasted women, and muscular, well-endowed men, and groups of men and women, with purple, orange, red, pink, mauve, green, blue limbs. Her style was reminiscent of the Fauves but it was very modern and distinctive, very Julia.

"You know," she said to me after she had completed her first year, "if the paintings don't sell, I could maybe become a sex therapist."

"Your paintings are going to sell, Julia, no way they won't," I had told her, and believed it. She was uncommonly talented. Her work was magnificent, as her singing had always been.

*   *   *

Now she gave me a grin across the table. "You look hassled. What's up?"

"The Newborns—how does that sound for hassled?"

A young woman rolled the cart to our table. It was laden with scones, tea, drinks, and finger sandwiches. Laura Ashley–print cozies coddled the teapots. English Breakfast, India, Lady Londonderry, and Constant Comment sat on the trays, snug in their pastel boxes. Although I knew it would calm me, I decided against gin, and Julia and I both ordered Lady Londonderry tea.

"Isn't that the group Edward's daughter is in?" Julia said. "That beautiful girl you were helping a while back? Malinda, isn't that her name? How old is she now?"

I told her Malinda was twenty-two.

"So," Julia said, taking a breath and regaining her composure, "what are the rest of the Newborns like? Are they . . . normal?"

"They're sexy, they're loaded," I said, "they're going to walk away with a ton of Grammys, and at least one of them is a wacked-out drug addict who may take the group down in flames." The waitress placed two pots of tea, each covered with a lavender cozy, on the little table in front of us. There were two Limoges cups with silver strainers bridging the fragile porcelain, and lemon wedges on the matching flowered plates.

"I wonder if Edward minds his daughter hanging out with an addict," Julia said, a wistful look on her face.

"Probably as much as he likes her being in a rock-and-roll band," I said. "I think it's all the same to Edward."

"I don't know," Julia said, sipping the refreshing tea delicately, holding the cup in her fingers, still beautiful despite the paint, the occasional splinters, and the constant washing off with turpentine that went with her new work. "The addict may be able to keep the circus going," Julia went on. "A lot of strange people wind up on the stage, getting paid for being dysfunctional."

It was true. I had seen a lot of strung-out rock-and-rollers who nevertheless kept up brilliant careers.

"Are they any good?" Julia asked, trying to sound disinterested. I smiled at her. "Is *Malinda* any good?"

"Professional rivalry?" I kidded. "You saw her. She's good, and so is the rest of the group." I smiled at my friend. "But I thought you'd put all that behind you." It had been a year since Julia sang in public—at a farewell concert at Madison Square Garden in New York.

"I don't really care," Julia said, "I'm curious, that's all. You know, I'm through with rock and roll in all its forms."

"Right." I smiled. "And I'm the Queen of England." I sipped the tea, letting the amber liquid soothe my stomach. "Maybe it's because Edward's daughter is in the group, but I feel so strongly about these kids, Julia. I've been around a lot of junkie bands," I said. "This one I care about. I'd hate to see them blow it all to hell."

"If they've got the talent, they'll survive," she said.

I nodded. The tea was good and warming. I realized my fingers and my face were cold, as though I had been walking in a cold wind. With a shudder of recognition I remembered why I felt cold—that note sitting on my desk. Manila, frightening.

"Catherine, you look pale. Are you all right?" Julia knew me well.

I told her about the note, what it said, how I had called the police.

"Maybe it was a crank letter. Or maybe it was written by somebody you photographed," she said, tapping her nails on the white embossed tablecloth. "People can become *enraged* if you don't make them look exactly the way they think they look—haven't you told me that?" She smiled what I knew she meant to be a reassuring smile. Soaking in the surrounding opulence of the Mayfair, I was feeling more relaxed. Nothing better than money and success, I thought, to take away the sting of fear.

"I was frightened," I said. "It was a shock." I couldn't think of anyone who was angry about my photographs.

"Well, it gives you such a feeling of invasion. It's such a personal thing, a threat like that."

"The policeman said I should bring the letter in. They'll look at the writing, check it for fingerprints."

"Right. You'll do that?" Julia asked.

I nodded. "Stan said I should let my new assistant open all my mail, and to send anything strange right over to his office. I'm sure it was just a crank letter."

"As long as you take it to the police." I nodded that I would and Julia knocked three times on the table as the young waitress poured from steaming ceramic pots. "For divine protection, whether it's needed or not," she said.

I repeated her superstitious gesture. "Hopefully, if I ignore it, it will go away." Julia was always telling me I had a reality-avoidance problem. I always said that was the reason I took pictures—because I'm a voyeur at heart. A voyeur rather than a participant.

Now, she shook her long, pretty fingers at me. "Catherine, maybe you could use a shrink again." We both laughed. "Find a new one, not like that awful man," Julia said.

"Speaking of Wheeling, guess whose name I found on my new assistant's résumé," I said.

"No!" Julia put her hand over mine on the table.

She asked if I had used Ellen's agency, and I nodded assent. "Does Ellen know Wheeling?" she asked.

"I don't think so," I replied. "And Stan says he never mentioned it to her. Renaldo saw Wheeling for therapy and did some office work for him. Enough for Wheeling to give him a reference, that's all," I said.

"Wheeling should have lost his license—or worse," Julia said. "It's too bad you settled out of court."

"Shrinks may come and go, but a good friend is forever," I said. "And that shrink is gone. For good." I wanted so much to believe it, that Wheeling was part of my past.

"What's your new assistant like?" she asked brightly.

I fumbled in my purse for my cigarettes and lit up, drawing in a deep lungful of smoke. From the other side of the room the waitress looked at me disapprovingly. I took another puff and smudged the Pall Mall out in the ashtray. A character defect, cigarettes. I smiled and described Renaldo to her.

"He sounds perfect. Maybe you'll bring him to the opening." This was the week of Julia's first painting show. The opening the next night would be at a very hip SoHo gallery called the Siren.

I asked Julia if she was excited about her show. I certainly was.

"Nervous as a cat!" she said. "And much more anxious than I used to be about singing. The surfaces are dry, the paintings look great, everything is set for tomorrow night, and I'm still shaking in my boots." She sighed. "You know, when I listen to my old records now, I always hear the flaws. No one else does, I know, but I do. It has me worried. Will I see nothing but flaws in my paintings in ten years?"

"You're a perfectionist, Julia." I was too.

"How could I avoid it, having you for a friend?" We both laughed.

Although *Elle* magazine had asked me to cover Julia's opening as an exclusive, I wouldn't commit myself. I wanted to see the finished piece before I sold it. It was not every day that your best friend put herself on the line the way Julia was doing.

Julia sipped her tea, taking a deep draught, and settled back in her chair.

"All this painting and learning about sex and the human body," she went on, "what's it doing for me? It's been months since I got laid."

Good old Julia, always thinking about sex. "I understand," I said calmly.

"No you don't, either. You're perfectly taken care of, Catherine."

She meant sexually. Julia didn't think much of Edward. Just a feeling, she said. It was a subject we didn't discuss. Most of my friends didn't like Edward, but I had decided three years ago that that didn't matter. The sex was incredible, even though I felt sometimes he wasn't quite there with me, that we weren't soulmates. But he handled my finances as well as he handled me sexually, so I felt well cared for, and that meant a lot to me. I never wanted to even *look* at my bank statements; Edward did that for me.

I was looking forward to seeing him tonight and realized that this conversation with Julia was turning me on. Did I love Edward? I wondered suddenly, thinking about our phone conversation that morning.

Julia's husband, Jim, was a playwright. He had run off with a new soap-opera star in spite of twelve years of what had looked like a happy marriage. Julia had dismissed Jim's drinking and erratic behavior as career stress. She hadn't worried when the pretty twenty-year-old appeared and refused to disappear—until it was too late.

"Let's change the subject," Julia said. "Are you going to the Grammys?"

The Grammys, the recording industry's most prestigious award show, would be held in New York in two weeks. I already had half a dozen invitations on my desk to the glitzy social and music-business parties that surrounded the event. Julia was nominated for a Grammy for "Melody." Most of the parties would be loaded with stars in town for the big event, and some of them I should really go to, including the big fundraiser for AIDS the following Friday.

I told Julia I wanted her to go to the Grammys with me.

Julia looked nostalgic, then realized that I had noticed, and looked quickly away. "I'd love to see the Newborns," she said. I remembered the last time we were at the Grammys. Then it was Julia who had walked away with half a dozen bronze-cast replicas of a gramophone. That night she was buoyed by the standing ovations that had sent her off the stage with her trophies. We had celebrated all night—Julia, Jim, Edward, and I. "Are all the guys in the group as young as Malinda?"

Suddenly I realized Julia was thinking about that subject again. "Yes, Julia, too young for you," I joked.

"Are you sure?"

"Well, they're in their early twenties," I said. "But, come to think of it, seventeen years' difference is not a lot," I conceded, thinking of the virile Reed. "I'll introduce you to the leader of the group," I said. "You might like him." Reed would be floored by Julia. It might be fun to watch.

"Younger men never interested me, Catherine," Julia said, shaking her head.

I smiled. "You never know," I said. "Younger men might be just the answer." I remembered what I had said when Jim had left her: "Younger men, younger women make the heart grow stronger." "Loosen up, go out on some dates, for God's sake," I said, feeling a little strong giving her this advice.

"Do you know what dating is like today? Especially for me?" she said.

Julia was physically as attractive as any woman I had ever met. And I sensed in her a great sexual energy on top of her beauty and talent.

"First there's safe sex," she said, "that's bad enough. But then try to find somebody who can deal with the fact that he's been listening to you sing on the radio for fifteen years." She sighed, shaking her head. I looked across the table at her beautiful, suddenly lonely face, the face of a star and a nineties woman: fresh and vibrant, carefully tended at Georgette Klinger's, treated to the best of cosmetics, injected with collagen, steamed at the Health and Racquet Club, protected from the sun with PABA-free moisturizing sunscreen, glazed with a film of hypoallergenic makeup—a face, finally, to be admired by a lover and told it was prettiest without makeup, wearing nothing but a smile.

"You'll find someone, Julia," I said. "The goddess loathes a vacuum."

She shook her head. "The trouble is, I don't have time to look, really. I wish Jim had left *before* I changed careers. Then I could honestly blame my divorce on show business."

"He was probably upset that you became a painter," I said. "It's almost as bad as being an astrologer." We both laughed. The young actress Frank had run off with was an astrologer as well as a starlet.

"At least Jim and I have remained friends. Friday he came by for coffee, to see Jenny," she said. Julia's adorable, weedy, red-headed daughter was very bright, an excellent student in the ninth grade at Hawthorne, a private school in Manhattan. "But what he really came for was to get my advice. He knows I'm taking those classes in sex therapy. What do you think he wanted to talk about?"

"His work?" I guessed hopefully.

"The bastard wanted some advice about his sex life with the nymphet. Seems he's having trouble getting it up!"

"I hope you told him to go to hell," I said.

Julia ran her finger around the edge of the elegant translucent plate where the last crumbs of the fruit pastry lay, as though she were reading the future in them. She looked at me from under her long eyelashes. Beautiful. Guilty. "I told him what to nuzzle and what to press. And what to ask her to nuzzle and press. I told him what to do that he'd never done with me. I told him how to make Celia happy in bed." She made a defeated face. The women's movement had made us so free we were terrifying.

"Julia, I think *you* need a shrink." We both laughed.

13

WHEN ONE MOVES TO NEW YORK, ARMED WITH A SUB-way map, a bottle of antacid, and a thesaurus of clever retorts to insults, one should also be provided with a list of the various types of therapy that are available in the concrete jungle. There are any number of treatments for the wild occasional feeling of total insanity that overcomes those of us who live here.

You can take drugs and drink, and that sometimes seems to help. Or you can go to a Freudian, a Jungian, a William Alanson White devotee, a Reichian, a Sullivanian, or a mixture of all of these. Chiropractic techniques are considered strictly body therapy, and you can get Tragered (a massage where you are rocked like a baby), or shiatsued, a massage therapy that concentrates on the pressure points. There is scream therapy, and body work therapy; and Alexander, Feldenkreis, Fritz Perls, Rolfing, and Rubenfeld Synergy, as well as Alexander Lowen therapy.

After Sally Broomfield died, I was terribly anxious and depressed. I couldn't work, couldn't sleep. The horrible dreams that followed her funeral increased my isolation and my feeling of being abandoned. I started to consider suicide as an answer to my problems.

At first I drank a lot, but booze just made me sick. I had tried to kill myself when I was a teenager in some forgotten rage over my parents' anger. My father kept sleeping pills in the house and I took them, but they only knocked me out. I was taken to the hospital and my stomach was pumped.

People are embarrassed when you survive a suicide attempt. It is as though you have insulted them by giving them less than your real death, as though you're letting them know that they did not deserve your best efforts. I didn't want any embarrassment on my hands again, but still the thought of taking my own life haunted me.

One night I took a lot of pills on top of a lot of booze, and that landed me in St. Vincent's Hospital. When I came to, I was looking into the broadly smiling face of a nurse. Behind her stood my friend and lawyer Stan Shultz—scowling.

The nurse was an angel. People in hospitals in those days were still sympathetic, in the tradition of Florence Nightingale. Even with a would-be suicide.

"You idiot," said Stan, brushing the nurse aside as he advanced to the edge of the bed. His face leaned over me; he looked like he was going to explode.

"That's all we need right now—to have both of you dead." Behind him I could see Ellen, with her face beautifully made up, wearing three-inch heels, a black wool Saint Laurent suit, and carrying a black alligator Chanel purse. The height of fashion, even at this hour.

"How did you know I was here?" I asked weakly.

"You called us, and thanks a lot," Ellen said, "it was four-thirty in the morning." Despite her words, she smiled sympathetically. Her scarlet mouth was gentle, and although I had felt that Ellen judged me for having lived with Sally, she seemed genuinely concerned over me now.

Stan and Ellen took me home with them to their West Broadway apartment, a six-room penthouse they had bought at the start of the co-op boom. Stan and Ellen were married professionals, each with a budding career. Stan was a junior agent at William Morris and Ellen was working feverishly to keep her own new agency running at any cost. Meanwhile they had two empty bedrooms, waiting for babies. Stan said I could stay with them until I recovered.

"I don't want you going home by yourself," Stan told me. "We'll take care of you for a few days."

"We just want you to rest," Ellen said.

The doctor who pumped my stomach suggested I "see someone"—as close as they came in those days to telling you they thought you were a lunatic. It was then that I began to hear of the varieties of therapy that were available in New York, mecca of mental unwellness.

Ellen had started seeing a shrink after several miscarriages and suggested I see her counselor. It was there, in the office of a woman social worker, that I began my adventures in the psychiatric community.

Then someone at *Thunder and Lightning* offered me a choice assignment that got me out of town and gave me a leave from my problems. I was off to San Francisco to cover a rock-and-roll festival.

New York was hot and humid, and I packed my bags happily, glad for the opportunity to leave the city and to think about something other than Sally's death. I got great photographs in Monterey. It was the mid-seventies, and in those days you had a week or two to file a story, so before returning to New York I made my way down the Pacific Coast Highway to Esalen, the home of hot baths, brilliant California sunsets, and alternative therapies. Built on the edge of the sea overlooking the vast Pacific, Esalen is a group of wind-and-weather-beaten structures, a lodge and several cottages. Down the road a mile or so from the center is the ramshackle house where Henry Miller was living then, and where he wrote *Big Sur and the Oranges of Hieronymus Bosch* in between trips to those same hot tubs in which I basked. I inhaled the scent of the flowering ice plant and ingested as many drugs as I could, hoping to hear the rocks speak.

At Esalen, one has a choice of New Age therapies and healthy—if unpalatable—organic foods, prepared by earthy men and women of indeterminate sex dressed in thongs and wearing their hair long. I swam naked in the pool above the ocean and ate lotus leaves with the lover I had met in Monterey and transported with me to the magical mountainside above the sea. A flower child named Pythian, with yellow hair and beautiful, vacant green eyes, he had an endless supply of lysergic acid, cocaine, mushrooms, and psilocybin, and a myriad of mysterious pills like jelly beans, every color of the rainbow. I was in a mood to take every pill he offered me, feeling there were no rules out here in our sea otter heaven.

Pythian smiled all the time and I knew I wasn't in love, but he was great in bed, sensual in the baths, and he knew all the words to the Grateful Dead songs—plus he had slept with Janis Joplin and didn't like to talk about it. He had never been to a therapist in his life.

Between periods of lusting after Pythian and meditating on the rocks over the ocean, I was given a Practicalizing session with the woman who had developed the technique.

Helen Grant lived in a house not far from the main Esalen buildings within a grove of large maples. One big specimen towered over her little house.

A migration of butterflies had come through Big Sur that day and the tree was heavy with the weight of a thousand black-and-orange-winged insect bodies.

"You're so tense. What do you do for a living?" she asked.

I was far away, drifting among the black-and-orange butterfly wings. "I write about music," I said, after a pause that seemed like an eternity.

"Just let your body go, Catherine, feel the pressure of my fingers on your back." She told me I must imagine myself as a human *being,* not a human *doing,* I must tell myself I existed for a living, that I was not my work, but my breathing, my feeling, my being. I asked her why I couldn't forget Sally.

"The memory of the relationship is instilled in your

body. In order to free you to love again, we will have to work it out." I told her I had to go back to New York and file my story, get some photographs from photographer friends who had been at the festival, and get back to the real world.

"The real world is inside you," she said, her salt-and-pepper hair brushing my face as she leaned over me, pushing into my chest with the palms of her hands, pushing into my abdomen with her elbow. Her hair smelled of musk and patchouli. Her yellow silk robe brushed my body. "There are people I know who have traveled all over the world—to Katmandu, to the depths of Africa," she said. "Most of them know nothing of geography. The unknown and uncharted is not out there in the world. It is inside your own body. No matter where you go, there you are." Her hands moved on me and I felt like singing, which was strange, for I rarely sang. But I knew she was speaking the truth.

I headed back to New York, returning from paradise. I left Pythian standing in the airport in San Francisco looking spaced out, waving to me as I boarded my plane. He had promised he would write; he never did. I wondered if he knew how.

I smoked a lot more cigarettes after that, and I joined a karate class and intended to start doing yoga. For a few years, I just rode the surface of a sometimes rough, sometimes easy depression. I went to a Jungian analyst for a while, then to a strict Freudian. Each helped a little.

But even so, it seemed to me that nothing really mattered anymore.

14

*I dream I see my brother Ben riding his horse along
the horizon in the afternoon light. His lanky, tall
body is bent over the palomino stallion's neck, his
face looking out across the prairie, where the sun
is setting red and orange, blazing with color across
the plains. A thousand head of Black Angus dot
the horizon, black spots in a field of orange. Ben
leans over his horse's neck and races the freight
train that moans and whistles on its course along the
prairie, pulling a hundred black cars down the
stretch of silver track across the dirt highway from
our ranch. He parallels the fence, keeping up with
the rolling freight, then moves up along the border
between the road and the track, pulls his hat off
his head, waving it in the air, spurring his horse. He
gallops and whoops, racing the train for the sunset, riding for all he is worth, going so far that soon
I can see only his figure, burning in the light of
the sun, burning alongside the freight cars, going
like thunder.*

I was back at my apartment after tea with Julia, trying not to think about the manila envelope in my desk drawer. To ease my nerves, I printed some pictures from the afternoon shoot with the Newborns.

The phone rang. I picked it up before the machine went on.

"How did the rest of the shoot go?" Stan's voice said cheerfully. "Get anything good?"

"Yes, I think so," I said, juggling the telephone receiver under my chin and trying to pull on a pair of lycra exercise tights for my six-thirty aerobics class at Valentine's Health Spa. I geared up my courage and asked, "Stan, are you aware that Fred has a problem?" There was an uncomfortable silence. "And it's not going to just go away."

"He didn't look bad today, Catherine," Stan said. "He promised he'll stay straight." Stan didn't really sound convinced.

"Stan, it's not that easy."

"Well, you can work with them, Catherine, can't you? You can get some good pictures?"

"You know I can," I said. "But I'm telling you, he's going to crash. At the very least he's going to make life difficult for the band. He was barely conscious today."

Stan's voice sounded edgy. "I don't know what to do, I really don't."

I thought of my cousin Marty and frowned at the memory, thinking of the waste, the sorrow his family had suffered. My own sorrow. I told Stan I could put Fred in touch with someone who could help.

"Catherine," Stan said. "I just don't want Fred going on *20/20* talking about his drug problem, how he went to the Betty Ford Clinic and how his life was changed, and then have him get loaded again." Stan sounded frantic, frazzled, not his usual cool self.

"I'll get in touch with Denzel in the morning," I said. "I'll try to put him together with Fred." I left it at that.

After I hung up, I punched the rewind button on my answering machine, then pushed play and turned up the volume.

"This is Renaldo Pierce, Ms. Saint. I'm so excited about the job! I'll see you at ten on the dot."

What a lovely voice. No wonder I hired him. I grinned, looking forward to tomorrow. Next was a deep-voiced message from Edward. "See you at Enrico's at eight-thirty, darling."

The next message came on with a voice that shouted into the room with a manic intensity.

"I'm going to kill you, Catherine! You can't escape!"

I felt a rush of adrenaline. Fear gripped my chest, tightening like a fist, as though I had been punched, the wind knocked out of me. I rewound the tape, playing the message again, then a third time. Something in the voice, the phrasing, was familiar but I couldn't put my finger on it. A man with a high-pitched voice? Or a low-voiced woman? I knew there was something . . .

My hands were shaking, and I said to myself, *Oh my God, this is getting serious.* I sat down at my desk and looked hard at the answering machine while I played the tape a few more times, obsessively, with mounting terror. I was cold and shivered violently.

I needed consolation. I dialed my parents' number in Kansas, a number I knew by heart.

My mother answered, and I told her about the phone call and note. As always, just talking with Elizabeth, just hearing her sympathetic voice, helped. She asked me what she could do—if I wanted her to come to New York.

"No, it's all right," I said. "Give Buster and Ben my love, will you?" Since my father had broken his leg the year before, Ben was running the ranch.

Feeling somewhat comforted, I pulled the desk drawer open and retrieved the manila envelope. I put it on the desk beside the tape. I swallowed my fears, pushed down the button on the phone and lifted it to dial the phone number again for the precinct I had called that morning, the Twentieth Precinct on Eighty-second Street. I told the sleepy desk sergeant about the letter and phone call.

"Why don't you bring the tape and the letter in tomorrow morning?" he said, coming to life. He had a kind, nonsexist voice, not condescending like the first officer I had talked to.

I thanked him and told him I would. I hung up and felt better. I had done the next right thing, as they say. I willed myself to relax, to forget the phone call and letter till the morning.

At the gym I sweated through class, then showered and dressed and went to meet Edward for dinner, feeling much better after an icy shower. Like a new woman—one who didn't have threatening notes and phone calls. And yet somehow I felt a sense of shame, as if I had brought whatever was happening upon myself.

Edward met me at the door to the bar at Enrico's and kissed me. It was a sensual kiss, a magic kiss, and I remembered why I had been with him for three years. The headwaiter, Giorgio, whom we called George, stood patiently until the ceremony was finished before he approached us with his usual warm greeting.

"Buona sera, Ms. Saint, Mr. Valarian." He saw us to our table, nodding to other customers along the way, as though they were members of his family. I absorbed the familiar look of the Italian plates and sugar bowls, with their brightly ringed flowers and birds. They made me feel more like myself, distanced from the threats, from a vague feeling in some recess of my brain that I knew who was calling me—from a vague sense of shame.

George signaled to our waiter to bring us our drinks without asking. He knew it would be San Pellegrino water for me and Veuve Cliquot champagne for Edward. We came here a lot.

George didn't bat an eye at my outfit of running gear complete with leotard and sweat jacket. The silk-, pearl-, and diamond-clad customers at other tables glanced over casually, accustomed to the incredibly democratic city, where even someone who looked like a bum might be a countess, where the rich and famous occasionally wore holes in their Levi's.

"How was my daughter?" Edward said sheepishly as we sat down.

"Beautiful and talented as usual," I said. "She sent her regards."

"She actually called me," Edward said. He looked pleased, like a little boy. "You know how long it's been since she called? Months."

"I'm glad she called you. Does she know you're doing their taxes?" I asked.

"I'm sure she does. Stan wants things to be right

for the group financially." I frowned at Edward, thinking it must be painful for him not to see Malinda more often than he did.

"She asked me if I would come to the Grammys," Edward said. He seemed less sure of himself tonight, less the smooth, sexy, successful professional man he always appeared to be. Perhaps he was feeling vulnerable because Malinda was in town and on speaking terms with him. He smiled gently as he studied my face over his glass, and then his expression changed. "You seem agitated, Catherine," he said.

I grimaced. "I am. Somebody sent me a note with the doorman saying they were going to find me and kill me." I shivered as I described the rest—the telephone call that evening, my feelings of shame and fear. I told him I had called the police twice, and that I would go to the station in the morning with the tape and the letter.

Edward squeezed my knee under the table. "I'm sure the police will handle it," he said, looking serious and concerned. "Sorry I was short with you this afternoon, darling, I was just preoccupied," he said. "I've got a client in from Chicago. We're working on a big merger and they are driving me nuts."

"I understand," I said, feeling better just to be with him. I shook off the feelings of fear, took a deep breath, and dug into the fresh Italian bread and rosemary-scented olive oil that George had brought with our drinks. I was glad to be at Enrico's, surrounded by quiet, nonthreatening people.

My thoughts turned to Fred. "One of those kids in the band has a problem with drugs. Fred. You know, the one with the silver hair?" Edward nodded.

"I know, I saw them on the MTV special," he said. I was touched by the idea that Edward had watched his daughter on the tube.

"Malinda doesn't use drugs, does she?" I asked, suddenly worried.

"No, her mother would kill her," he said.

I nodded in agreement, knowing that Malinda's mother, Jane, who now ran a meditation and fasting farm in the Berkshires with her second husband, the yoga teacher, would be horrified at the thought of her daughter getting into drugs.

I smiled at Edward. "Well," I said, "I did something positive for myself today. I hired a new assistant," I said, "a young man from Ellen's agency."

Edward didn't look as happy as I thought he might. He was always complaining that all I did was work. "I hope he works out," he said rather gruffly. Then his tone changed and he joked, "I told you not to let strange men into your apartment. You see I can't leave you alone for a minute." Underneath the table, Edward's knee found mine and I felt the electricity that always surged through me at his touch. "You've had some day!" He drank from his glass, finishing off the effervescent topaz liquid and signaling to George to bring another champagne, as well as a Glenlivet and water.

I reached out with my free hand and picked up the crystal glass, drinking deeply from it as I looked across the table at my lover. Edward straightened his cuffs, pulling them down from under the sleeves of his cashmere houndstooth jacket, fingering the three-color Cartier love knots I had given him on the anniversary of our first year together. I was pleased that he chose to wear them often.

"You look beat, Catherine. Beautiful, but beat."

"I am. It's been a heavy day." He leaned his face nearer; his cheek brushed mine. George poured more champagne in Edward's glass and it shimmered, the bubbles rising like rows of diamonds in the candlelight. He picked up the short glass of scotch and downed the remains of it in one gulp as George stood poised with pencil and pad.

"Signora?" He lifted his eyebrows. "The usual?"

"Yes, thank you, George." He knew I wanted the succulent porcini mushrooms, the radicchio and endive salad, and the garlicky chicken piccata.

"Ditto," Edward said. We ordered another bottle of sparkling water, a second scotch for Edward, and a half-bottle of '85 Pauillac, which Edward would drink with his dinner.

Edward didn't usually drink this much. He must be feeling stressed out, I thought. He seemed a little more affectionate than usual, but we were silent while we ate. Life was going on, civilization was clicking, in spite of the threatening note and phone call, in spite of Wheeling's name on Renaldo's résumé.

We finished off with espresso and buttery caramelized apple tarts. The meal had been served quickly and elegantly.

I sat back, sighed, and looked around at the faces of people at the other small, round tables, many of them set with brandy snifters and pots of espresso. The restaurant was noisier, the decibels rising with the consumption of alcohol.

"Let's get out of here, shall we?" Edward said with sexual urgency.

"Yes, I'm ready," I said, laying my napkin aside. In spite of my fears, all during dessert I had been fantasizing about the night ahead. Sex with Edward would be an antidote to my fears.

"I'll try to take your mind off your troubles," he said. Edward pressed his knee more tightly to mine, and I thought of his duplex in Tribeca, all glass and aluminum, with its huge bed, Brancusi stone sculpture, emerald leather furniture with rough hand-woven covers, and tanks of tropical fish. His bed, the size of a swimming pool, enhanced the architectural beauty of the sleeping area—as did the beautiful dance we performed in that bed.

Tonight, the cost of our decision not to live together seemed high.

"I can't stay downtown," I said, disappointed. "I've got Renaldo starting in the morning and I have to organize my papers for him." A vision of our pleasures passed over Edward's face.

"And I can't stay uptown," he said. "This thing I'm working on is going to get me up very early. I've got to be on my toes. But I would love to see you naked, in bed," he said, lowering his voice.

I had known from the first that my attraction for Edward was primarily a sexual one. The sex was divine. "Take me home, Edward, and tuck me in," I said suggestively.

Edward put his platinum American Express card back in his wallet, neatly folding up the receipt. I envisioned my own receipts, crumpled up in the side pocket of my shoulder bag, next to the rolls of film, packs of cigarettes, and matches, the credit card somewhere nearby, available only after a desperate search. I vowed once more to become neat—tomorrow.

"You come late, you go early," George said, helping me with my coat. "You look worried, I hope everything all right, no?" I smiled as reassuringly as I could.

"Thank you, George, everything's fine." Think positive, I thought.

At my place, I unlocked the door and pulled Edward in after me. I was ravenous. With the door barely shut behind us, we went at each other, unwrapping, stripping away our clothes in the dark. Blue played bat-the-ball with Edward's shirt. Layers of fabric and my emerald earrings found their way to the carpet; under my bare feet as we moved, I felt the cloth of Edward's houndstooth jacket and flannel trousers, the gold love knots, gold belt buckle, hand-tailored cotton shirt, striped silk tie, my red-and-white Reeboks, my black leather bag, purple jacket, violet and red leotard, and purple tights. My mouth was on his and I clung to his body, unencumbered from the tangled heap of silk and cashmere, English wool, lycra, and flannel.

"My God, Catherine, you are *so* ready, and I wondered if you would even want to make love at all tonight," Edward whispered, and I felt him naked and hard and supple and rigid, felt every muscle in his body press against me, against my breasts, my neck, my hips, my bare loins.

He found his way into me, carrying me on him like a shield, darkness covering us.

We fell onto the bed and he moved his hands over my body, exciting me, squeezing my nipples in his fingers and then between his teeth gently, growling in his throat as we first giggled and then moaned deeply, our bodies moving together, diving into the middle of each other, he riding in and out of me, pounding me through the bottom of the darkness to a bright and sweet light. The fears I had felt earlier in the day were overladen by sexual ecstasy as we floated and rode, intertwining, forging our flesh, Edward's body sharp and fine yet soft as silk. He held my softness, hardening it, bending it, pulsing with it, pulling himself even more into me as he rode with me, my groin tightening around him, fear and pleasure linked, galloping together to where the sweetness lay, finally, upon us, raw and free and unleashed.

Edward gasped and fell on me as I bit my lip to keep from screaming. My release came hard, over and over again, waves of pleasure on a shore that went on and on into memory, like my past and future, like my genes, like long legs, like the ability to draw or make pictures or smile, and in the room's lighted darkness, my own pleasure floated upon the face of Sally, who could bring me to completion without touching me at times, just her eyes finding mine over the width of a bed, or a lifetime.

Afterward, our faces were damp against each other, my hair damp upon my cheeks. We rose back into consciousness, our heads on the pillow together, and I found Edward's wide, dark eyes looking into mine, satisfied, hungry for me again in the darkness.

I thought how complicated a thing is passion.

I was weak as a kitten. Wasted. The sex we had was always magnificent, but tonight was the best ever. I rose on one elbow.

He kissed me on the neck, pushing back the damp hair from my shoulders. "I'll make it all right," he said, "I can see in the dark, you know." Like a cat.

We kissed good night and I felt rather than saw him in shadow, padding about, picking up clothes, dressing backward to the door. I got up quickly, stumbled over a table, swore, and made my way across the room and into the hallway to kiss him hungrily again at the front door. He looked at me, raising his eyebrows. I handed him a gold cufflink which I had found under my foot, all of a sudden terribly sad he had to leave.

"Good night, darling. You're amazing. I love you so much I can't believe it," he said fluidly.

At times I thought I loved him too.

16

I GREW UP ON A RANCH THAT STRETCHED AS FAR AS the eye could see. My dad, Buster Saint, raised quarter horses and Black Angus cattle, with the help, he always said, of the woman behind the throne, my mother, Elizabeth. He credited my mother for a good crop of ponies, mild haying weather, and much of the work that went into the running of the ranch.

I worked hard too, along with my brother, Ben, who was two years younger than I. It was our ranch, our life, our horses, and our big, shiny Black Angus cattle that dotted the brown grazing land, and I gazed at them with wonder when they calved, or when they routed with the bulls in the spring.

My father ran about three thousand Kansas acres to wheat, and the rest to grazing land for the Angus, which brought in a substantial yearly income. My father also raised quarter horses. I knew he loved all the animals, whether they were for eating or riding.

My mother and father both rode well, and Bengie and I were taught early, put in the saddle, and given our own horses, colts, at their birth. We helped my father bring the wet, skinny-legged creatures out of their mothers' wombs in the slick and shiny envelopes while she writhed on the bed of straw, and then we would watch her pull off the membranes with her teeth, biting through them to lick the colt dry while we helped him climb to his shaky legs.

Training and raising an animal up to the standards of quality my father set was about a two-year job. As soon as the animal was ready for the feel of a rope on his shoulders to guide him in circles around the corral, Dad would be out there with us, bringing our training up to snuff, coaching, yelling, chasing a gangly kid and a barely grown horse around in circles till we all got the hang of it.

After our workouts with the animals, Dad would often lean up against the wood fence of the corral, his legs bowed in his washed-out Levi's, his Stetson set at an angle on his head. Above his tanned face, with his hat off, his forehead was white where the sun never reached under the brim.

Buster was very particular about the animals, and he cared about them both during the time he had them and after they belonged to somebody else. "Honey," he would say, "you never want to sell a horse to a man who rides his mount till the horse is all lathered with sweat. That man will ruin a good horse."

When a man bought, Buster always invited them to stay to dinner. "Always feed a man who gives you money," he would say.

It was always men, not their wives, who paid for the horses and made the decisions about the livestock. I learned that men had most of the power in financial matters and wondered why Buster had so much confidence in me. I realized as I grew up that to Buster I was different. Special. No matter that I was a girl, my father thought I could do anything.

Although he included my younger brother, Ben, as well as our cousin, Marty, in his lessons about ranching and living, I always knew Buster was talking mostly to me. Marty wasn't much interested in our ranch, or even his father's; he and Ben were always inventing things like boomerangs and chasing the calves around the corral. When he was a teenager, Marty liked to drive fast cars, although by that point he and Ben had parted company. Ben was the artist, Marty was the fast liver.

I knew Buster's teaching was meant for me, his oldest child.

In addition to being a successful rancher, my father was a tough and demanding parent; he challenged my brother and me on every little detail of our lives. Whether we had done something right or wrong, he had the same advice: "If you're number two, why aren't you number one? And if you're number one, the club's too small." I never dared to come home with a C on a report card—he would have whaled the daylights out of me.

I absorbed my father's criticism and his praise, either basking or cringing. When Ben was little, he never seemed to let my father's perfectionism bruise or bother him. His freckled face, brown cowlick of hair, and cornflower blue eyes registered no reaction to Buster's brusque style. Later on I realized that the hurt had gone inside, forming my brother's quiet and brooding nature, feeding his art. But when we were young, it seemed to me I was the one who reacted, while with Ben it rolled over his smooth cheeks and his pale, pretty face. Ben was so artistic, so good with his hands. He had a forgiving, easy personality. He played the guitar; and he loved to draw, paint in oils, and whittle animals out of scraps of wood. I realized in my teens that Ben was a philosopher, a dreamer. He wanted to be a sculptor, and he spent hours in his room or out in the back of the barns, sketching the wide prairie, the low barbed wire fences, and the long Kansas grass that seemed to blow in the wind whether or not there *was* any wind.

I knew I was my dad's great hope for the ranch, that he counted on me to stay on in Kansas and look after his beloved cattle and horses. He wanted me to know everything there was to know.

It was hard for me to understand that my father's tough hide had anything to do with love, but it was clear that Buster loved the animals, and wanted them trained right, so somehow, although he never said it, I knew he must love me. I was an eager learner. I loved the horses and the big Black Angus bulls, their horns angled from their heads, their black eyes lowering at me under silky lashes as long as a girl's.

One of my jobs was to fill their feeding troughs with steaming mash in the morning, the cold air biting my cheeks, the breath of the bulls making tiny clouds in the bullpen.

"Always keep those babies calm," my father would

say. "Just you move easy and slow in that pen, I don't want that seed all shaken up so they can't do their work." The Anguses' work—so I learned before I could walk—was to mount the three hundred or so females in the herd. They raked the air with their hooves, the females snorted and sometimes ran away, the big bulls scuffled and chased, mounting often a dozen times before their purpose was accomplished. The ultimate moment was penetration, and my dad said that penetration—"with that bull right up there on her, and in her"—was what kept his ranch in the black and his quarter horse business out of the red.

The wide space that met my eye at the door to our ranch house was all mine, that vast expanse of land that stretched west to the Rockies and east to the Atlantic Ocean. I couldn't imagine it ending anywhere before it came to mountains or water. In my mind's eye, the land beyond our ranch belonged to no one else but me.

Buster Saint was a handsome man. I was attuned to my mother Elizabeth's every sly glance at him. He treated my mother lovingly, roughly, as he did the horses, slapping her on the behind, putting his arms around her at off times, in front of company, even in private. He would come into the kitchen before dinner, still smelling of horses and sweat, grab her around the waist, lift her off the ground and spin her, his rough-out boot heels making circles on the linoleum floor.

"Buster, stop it, you're mussing my hair!" my

mother would say, sliding out from under his arms, her elbows white with flour from the biscuits she was making, her mouth in a sweet smile that belied her harsh words and bespoke a promise for later, after the kids were asleep, after the crew was off in the bunkhouse, fed and contented.

At night as I lay in my bed in the room I shared with Bengie, who I knew didn't understand a thing about what was going on, I would hear noises from my parents' bedroom, squeaking springs, and groans from my father. Even in the big ranch house, the sound traveled, and some nights I would hear my mother, if she thought we were asleep, giggle and make a high-pitched sound as though she were in pain, and when she knew we weren't, she would whisper, "Shhhh, Buster, *don't!*" and then couldn't keep her squeals from reaching my burning, waiting ears. Love sounded sweet and painful like the mating of the bulls. I thought I understood what love was, and I knew that Buster and Elizabeth were in love.

The year I was ten my parents' relationship changed forever in my mind. There was an extra heavy fall harvest and the weather was threatening rain. One day at lunch, the big meal of the day on the ranch, we got word that Mother would have to go to Kansas City because Grandma Wilson had taken ill. My mother was silent over lunch, sadness in her face.

"Elizabeth, you go on to Kansas City to your mother, the kids and I will be just fine here," my father said, passing the plate of steaming Silverlake corn that had been picked right off the back acre we had planted with food for our own table. Out there, behind a fence to keep off the deer, were heavy red tomatoes, beets and cauliflower, beans, and big green cucumbers twice the size of your foot. Practically everything we ate in the late summer and fall came fresh from that garden. Butter ran down the corners of my father's mouth, and he wiped his face with a linen-stitched napkin.

"But you've got your hands full now, Buster," Mother said. "Why don't we send Ben and Catherine over to Gene's place? They can catch the bus to school from there, and I'll feel better knowing they've got Marty to play with, that they're not here distracting you." We all played together a lot anyway, so it would make sense that Ben and I should go to Uncle Gene's ranch, which was three miles down the road from ours.

It was late August. The hay was due for cutting and rain was in the air, a damp, unseasonable wetness; my father said we would have to push to get the harvest in before the grasses were mildewed—before the winter feed, which we both used and sold for profit, was ruined. We had a crew of five or six regular fellows working all year on the ranch, more during calving time and at harvest. Twelve extra fellows were out in the bunk along with the regulars. I knew all the men liked my father, they would do anything for him.

We finished our meal and the issue seemed to be settled. I went out to the barn to talk to Charlie, our ranch foreman. He and I were working the rough spots out of a little mare my father had given me, and I wanted to see how she was doing and tell Charlie just to go on with the training sessions while I was at my cousin's. I was ten years old and this was the first horse my father had said was mine and mine alone. Charlie wasn't in the barn and I continued on over to the shed where the men ate and slept to search him out. From the weathered wood barn came the familiar sound of deep male laughter and, in the wake of its roll, the high-pitched voice of a woman.

I mounted the three steps onto the porch of the bunkhouse and looked in through the screen, pressing my nose so the hatched brown surface dented inward. Inside, at a long table, was the crew, finishing their big midday meal. Plates of bare corn cobs littered the scarred wood table. Depleted bowls of whipped Idaho spuds, as my dad called them, dotted the table's length. A single chicken back, fried crisp and brown, lay alone on a huge white porcelain platter in the center of the table. I knew that plate had been stacked high at the beginning of lunch. The crew, like everyone on Buster Saint's ranch, ate well.

"Hi, little lady, how's it going?" Charlie, the head wrangler, called out, waving me down to his end of the table. I swung through the screen door and it shut behind me, rocking for a moment on its springs, sending little squeaks into the room. Men in rough-out boots were leaning their chairs back, picking their teeth, their Stetsons tilted back on their heads. Charlie sat at the end of the table; he shook a white cloth pouch of loose tobacco over a thin cigarette paper, rolling it tight with the fingers of a brown hand whose nails were cracked right down to the half moons near the quicks.

"Come on in, honey, and meet Lou-Lou," he said, setting a flame to the end of the hand-rolled cigarette and beckoning me farther into the room. A woman's yellow hair bobbed up and down amidst the Stetsons, her hands fluttering above the table like loose birds, her face powder giving off a scent I took in all the way from the screen door. My mother didn't use powder or scent. Perfume in the bunkhouse, a whiff of spicy flowers, seemed to insult the pungency of manure that always permeated the barn and the bunk quarters.

"This here's Catherine, Lou-Lou." Sam, one of my father's full-time crew, slapped at a fly that buzzed around his face and put an arm around Lou-Lou's shoulders.

"Pleased to meet you, honey." I looked away from Lou-Lou's face, a landscape of reds and blush pinks with two bright sapphire eyes looking out. I had never seen a woman in the bunkhouse, except for my mother, who came into that male haven only to check that the boys had enough to eat.

Lou-Lou wore a white-lace, off-the-shoulder blouse. Her earrings were big gold hoops, and the polish on her fingernails was bright pink, cracked and flaking off in some places. She ran one hand over Sam's hand while the other caressed a glass of what looked like lemonade. Her fingers were the color of faded silk.

My embarrassed eyes focused on the fly strip that hung down from the ceiling, nearly touching the platter of clean chicken bones in the middle of the table. On the yellow surface of the fly strip, black creatures were fastened, their opalescent bodies glinting in the light as the strip turned slowly in the air from the ceiling fan.

The boys were standing up, shuffling out the door, heading for the haying rigs and the trucks. Hay to be cut, work to be done, noon respite over.

"The men need that hot meal, Buster," my mother would say whenever Buster talked of cutting back and putting out sandwiches for the men. I wondered if my mother would be as concerned about Lou-Lou getting a hot lunch.

Sam turned to me with a funny look. "Your mom still here?"

The men knew that Grandma Wilson was in the hospital and that my mother was going to Kansas City. They knew everything, I was quite sure. "Yes," I said.

"Sam and Lou-Lou's engaged to be married," Charlie offered. I nodded in their direction. Lou-Lou's hand was entangled with Sam's as it lay beside his empty coffee cup on the table. Their twining fingers reminded me of snakes.

"Ha!" Lou-Lou laughed a loud laugh like a big cow bell.

"Well, ain't you getting married? That's what Sam told me, eh Sam?" Charlie went on.

"He's lucky I still come to see him, if he's thinking of marryin'. I'm a single woman, by God, and intend to stay such." Her pale fingers freed themselves from Sam's. "This is just a casual social visit, ain't it, Sam honey?"

Sam looked at me sheepishly, looked at his abandoned hand on the table, then at his coffee cup. Charlie patted Lou-Lou on the shoulder and stood up.

"I've got work to do, and so do you, Sam." The men went out the door, letting it slam behind their backs.

Lou-Lou picked up her coffee mug, looked at me, and said, "You never ought to get married, either, sugar. How old are you?"

I told her I was eleven, which was a lie.

"Well, I'm a lot older, so listen to me," the yellow-haired woman said. "Reckon your daddy'd mind if I bunked over here with Sam a couple nights?"

I was so shocked I nodded. I don't know if I nodded yes or no. I backed out through the door and off the porch.

I didn't mention Lou-Lou at all—not to my mother, not to Daddy. My brother and I went to stay at Uncle Gene's, and Mother left for Kansas City.

Two nights later, while I was riding at dusk with Ben and Marty, my horse stumbled in a gopher hole, lurched, and threw me off. I broke my arm in the fall, and Uncle Gene drove me in his station wagon to the hospital in Moline, where they set the bone in a plaster cast. On the way back from the hospital, Uncle Gene pulled off the highway onto our ranch road.

"I suppose we ought to let your daddy know you're busted up, Cath honey," he said. "You go in and tell him what happened, show him your cast and all. I want him to know I done the right thing, getting you straight to the hospital. Me and Ben and Marty'll wait in the car. There's no need for us all to make a fuss."

It was late, around ten. Ranching families were early to bed, earlier to rise. We came to a stop on the gravel circle outside the back door of the house.

Everything was dark—the house, the bunkhouse. Alongside the main house, long shadows pulled in against the walls, wrapping like leaves across the front door, hiding the windows. The wind was blowing hard, the way it seems to on most Kansas summer nights. Either a howling wind or as still as sleep.

I walked in through the back door and into the kitchen.

"Daddy," I called out. I didn't hear the dogs; they usually made a racket. The house was quiet as a tomb. I figured Buster was asleep: sometimes he would take a little whiskey after a day's work, and then he'd be out like a couple of lights. I went tiptoeing through the kitchen toward the living room, which opened onto my parents' bedroom.

"Pa!" I called him that sometimes, especially when I was upset. A familiar creaking sound put a knot in my stomach. My father's groan, the sound of laughter like a heifer's neck bell, the slap of sweetness, a howl of pain and pleasure as I twisted open the doorknob, refusing to believe, putting away the familiar flower scent that poked its way to my nostrils.

"Oh God, Buster," a voice squealed and a body slipped out from under the sheet and hunkered down by the top corner of the bed, pulling the sheet over her shining white breasts a moment too late. Two sapphires gleamed at me through the semidarkness.

"Is that you, Charlie? Who's there?" My father's

hand was groping under the bed, where he kept a shotgun. His voice was loud and husky and, to my ears, horrible.

"It's me," I said, to save myself from having my head blown off as an intruder, yet not wanting to give away my presence, hating him suddenly, completely, irrevocably.

"Catherine," he said plaintively, his voice reflecting the end of something, the end of everything. My father, Lou-Lou, and I were frozen in a tableau, like a surreal photograph, me in the soft light framed by the door to the kitchen, she, kneeling with the sheet hiding her nakedness, my father sitting upright, his chest bare, his eyes staring at me in the dark room, his hand hanging limp over the side of the bed, the shotgun still in his grip. It seemed an eternity we three surveyed the timeless wreckage.

I backed out the door, pulling it closed, softly, my broken arm throbbing in the cast. I stood in the kitchen for a moment, then went to the stove and switched out the light. I tiptoed to the back door and stepped out into the windy moonlight. The shadows stole back across the door, like a pair of wings wrapping the house up behind me. I walked to Uncle Gene's station wagon and got into the back seat, slamming the door behind me.

"He's asleep, Uncle Gene, and I don't want to wake him." I was aware that my voice was trembling, and I tried to hold it steady. "He's tired. You know, he's been having a hard season."

17

I dream of a white, shuttered house with dozens of windows facing the sea. The sky is purpled and blackened with dark rolling clouds that thunder as lightning breaks the sky, slicing the air with silver ribbons above the long green lawn and the rows of flower beds that roll down to the sea from the long porch of the sea-bound house. In each window, looking out toward the breaking, flooding waters and the rolling clouds of thunder, is the face of a man, larger than life, as though a photographer had snapped a picture and then developed the photograph five feet high.

My father Buster, his scowl deep and tanned, his chin fixed like a fist as though he would pound down the dark clouds on the horizon and stop the rain from falling in dark shining lines on the sea; my brother Ben's face, gentle and thoughtful, his eyes moist and kind, his smile soft; Stan, with his lean jawbone, his piercing eyes, his intelligent brow, staring intently toward me, searching out my thoughts, knowing my secrets, sharing my confidence.

And then my lovers: Gavin, his long blond hair blowing in the wind from the sea, his bright, schoolboy looks accentuated in the lightning's *flashes, his charm radiating from the window, his finally shallow concerns as vivid now as they were the day we parted; John, dark and brooding like my father, John, the oldest of my lovers, an art dealer and wine connoisseur, swollen with money and power and a bad temper that eventually took over our time together and brought it to an end; James, who was dead now of AIDS, brown curls framing an angelic face that still moved me to tenderness, and would have continued to if he, and his needs, hadn't changed. And Edward, his handsome face and sexy eyes gleaming at me through the falling rain, promising, seducing, luring, satisfying all physical needs.*

Each of the men in the house, from his window, watches me through the rain, bigger than life, stranger than life. The wind howls and the rain pours down and the claps of thunder shake the shutters around their faces. The sea grows deeper and deeper from the rain and begins to move up the lawn toward the house, until it covers the flower beds with their peony and pansy faces and Johnny jump-ups, wild, woozy lilac, and white ranunculus. The water moves over these flowers, up the steps to the porch, through the screen doors, up the walls of the house, up the sides to the windows. The faces begin to drown in the rain, the water a deeper and deeper sea. The chins, the lips, the noses, the eyes, still watch me from each window of the house, until all are gone, all are drowned, all are under deep, swirling water.

18

The next morning, I threw on a pair of heavy black running pants, a thick black wool sweater, running shoes, and a fanny pack, into which I put my driver's license, a few bucks, and the tape and letter. I pulled a warm hat over my piled-up hair, threw on my black parka, and headed out the door.

Once on the street, I loped the ten blocks to the police precinct house between Amsterdam and Columbus on Eighty-second, figuring I could use the exercise, hurrying in the cold March wind. At the red brick building police officers ran in and out of the doors. I was shown to a desk in a big room filled with men and women in blue talking on the phone, drinking coffee, yelling at each other. The lieutenant who introduced himself and asked me to take a seat was very fat. While we talked, he drank coffee out of a cardboard cup and took bites out of a sticky-looking lemon Danish. He looked the letter over and played the tape on a scratchy-sounding Walkman attached to a pair of small speakers mounted on his cluttered desk. He told me there was not enough evidence to go on, that he doubted he could help me. But he said he wanted to hang on to the tape and the manila envelope and told me to call him if I received any more letters or calls; then he pulled out another Danish and ripped open the clear plastic. As he said good-bye he took a bite out of the pastry. This one was raspberry and dripped down on the paper-strewn desk as he waved after me.

I ran all the way back to my apartment building on Central Park West, relieved. At least, I thought, shrugging out of my heavy parka and shaking my hair out of my hat, even if the law was not very cooperative, I had taken the action. The rest was not my business—was it?

Renaldo arrived at ten sharp, looking fresh and hand-some. I didn't tell him about the threatening call or the note; I didn't want to frighten him. We went through my files and bills and I told him about the procedures I use for photographing and writing a piece, for paying my bills, making contacts, and keeping track of my shooting schedule.

When I turned on the computer and brought up the Rolodex function, Renaldo's mouth dropped open. "You know *everyone!*" he said. I smiled.

"Well, maybe in the music business," I said. "I suppose most of them have been here for dinner at least once."

He laughed. "Everyone who is in *Hit Men* is in here," he said, continuing to look down the lists.

"You *have* been doing your homework, haven't you?"

"The music business is where I want to work, Ms. Saint, and these are the people in it. I like to know the players." *Hit Men*, the scathing book about law-yers and managers who make the merry world of rock-and-roll deals go round, was indeed a script version of my Rolodex. "Are they as terrible as the book says they are?" he asked.

"They're not so bad," I said, "if you don't have to dance with them." Flawed, frail, fabulous, there were all kinds in the music business, as in every business. "Tell me," I continued, "you don't harbor the desire to be a stand-up comic or a singer, do you?"

"Ha," Renaldo said, scrolling through the entries, "I'm too shy for any of that. This is where I want to be—behind this desk." He smiled.

By the time we had gone through my files and the schedule of shoots for the next few months, and after I had given Renaldo the names of my key friends and associates in the business—the people he would have to get to know if he were to be a real help to me—it was lunchtime.

So far, the phone had brought only innocent, known callers: Stan, Julia, and Edna Shapiro, my photo editor at Random House. I was breathing easier.

I was going to like working with Renaldo. He didn't bullshit, he got right down to business, and he seemed to grasp a lot right away. I liked the way he took the calls, saying, "Ms. Saint will have to call you back. May I help you with anything? I'm her new assistant, Mr. Pierce." His English accent was so suave, I felt like swooning.

"I hate to say this," he said after we cleared away the lunch things. "Maybe you'll fire me, but for an organized person you seem kind of messy."

"That's putting it mildly," I said, a little testily. "That's why *you're* here, to clean up my act, make it smooth and seamless." When we got to the bookkeeping, I told Renaldo that Edward would explain the investment account to him. There was a portrait of Edward on my desk in a silver frame, signed *"To Catherine, with all my love."*

There was another picture of me and Edward with Malinda on one of the only trips we took together— to Aspen, before she went to Vermont for her first year of school, back when she still seemed to be feeling all right about her father. A field of snow behind our squinting, smiling faces and bright-colored parkas.

Renaldo said he would go to the bank later, introduce himself to the manager, and get the forms he would need to do my banking.

As I moved into the darkroom, Renaldo looked totally at ease, as though he had been here with me for years. I gave him a grateful smile as I pulled the door closed.

"Welcome to the music business, Renaldo," I said to myself.

Satisfied that I had hired exactly the right person, I shut the door to the darkroom and reviewed the pictures I had printed up the night before, of Kurt Cobain and Nirvana at a recording session the previous month. The piece was due in two days. Cobain looked beautiful, spiritual—and clearly troubled. His mumbling, practically unintelligible lyrics were sung with his head hung over his guitar, his stringy light-blond hair falling down over his Christlike face. I had worried about him even while I shot the performance, nervous about his behavior, aware, as everyone in the business was, that this group was unable to tour very much, in spite of their enormous record sales, because some of the members were on drugs. I looked over all the color and black-and-white prints, wondering what it was about this business. So many brilliant young people dead: Jimi, Janis, Jim Morrison. What was a girl like me doing in this menagerie? But I knew that in spite of the drugs and the drama, there was genius. I loved it all despite the trouble, the insanity, the death.

When I finished going over the pictures, Renaldo knocked softly on the door to the adjoining room, where I was working, to say he was going to the bank. I sat down at the computer and did a rough draft of the Cobain article, then headed for Valentine's, the swanky gym around the corner from me.

That day, like every day, the health club was crawling with good-looking hunks and curvy women who had last been seen on the talk shows, in the latest movies, and in the best New York stage shows. I knew some of these beautiful people. I considered Valentine's a sort of therapy group of unique creatures who were just as camera-conscious when they were naked as when they were dressed.

I spent an hour gasping and sweating with my aerobics instructor, Linda the bun-burner, hoping to lose the five extra pounds I always carried no matter how much I exercised or what I ate. I took a long swim and sat in the sauna. I dressed in a leisurely fashion, really taking my time for once. I blow-dried my hair and put on fresh makeup while gossiping in the women's locker room, catching up on who was doing what, who was sick, who was going to be appearing at the Grammys, who was in Los Angeles, and discussing the fact that the awards show was in New York this year.

Refreshed, I walked the few blocks home, stopping into Barnes and Noble to buy a copy of a new novel reviewed in the *Times* that morning, browsing with a cup of Starbucks coffee. At the Korean-run market on Columbus Avenue I bought rice cakes, dried fruit, fig bars, six big Golden Delicious apples, and two bunches of purple and white tulips; in the Capezio shop on Broadway I bought a new pair of bright-pink tights for my workouts; at a novelty shop, a pretty card for my mother's birthday.

I let my mind wander and my feet take me where they would. Having this kind of time was a total luxury for me. I knew that Renaldo was working in the office and it made me feel free, giddy and light, like a schoolgirl instead of an overworked photographer. As I wandered in and out of shops, nodding to acquaintances, enjoying the cool, wet air that promised rain, I felt as though I was having a wild, irresponsible love affair. With somebody other than Edward. I felt renewed.

And in the entire afternoon I had thought only twice of the threatening note and phone call.

The light was going fast in the mid-March evening, and by the time I reached the entrance to my building on Central Park West, it was after six and quite dark. One of the doormen helped me up the elevator, relieving me of some of the packages in my arms.

There was a note from Renaldo on my desk. "I found a small problem with an account," it said, "which I'm sure I'll be able to sort out in the morning. So long for today. See you tomorrow at ten. I'm so happy to be here—Renaldo. PS: If you need me, you can call me at home."

Renaldo's signature was elegant, like his clothes. I was glad he was in my life and glad there were no lights on my machine reminding me of terrible strangers.

19

It was 1991, three years before. My work was going well, I had money in the bank, sex with Edward was great, but there it was again, that old pang, a desire to take every pill I could get my hands on and end it all if I couldn't have Sally Broomfield. I felt mad, out of sync with everything around me. I started dreaming about Sally again, reliving the accident in which she was killed.

I went to see Dr. Victoria Friedman, the smart, savvy woman who was my internist. During my annual physical I had complained to her of the recurring nightmares, my depression, and my nervousness about traveling by airplane. (For months I had been so anxious at takeoffs and landings that I practically leapt into my fellow passengers' laps. Finding myself in the lap of a kind-looking Italian man after one particularly difficult landing, I had looked him in the eye, smiled, and said, *"Te amo."*) Dr. Friedman said that she didn't want to put me on medication. She thought that I should see a psychiatrist.

A male acquaintance at *Vanity Fair* had been seeing a shrink, and recommended Dr. Ernest Wheeling.

When I called for an appointment, I was told that it would be a few weeks before Dr. Wheeling could see me. But having made the call, my need diminished a bit, as it tends to do when you finally take an action, and getting to a shrink didn't seem quite so urgent. I said I could wait what seemed an awfully long time for what his secretary called an "assessment."

When I finally saw Wheeling, the summer was nearly over. Wheeling's office was on the East Side, a block from Bloomingdale's. I walked into the coolness of the lobby of the impressive prewar building on a quiet side street. I announced myself and was buzzed inside; I took the elevator to the eleventh floor and walked into a designer room of bright shapes, bold rugs, big square-framed posters of work by Mondrian and Hans Hofmann.

I sat in Wheeling's office, staring into the potted scheflera plant with its shiny leaves, looking at the prints on the wall, and listening to the hum of the white-noise machine that whirred outside the closed door to his inner sanctum. I thought about the ranch, about my photographs, about rock and roll. I tried to organize my thoughts, knowing they would have an important influence on what might go on in my session. I tried to remember my dreams of the night before, but except for a general feeling of terror, couldn't remember the details.

At ten minutes before the hour, a tall man wearing a gray tweed sport jacket stepped out and said good-bye to a well-dressed blond-haired woman. I couldn't see her face, but as she left the room I observed her elegance—high Jourdan heels, long shapely legs, a short skirt, a smart beige jacket.

Dr. Wheeling beckoned me into his office and closed the door. He gestured to a black leather, deeply cushioned chair, into which I sank, looking around the high-ceilinged chamber whose walls were painted glossy white. The shelves, full of medical texts and art books, were also white, with scrolling on the ledges and at the base of each row of gold-embossed, thick-spined volumes.

I scrutinized this new shrink as he took a seat on a Mies van der Rohe chair at a carved wooden desk, bare of any ornament except a Naguchi lamp, which shone a pool of yellow light on Wheeling's hands and face.

Wheeling had a pale, thin face with a pointed chin and a high forehead. His tortoiseshell reading glasses, which were pushed far up on his head, contrasted sharply with his black hair. He was handsome in a forbidding way.

"Please call me Ernest. May I call you Catherine?"

I nodded, surprised at his directness and casualness. I hadn't been to a shrink in a long time. Perhaps this was the new fashion in therapy. We're all friends here.

"Is there anything in particular bothering you?" Wheeling's voice was sharp, almost piercing. He was dressed in a white shirt open at the neck. I could see black and gray hairs curling up from his chest out his shirtfront. On the elbows of his jacket were black leather patches. The backs of his hands were covered with the same curly hair that stood out from the front of his shirt. He was wearing dark-brown tweed trousers and black ostrich-leather shoes. He seemed well built.

Yet this otherwise healthy-looking person might never have seen the sun. I assume that he never got out of this chair, that he was always working.

I felt a cold wind blow through the room and shivered. There was something chilly about Wheeling, something unfriendly about his friendly manner, something cold in his warmth. I took this in as I sat on the cushioned chair, reconsidering. He was continuing to speak, but I was barely listening. I realized I had a window of grace during which I might just say I had made a mistake, go out the door, and I would only have to pay for the hour I hadn't used, but no more than that. I wasn't sure I wanted this man in my life, for therapy or any other reason. "You said on the phone that you were suffering from depression?"

"Yes," I said, despite myself. "I'm terribly depressed." I was suddenly confused about why I had come.

"I charge a hundred twenty-five dollars a fifty-minute session," Wheeling said, then described the other logistics of our therapy. "Where were you born?" he asked suddenly.

"Kansas," I said.

It wasn't the price that was making me nervous, or the prospect of talking about my past, my family, and my dreams. Wheeling picked up a silver pen, waved it at me, pointing it as though I were a map and he were indicating mountain ranges, rivers, continents.

Suddenly I had completely forgotten about leaving; I found myself talking, explaining to Wheeling all the reasons I had come to see him.

"I have this thing I call 'the committee' in my head," I said as though speaking under water, or in a dream, almost against my will. "They meet in the middle of the night. They wake me up. They ask me about my sexual identity. I don't have any answers, and I find it confusing." I paused and took a deep breath.

Wheeling waved the silver pen in the air in a little circle above his desk, waiting for me to continue. The silver pen was strange, like a winding snake in the doctor's hand. I averted my eyes and continued speaking.

I told him that in my relationships with James, John, and Gavin, the three serious boyfriends I had before meeting Edward, I didn't feel much connection. I just felt lonely, even when I was with them. I said I had had an affair with a woman years before and was having nightmares about her death in an automobile accident. I said I didn't think I was lesbian, that I never had been particularly attracted to other women. I said I had had other boyfriends, other men in my life. And I confessed that I wondered sometimes whether I had had an incestuous relationship with my father. I told Wheeling things I had never talked about, even to Julia.

"Now I go out with a man named Edward," I said. "The sex is great and Edward helps me in other ways, with my investments, and we do a lot of things together. But in some ways the relationship doesn't seem to be enough. Do I hate men, is that it? I have good men friends, and good women friends. Is it that I can't really commit myself to Edward?" I stopped talking and realized that I had specifically wanted to see a male shrink, not a woman, to confirm to myself that I did in fact know how to get along with men.

Wheeling wrote a great deal in his black leather notebook. As he wrote, the room started to darken. It was early evening, and Wheeling's hands were illuminated now by the soft glow from the rice-paper lamp. His fingers held the pen over the paper, a black line twirling under its nib. Dr. Ernest Wheeling, Boswell to my Johnson, chronicling my life. We talked for fifty minutes and I wrote him a check for a hundred twenty-five dollars.

"I can give you something for the depression," Wheeling said as he saw me to the door, "if you're feeling depressed."

"Not now," I said, shaking my head. "I want to find out what is going on with me. If you give me a pill, I may not be depressed, but on the other hand, I won't know what's bothering me."

"It is always a possibility," he told me, "but just remember, you don't have to experience these feelings without help." The door shut behind him and the white-noise machine took over as I walked through his waiting room.

I continued to see Wheeling for over a year. Talking to him made me think of things, say things, that surprised me. There was something about the pen, the

light, the Naguchi lamp, his arms, the hair curling up
from his shirt, the little mushroom sound machine,
the plants like big green hands, the easiness of his
discomfort, the way the hair curled onto his fingers
from the backs of his hands. I found him at once re-
pulsive and extremely sexy.

Since our first session, I wasn't having terrible
dreams—at least I couldn't remember them. I felt better.
I lay down on the black leather couch with its deep
cushions similar to those in the chair I had sat in for a
month, staring at the high beamed ceiling. I couldn't see
Wheeling's face but I could hear his sharp, precise voice.

"I want you to go back to your earliest dream,"
he prodded.

"I don't remember my earliest dreams, Dr. Wheeling."

"Do you mind if we try a little experiment?" he
asked. "Sometimes I use a little hypnosis."

I was suddenly frightened. I had been taught that
hypnosis was not good for the soul, that it stole your
powers of self-determination.

"Do you really think it's necessary?" I said.

"It might help," he said, moving his chair so that he
could sit near my head and holding a silver pen before
my eyes. "Just follow the movement of the pen." I followed the moving pen back and forth, back and forth.

"You see," his voice was saying from somewhere,
"this can't hurt you." The pen moved slowly, and then
stopped in front of my eyes.

"How do you feel now, Catherine?"

When I answered, my lips felt as though they had
been glued together. I had to clear my throat. "I feel
thirsty," I said.

"Now," he said, "you will remember your dream in great detail, and when you have told me all about it, I will snap my fingers and you will remember everything we have said together. Let us begin." A memory, fleeting at first like a far-off vision, then becoming a whole, Technicolor dream, quite clear and vivid—a dream I had never before remembered.

I am in a big house, a house with many rooms. I am on the very top floor of the house, and I can hear the sound of pounding, a terrible, loud sound. I run to the window and see my father standing on the lawn, looking toward me, holding a hammer. His hands are made of bone. I run out of the house and down the steps as fast as I can, and I'm screaming. We have a watchdog, a German shepherd. My brother Ben and I both love the dog. My father takes my brother and me out to a big field near the house. He has brought his shotgun, and he tells us the dog has misbehaved. He makes us watch while he shoots the dog. The shepherd jumps once, but it is a clean hit and the dog just slumps his head, like he is going to sleep, and there is a red line running down through the honey-colored hair on his head.

"I am going to snap my fingers now," Wheeling said, holding his right hand in front of my face. "How do you feel?"

"I feel like a red bullet wound bleeding into the room," I said. "I feel my life is trickling away into the carpet, into the leather couch, into the empty coffee cup."

"You see how well it worked?" Wheeling said. "This is the dream that shaped your sexual feelings and formed your incestuous feelings toward your father. You will need a lot of work on it. All girls want to take their fathers away from their mothers. See you next week," he said.

Wheeling looked as though he had just had an injection. His face was less pale, his eyes brighter—dancing, almost.

As I left his office that day, I thought of Wheeling as a vampire lover needing the blood of my life's story to keep him from death; a vampire that haunted the room, absorbing my dreams, again and again, in the fading light of evening.

20

*I dream of my cousin, Marty Saint, a vivid dream
so real I awake weeping. We are in Kansas City,
where Marty is living. We are having coffee in a
diner near his one-bedroom apartment close to
the stockyards and train tracks at the outskirts
of town.*

*Marty looks terrible, not the handsome, dashing
man I had grown up with. His hair is long and
stringy and he is all bones. He tells me, sipping
coffee and trying to keep his hands from shaking, avoiding looking me in the eye, that he is
afraid. He came home high the night before, he
says, and thought he had just gone to bed. But
when he awoke the next morning he didn't
recognize the room; there were broken bottles and
the furniture was moved all around. There was
a pile of cigarette butts in the ashtray. Mixed
among his own were a brand he doesn't smoke,
and he has no memory of the stranger, or strangers, who must have been with him. Bottles of
booze, works for shooting heroin, drugs of every
kind, are scattered among the ruins of his
apartment.*

My cousin is a ruin himself as he tells me about what has happened. I tell him in the dream to go into the hospital, and he says he will. Soon. As soon as he gets himself together.

The next time I see him, three weeks later, is at his funeral.

21

At six-thirty I was dressed in an amethyst sequined top and a long peridot velvet skirt, and black high-heeled boots. My hair was piled up on my head, and it curled around my face, the way it often looks fresh out of the shower or the sauna. I was ready for Julia's opening.

Lingering fears about the threatening calls rumbled through my mind.

I put on my long black velvet cape and made sure I had plenty of film. I would be using a strobe, and I threw in my trusty Minolta light meter, the Nikon camera with a long lens as well as the short-lensed Leica. In my party dress and ready to shoot whatever was going on—I called this form "grin and grab it."

As I left, it was raining again, now a cold, drizzly sleet. I hailed a yellow cab on Central Park West and told the driver to head to SoHo, and to take the West Side Highway, downstream along the Hudson. I watched the surface of the river through the steamy windows of the cab. The Hudson River had always intrigued me and my mind hovered over the surface tonight while the sleet fell, making glass of the asphalt.

On Wooster between Spring and Prince the limos were lined up three deep in front of the Siren gallery. The Siren was tucked between two former warehouses now sporting the names Zebra and Petrucia, where you could buy beach glass bowls in rainbow colors, hand-woven fabrics from the Southwest, peaches made of cement, knotty-pine beds with green linen covers, dried wreaths of roses, anemones, freesia, lilacs, heather, and milkweed pods, chandeliers hand-carved from applewood, angels in papier-mâché and bright silk, copper-bottomed fish pans, and sieves made of gold. Then you could go next door and buy a Julia Clearwater painting. I loved SoHo—its contrasts, the evidence of artists working everywhere among the tin-roofed buildings and the cobblestoned streets.

I struggled out of the cab, juggling my bags and trying not to get soaked, avoiding the puddles that splashed up my long skirt in spite of my high-heeled boots, slinging my purse and bag over my velvet cape, feeling like a rock-and-roll pack rat.

Inside the three enormous white rooms of the Siren I searched for Edward. The gallery was jammed with people, but he was not among them. I felt a sudden irritation, my tranquil traveling mood broken. I also needed a cigarette. For some reason, I hadn't smoked in the cab, hadn't had a cigarette since coming home from the gym.

Julia's paintings were hung beautifully, and many already had dots next to them indicating that they were sold. There was a big blow-up of a recent interview with Julia in the *New York Times Magazine;* the interview had been done by Norman Mailer. Mailer called Julia's voice "the graceful accompaniment to contemporary life in all its gracelessness" and he said her paintings were "brilliantly sensual." Now, Mailer, holding a shapely plastic cup of champagne, was chatting with Julia.

"So, how is Renaldo working out?" Ellen's voice sounded full of energy, almost flying. I was not surprised to see her here. Ellen was always working the room. It was her business.

I told her he would be great and thanked Ellen, giving her a hug. "I should have brought Renaldo tonight," I said.

"Yes," she said, "you could have introduced him to my husband and all the other stars." Ellen smiled a strange smile. Ellen was dressed in black stockings, high, black, open-backed velvet shoes with tiny bows at the heel, a tight black skirt, and a silk jacket with black piping. She had always known how to enhance her somewhat plain looks, and tonight she looked as though she were ready for a night on the town.

"I think Renaldo is going to be worth the price," I said, thinking of the huge agency fee I would be paying Ellen in a few days if Renaldo liked the job and if I liked Renaldo. "Where's your husband?" I looked around the room, searching for Stan, but I didn't see him.

"He's with the Newborns," Ellen said. "They had to tape *Geraldo* this evening, so they're on their way back from Jersey."

"The Newborns, of course," I said. The heavy press schedule would have started already for the Newborns. Every television show in town, plus satellites, plus all the print work they could do. Including mine.

A shadow crossed my mind as I remembered Renaldo's résumé. "By the way, Ellen," I said, "do you know a psychiatrist named Ernest Wheeling?"

A blank look came over her face. "Oh, yes," she said, "the doctor who sent Renaldo to see me, right?"

"That's the one," I said.

"I called both of Renaldo's references, and they both said he's the tops."

"But," I pressed Ellen, "you didn't know Dr. Wheeling before?"

"Why do you ask?" Ellen smiled an enigmatic

smile, shaking her head, and drifted away from me, appearing to gaze at the big nude paintings on the wall. For some reason, I didn't believe that Ellen didn't know Wheeling and wondered why she would evade answering my question.

Jenny Clearwater moved into the room, accompanied by a gaggle of her fifteen-year-old girlfriends from Hawthorne, some of whom I recognized from Friday night pajama parties at Julia's. The girls chatted and socialized in the room, both among themselves and with the adults; each seemed totally at ease with the big, bright-colored nudes, as well as with the big, bright-colored stars.

"Darling, how are you?" Cher greeted me enthusiastically, shaking her head of magnificent curls. Her signature scent, something sweet and at the same time primitive and animal, enveloped the room.

I struggled for breath in her hug and unwound myself—cameras, legs, arms, and finally my head—long enough to reply.

"I feel like an octopus," I said.

Cher laughed, and her laugh included the room. All the men, scattered as they were between waiters serving drinks, women as well in fabulous, politically correct outfits (*sans* fur), politicians, movie stars, and music-business moguls, turned their heads to look toward Cher's laughter. Winona Ryder, Dennis Quaid, and Meryl Streep (bone-thin beautiful with skin so translucent you could almost see the paintings through her body) were among the crowd, exclaiming over Julia's pictures and drinking out of plastic champagne glasses; Pierre Cossette, producer of the Grammys, Phil Ramone, a great musician who had produced a lot of Julia's records over the years; Don Was, Tommy Tune, Bonnie Raitt, Keith Richards, David Geffen, George Harrison—all of Hollywood and Broadway and the music world seemed to be squeezed into the Siren to applaud Julia's new career.

Cher and Julia held center stage among the illustrious group. Cher was dressed in black lace. I could see goosebumps on her perfect shoulders, under the lacy top. She looked completely sexual, and Robert De Niro began to speak to her, enthralled. I photographed some of the other men and women in the room who were looking hungrily at Cher. She broke away from her old lover David Geffen and returned to my side.

"Was there anything in those pictures that I should see, sweetheart?" Cher asked me conspiratorially. I had shot some photographs for *Elle* at Cher's last recording sessions, and they had come out beautifully pouty, her curls thrown back as she seduced the microphone, her lanky body, as young as it had ever looked, bending over the control board to talk to her most recent producer, Quincy Jones. I was craning my neck to find Julia in the midst of the crowd—now she was talking to the gorgeous Rob Lowe—when Quincy gave me a kiss on the neck.

"Where do you find models in those colors?" Quincy asked, laughing his big, infectious laugh and moving on, accompanied by a clique of good-looking people who danced across the room in his wake.

I wondered where Edward could be. What could be keeping him?

George Christy from the *Hollywood Reporter* had cornered Julia and was leaning over her, a notepad in his hand. The noise level of the room, fueled, no doubt, by the endless supply of champagne, had risen to a screaming pitch. You could hardly hear yourself think as people shouted to one another over the tumult of praise and enthusiasm for Julia's paintings, as well as for one another's recent and future successes.

"Promise you'll call, you know the number!" Cher

threw her head back, shaking the rolls of curls that framed her beautiful skin. No plastic surgeon had created that skin, I was sure—it was just something magical, the way her inner energy showed through the fine surface of ivory, something you couldn't invent.

Industry parties, I thought as I took one picture after another, are in some ways all the same, whether it's the art crowd, the music crowd, the magazine crowd, the movie crowd, or the book publishing crowd. Everyone in the room was there to be seen and photographed—by me or by anyone else with a camera. Not exactly what you would call a higher plane of life. But what the hell, I thought, I just got another dozen superb pictures of Cher and Rob Lowe, Meg Ryan, and Dennis Quaid, and it's not a bad way to make a living.

"How's my favorite paparazza?" Stan said, grabbing me around the waist in an embrace that threatened to squash my cameras between us.

I slipped out of Stan's arms, protecting the cameras and feeling my shoulders ache from the burden of bags I perpetually carried. I asked how *Geraldo* went.

The Newborns were doing the publicity circuit— David Letterman, Charlie Rose, Jay Leno, Oprah Winfrey, Sally Jessy—it was important that they should hit all the talk shows they could with the Grammys coming up, and their publicist was doing a bang-up job of getting them on prime-time television. It was now about seven-thirty and I figured that the *Geraldo* show had been taped earlier.

"I heard they shone like diamonds." Stan winked at me. "Including Fred." He rushed on, seeming to be out of breath.

"I thought you were going," I said casually. I got a good shot of Stan, thinking I didn't have one and that I wanted a picture of him alone for my office.

"I sent Janine," he said, nodding in the direction of

the tall publicist with a lot of black hair who was popping her head in and out of conversations with the group, introducing them to various stars. Stan hesitated a moment before continuing. "I had some other business to attend to," he said.

Near the entrance, the boys and Malinda looked bewitched as they stood gazing mutely at Julia's brightly colored, mammoth nudes covering the four walls of the gallery. Fred, I thought with relief, looked straight. Sober, he was mild, humble, and sweet, his silver hair framing his lovely face. Z-Train sidled up to me and gave me a hug. The other Newborns approached.

I greeted the kids, my camera going the whole time.

"Get a lot of pictures, Catherine," Stan said as he spotted Ellen and waved, continuing to talk a mile a minute—like an agent. "Can you pose Z-Train with Quincy, Catherine?" he said.

I nodded agreement and maneuvered Z-Train over to Quincy Jones's side, indicated they were to look like good friends, and snapped a photograph: Z-Train in his dreadlocks, Quincy in his short, cropped hair.

"Quincy should produce their next album, don't you think?" Stan asked no one in particular.

I snapped more impromptu photographs of the boys as they looked in awe at Julia's nudes. "Do you think they ever saw anybody naked before?" I whispered to Stan, who was smiling at his charges. I knew Malinda was sophisticated enough, but if the boys were, they didn't show it.

"Certainly nobody naked who was purple and green and crimson," he replied.

"Catherine, how are you?" Sahid slid his arm around me, and I gave him a kiss on the cheek in spite of myself, thinking, Watch it, Catherine, remember the straight and narrow path, as my father would have put it. I gestured to Julia, who was now talking with Winona Ryder. After an animated conversation Julia came over and joined us.

I introduced Julia to Malinda. "Of course I remember you, we met at Catherine's," Julia said. "Congratulations on the success of the band! I listened to *Birth Canal*—it's great."

Malinda thanked her, looking embarrassed, and waved her hand in the direction of the paintings. "Awesome," Malinda said, taking Julia's outstretched hand. "I have always loved your records, Julia. And your paintings are so good! I really like that one," she said, pointing to a big painting of a woman with green breasts. "It's so sexy!"

"It's all yours, for a price," Julia said, smiling at Malinda, thanking her for the compliment. Julia then turned to speak with Stan and Malinda pulled me a little closer to her.

"Catherine," Malinda said with an edge, "I thought my dad would be here."

"I'm sure he'll be here, Malinda." I turned to the painter and introduced her to the rest of the band.

I knew by now that the holes in the kids' jeans and the wild hair were, for the most part, a cover for bright, interesting people. The look on Fred's face was not drugs, not tonight.

Malinda lifted her newly filled glass to the paintings on the wall. "Here's to art, the mother of us all," she said, winking.

"Catherine." Fred had moved up beside me, his voice low and confidential, his back to the crowd around Julia. "I was an idiot yesterday and I apologize."

I smiled at him and gave him an affectionate squeeze, juggling my cameras. I was amazed he apologized. It was uncanny that somebody who had seemed that gone one day could be like another person the next—Jekyll and Hyde. "I'm glad to see you in good shape today, Fred," I said. He looked sheepish and nodded his head.

The party yelled and screamed and shouted about us, like a whirlwind.

Out of the corner of my eye I could see Max watching how many glasses of champagne the group was drinking, shaking his head now and then in the direction of Fred.

"You know, I got sober a while back," Fred said, "I mean, really sober. I mean, I got into treatment. In Atlanta." He lowered his voice. "I got some blow from someone two days ago—but I'm not going to see him again, I'll be all right. I'm okay, I can stay straight, I know I can." His eyes looked like those of a hungry, wet, homeless puppy. The rest of him was pure rock-and-roll bullshit.

I remembered what Denzel's wife, Alicia, said when I heard her story a few years ago. "If you always do what you always did, you're gonna always get what you always got." I hoped this vulnerable, gifted young man was really going to be able to get himself together. I kept my doubts to myself.

"Fred, if there is anything I can ever do for you, if I can be of any help, would you ask, please?" I smiled at him gently.

"Yeah, well, I'm all right. It was just a little slip," he said.

A little slip. That's what they all say. "I know someone who might help, if you have any more trouble," I said, speaking softly, gently. "I'm going to give you a card with my friend Denzel Keating's name and number on it. New York is a scary city. Denzel will help you if you want help."

Fred took the card, burying it deep in one of the ragged pockets in his Levi's. It would probably drop out of one of the holes.

"Thanks. I may call him, maybe tomorrow. I appreciate your offer."

I smiled benignly at him and turned back to the crowd around Julia. Cher, flanked by the twenty-year-old weightlifter who doubled as her bodyguard, wandered over to talk to Julia. I knew she was taking in the Newborns with territorial interest, and I introduced her to Max and the group.

"I love your record," Cher said.

"Thanks," Reed said. "We all use Equal," he added, smiling brightly. Cher and Malinda had exchanged compliments, circling each other like two lionesses in a pride, sizing each other up.

"You're cute," Cher said to Reed after a few moments. "Where do you live?"

Before he could answer I gently moved Reed nearer to Julia, maneuvering him away from Cher. Reed's attention veered from Cher, where his eyes had been riveted.

"Julia Clearwater?" Reed said, as though waking from a dream. "The singer? Of course it's you. I didn't realize who you were—*are*. I mean, I know your music." Reed looked enthralled. "I love your singing." Reed's biceps showed through the ragged denim of his clothes and I suspected he had spent three hours on the Nautilus before going out to do Geraldo's show.

Julia was wearing an emerald-green satin dress that fit her as though she had been poured into it. Her neck and shoulders were bare and she wore long, aquamarine silk gloves that stretched from her fingertips to midway between her elbows and her shoulders. The dress moved like water on her body from just above her breasts down to the tops of her high-heeled, green satin Jourdan shoes. Highlights played on her high cheekbones from the sheen of her emerald-and-blue-green outfit. Julia's eyes were like aquamarine jewels and she looked very hard at Reed and took it all in—biceps, hair, wild energy. I saw sparks fly between the two of them. These things don't take long.

I got more good pictures. The Grammys and Julia's opening night would look good together in the *Elle* piece, I thought, and I kept the flash going. Five heads of tangled hair made room for Julia, who was flanked by Cher, with Quincy in the middle. Reed, the tallest of the group, put his arm protectively around Julia's waist and pulled her slight figure toward him.

"I doubt if my mother would approve of these paintings, Ms. Clearwater," Reed said. "But she loves your singing, that's for sure."

"Call me Julia, please," she said, lapping up Reed's southern drawl like it was a warm pint of moonshine. I could see in her face that she knew there was more to Reed than just a southern accent and long hair.

Julia gave me a glance that told me she had just changed her mind about younger men. She let her hand stay in Reed's until it looked awkward, withdrawing it only reluctantly. I saw the reluctance was mutual. Julia was hooked.

"Have you seen Edward?" I asked Stan. To my shrug, he raised his eyebrows.

"I haven't," Stan said. The gallery was wall-to-wall celebrities. Robert Redford, Gloria Estefan, Emma Thompson with Kenneth Branagh. Nicholas Cage came up behind Julia and put his arms around her slim waist. After her marriage fell apart, Julia had had an affair with the sexy Nicholas. Anjelica Huston was with him tonight, looking tall and smart and intelligent, as always. I took some pictures of Julia with Nicholas and Anjelica as Arnold Schwarzenegger and Maria Shriver arrived fashionably late.

Everyone was here, it seemed—except Edward. I was getting angry. I was ready to be rescued from this maze of people, ready to see my lover's face, feel his body against mine, instead of the crush of the famous, the heat of the well-known pretending to be at Julia's opening just to see the art. But Edward was nowhere to be seen, and I felt more irritated by the moment.

At that moment, my lover put his arm around my waist, and I nearly jumped out of my skin.

"God, Edward, don't do that!" I said, scared and then relieved. I dropped my light meter and was glad for the straps that held my cameras and gear on my body.

"I didn't mean to frighten you," he said, apologetically.

"Where have you been?" I asked, unsettled, trying to put everything back in my bags.

Edward shrugged his shoulders. "Late work at the office, Catherine." He helped me get my cameras re-organized after his sudden boisterous greeting. "That was sweet last night, wasn't it?"

"It was wonderful," I agreed. "I wish there were more like it lately."

"Me too," he said. "Is Malinda here?"

I pointed to the other side of the room where the tall rock-and-roll star was fending off a gaggle of press, her blond hair like a torch in the middle of the room. She and Julia were being interviewed together by someone with a video crew shining bright television lights in their faces.

"I think I'll say hello to the stars," Edward said and was gone, making his way among the warm, famous bodies. I watched him with a feeling of uncertainty. Edward was never late; it wasn't his style.

I finished shooting. With good material in the cameras and on tape, I was determined to write a comprehensive article about Julia's latest voyage.

I was packing up my equipment as the crowd thinned out when Ellen Carney swept past me on her way to the door.

"Great paintings, aren't they, Catherine?" she said. "I'm *so* glad Renaldo has worked out. I'll call you in the morning. Let's have coffee this week."

"Right, Ellen," I said. "Dinner still on?" Ellen and Stan's big Grammy party would be held the following week on the eve of the recording-industry event.

"Yes. Stan will tell you who's coming," she said. "You'll bring Edward, right? He'll want to see his daughter, I'm sure."

Ellen was gone with a wave of her hand. I was grateful Ellen had found Renaldo for me, glad she was married to Stan. But I hadn't seen them together all evening; I wondered what kind of domestic wars they were engaged in. Stan had hinted there were problems lately. I knew if I waited long enough he would tell me. Eventually, like all good friends, we told each other everything.

At eight o'clock a few shouting, champagne-drinking stragglers were still in the gallery looking at pictures, pouring down the Dom Pérignon, offering toasts to Julia and the brilliant nudes. The red dots were all in place, and my friend had a huge smile on her face.

Edward came up behind me as I zipped the last camera bag closed. He embraced me tenderly, turned me around, and gave me a long, lingering kiss, then told me he had to get back to the office to work. I was dumbstruck and said as much.

"I've got work still to do tonight and a late meeting, Catherine," he said, heading out the door. "I'll call." I couldn't help feeling disappointed, but I understood.

Malinda caught Edward at the door. "Bye, Dad," she said, giving him a peck on the cheek. "You look pretty good for an old fart."

Malinda and I watched Edward sprint into the street, his footsteps echoing between warehouse walls, his shadow dancing across the wet SoHo cobblestones that shone like mirrors. I stepped back into the gallery.

"I don't know what is going on with your dad, do you?" I said. "He seems so preoccupied lately."

Malinda shrugged. "My father is a strange man, in case you're just noticing, Catherine." She gave me a sympathetic look. "Thank you again for being so great to me last year." She shrugged into her coat. "You really saved my life. And I don't just mean getting me into the band." She smiled. "I hope my father is treating you right." Malinda hugged me with her slender arms before disappearing in a cloud of blond hair.

Z-Train's beautiful black face nuzzled mine as I stood, a little numbed, by the door. "We'll see you at the Meadowlands tomorrow, right?" Z-Train put his lips to my ear and his body to mine, letting me feel the length of his tall, sexy young form. His lips found mine, and I didn't fight it. He took my lower lip in his and delicately ran his tongue over it, taking my breath away.

"Stop it, I can't deal with this," I said, wondering if I meant it. Z-Train was built—he was pure energy and fiery beauty. I felt my pulse jump-start to racing speed. It would be nice, I knew, very nice. It was the kind of thing I had done before I met Edward. Find a beautiful singer, lose your troubles in a night of a little too much champagne, a line or two or six of coke, a little too much fantasy—and not be able the next morning to remember anything about it, even the sex.

"One of these days, Catherine," he said, smiling at me from behind his dreadlocks.

I pulled back, realizing Z-Train was quite drunk. His black eyes were shining. He sang his comment, slapping his hands against the wall, pounding out a rhythm. I sidestepped his lean body and used the last of the black-and-white roll in my Leica to take close-ups of his wild hair and face. Max pulled Z-Train away from me, edging him toward the door.

"Z-Train, cool it. Catherine, these kids have had too much to drink," he said.

"Don't get into any trouble, Catherine," Sahid purred like a gorgeous cat as he joined the group on their way out. "I want to see you soon. Please come hear us sing and take our pictures."

"I'm gonna call your friend, hear? The one in the program?" Fred told me, scrambling to get out the door.

I smiled and nodded goodbye. In the gallery Reed held Julia in a soft embrace. Her head was thrown back, her body leaning against the wall.

Max walked purposefully toward his fifth rock-and-roller and Reed surrendered Julia's torso reluctantly and joined the group at the door. "You seem to have a good effect on Fred, Catherine," Max said. "I hope you'll be at the Meadowlands for their big concert tomorrow night. They said they can't think of singing without you there!" Max lifted his fist, his thumb in the air, and with the other hand fed the quintuplets into the mouth of the big black limousine.

Max jumped into the front seat and the limo doors slammed. Z-Train rolled down the smoked window to throw me a kiss as the black stretch pulled away from the curb.

The driver of Julia's limo held the door open for me and I loaded my gear and myself into the back seat of the car.

I eased into the plush burgundy leather seat of the limousine. Jenny was already inside, looking tired but happy. She was sitting close to her mother, giving her a reassuring hug, and getting one in return. They nodded in the glow of the soft lights that ran around the ceiling of the car like a row of glowing pearls.

I suddenly thought about the wonderful sex Edward

and I had had the night before and felt an intense melancholy. "Edward had to work," I said sadly to mother and daughter. Jenny looked concerned and Julia squeezed my knee with her gloved hand.

We were heading north on the wet asphalt of the West Side Highway.

After a pause I congratulated Julia on the show.

"Yes, it was wonderful," she said, coloring slightly in the soft light. She looked across the seat at me. "Reed's going to come to the apartment to talk about my doing a painting of the group, nude. Maybe he'll come by later tonight." She glanced at her daughter. "You wouldn't mind, would you, honey?"

Jenny shook her head of red hair and I thought, What a good idea, the Newborns without their clothes on. I could almost hear Julia blushing.

"Thanks for playing cupid," she said, looking fifteen. She gave my arm a squeeze. I settled back in the plush back seat of the big Cadillac. Julia was silent, her eyes looking out the window.

Seventy blocks uptown, the driver swung off the highway and drove the few blocks to my building on Central Park West. I gave Julia a hug and headed upstairs.

Inside my door, I couldn't help wondering about Edward's sudden business. I let my black velvet cape slip to the ground and took off my damp boots. I greeted Blue, closed the shutters, and punched the play button on the answering machine. I was apprehensive, but my hands were not shaking. The police now had the letter and the tape. There was nothing to worry about.

A couple of hang-ups on my machine, and then an unfamiliar voice that boomed into the room, started, caught, then boomed again. A male voice, a stranger. But not the same stranger as before.

"Would you please call, ahem, Detective Zardos, at,

uh, the Twentieth Precinct, 580-6411, right away, please. It's a matter of, um, some urgency. Thank you."

Maybe the detective I had seen earlier that day had found fingerprints on the letter or the cassette and had identified the caller. I copied the number and called information to check the number of the Twentieth Precinct.

The computerized voice told me the number. All right, it's not a crank call, I thought, then took a deep breath and dialed.

"Twentieth," a resigned male voice answered.

I asked to speak with Detective Zardos. The phone clanked, as though it had been dropped. Then there were loud voices, the sound of a noisy, busy room. After what seemed an eternity, an extension was picked up.

"Zardos here," a voice said.

I introduced myself, speaking quickly, nervously.

"Thanks for calling back, Ms. Saint. We have a young man in Martindale Hospital with a bad bump on his head. Looks like he was attacked. He's unconscious. We found your card in his wallet. We'd like to talk to you."

"Who is it?" I knew a lot of young men. Musicians, singers, artists, writers. Maybe it was someone I'd photographed, some star who'd gotten into a fight with his coke dealer—it could be a thousand kids in the music business.

"His driver's license says his name is Renaldo Pierce."

22
~

I dream of a tall, dark, twisted man who has
threatened to kill the children. I know I have to
kill him, that I can't get rid of him any other way,
and that unless I do it soon he will get away
and I will never sleep easily again. The stranger is
sitting at the table, laughing and talking with the
children at breakfast as though nothing were the
matter.

I take the long, engraved sword that my grandfather left me, a relic from one of our ancestors
who fought in the Civil War. The blade has
been replaced with tempered steel so sharp that
it could peel the skin off a grape. The handle
is looped into some artistic message from the
previous century and the family crest is tangled
in those loops. I pull the sword out of its
black, weathered leather scabbard and creep into
the dining room, right behind the head of the
twisted, dark man. As he laughs, leaning his head
back, I plunge the sword into his neck up to
the hilt.

He doesn't even have time to scream. Scarlet
blood runs down the sleeves of his shirt and
onto the table, making shining vermilion pools

around the plates of toasted bagels. Among the cut-glass pot of honey, the silver coffee urn reflecting blood and flowers, the columbines, freesia, orchids, and lily of the valley in a bunch in the little crystal vase, he is dead before his head drops to the table.

23

I hung up the phone and took a deep breath, trying to absorb the shock. I dialed Edward's home number, almost as a reflex. I wanted him; at this moment I needed him. The machine started singing a song. I hung up on the recorded greeting and tried his office number. It rang and rang until the message for Winter, Valarian and Marshand came on and advised me to punch zero if I needed further assistance. I felt a sudden, violent impatience.

I dialed Stan's number at home. He answered immediately. "Stan, thank God you're still there," I said, relieved.

"Yes, I was pooped. I got the band back to the hotel and came home." I heard Ellen's bright laughter on the other line. She would probably be pissed to know it was me. I was always calling Stan on some errand of mercy.

I thought how fortunate I was to have a friend like Stan, so dependable and successful, a good pal. He knew his own limits and didn't have contempt for the limits of others. Also, he had found a way to live with his wife and still have time for me.

I filled Stan in on what had happened to Renaldo and asked him to go with me to see the police.

"Why would the police want to talk to you?" Stan said. "You just hired Renaldo, right?"

"That's right, but I may have been the last person to see him before he was attacked."

"Maybe you need a lawyer," he said. Stan was a lawyer first, an agent second.

"Damn it, Stan, you *are* a lawyer—what's more, you're *my* lawyer. Anyway, I don't need a lawyer. This is routine. I'm sure they just want to know if I can give them any leads, that's all." We made arrangements to meet and Stan hung up before I could thank him.

I laid Renaldo's résumé out on the desk in front of me, turned the light on high and looked again at the carefully typed pages, hoping they could tell me more than I already knew. The chronology of his jobs, his education, a brief life in brief, the reference to Dr. Wheeling. Now this nearly total stranger was in a hospital, his life in a sort of suspension.

"Meow," said Blue, and he jumped up into my lap, disrupting my reading. I held Blue's soft, smoke-colored body and went on reading, stroking his silky fur.

Detective Zardos would want to see the résumé. I set Blue on the floor, switched on the Canon, and made a few copies. When the green light went off I called the number of Renaldo's home in lower Manhattan. No answer. No such luck.

Renaldo, let it not be you, I thought. Let it not be you.

I headed out the door, throwing my velvet cape back on over the outfit I had worn to Julia's opening.

Downstairs, Alberto, the night doorman, ran into Central Park West to get me a cab. The weather was still cold but the sleet had stopped and I leaned into the cover of the awning to avoid the wind that was whipping across the park. I hugged my cape close around me during the taxi ride to the police station.

It was not the cool temperature that made my teeth begin to chatter.

Stan was at the precinct house already, standing in front of the red-brick wall, shifting from one well-shod foot to the other. Squares of gold light shone from the building out onto the nearly empty, wet street. A few police cars were double-parked in front of the two-story brick structure.

"You look great. Not at all like a suspect," he said, hugging me and taking my arm.

I grimaced, knowing he would make a joke at his own funeral. "You don't look so bad yourself, for an agent," I said affectionately. I kissed him, reaching for the cheek he had shaved smooth at the office. "Thanks for coming, Stan," I said.

At the main desk a twentysomething woman in uniform smiled cheerily at me and Stan, telling us we could take a seat.

Stan and I found our way to a bench with knife wounds on its back and legs, hearts with initials, ragged arrows plunging into the raw wood. Pushing aside some magazines, we sat down together.

"I'm frightened," I confessed. "This is the second time I've been here today. This place gives me the creeps." We huddled together on the bench, and Stan put his arm around me, pulling me close. I put my face against his coat, and he slid his arm through mine. We had just left a completely different world. At the Siren gallery, the scene of Julia's opening, people's crimes might be of the heart, or the spreadsheet, but most of them were not going to jail.

I raised my eyes to the clock on the wall. It was only five minutes since we had arrived, but it seemed an eternity.

A figure moved before me and suddenly I was looking into the eyes of a tall, dark man. His rather serious face seemed somehow familiar, as though I had known him for years.

"Ms. Saint?" he asked gently. "I'm Detective Zardos."

I had forgotten that detectives do not necessarily dress in uniform. He wore a fawn-colored suit and a darker, cream-colored shirt.

"I'm Catherine Saint," I said, assessing this solid, interesting-looking man, wondering about his life, where that calm look that he wore in his eye came from. *I* didn't feel calm. I introduced Stan, who stuck out his hand, and we followed Zardos through the same busy squad room I had been in that morning.

Zardos opened the door to his office and waved us in, gesturing toward the hot plate where a pot of heavy black liquid steamed.

"Coffee?" he asked. "Or whatever it is now?" Zardos's voice had a charming hesitation, like Sam Shepard's. Stan and I shook our heads and took the proffered chairs. Zardos closed the office door and got himself situated behind the desk.

He told us a man was found at the bottom of the stairs to the subway at Seventy-second and Central Park West, that he had received a severe head injury when he was pushed down the stairs, and that he was unconscious. Zardos's eyes focused on mine. "We found your card in his pocket," he said. He sipped from his cup, grimaced, and put the mug down on the desk, intersecting an ancient ring of stains from what I presumed had been cups of similarly terrible coffee. "Yours was the last appointment in his calendar yesterday," he said, studying his notes. "What can you tell me about him?"

"I hired him yesterday," I said, very upset. "Today was his first day on the job as my assistant. Is he going to be all right?"

"I hope so."

Zardos wrapped the crumbs of what had probably been his dinner in its waxed paper and tossed it with a gentle arc, landing it in the corner wastebasket—a perfect shot. I thought of the knot in my stomach where dinner should be. Then he reached for the paper I clutched in my hand.

"I'll take that," he said, a bit rudely, I thought. I laid the résumé on the cleared desk and studied the detective as he bent his head over the story of Renaldo's life. Zardos's hair, black and thick and shiny, lay in a curve upon his head. As he raised his head from the paper, I looked into his blue-black eyes. Zardos ran his fingers through his hair.

"I know your work, actually," he said. "I saw you on television recently. You're a good photographer." He looked from my face back to Renaldo's résumé, clearing his throat. "Where were you at six-thirty this evening?"

"In SoHo," I said, "at an art opening." I should have taken Renaldo with me, I thought, then this never would have happened.

Zardos pulled two cards out of his jacket and laid them in front of him. "Mr. Pierce had a card in his wallet from the Ellen Carney Agency. Do you know anything about Ms. Carney?" Zardos's eyes found mine.

Stan chuckled and glanced at me, reassuringly, only slightly testily. "We both know Ellen quite well, officer," he said. "Ellen is my wife."

"You would know where we might find her?" Zardos asked.

Stan and I both answered, stumbling over each other's words, saying we had just been with Ellen at an art opening. "And I presume Ellen is at home, right, Stan?" I asked him.

Stan nodded. "I just left her." He looked at his watch. "She's still there, as far as I know."

"What's your phone number?" Zardos asked. "I'll have someone call her."

A strange look crossed Stan's face as he asked coldly, "Does my wife need a lawyer too?"

Zardos cleared his throat and said he didn't know. "Mr. Shultz, where were *you* at around six tonight?"

Stan replied gruffly that he was at the office, working, and Zardos wrote everything down, then said he wanted me to come to the hospital to identify the victim.

Zardos's gaze returned to my face. "Have you used Ellen Carney as an agent before, Ms. Saint?"

"No," I said, "but I've known her a long time—longer than I've known Stan."

Stan stood, scraping his chair on the floor, noticeably annoyed at the officer's pursuit of Ellen's involvement. I thought of Stan's wife with her ruby-red nails, bright-colored silk Versace blouses, Chanel suits, Jourdan pumps, purses from Bottega Veneta, and scarves from Hermès. Ellen dressed in a style that was the antithesis of the black leather, torn Levi's, and unkempt hair that was so fashionable in her husband's business. The opposite of my new friends the Newborns.

"I apologize for all these questions," Zardos said sincerely, looking from Stan to me. "But I have to ask them."

"Were there any witnesses?" Stan asked with concern, looking at Zardos intently.

"Yes," Zardos answered. "A guy at the newsstand near the top of the subway stairs saw Mr. Pierce with someone, and a woman called in to report what she thought was an attack on a young man. We're looking for others."

Stan started to speak, then appeared to change his mind.

I suddenly thought about the note and the phone call, and told Zardos about them.

"I know," he answered. "I wondered when you were going to tell me," Zardos said, smiling. "I was checking the log this evening and saw that another officer had interviewed you about a threatening letter and a phone call." He set his coffee cup down again on the old circular coffee stain, shaking his head. "Do you think there's any connection between what happened to Mr. Pierce and the letter and call?"

"I don't know," I said, feeling suddenly more frightened.

"Well," Zardos said, "we should check out any possible connections." Zardos lifted the cuff of his jacket, looked at his watch, and shook his head. "I can try to get some I.D. in the morning on the letter at least. The lab won't send their report until late tomorrow if I know them."

The tall officer put his pen away, stood up, and began to move toward the door. "I'll let the desk know I'm taking over your case, and I'll check with a guy I trust over at forensics. I'll see if he can lift some prints. He'll probably want to hear some samples of your other friends' voices if you have them on tape."

I told Zardos I had phone messages of some of my friends and family.

Zardos nodded. "Let's get over to the hospital," he said. "It's already pretty late. I'll call your wife after we see Mr. Pierce," he said, looking at Stan.

I shuddered as Stan helped me into my black velvet cape. Zardos hadn't blinked at my unusually festive outfit, as if everybody comes to the police station at night dolled up in velvet and sequins.

Zardos held the door, and he and Stan waited for me to proceed in front of them. "Let's find out whether this young man is your Renaldo Pierce," he said.

"Do you think it might be someone else?" I asked, risking a hopeful tone.

I felt Zardos's intelligent eyes looking deeply into mine. "I wouldn't want to bet on it," he said.

He didn't look like a betting man.

24

IT WAS MIDSUMMER ON THE RANCH. HEAT DEVILS ROSE
from the fields. The animals bent their heads over the
water troughs, drinking water to try to revive. Ben
and I, Mother, even Daddy tried running in the sprinkler, but there was no relief to be had from the hun-
dred-degree weather. The wheat was drying up, and
the horses and Black Angus were drooping, their
breath coming in hard pants. Dad hosed down the
animals in the bullpen. Then he packed me, Mom, and
Ben into the car. We stopped at my uncle's ranch to
pick up Gene and Cheryl and Marty and then headed
for Moline for a swim in the local pool to cool off.

The sun was bright on the water, bouncing off the
blue tiles on the sides of the pool. The smell of chlorine filled the sunlit air. I ran in my pink and white
bathing suit, skidding on the wet cement, nearly going
off into the deep end. My brother, Bengie, and my
cousin, Marty, could dive well and they climbed the
ladder to the highest diving board and made graceful
entries into the water, parting the crowds of children
screaming and shouting and bouncing balls back and
forth across the blue dancing light in the pool's deep

end. I didn't swim nearly as well as Ben and my cousin and I crept against the wall, staying close to the sides, ducking my head every once in a while to cool off.

I was still panting from the heat, even in deep water. The high temperatures had driven in the very farthest neighbors to the cooling water—kids from town, brats from the outskirts (as my mother called them), and the ones from the big ranch that adjoined ours. All the kids were in the pool, even the Thatcher boys, the town bullies.

I stayed away, eyeing them from afar, trying just to cool off and keep my head under the edge of the pool so they wouldn't see me.

The Thatchers were town boys with a reputation. Sexy, bad boys. They stole money from the store in town, and my mother swore they sometimes took our papers from the mailbox. They chased our dogs with their shotguns when they got the chance, and my father suspected them of shooting one of our animals two winters before. Now one was thirteen, the other fourteen, and they were both mean.

I had a run-in with the Thatcher boys in school that spring. They had caught me alone in the playground swinging on the rings. They pulled on my braids and then, when I broke away, chased me down the alley behind the school, scaring me nearly to death and threatening to do bad things to me when they saw me again.

That day at the pool I was hiding but they saw me. They both dove into the deep end, making a cannonball that soaked everyone sitting by the pool. My mother glanced up, then settled back to her conversation with Uncle Gene, Aunt Cheryl, and Buster as I paddled as near as I could to where my brother was swimming in the shallow end. The Thatchers laughed and splashed in the water, making a terrible racket so that all the other kids in the pool moved away from them. They yelled my name and shook their fists at me. One of them turned his bare white bottom at me, laughing and pointing.

I kept trying to hide, not wanting to get out of the pool for fear they would chase me, and not wanting my mother to know I was so frightened. I felt, from their taunting, that I had done something to warrant it, something bad, like they were bad. I moved to the edge of the pool, near the spot where my mother was fanning herself and drinking iced tea. Wanting to be brave. Not feeling brave. Getting as close as I could to Mother and safety.

The Thatchers got out of the water and then dove back in, near me in the shallow end, shouting, and then they came at me, and I didn't seem to be able to shout, I just winced. Suddenly they were grabbing my hair and pushing me under, and held me, while I thrashed and fought in the water, and then they let me up and I gasped and sputtered and tried to scream and they pushed me under again and let me up, barely breathing, chlorine in my nose, gasping and breathless, in time to see my father striding over the wet cement in his bare feet, coming toward me. Buster leaned over, grabbed both Thatcher boys by the hair, and shook them so hard their teeth rattled in their heads.

I caught my breath and watched as my father dropped them into the water and kicked one boy gently on the head, tapping him lightly—just to tell him who was bigger, who was stronger.

"Don't you come near Catherine again, you hear?" my father said, stooping down till he was eye level with the bullies. "I'll shoot the next one of you that does," he said, speaking softly. He just walked away calmly, and they moved on down to the other side of the pool.

They never did bother me again, not that summer or any other summer. I never did learn to swim very well, either, but that day in the heat, in the pool, my father became my hero again.

25
~

At Martindale Hospital, the person who was supposed to be Renaldo lay still as death behind the glass windows of the Intensive Care Unit, his eyes closed. I identified him immediately.

A green dot bounced across the black screen of the heart monitor. It was eerily quiet in the hallways, nurses in rubber soles silently moving among the patients in various rooms, delivering midnight tranquilizers, sleeping pills, injections, bedpans. The only steady sound was the sucking noise of respirators. Near the bed on a chair was a pile of things draped over a hanger. On top was Renaldo's tie, with its printed whales.

"There is a pair of glasses, with flared plastic frames. The lenses are smashed," a nurse said quietly.

"Has he regained consciousness at all?" I asked Dr. March, the doctor who had brought us to the ICU.

"No," he said. "I'm afraid the fall was hard and the damage to the head was very bad. I can't say when or if Mr. Pierce will regain consciousness." Dr. March looked concerned and, as he left, promised to keep Zardos posted on Renaldo's condition.

Zardos sighed and shook his head, then took my elbow, guiding me away from the glass partition and the vision of Renaldo's stillness. "There's a room over here where we can talk." Stan and I followed Zardos past a public telephone. I halted, remembering I still hadn't reached Edward to explain what was going on.

"I've got to make a call," I said to both men, pulling out my cellular phone and stepping a few paces away for a bit of privacy. I got Edward's answering machine and left a message. I felt sorrow, and wished I could reach my lover to tell him how sad and frightened I was.

After I returned the flip-phone to my purse, I went into a peach-colored waiting room; it was furnished with a long green couch and a couple of antiseptic-looking chairs. There was another NO SMOKING sign on the wall. I wanted a smoke badly and sat next to Stan in a low-backed, plastic-covered chair. He put his arm around me again, massaging my neck.

I closed my eyes and let Stan's fingers release the tension in my neck, breathing deeply and trying to get the image of Renaldo's still and injured body out of my mind. I tried to replace it with the image of his smile, of him sitting behind the desk in my office, speaking in his charming accent.

It didn't work. Zardos's voice brought me back abruptly and I opened my eyes.

"There was a note in Renaldo's pocket," he said. Zardos held up a manila envelope covered in plastic. It looked like the one I had received two days before. "It says, *'Catherine Saint, you're next.'*"

"It's crazy," I said, as if in a dream. "Who would want to kill me?"

"Can you think of anything that happened," Zardos prodded, "even a long time ago? Something that might have made somebody terribly angry?" He looked at me hard. "Even a small incident can mushroom in a disturbed person's mind."

"I'm sure I've pissed plenty of people off in my life," I said.

I told him about Dr. Wheeling and the fact that Wheeling's name was on Renaldo's résumé.

Zardos looked at me. "I'll see Dr. Wheeling tomorrow," he said evenly. He closed his notebook and we made our way to the elevators. "Is there a doorman at your building?" he asked.

"Yes," I said.

"I'll talk to him, ask some questions. I want to put security on your building and have an officer stay with you tonight, somewhere other than your apartment." His look was a question.

I took out my portable phone again. The battery was low and made a beeping sound as I dialed Julia's number. I paused, sitting down in a chair in the corridor as her phone rang. I left a message letting Julia know I would be coming—I was always welcome at her place, and I had a set of keys. Then I called Edward and told his machine I would be staying at Julia's.

I had taken the phone number for Renaldo's parents from his résumé and now, feeling terrible that it was me, a stranger, calling, I dialed the number. It was an early hour in London, and when a woman's voice came on the answering machine, I left the bad news as well as my home number.

I rejoined Zardos and Stan and the three of us moved through the hospital lobby. At the main desk a uniformed guard glanced at us, then returned his eyes to his paper. It was nearly eleven; visiting time was long over: all good patients were in bed trying to get some sleep—so that they could be awakened every hour or so for their medication, whether they needed it or not.

The three of us went out the hospital door into the dampness of a light rain. It had been over an hour since I'd had a cigarette, which was some kind of record. As I pulled a slightly squashed pack of Pall Malls out of my purse, a figure materialized out of the shadows like a hallucination, raising a battered hat.

"This is Jethro Martin—Ms. Saint, Mr. Shultz," Zardos said. "He'll drive us over and we'll have a look around your friend's place, and then I'm going to ask Jethro to stay with you for the evening. Keep his eye on things."

Jethro stuck his hand out from the frayed sleeve of his taupe raincoat. "I'll be here when you need me, ma'am," he said in a cracked voice reminiscent of Peter Falk's. His raincoat flapped open to reveal a brown, out-of-date suit. His black, crumpled hat sat atop eyes hooded with tired lids and shot with red lines—but I could see the eyes themselves were sparkling, blue and alert. He looked as though he had been awake for years. A reassuring quality shone from his face. You knew he would stay awake for another ten years if he had to.

I put my cigarette out on the heel of my red boot, thinking that after all the money I had spent on therapy, it had never helped me quit smoking. We said goodbye to Stan.

Jethro's car was parked in the yellow, no-parking zone in front of the hospital, a late-model Oldsmobile that looked as though it had been in multiple car races and lost every one. It was banged and dented and very undercover. We drove in silence the few blocks to Julia's apartment building.

Jethro parked right in front of the building alongside the yellow line. The uniformed doorman sprang to the door and held it open for me, Zardos, and Jethro with a greeting and waved us in. On the elevator ride up I wrote Julia's phone number on the back of one of my cards. "It's private, please don't give it to anyone else," I said, feeling foolish as I handed it to Zardos.

"And here are my numbers," Zardos said, smiling,

giving me his card. "They are very *un*private." He handed me a simple white card. "Call me in the middle of the night if you should think of anything," he said. "Even if it's three in the morning."

Three in the morning is the time when my committee often meets. Sometimes it's just the steering committee and sometimes it's the whole panel. I usually plead innocent and defend my case.

I had learned over the years that I couldn't call Edward in the middle of the night.

The elevator opened into the foyer of Julia's penthouse. She greeted us in a flowing, fuchsia silk robe.

"Howdy, ma'am." Jethro took his hat off and parked it on the table by the elevator. "I'm Officer Martin. Do you mind if I take a look around?" he asked politely, and before she could answer, he began peering into the long hallway that angled off the entrance.

"And I'm Lieutenant Zardos." I could see Julia taking Zardos in, his lean, intense face, his intelligent eyes, his dark hair.

"Pleased to meet you," Julia said to the detective, looking puzzled, then turned to me, with concern. "Catherine, I got your message. I'm so sorry to hear about Renaldo."

I began to answer, but Zardos broke in.

"Actually, Ms. Clearwater, we also think Catherine may be in some danger." Zardos turned his head, looking down the hallway from the foyer to take in what was visible of the apartment. "Is there anybody else here?" The rooms smelled of mahogany and silk and potpourri, of roses and expensive rugs and Old Master paintings, of money.

"Just me and Jenny, my daughter," Julia answered, hesitating slightly. "And my housekeeper, Martha." I could see Martha at the entrance to the kitchen, looking fed up at the midnight traffic on her clean floors.

I heard the teakettle whistling on the stove and knew that in spite of the interruptions Martha was already ministering to our needs, as usual. "And . . ." Julia hesitated, "Reed."

"Reed?" I smiled. *Already?* From the opposite direction, padding down a long, softly lighted corridor lined with Daumier prints, came a figure of beauty, a form that might have stepped out of one of the Old Master paintings: a head of curly golden ringlets, two long legs clothed in ripped jeans. Above the waist, an expanse of bare skin rose to a handsome pair of shoulders and a pair of arms that seemed to go on for miles and end in a pair of rugged, tanned hands that I recalled last seeing around Julia's waist.

"Anything wrong, Julia?" Reed said. "Oh, hi, Catherine. Ms. Saint. I was just leaving." He ducked around the corner and reappeared with his shirt on—what there was of it, with its ragged sleeves and torn pockets.

I introduced Reed to Zardos and Jethro, who had come back from the kitchen. Reed shook Zardos's hand. "Detective? What's going on? Is this a bust?" he asked.

"No, it's not a bust. Not yet, anyway," Zardos said.

"Reed is a member of a rock-and-roll band," Julia explained. "We were all at the opening of my painting exhibition tonight. We were . . . Reed and I were talking about a portrait." Julia spoke quickly, stuttering a bit, her embarrassment evident but her eyes bright and sparkling.

"The party's just continuing, officer," Reed said, "uh, in a quiet way. No funny stuff."

"Hi, who's here?" Julia's daughter, Jenny, asked, appearing in her nightgown out of the blue.

When Julia explained, Jenny shook her head of straight red hair that fell over one eye, turned on her bare feet, and disappeared back down the hallway.

Something tugged at my heartstrings watching Jenny retreat down the hall—would I never have a child? I felt that old pain.

"Jenny grew up in show business, you know. Nothing shocks her, Catherine," Julia said.

"God, I wish I could say the same about me!" I said, noticing that Jenny hadn't seemed surprised by Reed's presence.

"Everything looks okay," Jethro said, his voice coming from the area of the kitchen. He had a teacup in one hand, its rising vapor evidence of Martha's presence. Running his free hand through his rumpled sandy hair, Jethro looked flustered. I was sure he always did.

"I'll just stay here in the living room for the night," Jethro said. He didn't ask. He made himself comfortable on a mauve-damask easy chair in the living room in front of a mirror that reflected back down the hall and into the kitchen. Reed took a seat on the couch beside him and they began an earnest conversation about something. Rock and roll? Antique furniture? Perhaps Reed was telling him what it was like to play the guitar in public. Or about having a cocaine addict for a singing partner. Perhaps Jethro was talking about his various cars and raincoats. Perhaps they were discussing *Frasier*.

Zardos told me he would check on me in the morning and pulled the door closed gently behind him.

In the living room, Jethro had sunk further into the big chair, comfortable, as though he had always been there, but alert as a watchdog. Reed rose and padded into the foyer after Julia and me, looking concerned, his feet still bare.

Reed and Julia expressed their concern and asked if my new assistant was going to be all right. I shook my head, saying I didn't know and that the doctors had told us the injury was serious. I thanked them for their concern and Reed put his arm around my shoulders, gave me a hug, and then disappeared back down the hall to retrieve the rest of his clothes.

"You were right . . . *younger men!*" Julia whispered. She laughed a gutsy, deep laugh, one she would never have used in her concertizing days. Julia had always been protecting her voice, her jewel, on and off the stage. Now she sounded free.

Julia gave Reed a chaste kiss before seeing him out. Jethro hovered over her as she locked and bolted the inside door and guided me toward the guest bedroom.

"Now, Catherine, what do you think is going on?" Julia said, wrinkling her beautiful eyebrows and sitting down on the bed. I felt the frown return to my face. I shook my head, setting down the decaf Martha had made me in order to light a cigarette.

"I don't know," I said. "It's all very confusing. And alarming."

Julia waved the smoke aside. "Catherine, Renaldo will be all right, surely?"

"I hope so," I said, remembering the note. "But if someone is trying to frighten me, they've succeeded." I stubbed out the cigarette in a gold, leaf-shaped ashtray on a table beside the bed.

"Do you want me to get you something? Maybe a sleeping pill?" she asked somewhat helplessly.

I was not used to seeing my friend at a loss. "No, thanks. I'll be all right. I'm just so tired, and I can't bear to think about it anymore tonight." I smiled at Julia, who looked at me questioningly.

"You're going to let Edward know where you are, aren't you?" she asked.

I nodded. "I've been calling him tonight, but I haven't reached him," I said. I dialed Edward's number once again. The machine answered again and I hung up on it. "I don't know where he is," I said. I felt abandoned. It was not something I felt very often, and it hurt.

Julia tucked me into the queen-size bed and then smiled a nervous smile. "Good night, Catherine," she said, switching off the light and letting herself out the door. "I *know* everything is going to be all right." She didn't sound quite convinced, but I thanked her, and when the room went dark as the door shut behind her, I closed my eyes.

God, I prayed, let the committee be out of session for tonight. I need the rest. Let Renaldo regain consciousness. Help Zardos solve this mystery.

Willing trouble away, I let my grooved, embroidered memories take me on their journey. The ranch, the West, the long, flat, beautiful miles of Kansas reached out to comfort me, lulling me to sleep in their arms.

26

My mother sang in August, in the long days at the end of every summer. She sang the Rachmaninoff "Vocalise," and the "Kerry Dancers," and Irish songs, and Schumann lieder. She prepared herself by looking over the sheet music, then would sing in the kitchen while she baked bread and rustled up food for the ranch hands. She sang while she hung out the wash, while she shooed the dogs out of the house after dinner into the big yard for the night. She sang softly after she thought we children were asleep, and she sang when she thought no one was listening. She sang beautifully.

It was the time when the long ripe wheat began to shiver their golden heads in the afternoon wind; when the Angus took their time ambling home in the long shadows of sunset, the heat upon the horns of the bulls; when she and my father began to get us ready for our annual trip to Wyoming, to the mountains, up out of the flatness of Kansas to the green, clear mountain rivers, the peaks covered to their tips with glaciers like gloves, the rushing, silvery sound of aspen leaves shaking in the wind.

"Mother, let's shake a leg," Buster said. The car was piled heavy and hung low, an old black Packard touring car that looked almost like a limousine—it was long, sleek, and polished to a solid shine by our foreman, Charlie, so that you could see your face in the silver tire rims and in the massive doors. Buster trusted Charlie to run the ranch in his absence.

"Oh, Buster, hold your horses, I'm moving as fast as I can," Mother said, hauling my brother at the end of one arm and a net bag of peaches in the other. She always took the best of our early crop of fruit to Mr. Christian, her singing teacher, and to Miss Carolyn, the woman who owned the ranch in Wyoming where we rented a house every year. Miss Carolyn was my idol.

We traveled at night to avoid the heat. It was before air conditioning, and my father always said he wanted to beat that murderous sun. My brother, Ben, and I thought it a great treat to be in the car at bedtime, piled with pillows in the big back seat of the Packard. Ben drew pictures of the flat landscape even as we drove, working with pastels, later sketching the beautiful soft hills that led to the pointed, breathtaking highest peaks.

"Now, kids, I want you asleep, you hear? You're not to stay up. This is your bedtime—you're just in the car, that's the only difference." Ben and I tickled and teased each other for a hundred miles or so, incurring the occasional scolding from Mother and harrumphs from our father, but by the time we got to the Wyoming border, our giddiness at being up and out of bed was over and we were sound asleep amid the trunks and sweaters, the bag of peaches, the pillows askew under our heads, and the blankets we had tossed off in the growing heat. For as we rode across the prairies, the air indeed began to heat up, just as Buster had promised. "I've been making this trip since before you were born, Catherine," he said. "I know how this thing with the heat works."

On this trip, I awoke after the sun was up as we pulled into a gas station along the highway in eastern Wyoming. My father got out to stretch his legs, fill the gas tank, get his bearings. He sniffed the air and said he could smell the altitude.

It was a steady climb from Moline, and by the time we reached the outskirts of Moose, it seemed we were more than a mile high. Ben had a nosebleed by that time. There was a bag of water with a picture of a camel on it slung across the radiator of the old car, and steam rose from it with the sun's heat. In the dawn light, Burma Shave signs began to appear along the side of the road. We could look up from the plains and see our destination, where the Grand Teton, the highest of the Teton peaks, rose above the tops of the surrounding mountains. She was high and white as the Matterhorn, my father said.

Riding from the plateau up into the fresh pine scent of the Snake River, we began to smell the water and the ozone in the air. Outside of Jackson Hole we rode awhile on a dirt road, bouncing up and down on the Packard's springs toward our house—the summer-house, open and fresh. Miss Carolyn had aired it and made it ready for us.

Down below us, the Snake River rushed toward its destination, the great Pacific. At night I could hear the river, and sometimes we slept out in the pastures, and I would wake and see the Grand Teton shining in the starlight, its white point reaching into the black heavens.

Miss Carolyn wore a tattered hat, worn Levi's and work boots, a bright colored bandana wrapped around her leathery neck above her flannel shirt that was stained with salty sweat at the armpits. She had one old arthritic ranch hand, her only help, and with him, she herded her cattle in the acres on Antelope Ridge, where her parents had carved out their original fifty acres. She was black, a fierce African-American. Her father had taught her to ranch, and to hold out against every man who entered her life. He assured his daughter that every man who courted her was after money, not love.

I was seven, eager to see my idol again. I thought Miss Carolyn, who had never married, was the most incredible person I had ever met.

She drove the black Angus to pasture with a station wagon that had no back door; in that shattered vehicle she rode her fences and fed bales of hay to her herd. She was an inspiration to me, this maverick, this woman pioneer who didn't fit the mold of the western feminine ideal, who neither raised children nor sewed clothes for a husband. She was a woman who ran her own life, her own ranch, oversaw her own calving and harvesting, who wintered through the Wyoming mountain snows and freezing temperatures and sweated through the summer heat—this woman who was strong and yet totally female, like a great warrior queen ruling her kingdom. I wanted to be like Miss Carolyn; freezing and sweating, but in my kingdom and for my creatures.

I knew and didn't care that Miss Carolyn was terribly, beautifully alone. That was part of her bittersweet attraction for me, an old-fashioned girl wanting to be independent. Like Miss Carolyn. I knew the price was high. Still, I yearned for it. I thought the price of that freedom could never be too high.

27

The shrill sound of the intercom rattled me out of my sleep, slicing into my dreams of the past. Standing up to answer the call of the white metal box, I nearly knocked over one of Julia's antique porcelain lamps. Recovering my balance, I grabbed the receiver. Martha's voice came through the intercom, telling me there was a call for me. I fumbled with the buttons on the telephone by the bed and eventually succeeded in pressing one that brought a male voice on the line.

"Ms. Saint," a familiar voice said. "This is Zardos."

Zardos. "Hello," I croaked. I cleared my throat, reached out for my cigarettes, pulled out a Pall Mall, and snapped a green plastic lighter into flame. "Please call me Catherine."

"Good morning," he said. "Sorry to wake you so early."

"What time is it?" I said through smoke, thinking this was no good for my lungs and terrible for my voice. I could barely speak.

"It's seven-fifteen," said the voice. "Do you have a cold?"

"This is the way I sound at seven-fifteen in the morning," I said, inhaling deeply, getting my lungs going. I didn't like this guy. I hadn't slept well, tossing and turning all night. The French Impressionist paintings and the smooth fabric from Schumacher—none of it had helped me sleep. I felt nervous and scared.

"You sound like you are getting a cold," Zardos said.

"How is Renaldo? Has he regained consciousness?" I switched the subject.

"The same."

My mind was clearing up. The smoke and the telephone helped. Renaldo in the hospital. Someone threatening to kill me. I remembered Renaldo's parents and vowed to call them back, to speak to them in person.

"I was looking through our computers," Zardos continued, "and I found an article about your therapist, Dr. Ernest Wheeling."

"Former therapist," I said quickly.

"The article says three of Wheeling's patients sued him for malpractice," Zardos said. "You weren't the only one."

I was more awake by the minute. "I'm not surprised."

"So was he a little weird?" Zardos asked.

"You might say that," I said. "I didn't know much about Wheeling's private life," I answered after a moment, "or his other patients. I went to see him for about a year. I stopped two years ago. I haven't seen him since, except in front of a judge. He was my therapist," I said, "and now he isn't." I felt anger rising in my throat, fury and rage toward Wheeling, and toward Zardos for asking these questions. The feeling I had inherited from my father, the one he acted out when things didn't go his way. I felt it choking me, threatening to leave me speechless.

"Catherine, I am not the enemy," Zardos said.

"Sorry," I said, "you're right. I'm touchy this morning. It's early, and I'm upset."

"That I can hear." Zardos wasn't arguing with me. He was calm.

"Catherine, can you meet me at your place in an hour?" Zardos said. "I want to pick up the tapes I asked you about, the voices of your friends, acquaintances, so that I can get them to the forensics lab. Then I'm going to see Dr. Wheeling."

I sucked in my breath. "How can Wheeling help?" I didn't want the man in my life.

"I want to ask him about Renaldo," Zardos answered.

I wished Zardos luck, then hung up and called Edward, who answered the telephone at his apartment. He sounded sleepy too. I told him everything that had happened, crushing my cigarette out in the ashtray as I spoke. It felt so good to talk to him. "Edward," I told my handsome lover, "I would have liked to spend the night with you. It was not a great time to be alone."

"I'm so sorry, darling," Edward said. "I was going to call you in an hour. I was working till two last night." He sounded genuinely apologetic.

I thought of his sexy body and wished he were in bed with me.

I told Edward I was going out to the Meadowlands to shoot the Newborns and asked if he would like to come see Malinda perform. He seemed delighted and agreed to go.

"We'll come home and make love," he said, "and all this will be a memory." He sounded delicious, edible. His usual, seductive self. In control. "I'm sure the police will solve everything."

"Me too, Edward," I said, hopefully.

"Why don't you come to the office this afternoon before we go out to New Jersey? I have some tax papers for you to sign. Or do you want to send a messenger?"

"No, I'll come," I said. "I want to see you. Touch you. Hold your hand." I reached for the cigarettes, found the package empty and, crushing it in the palm of my hand, tossed it into the wastebasket.

I said I had missed him terribly.

"I can't wait," Edward said.

Somehow, although I hated to admit it to myself, I didn't entirely believe him.

28

*I dream that Edward is driving me over the pass on
Mount Fuji in Japan.*

*"I am so needy. I do not know how to give," he
says. We are driving in his Land Rover. "I am
going to leave, and I am going to take you with me."
We have packed our bags with sugar, white flour,
and chocolate, none of which Edward will eat, and
none of which I choose to eat. We are starving,
slowly. There are guns in the mounts of the car, and
though we do not say it, we both know we are
going into hiding. We are hurrying, followed by an
enormous truck that is moving up behind us, driving too quickly in spite of the snow, in spite of the
low visibility. Long Japanese scrolls rise in front
of the car, telling us where to go. On the radio is
koto music, playing very loud, the plucked strings
vibrating in the cab of the Land Rover. The truck
is gaining on us through the ice and the swirling
white flakes, narrowing the distance while the snow
continues to pile up on the mountain. The wind-
shield wipers are straining to remove the onslaught
of fresh snow. We cannot see the road.*

*"Don't run over your father," Edward says, yank-
ing the steering wheel.*

Out on the snow-covered mountain, Buster Saint

appears, standing in snow to his waist, naked. His hair is white, frozen in icicles on his head. Blood runs from his face where he has been cut. Looking like a clip from a Kurosawa movie, he is waving his arms at us.

"I can't stop. He will kill us, the truck will catch us," Buster says, then turns into a bear and lunges at the car. Edward opens fire with the guns. The bullets tear into the heavy coat of the bear but he keeps coming, forcing the Land Rover off the road, holding it up in huge, hairy arms, throwing it at the oncoming truck. The car tumbles into the snowfield and falls down the mountainside, and now, disembodied, I see the car shattering into a million pieces.

29

I lit a cigarette and balanced it on the side of the marble sink in the guest bathroom, ran cold water into my hands, and splashed my sleep-wrinkled face. I was smoking too much, I thought, looking into my reflection in the gold-framed mirror. The room had Grand Palais facades and gold-plated faucets. My face looked exhausted. I wanted a shower, but it would have to wait.

There was a nagging question in my mind this morning. As I made my way into the living room, it wouldn't go away. *What did Ellen know about Wheeling and Renaldo?* I asked myself. For the last few months I had increasingly felt as if she and I were on different wavelengths.

Martha's voice interrupted my anxious thoughts. "Ms. Saint," she said, turning off the vacuum and waving the *New York Times* in front of my eyes, "will you make Ms. Clearwater read this? She says she's nervous about it. It's just wonderful!" I took the paper Martha offered and began to read a long review of Julia's opening at the Siren. "She goes to all that trouble to paint them, she should read what the man says!" Martha's expression said she hadn't thought much of the purple and green nudes, but if the *New York Times* liked them, she did too.

I took the paper into the kitchen and showed the review to Julia, who was making our breakfast. "Michael Kimmelman loved the show," I said.

"Let me at it," she said, smiling with satisfaction, and folded back the *Times*. "This is wonderful," she said as she quickly read the three-column review. "I was more nervous about this show than I realized," she said at last. Julia began pouring espresso beans into the coffee grinder, then roared them into a fine powder. "It's amazing what a good review will do. I feel high, like I'm on something." I sat down on one of the tall stools and watched Julia manipulate the high-tech German coffee equipment. I knew that after breakfast, Julia would make her way to the three rooms she had turned into a vast painting studio at the back of her sprawling apartment.

The coffee machine began to make promising noises as soon as Julia pushed the on button. "Was that the detective who called this morning? Has your assistant regained consciousness?"

"There's no change," I said. "And I'm scared. This thing has really got me confused, Julia." I was feeling at a loss.

"What you need is a good breakfast and a few laughs," Julia said and I smiled at my friend.

I asked for coffee—my greatest passion after sex but before cigarettes, I said, only half-jokingly.

"It won't be long," Julia said. A slender trickle of the rich black liquid was seeping into the glass pot. A divine smell suffused the kitchen. Julia slipped a cup under the stream of coffee to give me my first strong cup of the day, which I drank gratefully.

Julia reached into a glass-doored cupboard above her head, took four Venetian glasses down, and set them on the counter.

"Zardos is going to talk to Wheeling today," I said, watching Julia work, "because Wheeling's name was on Renaldo's résumé. I hate having to think about Wheeling."

"But you *do* have to think about him," Julia said. "You can't ignore what he did to you." Julia poured orange juice into the glasses. The juice turned the blue-green color of the glasses aqua. I changed the subject, and told Julia that I wished I had been able to reach Edward last night. "Not that you aren't a perfect date, but I could have done with a warm body next to mine." I sighed, licking an orange juice mustache off my lip. "Sometimes Edward is difficult."

"Most men are difficult, Catherine," Julia said, busying herself with breakfast. "I'm waiting to find the one who isn't."

Martha came into the kitchen with a basket of flowers—pink roses, long-stemmed tulips, elegant white freesia, long stems of orchids, and fresh greenery spread through the basket. It was a magnificent bouquet.

"Flowers," Martha said perfunctorily. She set the big bouquet down on the chopping board in the middle of the kitchen and handed Julia the note.

" 'You're the greatest painter and singer, and we love you. Congratulations—Stan and Ellen,' " Julia read. " 'PS: Now, will you go back to singing, pretty please?' " She laughed and shook her head.

"Good old Stan, forever the agent, right?"

She smelled the roses and rearranged a stem or two, then gave me a sly look.

"How did Stan get these delivered so early?" she said, looking at the clock. It was barely eight-thirty. "He probably had them sent last night, and they just came up."

I remembered it had been months since my lover had sent me flowers.

"Maybe Edward's having an affair, Catherine," Julia said out of the blue, nodding with conviction.

"He wouldn't do that," I said securely. She was wrong, no doubt about it.

"Why should Edward be different?" Julia asked skeptically and opened the door of the eight-foot-tall, shiny-white refrigerator. She took out a rack of brown eggs and set it on the counter.

"If Edward's having an affair, he's a pretty good actor," I said, smiling at her, "at least when we're together. Though that isn't as much as I would like." I changed the subject again, realizing there were a lot of things lately I didn't want to meet head on. "And what about Reed, Julia?" She giggled like a schoolgirl. "Don't let him fall in love with you, he'll never get over it."

"Oh God, he's cute. I suppose I'm corrupting a minor," Julia said and smiled at me.

I managed a smile at my sexy friend, who was looking attractive, as she always did, and available, as she hadn't since her husband's departure three years before.

"Reed's really very prim," Julia said defensively, "in spite of the way he dresses." She began cracking half a dozen eggs on the side of a bowl, separating the whites from the yolks while she talked, and scraping the shells on the rim to get the last drop.

"Did you know Reed is in Al-Anon?" she asked, concentrating on cracking the eggs cleanly. Julia's ex-husband, Jim, had been a heavy drinker. "Reed said he'd take me to a meeting." Julia made a face, then laughed. "Isn't that a hoot? Me going to Al-Anon meetings? Now that I'm divorced from the problem? Talk about closing the barn door after the horse is out."

"Reed's a doll," I said. "I like him. But look out for yourself, okay?"

"Right," Julia said, reaching for the electric egg-beater. "I never met a man before Reed who was already getting help," she said, smiling. "In the past, it was always me, insisting some man get a shrink or go to some kind of program."

"We could double date!" I said, only half-joking.

"What does your detective have planned for you today?" Julia asked. Her tone spoke volumes. She saw my look of disapproval and reached into the silver drawer in front of me, pulling out silver forks and knives and a serving spoon and fork.

"He's not *my* detective," I said. After a pause, I asked, "Do you think he's good-looking?" feeling uncomfortable.

"Well," Julia replied, setting a silver fork, knife, and spoon and an ecru linen napkin in front of me on the counter, "on a scale of one to ten I'd say he's just about nine."

I glanced at her sternly and shook my head. "I want Zardos to solve this thing, not to be interested in me," I said. "He has work to do. He's got to figure out what's going on." I refilled my coffee cup from the glass pot and took a mouthful.

The whir of the electric beater filled the kitchen as Julia began whipping egg whites to a stiff peak, beginning the preparation of a "svomlet," as she called it—an omelet-soufflé, one of her specialties. She grated Black Diamond cheddar into the yolks, which she had set aside in a white porcelain bowl, sprinkled salt and pepper over them, and then folded the egg whites into the yolks-and-cheese mixture. She poured the svomlet into a shallow Pyrex dish in which the butter she had heated made a gentle bubbling, sizzling sound. Finally she slid the whole yellow-white, delicious-looking, frothy mixture under the flame of the oven grill.

I peered into the glass door of the oven as the svomlet rose, turned brown, and began to bubble. It didn't seem fair that Julia, who was a great star, a fabulous singer, a painter, and just plain beautiful, should also be a hell of a cook.

I thought of my plans for the day. "I'm supposed to go to the Meadowlands tonight," I said, "to shoot the Newborns." I inhaled a whiff of the mouthwatering smell of eggs and butter and cheese.

Julia looked concerned.

"I have to keep working," I said, my eye on the magical egg dish. "Don't you agree?"

"The show must go on," Julia reluctantly agreed, "that's what we all say. Just be careful, all right?" She took out the dish, laid the hot pads down on the counter beside the svomlet, and began to cut it into pieces.

"You know, Z-Train made a pass at me last night," I said. "I was sure it was going to be Sahid."

Julia laughed. "We've both put in time with men our own age," Julia said, "we can't be thought of as cradle robbers. So now, a little variety, younger men. Isn't that what you told me? Get a little involved with Z-Train and watch Edward come around."

"Maybe you're right," I said.

Julia asked if she could come to the shoot tonight. I guessed Reed was the reason for her interest, but I was still pleased. "Of course," I said. "Edward is coming too, we'll have fun. He hasn't seen the group at work, you know." Malinda, in all her blond rock-and-roll fury, would blow Edward's mind. It would be a pleasure to watch, and maybe I could get some intimate pictures for *People*—dad-and-daughter stuff. "It will take my mind off the trouble," I said.

Julia hesitated. "I don't want to alarm you," she said gently, "but I have wondered if it might be Wheeling who is threatening you."

Wheeling. I couldn't escape. Shame coursed like acid through my veins. My breath caught, I felt a hot burning in my face. "Yes," I said, "and I don't even want to think about it."

"Did you tell Zardos what Wheeling did? I mean everything?"

I shook my head. "That's nobody's business, Julia."

"I disagree," Julia said. "Zardos believes you're in danger, Catherine." She ran water into the sink. "Tell him what Wheeling did." I had been skirting that thought, afraid to put a name to my fears.

"Promise me you'll do that?"

I nodded, regretfully, but I knew she was right.

"Of course I'm right," Julia said. She put the coffee pot under the tap and rinsed it out. "You had more than a transference with Wheeling. It was a search for catharsis." I managed a laugh and she smiled. "Not the kind of catharsis you got, of course."

"No," I agreed.

The phone rang and Julia, after wiping her hands with a raspberry-colored tea towel, answered it. She handed me the phone.

It was Stan. "Catherine, Fred's gone!" he said bluntly.

"What do you mean *gone?*" I asked, shocked.

"I mean he's gone," Stan said. "Run. Disappeared, any way you want to say it." Stan was a man who was never flustered or disturbed about anything, it seemed to me. Now he sounded fit to be tied. "I don't know what to do."

"The kids have the Meadowlands show tonight, right?" I asked. He hurriedly agreed.

"They're going to do the show without Fred?"

"Catherine, the show always goes on, you know that," Stan said, then hung up. I told Julia about Fred's disappearance.

Julia pressed her cheek to mine. "I used to know a priest," she said, "and when terrible things happened to people, he would say 'Even the devil works for God.' This will all come out right."

"Thanks for the optimism," I said. "And the breakfast."

Julia gave me a hug and looked one last time around the kitchen to make sure she had left it clean as a whistle before Martha's return. She was like that, I thought.

It reminded me of how different we were. And how much the same.

30

I dream I am alone, floating on a board in the middle of a vast sea. There are islands all around me, and on a dark night with no moon, Edward and Dr. Wheeling come flying toward me in the shadow of a great cloud. They take me down into the dark caves of the sea, where we are to look for shells, the doctor says. The floor of the cave is lit from below with a bright, shimmering, tremendous light as though from a great captive star. We find rings and necklaces, starlight memorized as diamonds, twists of gold, shooting-star hoops, moonstones in platinum settings, sapphires surrounded with gold thread, amethyst bracelets with gold-inlay work, bright rubies in emerald-clustered swirls, pearls in every size and shape, pale white, bright white, tiny, huge, and in long strands; pins that sparkle on embroidered, deep-blue velvet. I put them in my hair, put the rings on my fingers, settle the strands of pearls around my neck, pin the pins on my long velvet gown, fill my hands and my bags and my shoes with jewels and shells; conch and double sunrise, periwinkle and oyster, mother-of-pearl-blue and purple-veined.

Suddenly I am ice skating away from the island on a pair of skates made of gold and inlaid with *intricate patterns of pearls and diamonds, rubies and amethysts. On my legs are pure gold leggings. I am wearing a skintight suit of pearls crushed and poured over my body. My hair is flying, filled with jeweled combs to hold the wind back. Dr. Wheeling is skating beside me, and Edward, skating away to his own island, carries the list of the jewels.*

Suddenly a dinosaur-sized creature, all mouth and arms and head and slime, oozes out of the depths of the icy sea; the monster takes my glittering, jewel-bedecked body, moving around me like some primordial nightmare and pulling me from the bright sun of the water's surface and the dazzling lights of diamonds and the protection of amethyst, down to the ugly, drowning, final, black death of the heart.

31

At my building on Central Park West, Philippe, my doorman, was standing outside talking to Zardos. They seemed engrossed, watching the children play in the little park opposite my building.

Zardos's body was relaxed against the gray marble as he talked to Philippe. It hadn't occurred to me the night before, but I had to agree with Julia that Zardos was indeed handsome. When we pulled up, he stepped over to the car, leaned in the front window and said a few words to Jethro. He held the door for me and I climbed out, fumbling in my purse for my keys.

"They love you in this building," Zardos said. "They say you always give them a good Christmas tip and you don't whine when the water is shut off. Apparently that's the crucial test. They say the water is off a lot."

"I hope it isn't off today," I said. "I need a shower." I headed toward the entrance. On the way up, I told Zardos about my strange new feelings about Ellen.

The elevator let us off at the fifteenth floor, and the sound of Blue's loud meow came through the door. I knew he had probably been tearing my favorite chair to shreds, wondering where I was, and where Flora was. It was long past his breakfast time.

The cat's enthusiasm for my return faded when he

saw I was not alone, and the big Himalayan pounded through the foyer into the living room in a cloud of fur.

"I have that effect on animals—they love me to the point of disappearance," Zardos said. "Catherine, have you noticed anything unusual about Ellen Carney's behavior lately?"

"Not really," I said. "I saw her at the opening last night, and she seemed nervous, but fine."

"She seemed tense this morning too," Zardos said. "Maybe she's just the high-strung type."

I threw off my black velvet cape and headed for the kitchen, where I grabbed a can of cat food from the stack in the corner near the refrigerator. "Stan and Ellen are having some marital trouble, I think," I added. I looked around the kitchen, then at Zardos. I didn't know what I could offer Zardos. Flora wasn't there to make coffee. Fortunately he didn't ask.

"I need the tape, please, Catherine," Zardos said, moving toward the door.

"Right," I said as Blue pounded in from wherever he was hiding, now too hungry to stay shy, and dug into his food.

I led Zardos through the big dining room, where one of Julia's vibrant nudes, a beautiful painting called *Shameless*, hung on the wall. *Shameless* was loud and sensual, green and orange, purple and red, limbs and lips and shoulders and thighs shouting of lust and joy. Zardos's eyebrows lifted but he didn't comment.

In my office things looked neater and much more organized than they had the day before Renaldo came. The light was blinking on my machine. I rewound the tape and played back the voice of a distraught woman who identified herself as Renaldo's mother. She said she and her husband would be anxiously awaiting further news of their son.

Zardos and I looked at each other when the message had finished playing.

I handed Zardos the old tape of messages. "There are a lot of other calls on this too," I said, "messages from my mother, a couple of messages from Ellen, one from Cher, one from Stan, one from Rob Lowe about a photo shoot. One from Julia, and, I think, one from my boyfriend Edward."

"That will help," Zardos said. "I'll give these to the lab. Do you happen to have any handwriting samples? Postcards, anything?"

I dug around clumsily and pulled out letters from my mother and Edward, a note from Ellen, one from Cher, postcards from Stan and Julia. There was also a letter from Dr. Wheeling about one of our therapy sessions. It was typed, but his signature was on the bottom.

"Great. That's a start." Zardos put the postcards and letters into the plastic bag and stepped into the darkroom. He gazed at the photographs pinned up on the wall, then picked one up and looked closer.

"I saw this picture of you in *People* magazine," he said, smiling. In the picture I am kneeling by a light setup, my hands are resting loosely on my knees, a smile on my face. "You're almost as famous as your subjects."

I shoved a group of the new photographs of the Newborns into an envelope to take to Edna. Zardos watched me lick the envelope and run my thumb over the flap, sealing it down. I felt warm.

"Not really," I answered after a long pause. "Anyway, fame isn't all it's cracked up to be," I said. "My father says fame is a profession, like having a ranch. If you've got it, you might want to try to be good at it." I put the envelope on the corner of the desk, sat down in the swivel chair, and turned to look at the detective. "What I really do is get *truly* famous people to relax when I'm behind the camera." Zardos looked at the wall calendar.

"Is this your schedule?" Zardos asked.

I nodded and he whistled through his teeth. I told him I still planned to do the shoot at the Newborns concert in the Meadowlands this evening.

His eye fell on a few press prints of the Newborns from the MTV concert they had done a week before, in full makeup.

"Oh, here are the Newborns, and here's Reed—you met him last night," I said, pointing. They looked like a quartet of Draculas plus Malinda, the angel. I fingered through the photos without makeup and pulled out a good portrait of Fred. These pictures would be in the *Vanity Fair* piece, along with the pictures I would get that night in New Jersey. "This is Fred," I said, "the one who's disappeared." Zardos nodded and told me Stan had called him earlier that morning to report Fred's disappearance.

"I would like to take this picture if I may," Zardos said. "God, he's just a boy," he added, holding up the eight-by-ten portrait of the silver-haired singer.

"I wish I could go with you to the concert tonight but I've got to interview Ellen Carney and try to see Wheeling today. Jethro will stay with you." He paused and looked at me. "Anyway, won't the Newborns have to cancel if they can't find Fred?" I shook my head.

I bit my lip, controlling the surge of emotion, and told him that the band had a stand-in keyboard player, and, anyway, they would never cancel. If Fred showed up and was too stoned to sing, the show would get a lot of press—if he showed up and sang well, they would also get a lot of press. And if he didn't show up at all, they would still get a lot of press.

"Stan Shultz can't lose," Zardos said. "I guess I have a lot to learn about show business. Look, Catherine, I'd rather not have you out there in such a big crowd, but if you insist on going, Jethro will be there with you."

Zardos reached down to pet the cat, who had followed us into the office after his meal and decided Zardos was okay after all. When Zardos straightened up from petting Blue's furry body, he was holding a piece of paper in his hand. "Is this anything important?" he asked.

"Oh," I said, looking at the folded white paper. "It must have slipped off the desk. It's a note Renaldo left for me after he worked here. He says he found a problem at the bank. I forgot all about it," I said.

"What kind of problem is he talking about?" He looked concerned. I shook my head.

"I don't know." Something new to worry about. "I'll call the bank this afternoon and find out what's going on."

"I'll take this, too, if you don't mind. I want the lab guys to have a look at it." Zardos smiled and turned to the telephone.

I headed for the bathroom where I stripped off the velvet and sequins, doused my body with soap and water, ran a comb through my hair, and put on fresh underwear and a pair of gray suede pants and a cashmere sweater of the same smoky color. When I rejoined Zardos, he was sitting in the living room, studying Julia's lewd painting. He looked up at me and smiled approvingly.

"You look better," Zardos said gently. "Let's get some fresh air." It didn't sound like he was asking.

I pulled my purple wool jacket out of the closet and we rode the elevator down and went out into the sunlight.

On the lawns in Central Park were magical-looking figures—children—chasing balls, and dogs running around in circles. The trees were lean and bare against the blue sky, and the kids' voices called to each other in the clean air. They seemed so innocent. I had gotten involved in something deep and dark, I felt, shivering at the thought of Renaldo lying in the hospital, and the notes and calls threatening my life. I felt a couple of tears run down my cheeks. Ashamed to cry in front of Zardos, I squinted at the sun. Perhaps he would think the cold air had caused my eyes to water.

We sat down on a bench, self-consciously, just far enough apart. Embarrassed at the emotion I was feeling, I pulled the package of Pall Malls out of my pocket, lit up, drew in the smoke.

"Did you ever smoke?" I asked after I had exhaled the first, grateful lungful of smoke.

"Three packs a day," he said. "If I have another heart attack the force will retire me—against my will, whether it's serious or not. The first thing I said to my wife in the hospital when I woke up was, 'I'm an ex-smoker.' That did it. The compulsion was completely gone."

I glanced at his long, strong-looking fingers, remembering that long fingers in a well-proportioned man are usually the sign of other well-proportioned appendages. "How long have you been in the police force?" I asked.

"Seventeen years," Zardos replied.

I wanted to ask if his wife was on the police force or if she just stayed home taking care of his beautiful children, two boys and two girls, in their home in the suburbs. PTA meetings, community functions, dinner by candlelight when he could make it home for dinner from his demanding police schedule. "So you like your work?" I managed to ask. Polite talk.

"I've been wounded twice," Zardos said, "but they pay me well, for a New York City detective." He smiled, and I smiled back. "I like my work."

"Does your wife like your work?" I asked, keeping my voice even.

"She did," Zardos replied. "Before she died."

I took in a breath and held it. "I'm sorry," I said, "I don't mean to pry. Forgive me." I took a long drag on my cigarette.

"It's all right," Zardos said. He spoke as if of an old wound, one that still throbbed, the scars unfaded. "Margaret was killed three years ago by an ex-con who got out of jail with nothing but me on his mind." He looked up at the blue sky, squinting his beautiful blue eyes.

How, I wondered, did I get into this grisly situation, where I could even *hear* of such a thing? I was used to good, clean rock and roll, where people were occasionally trampled to death at a Grateful Dead concert, but they died happy, doing what they wanted to. Yes, it was true, there was suicide, dope, accidents like Sally's, failure in the music business—things that could kill you. But those were my deaths, in my own business. These were the deaths of strangers, and they seemed much more real, much more horrible. I resented Zardos somehow for bringing this into my life.

He cleared his throat and pulled out his notebook. He asked me questions about Stan, Ellen, Renaldo, Edward, and Julia—when I met them, what I thought of them, if there had been any changes in their behavior recently that I had failed to mention.

Finally Zardos zoomed in. "And Dr. Wheeling. Your shrink."

"Former shrink."

"What happened? I think you should tell me why you sued him. This is the article from the *Times,* about the other people who sued Wheeling." He pulled out a folded piece of newsprint and opened it up for me to look at.

THERAPIST SUED, the heading said. The article

quoted three anonymous former patients who had made accusations of malpractice against Wheeling. In his defense, the doctor was quoted as saying his patients benefited from his "brilliant new therapy"; he dismissed his accusers, calling them "liars, paranoid schizophrenics, and political opponents." The date of the piece was one year after my last session with Wheeling.

As I read the *New York Times* article, I realized Wheeling had many reasons to settle his dispute with me out of court. The thought of him still made my skin crawl. Wheeling had paid me a lot of money. Now I thought I knew why.

"You weren't aware of this article?" Zardos asked.

I squinted my eyes against the bright sunlight, feeling very uncomfortable. I told Zardos I had seen Wheeling for almost a year and that I didn't know anything about his professional practice beyond my own experience as a patient.

"I am going to talk to Dr. Wheeling about his relationship with your assistant, and to find out if he has an alibi for the night Renaldo was attacked. Of course," Zardos went on, "who knows whether anything in his personal and professional life may be relevant. But if you had some kind of difficulties with him, it might shed some light on what makes Wheeling tick," Zardos said, folding the newspaper article and putting it into his pocket. He raised his black eyebrows. "And perhaps what makes you tick, Catherine," he said. "Why did you take Wheeling to court?"

I laughed nervously and took a deep breath.

There comes a point in the photographic development process when vague and shadowy edges start to come into focus. When the image is nearly there. The shadowy edges had to fall off now, I knew. I had to tell Zardos. Now.

32

It was late, nearly six-thirty, on our usual Thursday-night double session. I walked into Wheeling's office, laid my purse on the ottoman and settled down on the patient's chair, my face turned toward him as he sat in his Mies van der Rohe chair. I was expecting the usual harangue about what I should and should not do. This time he surprised me.

"I think today we will work on the couch, Catherine," Wheeling said. "And I'd like to hear once more about your father's indiscretion. I think there are some things you are blocking about that incident."

"I think I've told you everything I know about it," I said, resisting his prodding.

"Yes, but what about what you don't know, what your subconscious is holding back?"

"I'm not holding back anything," I said.

"I'd like to hypnotize you, Catherine, to see if we can have you remember any more of that night." He moved toward me until he was sitting next to me on the couch. His eyes were pointed at me; his pen was silver and as smooth as a snake. It was as if I had no power of my own; I couldn't seem to refuse. I lay back on the couch and watched the pen in its slow rhythm before my eyes for what seemed like a long time. I spoke of the night, the wind, the naked woman in my father's bed, his hands on the gun, and my unsettling rush out of the house.

Wheeling's voice cut into my reverie. "Catherine, I am sure we have found the source of your trouble with men." As if in a dream, I watched his fingers fumble on the front of his tweed trousers, searching beneath the black leather of his belt.

I couldn't seem to move out of his gaze, the trance. Whether I was awake or not I will never know, but afterward I would always remember Wheeling's eyes, and the haze of that faraway night, the night of my father's sexual voyage with the stranger, the hypnotic power Wheeling held over me, lulling me, rendering me spellbound with the stranger's breasts, the sound of the lovers' ragged voices in the dark.

Wheeling had his trousers off and in one movement bent his chest to mine, reached his arms around my waist, slipped a band of tough, lightweight twine under my body and slid the two loops over my wrists. He had accomplished this in one sure motion, as if he had practiced it a thousand times, and when the loops caught, he lifted my hands behind my head, where he bound them together tightly.

I was lying on my back, my arms up. Wheeling's fingers moved quickly on my skin, up my legs and along my inner thighs, till he reached his arms around my waist, pulling my back up toward him, off the leather couch. He threw my rope-bound body onto the floor and I could hear my voice screaming but couldn't move out of his grasp and he shook me and shook me till my neck swung back, snapping as though it might break, his black eyes piercing down, his voice screaming over and over, "I know what you want, Catherine, I know what you need, I am giving it to you," while he opened my blouse and yanked my skirt up along my hips and forced down my nylons, running his hands up my ribs and holding my breasts, squeezing the nipples with his fingernails. I could feel his maleness, hot and ready and filled with his fire, and he thrust himself into me, over and over, pounding, pressing, driving. I could hear his voice and feel the fight in my loins, my revulsion and the struggle to free myself, tugging at the rope ties, fighting the pounding of his body against mine, filled with revulsion at the thought of his seed, my fight nothing to the power of his domination over me as I lay under him, suddenly weak and not able to fight, my energy spent, my face cold and sweaty, the rope ties down around my throat, my wrists limp and weak, praying for it to be over.

This couldn't last forever. Was it war or rape—or both? The ties, as though made of steel wire, still held tight as I struggled to get away. I screamed in rage and fury, a primeval surge fueling my energy to resist again. I was fighting even as I felt his orgasm.

Wheeling pulled himself out of me, raised himself up on his arms over my struggling limbs, lifted his body off mine, undid the rope from my wrists, and stood, half-naked, clapping his hands together, laughing. As soon as I was free, my body began to shake and I felt the nubby rug beneath my back, under my body.

"Come back, Catherine, the hypnosis is over!" He smiled.

"You bastard," I said, coming to with a shock, feeling the surge of revulsion in my throat, in my whole being. My voice came out soft, almost whimpering. Wheeling was still laughing and looking down at me as I struggled up off the floor toward the couch, his face pressing close to mine like a dark, clouded sky. I was wounded, but I knew I had not surrendered. I shifted into a curve, like a half-moon, to hide my breasts and my body and reached for my blouse and skirt.

"It was what you wanted, Catherine, what you have always wanted, ever since you came to see me."

"That's crazy. *You're* crazy!" I shouted, my voice stronger, my hands shaking. I must get out of this animal's cage alive, I thought.

Wheeling laughed again. "Catherine, you could never have gotten well without this. I am giving you the kind of therapy you need."

I stood up in my rumpled blouse, adjusted my skirt, and reached for my purse. "I'm leaving."

"You can't leave, Catherine. We have only begun to solve your problems." He smiled at me, the smile that said, I have you completely, you loved it, you will never leave. "I shall see you Thursday at eight-thirty. I will rouse you again from your sleep. Please be prompt."

I felt stronger, and even in the presence of this mad,

sick animal, I was near enough to the door to be brave. "You're history, Wheeling," I said with hatred.

Wheeling looked at me through narrowing eyes and bellowed in someone else's voice, "You cannot quit. I'm warning you. You have no idea what I can do to you if you leave."

I slammed the door, angry and frightened.

33

I had broken the seal, let the genie out of the bottle, let in the air, and, somehow, rather than feeling sorry I had shared this experience with Zardos, I felt relieved, felt the shame and guilt of the rape lifting. When I had finished telling the story, he looked at me with sympathy.

"What happened must have been terrible for you," he said. "Thank you for trusting me enough to tell me, though I know I didn't give you much of a choice."

"Stan represented me in the malpractice suit," I said. "I didn't want the publicity of a criminal case. Wheeling settled with me out of court, for a lot of money."

As we crossed the street, I felt a heavy burden lifted from my shoulders.

34

*I dream of life at home on the ranch, of the long
wheat waving in the fields, the crickets calling
from the patch of brown weeds by the fence, and
under the big cottonwood in the front yard, the
lumbering Angus and the little calves, their tongues
pink, their coats shiny and rich from the milk they
suck from their mother's full udders. I am watching
Charlie, the foreman, mount his horse to ride the
fences, sitting like he was born on that horse, riding
off in faded Levi's that cling to his body like blue
skin and the old rough-out boots he wears, dusty
and brown, the tops soft and stained, folding
gently down beneath his long legs.*

   *I am fifteen—school out and chores done—long-
ing in some deep inner part of me to do more
than watch the handsome ranch foreman riding on
an Indian summer afternoon. I swing in the porch
swing, cooling my sweaty face with the red and green
flower–painted rattan fan my mother had brought
back from her visit to California—when she was
young, before she married my father, her dad had
sent her out to try schooling in the far, far West. But
she soon came home and married Buster, her high
school sweetheart, and had me and Ben, and settled
down to life with us and with Buster's brother*

and his wife, Cheryl, and their son, Marty, and the black Angus, hot summers, wet bundles of laundry that have to be hung out to dry on a line strung in our back yard over the withering Kansas lawn that stays brown no matter how much you water it, no matter how much you fertilize it.

My mother's dreams, her visits to her singing teacher in Wyoming, her love for my father and Ben and me, all hover over me as I swing in this dream. I know someday I will have a place somewhere else, somewhere wet and green, somewhere far away from the heat and the horses, from the sting of the Kansas wind, from the long summers with their dry sun parching down on my face. I smiled toward the horizon, and when mother calls dinner, I go in, knowing I will not always be there for supper, not always be a girl on a ranch in the middle of the great wheat fields, in the heat and the snow on a ranch in Kansas, the feel of lemonade running down my dry, parched throat, the sense of owning the world in my gut, where it matters.

35

The Newborns' long, sleek stretch limo was parked in front of my apartment building as we crossed Central Park West. Zardos and Max spoke briefly, then the detective gave my hand a gentle squeeze as he said goodbye. Zardos traded places with Jethro behind the wheel of the unmarked car and drove off.

As I watched Zardos drive away, I knew something about him that I hadn't known.

I knew I liked him.

Max joined Jethro and me as we entered the lobby. Inside we came upon Reed slumped on the red leather couch, tapping the floor with his foot. When he saw me, he leapt to his feet.

"Catherine," Reed said, attempting a smile. "Catherine, I trust you, and I need your advice. I can't really talk to the police. I don't know what to do," he said, putting his head in his hands. Reed was a different person from the sexy man I had seen the night before in Julia's apartment. Now, he was vulnerable and meek, and he tucked his head down. "Fred and I had **a terrible fight last night**," Reed said. "It was about who wrote the big songs. Then he left. I'm afraid I made him do it."

"You can't do that to yourself," Max said. "This isn't your fault."

Reed's face twisted in a grimace. "But now he's disappeared," he rambled on, "and now it's in all the papers. My mother called me from Georgia this morning. Somebody saw the piece in the *Daily News* and called her. We were supposed to shoot a piece for MTV this afternoon, some kind of portrait for the Grammys. And we have the concert tonight at the Meadowlands."

Max, Reed, Jethro, and I headed up the elevator to my apartment. "Catherine," Reed said, continuing to speak agitatedly as the elevator settled on my floor, "when we find Fred, I'm going to have him committed."

"You can't commit someone against his will," I said.

"Well, then I'm going to break his neck. He's jeopardizing all of our careers, not just his. He's selfish, self-centered, and arrogant. I'll kill him, I'll beat him to a pulp." Reed's face was red, his guilt having turned to anger.

"He's also sick, Reed, you know that," I said. "And you have to stay calm and do your show tonight, whether he shows or not."

He nodded, clenching his teeth. "But how can I stay calm?"

Flora took one look at us and made her way to the kitchen and returned with a tray containing four mugs of coffee and a plate of freshly baked butter cookies, four tiny spoons, cream, sugar, and a pile of flower-print paper napkins. We sat down in the living room under Julia's painting. I drank my coffee black, then wanted to pull a Pall Mall from a marble inlaid box on the glass table but resisted as I watched Reed try to get coffee from his mug into his mouth. His hands were shaking; he spilled half the liquid onto the table as he set it down.

"You know what to do to get through the show without Fred," I said, as comfortingly as I could.

Reed mopped up the spilled coffee with a napkin. "Sure. We'll split up Fred's solos. We've done it before. We'll have our sub, Pete Sky, on keyboards, so the arrangements won't suffer. But Peter can't sing. No, this is one time too many for Fred." I reached out a hand and put it over his.

Max quickly downed three cookies. "Fred can make it very hard for us this week, there will be all kinds of talk. But you can handle it, Reed," Max said, his mouth dusted with cookie crumbs. He was trying to be positive, but I knew a manager could do just so much.

Reed continued. "I'm really worried about the reputation of the group. Don't you think we may lose some of the awards if he doesn't turn up before the Grammys next week? Isn't that possible? This could hurt our chances." Reed had a lot at stake.

I stood up and paced the floor in front of Julia's painting.

"You know," Reed said, "when Fred was in treatment for a month, we canceled all our shows and waited it out."

Max was nodding his head. "All of us." Max smiled. "Fred was in terrible shape last year. We had to confront him. Malinda nearly tore her hair out, trying to explain to him that we're all his family and what he does affects all of us." Max put his mug to his lips again. It looked like a cup from a child's tea set in his enormous hand.

"My daddy is a drunk and my family has suffered for years," Reed said. "Fred's no different just because it's cocaine and not alcohol. They're the same thing."

"Is there an Al-Anon meeting near your hotel, Reed?" I asked.

Reed looked up at me sheepishly. "I don't know. I do go, normally. At home. Even sometimes on the road. It's just that I'm too angry. Too mad at him."

Max nodded.

"Isn't Al-Anon for *you?*" I asked. "To make *you* feel better? Put the focus on yourself?" He sat with his fists clenched, but the normal color had begun to come back into his face. It was nearly eleven and the sun was a bright lemon wedge on the rug. The rays lit up Reed's golden hair. The coffee was gone and a few crumbs remained on the plate where the cookies had been.

"Why don't I ask Denzel to take you to a meeting?" I remembered there was a noon meeting somewhere near the Plaza. I had sat in those meetings, trying to get through the pain of my cousin Marty's drug use, and, later, trying to deal with his death. "Then you could get in the limo and drive out to the Meadowlands for your sound check. You'll feel better no matter what happens." I hoped I was helping. "I lost my favorite cousin to drugs, Reed," I said, putting my hand over his agitated fingers. Remembering Marty's face, his energy, his beauty, I knew I still missed him and always would. "It took me a long time to heal and realize my cousin's death wasn't my fault."

Reed stopped drumming his fingers on the table and let out a breath, stood, and put his coffee mug back on the tray, shaking his mane of bright curls. "God, Catherine, Fred's not dead, he's just using, right?" Reed said with panic, then calmed himself. "I hope it's a good meeting." Reed managed a smile. "Of course, I never went to a bad meeting, now that I think of it."

When I phoned Denzel, he was in the editing room, but he said he could meet Reed at Fifty-fifth and Park.

As he left, I got a smile out of Reed and a kiss on the cheek.

Before hanging up, I told Denzel he should look for the angry boy with lots of hair who appeared ready to kill.

36

IN 1962 I WAS TWELVE YEARS OLD. THAT YEAR, WHEN the wind began to blow hard across the Kansas plains and the Black Angus stood with their backs against the cold, when the long wheat was brown and top-heavy and the brown-faced owls and wide-winged eagles raced the smallest rabbits and mice across the ground, clutching them in deadly talons and flying them to nests in sparse willow groves beside the drying beds of rivers where their adolescent offspring waited, ever hungry; when the milkweed pods were drying in the wind and shaking like pages of Quaker prayer in the hands of the devout, when the berries of the red-weed bush stood out in crimson clusters for the birds to find with their calling mouths; when diamond hoods covered the heads of the wheat on the coldest mornings after the rain had turned to sleet and frozen in the early hours, when the frost bit deep into the green and orange hard-skinned squash that still lay on the ground in my mother's big garden; when winter sweaters pulled down hard over thin summer shirts gave your nose a sharp whiff of camphor; when plaid wool jackets appeared on the wide plains upon the shoul-

ders of men riding behind frosty clouds of breath from
horses running down the October wind; when the
scent of the land, bittersweet, of burning leaves and
fires of smudging pots in scanty orchards, of the vine-
gar smell of hides tanning and the steaming smell of
horses and cattle, the working smell of the ranch, said
the winter to follow would be bitter; when my father
made home-brewed beer in big brown- and cream-
colored crocks, adding sugar at the last minute and
capping it in dark bottles that sometimes burst in the
cellar, causing my mother to jump with a start, to bless
herself and curse my father's drinking; when the rest
of the cellar was filled with roots and musky-smelling
potatoes, turnips with the dirt still in their skins and
blushing, shining jars filled with purple and red and
crimson and orange jams, tomato preserves, yellow
peaches in sweet syrup, beans boiled, cucumbers pick-
led, relishes and white cabbage sliced with onions and
waiting for the brisket of beef to come in January;
when the pumpkins glowed with eyes and candles and
the littlest neighbors came in groups of ghosts and
ballerinas to beg for sugar and chocolate on the porch,
posing in their makeshift costumes of sheets and shining sequins; when the light on the porch drew only a
few insects at night and the low moaning, beckoning
sound of the train could be heard for nearly a hundred
miles across the plains between us and Moline—this
was when my father's brother was killed in a hunting
accident not twenty miles away, in a big clump of pine
that was one of the only forests in the state.

Uncle Gene was drunk, and the man with him, his

best friend, was also drunk and shot him accidentally, it was thought, then sank to his knees in the dry twigs and pine needles and wept, and then put the gun to his own head and killed himself.

Uncle Gene was the oldest of my father's brothers and his favorite.

It was the first death I had ever experienced. I knew my father loved his brother, but I was not prepared for his tears, for his emotion.

We went to the friend's funeral in Moline. Everyone was a stranger to us. The next day we packed up our black clothes and went down to Georgia for Gene's funeral. We rode on the train from Moline, and my father was quiet and tearful. Over our dinner in the dining car—served by a black man who put a pink rose on the table and called me "Miss" and served me and my brother a pink drink called a Shirley Temple—my father said, over his second scotch whiskey, and mopping his eyes with the white linen handkerchief that my mother had ironed and put in the pocket of his black suit, that his brother, who was three years older, had taken care of him when they were children and their father died, and that he had never properly thanked Gene for that gift. He kept speaking of gifts, but all I could think of was my uncle, once warm and kind to me and now cold and of no use whatsoever to anyone.

Cheryl and my father wanted Uncle Gene buried next to his parents and the brothers' other ancestors in the tiny tree-shaded cemetery near the old Methodist church in Atlanta. At the funeral in the small white church, my father recited a poem by Gerard Manley Hopkins that I had no idea he even knew. There was a great deal of black crepe and dozens of white roses and no children our age, and Ben and Marty and I kept to ourselves and listened to Cheryl and a lot of other adults talk about how Gene's time had come, and that was that. I remember wondering how you can tell when someone had gone when they were supposed to go, and if it was different from the times when they had gone when they were not supposed to go. It seemed to make a good deal of difference to everyone that Gene was meant to go when he went— not a moment before and not a moment after.

As I grew older, I remembered these people— ranchers from Kansas, farmers from Georgia, shopkeepers, some preachers, men and women who had known what it was to lose crops, lose animals, lose children to disease, lose loved ones to accidents, lightning. They knew the earth, and knew that each and every life has its season, and that God dictates that season and that time.

I remember wondering, in that time of sorrow and memory, if my father had ever told my mother about Lou-Lou. I also knew this wasn't the time to ask.

The first dream I had after my uncle's death was of my Aunt Cheryl, Gene's widow. She and I were slogging downhill through mud in high boots, snakes writhing on the ground beneath our feet. We went so far and could go no farther, and we had to tell my father that we would be unable to complete the journey for him.

Back home on our ranch, in the kitchen a week after the funeral, I told my father about the dream.

"The great way is not difficult if you have no preferences," he said. I said I didn't understand. "Everyone has a path," Buster explained, "and if you accept your path, that means you accept your life, and don't squawk over death, over loss. Life is mysterious, Catherine. If you assume you know where you are going and what is going to happen, your life will be full of pain. Life can never meet all our expectations. If you expect nothing, all will be velvet." Although my father's voice was calm and level, I saw his cheeks were damp. He didn't raise his handkerchief to dry them and his tears fell, round and wet, on the top of the table as his eyes looked out the kitchen window across the late fall landscape, over the stretching acres, mile after mile, across the last few waving wheat stalks with their crystal, shaking covers.

37

Jethro drove me to midtown. I was beginning to feel joined at the hip to this methodical, Columbo-like detective, and although I was grateful for his concern for me, and for his constancy, I couldn't figure out how he had been able to go day to day with so little sleep. I had to admit to myself that Jethro probably looked as fresh as he was ever going to look, stained raincoat and all.

He pulled up in front of Trump Tower, cut the engine in the middle of the NO PARKING zone, and stuck his police parking pass in the window. Passersby looked at him with ill-concealed hostility. "They hate us for it, but it's the perks," he said, smiling at their looks.

It was near noon. The streets of midtown Manhattan were filled with pedestrians rushing to make the WALK lights, hurrying by the flashy windows filled with designer silks and high-priced art, furs, and glittering jewels. Each was headed to some seemingly all-important destination, daring cars to jump the intersections, rushing with that tilted, preoccupied, urgent look found only on the faces of New Yorkers—the mark of the members of some exotic tribe seeking who-knows-what. They hurried and hurried, dressed in silk and the skins of endangered species, in rough leathers and wools and smooth satins and cottons, in polyester suits and Ferragamo heels and Nike tennis shoes and army fatigues. Homeless people in rags were on the street among corporate giants in two-thousand-dollar Armani suits.

There was a blind beggar with a dog and a tin cup; his sign read: I CANNOT SEE. PLEASE BE GENEROUS AND MAY GOD BLESS YOU. A blond woman in an ivory-colored coat and purple boots got out of a silver limo that pulled up to the curb behind Jethro's unmarked car. She rushed for the door to Tiffany's, brushing shoulders with a black dude in shiny red leather who was selling fake "gold" watches in front of the house of priceless jewels.

How I loved New York, its decadence, its unpredictability. Jethro followed me across the sidewalk and into the main lobby of the Tower, past water walls and dripping green ivy plants. Everything smelled of money. We stepped to the bank of elevators and got on with men in business suits and women in suits and heels, many of them carrying soft leather briefcases.

At the forty-ninth floor the elevator opened directly onto the floor of Winter, Valarian, and Marshand. Edward's office was surrounded by an enormous tank of tropical fish—exotic creatures floating under the lights, their dazzling colors shimmering through the glass. French angelfish, wrasses, blue Tang, drumfish, and winged tigerfish waved their exotic red and orange fringes in the floor-to-ceiling aquamarine water.

Bella, Edward's secretary, leapt up from behind her desk. "Catherine, I've got to talk to you! Did Flora give you my message?" Bella was agitated, wired, close to hysteria. In the last few months, I thought Bella had lost weight, her usually buxom figure at least a size smaller. She bolted across the room in front of the fish tank, waving her arms among the bright colored fish. A pair of Tang made for the other side of the tank at her sudden movement.

"Bella," I said as comfortingly as I could, "take it easy. I got your message but I couldn't call back right away. It's been a busy morning," I said, though that was something of an understatement. Bella had in fact called, and I had assumed it was the usual—tax extensions or other papers that had to be signed. She was always overwrought. "It can't be all that bad." I glanced around the empty waiting room. Flowered fabrics covered the contemporary-style couches flanking Bella's desk. A tall, multiblossomed white orchid sat in a Sioux Indian pot on a low table; a fresco of naked warriors in chariots waved their whips over massive, forever-galloping horses.

"What I have to tell you is very important," Bella said. She looked at me intensely, then turned her gaze to the angelfish swimming in slow, elegant movements.

"What's the problem, Bella?" I introduced Jethro, and she barely glanced at him. She really did look upset. Clearly something was wrong.

Bella smiled a hard smile, then suddenly seemed to remember something. "Edward said your new assistant was attacked. Is it true?" She peered at me from her deep, brown, heavily made-up eyes. Her pupils were tiny, as if she were looking into a spotlight.

"Yes. He's in the hospital, still unconscious."

Bella shook her black head of hair. "I'm so sorry. And I'm sorry to have this bad piece of news for you." She looked over at Jethro, who was checking the room out, peering into corners, and was at present looking at the fish, too far from us to hear our voices. Bella lowered her voice anyway. "I like you, Catherine, I always have." She seemed to hold her breath for an instant before she went on. "Edward is having an affair," she said.

I backed away a step as though I had been punched.

"How do you know? How can you be sure?" Even though something had been telling me that things were not well, Bella's manic energy was almost as upsetting as her news.

"She calls all the time on his private line and sometimes I overhear their voices, what they're saying," she said. "The voice is familiar." She looked at me sympathetically, like a sister. "And," she added, keeping her voice down, "I have a feeling Edward is in some other kind of trouble too."

Before I could respond, Edward's voice came over the intercom. "Bella, can you get Stan Shultz on the phone for me, please?"

I was startled by Edward's instructions to Bella, then remembered that Edward was doing the Newborns' taxes. I wondered if he had heard Bella's last words.

"Catherine's here, Mr. Valarian," Bella said crisply into the intercom, giving me a look. She pulled a sheaf of papers off her desk in a flurry of activity, shaking her head. "Do you still want me to get Stan for you?" Bella asked crisply, as though nothing were amiss.

"No, I'll call him later. Send Catherine in, Bella." Edward's deep voice sounded sexy even on the intercom.

Bella steered me toward the door to Edward's office, then continued in a loud whisper, "I'll see you when you come out."

Jethro frowned as I introduced him to Edward; they shook hands perfunctorily. Jethro looked concerned.

"Hello, darling," Edward said. *Cheat,* I thought. For a sickening moment I wondered if it was Julia. Hadn't Julia warned me Edward was having an affair?

Breathtaking views of upper Manhattan and Central **Park** filled the floor-to-ceiling windows of Edward's big office. The night we met he had brought me up here to look at the moon, and we made passionate love on the floor. Today there were bare trees, reservoirs like silver pools, and a pale gray sky. It looked as if it might snow.

Edward's wide cherry desk floated in space above the deep-piled cream-and-gray carpet. He rose from the desk as soon as the door was closed and came across the room toward me, putting his arms around me, trying to bury his face in my neck. I pulled away, tense and on guard. He put his hand on my elbow and I shook it off, and looked out the windows onto Central Park and around the familiar office, with its expensive bibelots scattered on smooth, hand-carved wood and marble surfaces. There were polished onyx shelves, heavy amethyst and seashell ashtrays, and statues, one in bronze of a naked man, and a tall urn from Yucatán, pillaged, no doubt, from some native Indian tribe.

"Listen," Edward said, his voice low, "I'm sorry I wasn't with you last night, darling. Is everything all right?"

"No, Edward, everything is *not* all right. Where have you been?" I picked up a conch shell twice the size of my hand with a shiny pink inside and ran my fingers into its smooth interior, thinking of sex with Edward, and at the same time raging at my feelings of sexual attraction. Why was I so drawn to a man who would cheat on me?

"What is her name?" I asked softly, with all the calm I could muster. Was it Julia? I tried to shake the thought off, but it persisted.

He looked at me. "What do you mean, 'What is her name?'" He paused, taking the temperature of the situation, wondering how much I knew, saying nothing for a moment. Then he said, "I've just been busy, Catherine. That's all."

I looked carefully at Edward. Bella might be a lot of things—pushy and heavy-handed at times, perhaps a bit neurotic—but crazy she was not. If she said Edward was having an affair, I was more than inclined to believe her. And Edward didn't sound like himself now. He started to say something and his voice trailed off. I reached into my purse to pull out a cigarette.

"Are you sure," I said, "that there isn't something you would like to tell me?"

My lover didn't respond. He took the matches out of my hand and lit my cigarette for me with his heavy gold lighter without looking into my eyes, watching the smoke rise from my Pall Mall. He crossed the lush carpet, picked up a heavy glass ashtray, and placed it beside me on the table. He didn't touch me again, didn't reach out with those sexy hands of his, and for once was silent and brooding.

He was not going to tell me, he was just going to avoid the issue. Edward's voice was low, nearly inaudible. "Why don't you go home, get in a hot tub, and get somebody else to do this shoot tonight?"

I shook my head. "I'm going, I've decided," I said.

"Do the police approve of your going?" he said, continuing the game of avoiding the question.

I ground my cigarette out in the beautiful glass. It would be my last cigarette, I decided.

I reached into my purse, pulled out the empty cigarette package and crushed the cellophane-covered wrapping in my fist. "I wouldn't say the police approve, exactly. But I'd rather be taking pictures than worrying about all of this," I said.

I would survive. I would work. That is what I had done before. That is what I would do now. I tossed the empty cigarette package into a wood-sided wastebasket.

Edward moved behind his desk and looked nervously at me. The old tone of confidence was not in his voice. "You're not a woman to argue with," he said.

"Well, you'll be with me, right, Edward?"

He had said he wanted to see Malinda. I couldn't help it. I sealed my hurt behind a bright face, shut my purse, and stood my ground.

Edward frowned, pulling at his burgundy lizard Cartier watchband. "I'm sorry, but I'm not going to be able to see Malinda sing," he said. "I have a business emergency today and I have to work all night." He paused and the impact of what he was saying hit me like a brick. He looked at me. "It's just as hard for me not to see Malinda, all right? Don't look so hurt. I have to finish this work. And I don't want to talk right now, Catherine, okay?" he said and reached out to take my face in his hands, to draw me to him. "You should understand—you're as career-driven as I am!"

I felt the surge of desire that was always there and tried to push it away. The lust boiled under my skin but I fought it down and moved firmly out of his embrace.

"To say I'm disappointed is putting it mildly," I said. I contemplated throwing the beautiful lavender ashtray across the room, right through the plate-glass windows. Edward tried to embrace me again. I stepped out of the formerly magic circle of his arms.

"Catherine, we have to talk. But later," he said, "when you're not so upset."

I felt a great emptiness growing in the place around my heart, and knew I was in danger of jumping into it and never coming out.

"Call me when you get back from the Meadowlands," he said and followed me as I moved toward the door.

"Goodbye, Edward," I said, closing the door behind me. Jethro was watching the fish. I waved to him and he joined me as I headed past the tanks to the elevator, looking around for Bella. Among the tigerfish, the rainbow wrasses, yellow butterfish, and pearl castles, among the angelfish and seahorses, Bella Windsor was nowhere to be seen.

As Edward's office door closed behind me, I stepped up to Bella's desk and looked down at the papers in disordered piles—multicolored eight-by-ten folders, a leather-bound date book, a magenta calculator, a small silver inlaid box—a pill box?—its lid laid to the side, its inner space empty. I wondered if Bella was taking pills, maybe some kind of speed. The desk was chaos. There was a red rose in a crystal vase, a picture in a mother-of-pearl frame of a man with glasses and gray hair. Everything seemed strewn randomly about, as though Bella had left in a hurry.

"The secretary said she had to go somewhere, Ms. Saint," Jethro said. "Anything wrong?"

Shaking my head, I flipped through the pages in the leather diary on Bella's desk, as if it would give me the answer I sought. The entries were almost illegible, but I recognized the hand that wrote many of the notes on my tax forms and financial papers.

The Rolodex at the corner of Bella's desk, bulging with cards, caught my eye. It lay open to a card I assumed would be Stan Shultz's. But then I looked more closely.

Facing me was the name, address, and telephone number of Dr. Ernest Wheeling.

38

I dream I am running through the streets of an unfamiliar city screaming Edward's name. I have lost him.

At the outskirts of the city is a long dirt road, at the end of which, in a dance hall, I find my cheating lover with a woman. He lives there with her in an attic, along with her seven-year-old child.

Suddenly we are riding in a carriage through a desert; we are dressed as if for an outing in severe weather, in heavy, insulated clothing. In the sand-colored landscape around us there are many men, naked to the waist, digging industriously in the sand, working up a sweat. I ask the driver of our buggy, who has turned into Dr. Wheeling, what the people are doing.

"Burying the dead," Wheeling replies. "First the dead are cremated and then they are put in these containers." He points to a series of large forms in the shape of human beings, fifteen or twenty feet tall, like Egyptian mummies, painted bright colors and stacked along the sandy road that cuts through the sand-filled landscape.

"Is this the way I will be buried?" I ask, knowing my spirit would wither and die and never rise to heaven from one of these dense, brightly painted

*containers. My remains would be trapped—no air
to breathe, no dreams to fly.*

*"Yes, all people here are buried in this way, it is
the custom." Wheeling looked surprised that I
should want to know.*

*"My ashes must be scattered to the wind," I said,
"so my soul can fly to heaven."*

*"It will be arranged," Wheeling says, his teeth
turning into fangs, his eyes to black holes, his
head to that of a monster.*

39

"Edward is having an affair," I said, surprised at the calm in my voice. Inside, my heart was racing. "Bella told me."

"Who is it? Do you know?" Julia asked. We were on our way to the Meadowlands. I was driving my Daimler, gripping the wheel too tight, going too fast.

"I don't," I said. The feeling of betrayal and hurt had settled into a steady anger.

"So it isn't Bella?" Julia said.

"I don't think so," I said, looking sideways at Julia and wondering again if—but I shook my suspicions aside. "Edward wouldn't answer me when I asked him who it was." I stared hard at the road in front of me. "He didn't admit anything."

"My suspicions were right," Julia said. "He *is* a jerk." She shook her head. "I'm sorry to say that about your lover."

"There was something else, something strange," I went on. "Bella's Rolodex was open to Wheeling's name when she left the office."

"That's bizarre," Julia said.

Her voice was filled with concern. I kept my eyes on the road, steering the black Daimler Princess—an impulsive purchase I had made on my last trip to England. The car had a wide back seat and a right-hand

207

drive with which I delighted in panicking other drivers in Manhattan.

I shook my head. "I don't know what to think."

"Are you sure you're all right to drive?" Julia asked.

I looked at Julia's face out of the corner of my eye and nodded. "Yes. But I'm angry at Edward. And hurt that he could be having an affair," I said. To myself I admitted I was also scared.

"That's a healthy feeling," Julia said. "I'm glad to hear you express it."

"I think in some way I feel relieved to find out that's what's probably been going on," I said. "It explains a lot." But there was sadness under the anger. "When Bella told me, I felt like a teenager dropped on the night of the prom."

Julia put her hand on my arm. "He's not good enough for you, Catherine," she said. I was grateful Julia had kept her promise to accompany me on this shoot. I knew she was coming mostly to see Reed, but I was grateful for her company no matter the reason.

I laughed. "No man is ever good enough for your best friend, Julia." But as I drove, I felt wary, vulnerable, depressed. I thought of Renaldo, and the threats on my life, then tried to shake off the black mood. Jethro, sitting in the back seat, was silent. I didn't care if he heard what we were saying. Let the whole world know, I thought. "Jethro, are you comfortable back there?" I asked.

"I'm fine." Our eyes connected in the rearview mirror. I had told Jethro about Bella having Wheeling's card on her desk, and he had immediately called Zardos to let him know.

"Anything new on Fred?" Julia asked.

"Nothing," Jethro said. "The whole police force is on the lookout."

"It's so sad, that boy," Julia said. "Stan says Malinda is in a snit, but the rest of them are handling it all right."

"They're brave to go on without Fred," I said. "He plays all the keyboards, he's such a strong part of the group, and he sings one of their big hits. But Stan says he can't afford to cancel them with the Grammys just around the corner."

"Reed sounded pretty calm," Julia said, "for somebody who has just lost his lead singer."

"Well," I glanced over at my friend, "Reed's life isn't that bad right now. He's mad about you."

She smiled.

On the New Jersey side of the Lincoln Tunnel I settled the Daimler into a gentle sixty-mile-an-hour cruise, relishing the feeling of being in control of something, anything. There were no phone-callers out here on the highway, no threatening notes, no assistants in comas. No Edward having an affair with someone.

There was just a band of kids missing another kid.

"Tell me about Zardos," Julia asked Jethro, looking at him over her shoulder. "What's he like?"

Jethro shifted forward so his head was nearer Julia's. "Zardos is one amazing cop," he said. "I've worked with a lot of them, and he's the best. And he always solves his cases," Jethro went on. "Do you remember that guy that was killing women in Central Park last year?"

"You mean the Dusk Murderer?" I said.

"That's the one," Jethro said. All the murders happened when it was nearly dark. "Zardos solved it, practically by himself, after everybody else had given up."

I tried to remember back to the fall, when the murders had occurred. "How did Zardos find the killer?" I asked.

"Blood sugar," Jethro said.

"What did blood sugar have to do with it?" I said, smiling in spite of the grotesque subject matter. It struck me as funny.

"Zardos found out that all the women had normal blood-sugar levels at the time of their death," he said. "He knew that when you're running, something happens to your blood sugar and it goes down. But the victims' blood sugars tested normal, and that's how Zardos figured it out. There was this kiosk that sold Italian ices not far from the scene of the murders. The vendor would sell an ice to a woman, close his kiosk, then take off after her and murder her."

I shook my head and Julia shuddered and pulled her sweater tighter around her shoulders.

"I brought something to eat," I said, speaking of food. "A little something. You can't get anything at the Meadowlands but junk food." In two shopping bags were a thermos of hot coffee, half a dozen bagels, roasted chicken with rosemary, mozzarella with sun-dried tomatoes, caviar cream-cheese spread, Carr's wheat crackers, sliced gravlax, and a tub of Greek olives, all bought by Flora at Zabar's.

Food, I thought. My friend. My nemesis. Even with everything that was going on, it seemed I had always thought of food in terms of either feast or famine. My boyfriends on the ranch and at school ate all the burgers and fries and malts they ever wanted and never gained an ounce. Sometimes I tried to keep up and then had to eat like a bird to lose the extra fat.

In my first year of college I started going on binges and then fasting for days to make up for the weight I had gained. Later, when I went on the road, following rock bands, I would eat junk food and make up for it with days of juice and tea and coffee. I got sick from all the ups and downs in my weight. I even found a diet doctor who gave me pills for a while, but they didn't work for long. Then, in many of my relation-

ships with men, food played a major role in the court-
ship—wine and fancy French food that I either picked
at, gorged on, or guzzled.

In the last ten years, I had learned to enjoy a little
of everything, avoid the fat, and work my buns off at
the gym. I wasn't cured of food, but the sex with Edward, along with long sessions at the gym, had made
me feel less afraid of it. I wondered whether breaking
up with Edward would make me gain weight or lose.

My thoughts returned to the road and I realized I
was speeding again, this time doing nearly eighty-five.
I brought the needle down close to the speed limit.

At the backstage entrance to the arena, Jethro, Julia,
and I grabbed shopping bags, camera bags, film,
purses, and coats. We piled through the performers'
entrance, past the security guard, down a length of
institutional corridor that echoed with our steps. I
reached the line of dressing rooms and almost ran into
Stan, who was going in the opposite direction in a
big hurry.

"Catherine, I'm glad you came. You're just in time
for the sound check," Stan said, breathlessly kissing
me on my cheek. "He hasn't turned up," he said, gri-
macing, and then looked at me as though seeing me
for the first time. "You look terrible," he said bluntly.
"Is something else going on? Other than Renaldo?
Other than Fred?"

I felt my face fall. "I found out Edward is having
an affair," I said bluntly.

Stan gave me a frown, stuck out his lower lip, and
took me in his arms. "Baby, I'm so sorry. You really
deserve better." He held me at arm's length. "Are
you all right to do some pictures?" he quickly asked.
I nodded and he looked concerned.

Instead of the usual suit and tie, Stan was wearing
a sand-washed, bright green silk shirt. In the pocket

of his shirt was a slender gold Tiffany pen bearing his initials, and a gold chain gleamed from the nest of black and silver hair visible at the open neck of his shirt. Stan's rock-and-roll look.

"I'll be all right," I said. "I've got so much on my mind, this is just one more thing."

Then Stan noticed Julia. "You came? What a good friend you are," Stan said, embracing Julia. "Isn't it the pits? Edward the Terrible," Stan went on, looking at me, "that's what we call him behind your back, Catherine. Don't we, Julia?" She nodded her head.

"Julia, when are we going to get you out here again, darling? Not painting, but singing!" Stan boomed. I thought I heard the sound of lost revenue in Stan's voice. He loved Julia, I knew, but he would have loved her even more with the concert checks coming in. "I know this is tacky, Julia," he continued, "and if you don't want to do it you can just say no." He put his hand on Julia's shoulder. "Would you open tonight's show? Just one song? You know, the audience would go crazy." With his free hand he played with the hair on his chest. "And it would help me out. The audience is going to miss Fred, even though the show is sold out. If you sing a song, it would take their mind off his absence for a while. For sure."

Julia looked at Stan with a glimmer in her eyes and said something that astonished me. "You know I'm retired, Stan." She ran her finger over her red lips. "But for you, and for Reed—is John Gilmore playing?" Julia asked. John was the lead keyboard player for Freedom, the band who was opening the show for the Newborns, a good, hot band, a favorite in the tri-state area. He had played many recording sessions with Julia.

"John's here all right," Stan said. "They're just finishing their rehearsal."

"If he'll play 'Melody' for me, then I'll sing it," Julia said.

I couldn't believe she was going on.

"Julia," I said, giving her a weak smile, "I'm shocked. You used to book a job two years in advance. You didn't even ask if the sound system's any good."

"Well, maybe I can cheer you up too, Catherine," Julia said. She put her arm around my shoulders. She knew I loved to hear her sing that song.

"Then it's a done deal?" Stan said. He couldn't believe his good luck.

Julia smiled at him. "It's a done deal," she said.

"Ain't love grand," I said to Stan, shaking off the anxiety in the pit of my stomach. "It must be hormones."

I looked around the production office in which Stan had settled us. The desktop was overflowing with papers and contracts, piles of magazines, promotional photographs, ticket stubs, packs of cigarettes, candy wrappers. Pieces of clothing were thrown over the chairs and couches. The walls were plastered with photographs of the major stars of rock and roll. I recognized some of the pictures as mine, a couple that hadn't been paid for. Rock-and-roll acts will do anything to save a buck.

Julia smiled angelically. "Stan, I've got to go somewhere to warm up."

Unlike Julia, I was far from relaxed. The arena was beginning to fill and I could hear the huge audience even here in the office. The sound reverberated off every wall in the performing center, and a twenty-thousand-strong audience was starting to pound up and down the stairs, buying hot dogs and T-shirts, hats and pins, popcorn and soft drinks, waiting for the music to start. I was nervous, frightened, and sad, all at the same time.

"Do you have a room where Ms. Clearwater can warm up?" Stan asked. Hank Cramer, one of the production crew, was a muscular man once under indictment for Mafia-related activities. He had been acquitted of wrongdoing, but the rumor persisted that he still palled around with a heavy crowd. Now, he ushered us—Julia, Stan, Jethro, and me—down a series of corridors, dodging groupies and people with press passes dangling around their necks. A few steps down from the office he opened the door into an enormous space clearly intended for a sports team, complete with cement floors, showers and urinals, rust-stained sinks, lockers half open and half shut, and overhead lighting that made you feel as though you were on display in a zoo. Bare cinder-block walls and the mingled smell of Dr. Scholl's, must, mildew, deodorant, soap, sweat, and nerves.

"Romantic," I said, looking around the bleak space. "Real glamorous." I wanted a cigarette. And I wanted to go home after shooting the photos tonight and make love to Edward. "I could use a cigarette," I said to no one in particular.

Julia went over to the floor-length mirror and ran a comb through her hair. "Have you quit smoking again?" she asked me over the sound of running water. "I notice the absence of the perpetual cloud of smoke around your head. Mad enough at Edward to quit?" she said, throwing me a conspiratorial grin.

"Just for this evening," I said, and returned the grin.

"Right," she said and laughed. "You've quit many times, as I remember. Good luck."

"Thanks. I need it." I wondered if I could do it.

I had smoked from the time I was fifteen, starting with the sneaked butts I gathered from Charlie, our foreman. My father used to call them "coffin nails";

he wouldn't let me near a cigarette, and if he saw me smoking, smoke would practically pour out of his ears and I would get the big cancer lecture. Buster seemed to know cigarettes were dangerous before anyone else tumbled to the health hazards of the "dread weed," as he called it. My father, of course, was an ex-smoker.

Partly because my father hated to see me smoke, I delighted in breaking his rules and smoked as often as possible. Now, more than twenty years later, I knew I was totally addicted and it was going to be a bitch to stop. But I swore I would do it. If only to prove to Edward, who had always hated my smoking, that I could.

Julia began her vocal warm-up with high-powered trilling sounds that would have peeled the paint off the walls, if there had been any paint. I threw my coat over a wooden athletic bench, pulled out my cameras and film bag, and headed for the door.

"See you in a little while," Julia said, then continued vocalizing. Jethro and I and the stadium's security officer left her singing among the mildew and cement, happy as a clam.

"This is the best part, Jethro," I said, as the three of us moved into the mob scene in the hallway, where by now hundreds of groupies were hanging out, talking, flashing backstage passes, buying hot dogs and popcorn and beer, sporting T-shirts and caps that said *The Newborns, New York's Number One*, waiting for the evening to begin. Jethro looked suspiciously at everyone in the crowd.

"All these people look like rock-and-rollers themselves," Jethro observed. Indeed, the Newborns' fans were indistinguishable from the Newborns themselves. Some were dramatically dressed in wrinkled army-surplus clothes or frilly lingerie with masses of beads and crosses. One fellow, in long robes and thongs, looked like an extra from the movie *Gandhi*, and a girl was dressed like Malinda, her body clad in a silvery leotard, her head a mass of lemon-blond curls. There was a Z-Train look-alike, his black skin gleaming like ebony, bits of turquoise in his dreadlocks.

As Jethro and I made our way through the crowd, I caught a glimpse of Stan, Hank, and a big, familiar man off to the side of the stadium. I tensed, recognizing one of Hank's friends, a powerful and reputedly dangerous man named Benhurst, a known mob lawyer. In the music business there was occasionally the suspicion of Mafia presence, with a link between payola and radio play. It could seldom be proved, but such lawyers were people to be avoided like the plague. The rumors about Hank must, I thought, be true, and shook myself as Jethro sniffed the air, giving the groupies the eye but staying close as I put them on film. "Don't you smell that?" he asked.

"I sure do," I said, inhaling the scent of marijuana. I was surprised. Fred's difficulties notwithstanding, the usual substance of choice at a Newborns concert was Snapple or Gatorade.

I had smoked my share of marijuana in my younger years and now the smell made me a little dizzy and reminded me of Gavin Richards, the Englishman I had gone with for a few years. Gavin always had a supply of hash and pot, and I finally realized he was enjoying the weed more than my company. The smell was evocative, and in spite of the tingle of fear that still lingered and my general state of nervous tension, the familiar thrill that made me love this crazy business began to run up my spine.

"Catherine!" a voice called and I turned to see Kathleen Turner. "Hi!" Her voice raised at the sight of the uniformed officer. Her big blond beautiful body was swathed in camel-colored suede.

"Hi, Kathleen," I said. Sting and Bette Midler were in the swarm of fans waiting to get into the private boxes near the stage, along with a half-dozen giant men, members of the New York Rangers still high from their recent Stanley Cup victory, their first in fifty-four years. The Newborns had a delicious bunch of fans, many of whom were famous in their own right. All were going to be disappointed that one of the group's singers was out of commission.

A guard let us through the curtain into the stage area and then dropped the black fabric back across the entrance. Inside the empty hall, light monkeys were still climbing amid the rigging, replacing gels, and the sound system roared, squealed, and spat guitar sounds and drum beats into the air. Freedom was completing their sound check, Mick Link's drums slapping against the walls. I kept the camera going as Malinda, Reed, Z-Train, and Sahid, as well as Pete Sky, who would be playing Fred's keyboard parts, clambered onto the stage in their street clothes for the rehearsal. They tuned guitars, adjusted amps, and yelled instructions to the sound crew. Reed waved to me and then got up close to the microphone. "Fred, if you're out there, you better get your ass on this stage!"

Malinda opened up the rehearsal with her wild, eerie voice. *"You're shameless, baby,"* she sang, *"you're a face without a heart."* Reed and Z-Train joined in on the chorus. Reed had written the new song after seeing Julia's painting of the same name in my apartment.

I had shot a lot of pictures by then and the thought of Edward and Renaldo and Wheeling and my other troubles took the wind out of my sails. I was suddenly tired and hungry.

"I've got enough pictures," I said to Jethro and the security officer, who had been quietly following me around as I shot. "Time for some food."

Back at the dressing room Julia was still singing and a gang of fans was outside the door screaming and waving programs, telling the guard they knew that Julia Clearwater was inside and would he please just get her to sign their programs. The uniformed guard stood his ground, and I could still hear Reed's voice echoing down the hall—*"shameless, you're shameless, you're tearin' me apart . . ."*

Finally Reed came back in, with Malinda on his arm. Z-Train and Sahid followed close behind to complete the quintet minus one.

Stan poked his head out the door of the dressing room and saw the six of us.

"Four out of five—at least I've got *you,*" Stan said, pulling us through the door. "They're legal, you can let them in," he said to the guard. "They're with the show."

I took Stan by the arm and asked him what he was doing talking to Benhurst.

"Nothing important," he said casually, shaking his head. "He was asking if we needed more legal representation." Stan smiled. "We don't," he said.

"I'm here to see Reed Wilton." I heard Denzel's voice outside the dressing room door.

"He's all right, let him in," Stan said over the commotion at the door and Denzel appeared in the room—tall, and with a great body from lifting weights as well as cameras.

I gave him a hug.

"Thanks for having Reed call me, Catherine," Denzel said.

"I don't talk the talk," Denzel had told me once. "Nobody wants to hear it. I just walk the walk."

"I'm glad you guys got together," I said.

Reed was not the wreck he had been earlier in the day. He planted a kiss on Julia's lips. Then he frowned, making his plans to work around his missing singer. "Z-Train, you can take Fred's solo on 'Southern Comfort.' I'll play his bass part. We'll get by."

Malinda came up and gave me a hug. "Where's my father?" She flashed me a gentle, expectant smile with a mile of white teeth, her hair a mass of golden curls on top of her head.

"He couldn't come, Malinda," I said, hiding my own fury at Edward. "He had business, he said."

"Dad hasn't ever seen me work with the band, you know," Malinda said, a sad, resigned look on her face, not what you would expect from a sexy, long-legged rock-and-roll beauty.

"*Entertainment Tonight* is here," Max said, gathering up the Newborns in his arms. "They want you on camera." I felt a sudden exasperation with the press, of which I was, after all, a part. We were always there, prying, pushing, getting into the act. I heard some shouting outside the door, the sound of equipment banging around and even louder voices than the fans', and then Fran, a blond television anchor, got her head in the door and called out Reed's name. Jethro kept nervously close, scrutinizing the whole situation with apprehension.

"Reed Wilton, I'd really like to talk to you," Fran said in a loud voice. "Malinda, where is Fred? Are you going to sing 'Southern Comfort' without him?" Fran was shouting, the lights on, the camera rolling.

"Of course. That's our big hit." Malinda smiled, a mile of teeth showing.

"Is it true what the *Post* said this morning—that Fred was nude in front of Bergdorf Goodman, that he has disappeared?" Fran went on. When no one answered her, she continued talking. "Do you like being called the Melanie Griffith of rock and roll?" Fran zoomed in on Malinda, whose wide smile kept on shining.

"I don't mind being called whatever they call me, as long as people buy my records!" Malinda said, laughing.

"But where is Fred? Is he going to sing tonight? Is he going to be at the Grammys?" Fran asked insistently.

"I think I'll let my manager answer that question," Malinda said, ducking out of camera range, pulling Max forward.

Max spoke with the voice of authority, his weight giving him the upper hand. "We've all heard the rumors, but that's just gossip," the huge man said. "Fred is ill right now," he went on. Of course, Max was right—Fred *was* ill. Max's voice was a cross between Edward R. Murrow and the Reverend Jesse Jackson, very reassuring, almost convincing.

But Fran wasn't convinced. The bright lights of the camera turned full on Max's face. "Let's get this show on the road, it's getting late," Max said, wanting out of the cameras, wanting off the hot seat.

Fran followed, poking the microphone in Max's face again and again as he tried to lead the group out of the room. I just kept taking pictures. Max, Z-Train, Malinda, and Reed tangling with the agitated anchor made a good picture.

"What do you mean, 'Fred's ill'?" Fran persisted.

"He's got the flu," Max answered, both his arms around the band members, getting nearer to the door. "He's not feeling well. He has some kind of a virus, he can't perform. He's lost his voice."

A likely story, I heard Fran mumble.

"Gotta go now, we're on in a few minutes," Malinda said, waving a thin, elegant arm at the cameras.

"See you." Reed kissed Julia wetly on the mouth and headed out the door after Malinda. Max followed, and Fran and the crew cornered Reed again but he just laughed merrily and squeezed past, shielded by Max, who lifted Reed's arms in the manner of a fight referee, and then brought them down to signal that the interview was at an end. The group exited the room in a flurry of lights and video equipment.

Jethro had been hovering near the door, plugging a finger in one ear to keep out the noise as he spoke into his cellular phone. Now, as the Newborns exited with Fran and the rest of the press in tow, Jethro took two quick steps toward me, a smile breaking out on his features. He looked excited and out of breath.

"I just heard from Zardos," he said. "Renaldo is conscious."

I grinned from ear to ear with relief.

Stan, overhearing, clapped Jethro on the shoulder. "That's great," he said.

"Yes," Jethro continued. "Renaldo remembers everything—getting roughed up, threatened, pushed down the subway stairs."

"Did he say why they pushed him?" I asked.

Jethro nodded. "He says whoever it was seemed to be trying to stop him from going back to work for you, something about him being too nosy. He says he would certainly remember his attacker. Zardos is going to show him some pictures in the morning."

"Pictures of whom?" I asked.

"Oh, you know, *everybody*," Jethro said, looking at me. "Your friends, Ms. Saint."

Stan smiled broadly. "Oh, Catherine," he said, giving me a tight hug, "this is wonderful. You must be so relieved." Smiling nervously, he raced out the door to be sure the Newborns got on stage.

I sighed with relief and stashed rolls of exposed film in my bags. I loaded fresh film and thought that in the morning, when Renaldo had identified his assailant, my life would get back to normal.

40

I dream of the night Sally is killed, a dream I have had many times, trying to make the ending come out different, trying to have Sally live instead of dying.

In this dream, I see her at a performance of the Invincible Myth Machine, the group she is touring with and writing about at the time of her death. The Invincible Myth Machine is three long-haired teenagers from Scotland with voices like angels who wear steel helmets and wire wings in their performances. Sally is writing the liner notes for their latest record, which they recorded live at a club in Santa Monica; now they are traveling to a small club on Long Island called The Weird Room to reenact the West Coast scene of the recording.

Their music fills the smoky club while Sally sits backstage with the road manager getting the lowdown on the band, and when the show is over, the road manager suggests that tonight, because the weather is bad, instead of driving back in the van, the group should stay overnight at a local hotel.

Sally drives back to New York with the band on a sunny morning after the storm. Sally lives. We

*meet in her apartment on Barrow Street and make
love until dusk, until all the light has drained
from her room, until we are exhausted and hungry.
We walk together, smoking and laughing,
through the fresh, rain-washed streets of Greenwich Village.*

41

Exultant over the news that Renaldo had regained consciousness, I hurried to the room where Julia was warming up, to tell her what I had learned.

"What a relief!" Julia said. "Does Zardos know who pushed him yet?"

I shook my head, and said I hadn't a clue, that I had to hold my breath until the morning, until Zardos showed Renaldo some pictures.

Julia gave me a hug and went on rehearsing, concentrating on making beautiful tones.

I have always thought that what performers do between shows is a dream. Their real lives happen, at least for real performers, only when they are on that magical stage, near the fumes of the smoke machines, the dust from cartons and curtains and crates, boxes, Haliburtons, costumes; the smell of greasepaint, the aura of nervous excitement.

With Jethro, I followed Julia from the dressing room through the crowds to the backstage area, snapping pictures of her.

In a quiet moment while she waited to go onstage, looking calm and beautiful, I got another good portrait.

The press had been evicted from the backstage area and everybody else was running to find their seats for the show. Fran's voice still echoed down the hall toward the stage. Reed walked up in full makeup, looking all hair, eyes, teeth, and arms, his torso pulsating beneath some rags of denim.

"You're on, sweetheart," Reed said to Julia. "Have a ball!" He kissed her, avoiding getting his makeup all over her. His guitar was strapped across his slim hips and he was absentmindedly tuning. Reed continued to look happy and calm. Denzel kept close to him.

Those meetings, I thought, are better than drugs.

John Gilmore and Freedom were onstage waiting for the surprise appearance of Julia Clearwater. The audience was a hip mixture of fans of the music from the sixties through the nineties. Now they quieted down expectantly.

"And now, ladies and gentlemen, a special surprise guest ... *Ms. Julia Clearwater!*" roared a voice through the hall as Julia stepped onto the stage to wild screams. Her voice soared, and the audience swooned at her sweet, powerful sound.

Julia's audience had made love to the sound of her voice for more than twenty years. They had smoked grass, graduated from college, gotten married; done drugs and gotten into recovery; gone from weed to juice to aerobics to codependency groups, listening to her songs. Her voice had accompanied their weddings and their divorces, soothed their broken hearts and accompanied the days when they spread their wings and took to the sky as well as the days their dreams were dashed to the ground. It was her voice that got them back on their feet, mended their hearts, and told them, in that subtle magic with which it was infused, that they were going to be all right again, fall in love again, live to fly again. They adored her.

I hunkered down under the apron of the stage, where I had a good view of my friend. John Gilmore played "Melody" and conducted the rest of the band in what had become the most popular big ballad of the early nineties, an even bigger hit than Bette's "From a Distance." When Julia finished her song the crowd went crazy trying to get her to sing again, but the announcer reintroduced Freedom and they began to play over the pounding of feet on the floor. The audience was still roaring as I made my way backstage.

"Julia, that was beautiful," I said, "I have never heard you sing better." Malinda, Z-Train, and Sahid were congratulating her.

Sahid turned from Julia toward me, a concerned look on his face. "Catherine," he whispered, putting his lips to my ear, "I think Reed is falling in love and it's got me worried." Sahid was one of those rockers who were convinced that Yoko had broken up the Beatles. Though I was fond of him, Sahid, I imagined, would prefer drug addiction to love.

"Please don't worry," I said. "Julia is a professional, she knows how it is."

He was only slightly reassured. "We're in trouble already," Sahid went on.

So was I. Today Zardos had been interviewing Wheeling, looking into every part of my life, while I was here at the Meadowlands taking pictures of a rock-and-roll band.

But I felt relief about Renaldo, and soon, I thought, we would know who had tried to kill him and perhaps who had made the threats on my life. I wondered if they were the same person, and looked around at the faces of my friends.

Were they my friends?

Zardos had wanted to know if the behavior of my friends had changed recently. Certainly I should tell the detective that in the case of Edward, the answer was yes.

Stan came up to Julia and put his arm around her. "You're better than ever, Julia," he said. "Let me

convince you to start singing again. You're the best."
He looked at his musicians, including Fred's sub,
wearing heavy makeup but clearly not Fred—Fred was
small with silver hair, Pete was big and blond. They all
got ready to go on. "You guys look great. Menacing!
Catherine, don't they look good, even without Fred?"
Reed threw Julia a kiss, mounting the stairs to the
stage.

"Wish us luck, Catherine," Sahid said.

Z-Train gave me a victory sign. His makeup was
ghastly, but the fans called it cool. He shook his dreadlocks and the turquoise and glass beads danced around
his face with its war paint. "Fred can't destroy this
group!" he shouted as Max moved in behind him,
gathering Sahid, Z-Train, Reed, Malinda, and Pete in
the circle of his arms.

"Just make music," Max said, "forget about everything else!"

Sahid ran onto the stage and began a drum beat for
their entrance; Malinda danced into the lights, twirling
strands of her hair in her fingers; she shone like a
long slender jewel in her silver costume. Z-Train loped
onstage, joining Malinda to Sahid's pounding drums,
followed by Reed and Pete Sky; and they were all
there—all but Fred, and God knew where he was.
Missing his life, I thought.

The audience was going crazy, screaming, shouting.

In their makeup the boys looked like demons; their
hair was pulled back from their faces in ghoulish colors, violet and black. Spikes standing out on wrists,
chests and arms tattooed with greasepaint, and black
leather pants so tight you could see bony kneecaps,
as well as some less-emaciated parts of their young
bodies.

Malinda was the glorious contrast, the beauty, her
slender silver figure casting rainbows from her sequins.

The four of them combined probably weighed as much as Max.

The Newborns sang most of the songs from *Birth Canal*, including their most recent platinum single, "Southern Comfort." Z-Train sang lead:

> *There's no more Southern Comfort, darlin',*
> *give yourself a break for today.*
> *There's no more Southern Comfort, darlin',*
> *nothing you can smoke, drink, or say.*
> *You're always used to running,*
> *standing still is not a price you can pay ...*

Then they did a great new song about Elvis Presley called "Poor Boy." Between songs, the crowd chanted "Fred, Fred, Fred, Fred," and I wondered how that would sound to a twenty-year-old who was probably passed out on the street somewhere in a cocaine blackout, to hear his name on the lips of thousands. It proved to me again that it wasn't success or lack of it that made people drug addicts and alcoholics.

Next was a terrific new song from the album. I was practically dancing on the ground trying to get as many pictures as I could. "Starbreaker" was a real rocker:

> *He likes to get paid and he likes to talk fast,*
> *likes to get laid, likes the flavor of cash.*
> *He likes to do deals that may never last.*
> *Likes his tuna raw,*
> *likes to break the law,*
> *and he'd sell his dad and he'd sell his ma.*
> *He's a deal maker,*
> *smile faker,*
> *starbreaker ...*

Then Malinda launched into "Shameless." From the first line of the song, the crowd was on its feet, shouting. It was an instant hit. The stage went dark, Malinda's voice came from everywhere onstage. The audience was hers as she sang in her wailing, tormenting voice:

"You're shameless, baby, you're tearin' me apart..."

Pete Sky was good on the keyboards, but he didn't sing, and Malinda took the entire solo. On stage she was radiant in silver boots with golden toes, a bosom of pointed, sensuous lines that reached out to the very last person in the audience, hips that squealed and jutted as her pelvis moved with the roar of hard rock and roll. Guitars wailed, Reed's wild guitar behind her, Z-Train's bass deep, rumbling, Sahid's drums sensuous, pounding, the rhythm taking the crowd with it, pulsing, throbbing.

"You're shameless, baby, you're a face without a heart..."

The show utilized state-of-the-art lighting that included a large complement of additional setups on the side sustained by a huge metal rigging system with a platform that could accommodate two or three people. Julia, Stan, and Jethro were standing beside me as I began pulling myself up on the metal bars of the super rig onto the wooden platform. As I started to climb, Jethro gasped.

"God, Ms. Saint, you aren't going up there, are you?" Jethro said.

"It's all right, I've done this many times before," I said reassuringly. I was famous for climbing the rigs. I wanted those pictures.

Julia understood and gave me a gentle boost. "Watch yourself, Catherine." My knees were a little shaky, but I knew it would be worth it to be up this high. I shook a smile from my face, and now from the height I had reached I had a much better view of the stage. Jethro and the officer were right below me, watching me.

Malinda's costume barely covered the tops of her thighs. From there on down to the tops of her glimmering silver boots, the silvery skin-tight leggings shone as if a thousand tourmalines were encrusted on their surface.

I had wanted Renaldo to see this group perform and now, thank God, he would.

"Watch it," I shouted to Jethro beneath me, "mind your head." Jethro was keeping his eyes on me instead of the show, ducking under the metal bars directly beneath my cameras. There was a crowd under the rigging.

Hank, the production man, had often assured me that the super rig's platform would hold an elephant upside down. Jethro looked as though he were going to scream. I went on shooting, entranced by the Newborns' show and Malinda's magical performance. They had the audience in a frenzy.

For an encore, the Newborns did a rock-and-roll snake dance with a twenty-foot-long black-and-silver feather boa that looked alive. Malinda was writhing and turning with the faux snake in the lights while the band played. The lighting made you think you were in Hades, on the River Styx, in *Paradise Lost*, watching Gounod's *Faust*, and riding a rollercoaster all at once. As a finale, Malinda, Z-Train, Reed, and Sahid cut off the snake's head and the crowd went crazy.

In the noise and smoke, the lights and tumult, the platform suddenly shook violently, the bar holding it slanted suddenly toward the floor and I plummeted, cameras flying, lenses smashing as I fell from the platform and hit the hard stage twenty feet below me, every bone in my body seeming to snap, conscious of chaos before a great pain shot through my body and the lights went out.

42

A MEMORY OF THE WEST DRIFTED INTO MY MIND, BACK to a winter morning in 1962—a morning of fear and revelation.

I was twelve that winter. I had always known that life on the ranch could be dangerous. My father told me ranching was the best way in the world for a man, or a woman, to make a living. He also told me of the hardships of ranching. By then I had seen animals die giving birth and winter storms with snow so deep the Black Angus cattle froze to death, and summers so hot the wheat withered and dust rose from the beds of the creeks and the fields and there was no food and no money to do anything but scrape through the best we could.

And I knew about rabies.

My father told me bats carried rabies and when they bit another animal they could pass the rabies along, and that a terrible death could follow a rabies bite in an animal or a human. Lockjaw and fever and pain, he said, and there was only one cure—a series of needles in the stomach that were excruciatingly painful—which might or might not save your life.

A pair of rabid coyotes was reported to be among the mice and rats and bats who bore the dread disease. These wolflike coyotes, silver with black streaks and huge heads, had been attacking other animals and children, prowling the neighboring ranches.

That winter morning the radio from Moline issued a warning that the animals should be shot on sight, that they were a danger to livestock and people. In the winter wheat their low-slung bodies could be difficult to spot on the ranch. They might prowl in dry fields, bellies to the ground; they might slither in the dry riverbeds among the milkweed and the rattling dead brush; or they might hide in shadows cast by the winter sun on short days near the barn or the house.

My father and mother and brother and I listened to the reporter from Moline say the coyotes were sick, they were probably foaming at the mouth, and that they were likely to attack without provocation. My father told me to keep an eye out for them and if I saw them to grab the shotgun he kept on the front porch for just such an occasion and to shoot first, ask questions later.

I knew how to shoot a gun, and how to clean it too. But I was frightened and that night I had nightmares and tossed in my feather bed on the second floor of our house, under the eaves. I dreamed the coyotes were in the attic and at dawn I tiptoed up the cold, narrow staircase to the attic to look for them, my feet and fingers shivering. Relieved to find only sagging mattresses, unused furniture, boxes of Christmas ornaments, and chests of mothballed summer clothing in the nooks and crannies in the creaky attic, I tiptoed downstairs again, my breath making white clouds in front of my face, the cold wooden stairs creaking with every step I took.

Back in bed, I shivered under the multicolored quilt my grandmother had stitched together by hand—squares of blue velvet, white silk, pink cotton, violet rayon, threaded together with a blue, green, and yellow embroidered pattern of stars and squares, done in what she called the "blind stitch," fine and almost invisible among the colors. But even under the reassuring warmth and weight of my beautiful comforter, I couldn't get back to sleep.

I ate breakfast that morning with my parents and my brother. Mother served a fluffy omelet and fresh-baked bread with homemade blueberry preserves, and I washed everything down with three glasses of milk before excusing myself from the table to go out for my morning ride and my chores. And to look for those rabid coyotes.

I mounted Duke, my favorite two-year-old, whom I had trained and ridden since he could take a saddle, and galloped to Uncle Gene's ranch and back, getting in a good loping run on the hill that separated our two houses.

I wound up outside the bullpen about seven-thirty. Instead of unsaddling Duke as I usually did, I tied his reins to the wooden part of the electric fence near the gate. I swung down, patted Duke's hind quarters, and eased around him, sliding open the lock that kept the pen closed. This was the time I usually went to prepare the bulls' breakfast.

I kept my eyes open for the coyotes. I looked for them everywhere I went that day. I scanned the horizon and the ground in front of me. Perhaps they were in the bullpen. My father would be furious if one of those coyotes were to attack a bull.

It was still cold, frightfully cold, and I took off my leather gloves to move my fingers around and maneuver the big quarts of raw oats, molasses, and nutrients into the feeding troughs. I had come by earlier to heat the molasses into a thick black goo under a burner on the big Coleman stove, then mixed it in with the oats. I turned the big wooden ladle in the mixture, the steam coming from the mash echoing the pattern of mist from the mouths of the bulls, who were by now edging around the sides of the long, narrow feed trough, breathing through their soft, velvety noses, grunting in anticipation. There were fifteen bulls inside, lowing and moving about peacefully.

They soon settled into their chewing, content, their horns down, their tails fanning away the flies that even the cold January air couldn't keep from their backs and underbellies.

I watched them awhile, and then turned back to where Duke was and faced him from inside the pen.

The electrified wire, something of which I was always careful and conscious, was on the inside of the pen. I moved familiarly around it, reaching out to touch the brown muzzle of Duke's nose, just to say hello to him.

"Good horse," I murmured. I would be beside myself if a coyote bit Duke, I thought. I loved him so much, my heart would break if he died of rabies.

Looking around again to check that the coyotes were not in the bullpen, somehow, at the same moment as I touched Duke I must have touched the live wire on the inside of the wooden-slatted fence. The jolt traveled straight through me to the horse, and he whinnied in terror at the full impact of the electric shock.

I fell backward onto the dirt of the bullpen. Duke threw his head back, ripped the reins from the bridle, and tore completely free of the loose knot I had used to tether him. He galloped off straight for the alfalfa fields at a greater speed than I had ever been able to pull out of him.

I forgot all about rabid coyotes. I was on the ground, my gloves beside me, my head spinning. When I caught my breath, I realized what had happened and knew I had to get Duke back before he tore into that field. There was a sprinkler system that watered the alfalfa fields in the summer. Buster kept the tubes out all winter in case he needed water for the winter wheat. They were exposed and Duke could easily break a leg or break one of the pipes—and get me in trouble with my father.

I tore out of the gate, forgetting the bulls, forgetting the steaming mash. I yelled, "Duke! Duke!" as I hightailed it for the alfalfa fields.

He was already into the field of watering pipe. Behind me the bulls were now moving, confused at first but then eager at their sudden opportunity. My face contorted with horror as I saw fifteen huge creatures leading with their horns, flowing like a black river into the barnyard toward the big horse ring, which I had also left open behind me, and then moving into the ranch-house yard that bordered on the dry alfalfa fields.

"And don't you run those bulls, hear, and shake up that seed!" I could hear Buster's voice in my head, but it did no good. I had managed to head Duke off as he came out of the first section of alfalfa, grabbing him by what was left of his bridle, and now I was running, pulling Duke behind me by a dangling rein, yelling at the bulls, "Get back! Get back!" trying to recall their names, most of which I had given them myself: Black Night, Ebony, Nighthood, Volcano, Pitch, Nightmares, White Face, Chocolate, Starry Starry Knight, Othello, Lake of Fire, Renegade, Tar— a mass of beautiful names pouring out of the gate and heading me into big trouble.

I got Duke into the barn, screaming all the while at the bulls, and picked up the nearest thing I could find, which happened to be a nine-foot pitchfork. Right after those bulls I went, running around them in a circle, herding them the way our black sheep dog, Sunny, would do, all the while shouting like mad. Where was Sam? And Charlie—where was he? Buster's voice suddenly cut through the sound of my own.

"You put that pitchfork down, hear, or I'll beat the living daylights out of you," Pa was shouting from the porch of the house. His shirt was unbuttoned and his shirttails were flying and his suspenders flapped down his go-to-town suit pants. I remembered he was on his way to the bank that morning in Moline, to get an extension on the mortgage.

"They got out. I'm just trying to get them back in," I shouted, and he kept waving to put the pitchfork down.

"Just let it go, let it go," he shouted again, running toward the bulls, sliding the suspenders up over his shoulders and slowing to a walk. He approached the big, lowing animals, by now in a haphazard bunch, nearer the gate but far from their destination, the big fields in which the female Anguses grazed. My father's voice was soothing, his arms wide and outspread as he moved along toward the animals, who turned their heads to him inquiringly and kept moving slowly. He herded them along, and said over his shoulder to me in a quieter voice, "Go get Charlie and your mother and Ben. And just move slow and easy, hear?" I did as he said, and we all moved around the bulls, saying soothing things until the fifteen horn-heavy heads were once again bowed over the steaming mash and the gate to the bullpen was safely shut.

The points of those horns were lethal. I had tried to challenge them with a meager pitchfork. Now I was glad they had not decided to run me down, pitchfork and all.

I was just recovering my breath when my father let me have it.

"I can't believe you did that, Catherine," he said. "You know how important it is to keep them calm!"

My protests were pointless. I remembered why I had been so distracted—I had been thinking about the rabid coyotes—but I was afraid to say anything now that Buster was so angry. Explanations would only draw more fire from my already irate father.

"I'll pay for the bridle," I offered, mumbling.

"I'll say you will, and you'll get a ride into town and have it done on your own, too. I think I have to go have a look at that sprinkler system. That's probably shot to hell." My mother, Elizabeth, was making consoling noises to me, rubbing my head.

"Are you all right, honey?" She sounded worried about me, and I thought again how often it was she who consoled me, and loved me. I wondered why my father couldn't—not in any way that seemed obvious, like letting me off the hook once in a while.

The sprinkler system, as it turned out, was not shot to hell, although Duke had stepped on it in a couple of places. The horse was fine physically; he hadn't broken any bones. By the end of the day I had forgotten all about coyotes and was thinking only about how I was going to get that bridle repaired. I got a ride into town with Charlie the next afternoon and took the bridle to the leathersmith to be fixed, and came home to a house that was quiet for a week.

There were no more harsh words; there were hardly any words at all.

The following Saturday morning I was in my room when I looked out the window and saw my father sitting in the sun by the barn, all alone, smoking his pipe. Over his shoulder I could see the bullpen. I still felt guilty about my adventure of the previous week. I knew he was sorry he'd been so hard on me but he didn't know how to say it.

As I watched, just absorbing my father's serene moment, I felt a horror come into my bones. From the side of the barn where there is a little space, where Ben and I always bet each other there were snakes and ghouls and witches, came sliding on his belly a silver, lean, big-headed, long-haired coyote, slithering along the ground toward my father, to a spot where the bright, warm morning sun was making a golden pool. The coyote crouched, a rabid beast, his mouth open, his fangs dripping an evil white foam. My father did not move or turn around; Pa was completely unaware that the coyote was making ready to strike at him.

In a flash I was out of my room, through the kitchen to the entryway that led to the backyard. My father had spent hours with me behind the barn teaching me to shoot cans off the tops of chopped-off logs, and I knew I was a good shot. It was only a question of how quickly I could get to the gun, and I moved like the wind down the stairs, warm from the heat of the stove and the sun shining on the house. My rifle was in the entryway between the kitchen and the back door on a shelf above hooks hung with leather overcoats and mackintoshes with oilcloth outer shells and woolen hats with long tie strings.

I pulled the familiar .22 off the shelf and, reminding myself to stay calm, loaded a single round in the chamber. I slipped out the back door and around the corner of the house, lifted the barrel of the gun, and aimed right between the coyote's eyes. He was still crouched and ready; my father still smoked his pipe. It was about forty feet from where I stood—silently, hardly breathing—to the coyote, which was only ten feet from the back of my father's neck.

I shot true, and the rabid animal instantly collapsed as the shot echoed against the barn and the back of the house. My father exclaimed loudly and looked behind him at the slumped, still form in the dirt.

"My God," my father said, now on his feet. The stump, the winter grass laid down across the lawn, the sudden quiet after the gunshot, and the coyote with a bloody mark on his head.

My father took in what had happened at once.

"Catherine, you saved my life." He picked me up in his arms, embracing me, hugging me. I was crying. My hand had been steady as a rock when I pulled the trigger, but now it was shaking. "That was a remarkable shot, Catherine."

My father had never paid me such a compliment before.

"Mother! Ben! Charlie! Everybody come see what this girl has done!" my father shouted.

The hurt of the week before, the angry silences of the past few days, were gone. Buster's pride bristled like a wave I could feel through my body. He picked me up and called everyone into the yard to see the coyote's corpse.

The sound of the shot had brought my mother out

from washing clothes in the pump room and Ben pounded down the stairs from his room where he had been hiding away, drawing; Charlie and three jacket-clad hired hands clumped through the back door of the barn, scraping their feet on the rough mat after rushing in from the bullpens. My father shouted my praises to the men and my brother and mother, the rest of the day calling me his "hero."

It felt very strange.

Later that afternoon the men shot the other coyote; she was slumping around in the dried brush in back of the barns looking for her mate. My father called the authorities and they came to pick up the dead coyotes. They praised the men and me for "ridding the community of a deadly menace."

That night, after dinner, my mother made my favorite, Toll House cookies, and my father held me in a tight embrace.

"I'm giving Catherine first prize for killing the coyote and saving her daddy's life," he said, handing me a blue ribbon he had crafted from some of the prizes our bulls had won at state farm shows over the years. I was flabbergasted. I had never received such praise from him and I beamed from my hard-won perch.

I realized I loved my father more than I hated him, and that I always would.

43

I remember a dream. It comes to me vividly.

*Ernest Wheeling, with his black mustache and lean
figure, is following me through the church where
we worshiped on Christmas and Easter Sundays in
Moline. In Wheeling's hands are a notebook and
a silver pen that he keeps moving in front of my
eyes, slowly, back and forth. On his face is a
smile.*

*"Have I told you my dreams lately, Catherine?"
he asks.*

*We fly up toward the rose window in the chapel
and Wheeling is holding silver tongs in his hands,
like scissored talons with which he cuts his way
through the colored glass. Then we are in New
York, and as we travel over the city he holds me,
flying with black, wide wings.*

*Wheeling's voice comes back to me on a foul
wind. "I starved in a ghetto in a dark northern
city, held hostage by a hunchback who cut off the
fingers and noses and ears of tramps and vaga-
bonds. I stayed alive while all around were dying. I
had no friends and no clothes. It was freezing in
the winter and the enemy tramped outside all night
while the fires burned and I rubbed my fingers
together to keep them warm and my mother died*

*one night and I could not bury her for fear of
them finding me and I shivered and hid but stayed
alive. When the siege was over, I was thin as a
rail and I had forgotten how to communicate in all
those years without talking to anyone. I was emaciated and speechless."*

*Wheeling keeps cutting among the cumulus, nim-
bus, and stratus clouds, holding me by the back
of the neck like a cat, talking all the while he flies—
over the mountains, over the red sea filled with
blood. The blue air is oxygen and the moon is a
scalpel and the sun is a burning sword that
scorches my eyes with its brilliant glow. There is a
cauldron of witches' brew beneath us and Wheeling drops me, letting me fall toward that seething,
stinking muck, and then swoops to grab me by
the neck again.*

*"I do not have to live in a dark hole now. I fly
through the rose window and reach the sky when
I hear the stories that happen in the room below
where the candles burn and the lilies bloom and
the light shines on me from the bits of colored
glass."*

*I struggle free as Wheeling flies on, over the moun-
tains, into the dark, boiling clouds that blacken
the horizon. I plunge out of his grip through bright
air to the snow-crowned, jagged peak and I find
my feet under me at last, still my wobbling knees,
and stand on top of the mountain as I watch
Wheeling fly, carrying his tongs, his black cape, his
silver pen, his terrible memories, into the bil-
lowing black clouds, disappearing.*

44

"Catherine, Catherine, can you hear me?" I looked up into Julia's face from where I lay on the ground. I nodded slowly as the words of Malinda's song kept going around in my head—"*You're* SHAME-LESS *baby, a face without a heart. Shameless ... shameless ...*"

"Are you all right, Ms. Saint?" Jethro ran a cool hand over my forehead, looking into my eyes. "Jesus, Mary, and Joseph!" he said, as close as I ever heard Jethro get to swearing.

"What happened?" I asked. I moved my legs and my right arm, and then my left and yelped with pain. It was my wrist, and it hurt. I couldn't tell it if was broken.

"You took a hell of a fall, Ms. Saint," Jethro said. "You're lucky to be alive." Jethro's voice was comforting, soothing.

Julia's face was there next to Jethro's. "Don't talk too much, Catherine," she said, "let's see if anything is broken." Her voice, like Jethro's, was a balm.

"I'm all right, Jethro." Looking up at the hanging bar, the platform from which I had fallen, I felt lucky. I could see the crowd around me now, the technical people, Z-Train with his dreadlocks, Malinda with her wide blue eyes, Reed with his virile beauty, Sahid looking like a young Omar Sharif without the mustache, all of them in their stage outfits, their makeup beginning to run, hovering above my body as I lay on the ground, all of them looking down at me with concerned faces.

I tried a smile, rolled over a bit, and felt some glass under my left hip. Reed and Sahid leaned down and began to brush away the glass from around me.

"You'll be fine," Reed said soothingly, and Denzel nodded his head. He had no idea if I would be fine or not, and neither did I.

"Just try to breathe deeply," Stan said, helping me get to my feet, picking up the strewn film canisters and light meters and the big soft shoulder bag that had fallen open, its contents scattered under me.

To my horror I saw my camera beside Sahid's foot. I reached out for it, and Sahid picked it up and showed it to me. "Damn, that lens is broken," I said.

"But are *you* all right?" Sahid had laid his guitar down beside me. He put the camera down and knelt, gently rubbing my legs.

"I don't know." I felt stunned rather than in pain. My wrist throbbed.

"Is your head okay?" Julia put her arm around my shoulder, rubbing the back of my neck.

"I think it's fine, I just feel a bit dizzy."

Really I felt scared to death, shaken up. I must be in mild shock, I thought. The sounds of the crowd were like water washing over me, the threats, the frightening events of the last few days. I remembered with gratitude that Renaldo was awake, out of danger.

"How did I fall?" I asked, looking up, trying to pull myself together and take stock of myself. I was still looking at the rigging when Hank, the stage manager, arrived at my side.

"It wasn't the platform rigging, Catherine," he said,

absolving himself of any responsibility for my fall. He sounded rather relieved.

I didn't believe him. I looked up to where my former perch was waving in the breeze. I could see that the metal bar supporting the secondary platform had been kicked or shoved off center; the metal support was now bending down like a willow tree to the ground. No wonder I had fallen.

"Those things are tough," Hank said, "but then if somebody wanted to pull them out from under you, I guess there would be nothing to stop them. Maybe it was one of the groupies. Thank God your camera bag broke your fall." He put the wrecked camera back in the bag. "I hope there's not going to be any more trouble," he said. I was sure he was thinking of crowds going wild at concerts, fans being trampled. It was impossible to say who among the crowd might have caused my fall.

The Newborns were milling around me, making consoling sounds, as I dusted off my pants and gathered things together. I was basically all right. Reed, Julia, Z-Train, and Sahid still stood around me with their roadies and a handful of groupies.

"I could look at that arm, we have a remedy," Sahid said in a soft voice. He was still in his makeup, ghoulishly adorable. Stan shook his head and helped me up.

"The first aid room is down the hall," Stan said. "Let's go."

I felt hurt and angry and confused as I tried to steady my hands, but they still shook and I held on to Julia as she put an arm around me. Stan's gold chain swung out from his open shirt as he helped me to my feet. I was wobbly and weak as we made our way to the room with the red cross above the door. Inside, a tall woman in a crisp white uniform was wrapping bandages.

She smiled at me, taking in the situation. She took my wrist in her hands and prodded it gently.

"I don't think it's broken. It's probably a bad sprain or a green stem fracture—where the bone bends but doesn't break," she said, looking into my eyes after prodding my wrist, elbow, arm, and shoulder. She wrapped an athletic support bandage around my wrist and handed me an envelope of codeine tablets and a paper cup of water. "I'm not supposed to give you these without a prescription, but here—they're double strength. Take two, and then if it continues hurting, take one more. That's the limit till you see somebody."

I gulped down two pills and told myself I would take as many as I needed to dull the pain. I thanked her. Feeling afraid, I was unsteady on my legs and feared I might be in shock. "Do you have a blanket?" I asked. "I feel cold."

She wrapped me in a soft blue wool blanket and my body began to warm up as Jethro and Stan walked me to the door.

Stan had his arm around my waist. "My lead singer missing in action and my friend an endangered species," he said, trying to smile, but looking uncomfortable.

I was shivering. I wanted a cigarette. I knew there were none in my purse and decided then and there that whoever had done this was not going to have the satisfaction of either seeing me dead or seeing me smoke.

Instead, I put another codeine pill in my mouth. I was safe. Pills were not a problem. Pain was, and the wrist hurt like hell. It was going to take a huge dose of painkiller to get me through this night. In some corner of my mind a suspicion of the truth glimmered.

"I'll bring your car around to the stage door, Catherine." Stan put out his hand for the car keys. "I'll drive it back into the city. I think you should go home with Max and the Newborns in the limousine. You'll be more comfortable."

"We'll have some champagne, we'll see to it that you feel no pain," Z-Train said. I hoped he was right.

The Newborns had taken off their makeup.

Z-Train's face seemed to float in the air. "I'm ready to feel no pain, Z-Train," I confessed. I realized I was a bit stoned. I smiled at him. The codeine was beginning to work.

"I'm staying with Ms. Saint," Jethro said.

"Will there be room?" Julia said, looking nervously at Reed. "The limo will take ten." We counted nine, including the driver. "We can all make it," Reed said. I was shaky on my feet, and Jethro took one arm, Stan took the other, and we made our way toward the stage entrance, picking up my equipment on the way.

"We'll sing to you on the way to the city," Malinda said. "My father is a monster not to be here with you!" Malinda's golden mass of curls brushed my face as she kissed my cheek.

Could it have been Edward who pushed me? Crazy thought. By now I didn't feel much. All my fears—the threats on my life, the attack on Renaldo, the infuriating fact that Edward had cheated on me and lied to me, and now, that somebody had caused me to fall from a platform and nearly break my neck—all of these were being soothed by the painkiller. Too bad I couldn't take these all the time.

Jethro helped me into the limo and then settled himself in front with the driver. Z-Train and Malinda put me between them on the back seat, Sahid by the window. Julia and Reed sat together facing backwards on the wraparound seat. There was still room in the limousine for a couple of swimming pools. Doors slammed, there was a scramble of vehicles, and the police escort of the Newborns led the way out of the parking lot toward Route 9, sirens screaming, red lights flashing. There was a loud pop in the car and I jumped, thinking a gun had gone off.

My fears broke through the codeine, and a feeling of terror filled my heart. I was about to fall again, I thought, and started forward in my seat.

"Champagne," Z-Train said, putting his arms around me, "that's all it is, Catherine. Don't be frightened." He poured champagne into a plastic cup and a slight mist rose from the bubbles as he steadied the glass. I felt a momentary nervousness about drinking on top of the codeine, but then thought, what the hell? The limousine swayed around a curve and hit the highway at sixty miles an hour. "I want you to drink this down."

Z-Train held the half-full glass out. I accepted the bubbling liquid as my heartbeat slowed down from a gallop. I drained the champagne, holding it out to be refilled. I was terribly thirsty and felt the bubbles hit the codeine. The high I was feeling was beginning to be euphoric.

"I want you to think positively, Catherine. Here's to love and friendship," Malinda said. I lifted my glass again and drank the sparkling champagne.

Malinda began to sing "Bright Morning Star." Sahid and Z-Train joined her, the champagne flowed, the codeine took the pain away, and my fears bundled themselves into a smaller group in the corner of my mind—waiting, hiding. My mind was liking the feeling of being more high than scared, more drunk than sober.

The music poured out in harmony, Sahid, Reed, Malinda, Z-Train, and Julia harmonizing on the old hymn.

Sahid's beautiful long hand found its way along my legs and up my side, touching me, soothing me, turning me on.

In the front seat the backs of Jethro's and Max's heads settled into a blur as the car rolled up the asphalt on the way into the city and the headlights of cars on the highway outside the smoked glass window blurred into a soft glow. I was softly glowing too, and I thought I felt Z-Train's hand running up and down my arm and along the side of my chest. I didn't move, didn't fight it. Edward's face, Renaldo's face, Wheeling's face, and the face of the crowd as I tumbled off the scaffolding all mixed in with a feeling of pure pleasure as a hand touched my body.

"Are you asleep?" Z-Train whispered to my ear.

"Almost," I whispered.

Z-Train's hands massaged my elbows, my neck, my face, my arms. My eyes began to droop as I felt the waves of physical pleasure from the gentle hands. Z-Train moved his fingers over my wrist and down my body as he rubbed the back of my neck and ran his fingers through my hair. I didn't know if I was dreaming . . . for a moment, Zardos's face hovered in my imagination and I felt the image of white wings against isinglass, torn between flying and staying, the unicorn hovered near the smoked window of the limousine . . .

Z-Train and Sahid fondled my neck, my ears, my shoulders . . . I was dreaming now . . . Sahid was touching my naked breasts and I didn't, couldn't protest; he then moved his fingers down my body and I floated with the music of his deep, sweet voice humming softly in my ears.

I knew I must be dreaming, my superego on hold for once.

My hands found Sahid's young body and returned his touch, his body feeling warm and full and my lips pressed against his neck and lips as I returned the caresses that moved over me. Sahid's hard body was next to me and the sweet smell of Z-Train's skin made me swoon. . . .

The Newborns' tender hands on my body floated me to a shuddering completion, a wave of pleasure over my whole being, my pain gone, hard reality gone, problems gone. I slipped into an exotic slumber.

45

O<small>N OUR TRIPS TO</small> W<small>YOMING,</small> <small>EACH SUMMER FOR THREE</small>
weeks, every other day, my mother took singing les-
sons at the Rolling Ridge Music School in Jackson
Hole, with Mr. Christian. She had been studying for
twenty years. Besides my father and her love for him,
those lessons were the high point of her life.

Rolling Ridge Music School was on the road between Jackson Hole and Moose, near the border of
the Grand Teton campground. Every other day my
mother would load me and Ben into the Packard and
head down the road.

"Now, you children amuse yourselves," she'd say.
"Read some magazines or go for a walk. I'll see you
when my lesson is finished."

The music school's lodge had big rocks for walls
and a floor made of logs stuck together in the end-up
way, what they call a "puncheon" floor. There was
also a fireplace so big my father could stand up in it,
and massive beams ran across the ceiling to support
the second story.

Students of all ages, carrying cellos and clarinets
and music stands, roamed in and out of the big main

lodge. Bengie and I kept to ourselves, watching the passing musicians, until Mother came out from her lesson, beaming and holding Mr. Christian by the hand.

"Here, children, say hello to Mr. Christian. You're glad to see him again, aren't you?" Mr. Christian was about fifty and extremely fat. He wore colorful, bright shirts with parrots and palm trees on them. His smile became larger and I grew taller as his body became bigger.

Once or twice during each vacation in Wyoming I was allowed to come to one of my mother's lessons with Mr. Christian. I watched my mother's face while he told her to sing this phrase or that one.

"Your mother is singing very well this year," he would say to me, and then turn back to my mother.

"You must make a clear sound, *ah,* when you sing that word," and he would demonstrate: *"O Danny Boy, the pipes, the pipes are calling."* You see, the *ah* must have no noise, and no consonant stopping the sound."

My mother sang a phrase again, and Mr. Christian listened totally, his face immersed in the sound of her voice. He took off his reading glasses, round glass orbs with silver frames, and wiped his eyes, as though he had been crying. He listened to the singing once more, put the thick glasses on again, and looked at my mother over the top of the silver rims.

"That is better, Mrs. Saint," he said, "but you stop the phrase there. It should flow completely." Mr. Christian demonstrated a note, his creaky voice lifted by the loveliness of the phrase.

"Lo, how a rose ere blooming," he sang. "It must be transparent, can you hear that? It must make the listener understand, even if he might be standing in the next room. The clarity must be that great." He looked across the piano lid to where my mother stood.

Again, Mother would sing, *"Lo, how a rose ere blooming."*

"Good. Now sing the entire phrase." She began, and Mr. Christian stopped her, raising a large hand, his nails clipped close to the pads of his fingers, the moons of the nails white and even along the pink surface.

"Singing is like speaking," Mr. Christian said. "You must be able to hear the phrase, the whole idea in the line, not just the word." He laughed. "Who would want to hear just *'Lo,'* just that word, or just any of the other words by themselves?" Then he and my mother laughed, as though they had come upon a private, erotic joke. They laughed together sensually, the way I imagined lovers would laugh at some small incident that made them happy.

"Mrs. Saint, you will make the meaning of the song completely understandable," he said, "even to someone who doesn't know the language, because it will be so clear, do you see? So that even if a person were standing in the next room, he would understand the meaning, because he would understand the phrasing, yes?"

It was as though he were speaking of the curve of her neck or the light in her hair, and they would smile at one another.

I think every idea I have about music came from being an eavesdropper on my mother's musical fantasy life with Mr. Christian. She leaned on his words and his voice as she would on the arm of a lover.

At the end of our stay, my father, Ben, and I went to a concert at Rolling Ridge. We sat on folding chairs under the aspens in the sunny courtyard behind the school and listened to all the students do their solos. Mother sang two numbers she had been working on with Mr. Christian. The Schubert songs were my favorites, for they were sweet and dramatic. My mother always translated the German for Ben and me beforehand, so we knew the stories. My very favorite was the one about the child who is carried on his father's horse as they ride at night, and the child is dead and the father doesn't know it.

When the concert was over, my father took us by the hands and led us up to where Mother talked with her head close to Mr. Christian's head. "Mother, I think you sang better this year than any other year," he said, shaking Mr. Christian's hand, and told him how much he had done for Elizabeth. I saw my father hesitate before speaking, trying not to get in the way. "Why, you wouldn't believe how much Mother looks forward to these lessons every year," he finally said. "It's a wonder I ever get her back to the ranch at all." His face had the look of a man who knows it's best to be positive and peaceful and count his blessings. Whatever Mr. Christian and Mother did together in August was a mystery and was best left so.

Even before our mountain retreat had come to an end, I could sense my father's impatience in the pines and clear air. He was waiting for the singing lessons to be over, for the vacation to be over, for August to be over, so that he could leave the green, holy Rocky Mountains and get back to the dry, parched Kansas ranch, where his Angus and his quarter horses waited.

I often wondered, in all those years, whether my mother ever made love with Mr. Christian. I doubted it. But she sang for him, oh, she sang for him every year in the summer.

46

I dream of the Snake River, and a snake, and biology class. I am ten or so, me with a boa constric-
tor on my shoulders. I have seen a snake as a pet—
tame, as much as any wild thing in captivity can
be tame. I am not repulsed by him as the other children are. He is strong and beautiful and powerful
and has clean, smooth, black and silver scales like
mica; they are cool and perfectly in order, and on
my shoulders he waits, watching with me.

I see the shock on the faces of the other children,
their surprise at my courage. But it is not courage,
here in the biology class in the big sunlight-filled
schoolroom in Moline, where plain ranch children
with blond hair look at this snake with distaste. I
accept the snake, and he and I form a bond.

The snake in mythology, in green tall weeds, in
the primordial ooze, from the darkness and moisture of the secret caves, lives and coils and waits for
the warmth, moving out of the garden, moving
from the apple into the flesh, that writhing creature
fathoming the deepest, darkest, most secret parts
of our dreams.

And there is a green snake on the water in the
clear hot springs near our ranch, skimming
through the steam on top of the water around my

naked body. He rises up from the surface of silver with his bright green head, with his clever, piercing eyes, looking at me as he slips through the water and up into the silver-covered grasses, as he slinks away into the green tall grasses by the mountain.

The snake knows me, recognizes me. He takes me to the apple, pointing out its color, a radiant red; he eats of the meat; the juice runs down his cheeks and we smile at each other at the sweetness. I see the snake like a slice of the darkest moonless night, the glint of steel on his belly reflected by the sharp edge of his scales.

I think I can feel the scales pulse against me, agitating and forcing me open to my own power; I am fevered, aroused. A great surge is forcing and plucking and biting and wriggling and growing, becoming bigger as my center is filled with a smoky sensual pleasure, and my own inner power, the hard, strong beauty of my history, is made clear. The smooth lines of the snake, as though he is drawing a lesson, unencumbered, caressing, moving into the very depths of me and finding his way deep into my center. Power—centered, raw, ripe, rich, my own.

The power I have not yet claimed. The snake is a teacher, shedding his own skin and flowering into a tree, blossoming on the vines like red, ripe, sweet, succulent fruit. I reach for it. I know it is my tree, my snake, my dream, my power.

47

"Hi," said Zardos's familiar voice over the phone. "I heard you had some trouble last night."

"Yes," I said, picking up an empty Pall Mall package from the bedside table. It was near dawn. I was in my own bed in the pale gray light that filtered onto the walls, their cream color glowing in the dawn. The glimmer of truth I had seen the night before had slipped away with the champagne. I knew I *knew* something . . . but I couldn't remember what. I thought of the exotic, dreamy trip home the night before—the silky feel of Sahid's hands on my body, the moisture of Z-Train's full, sensual lips in my ear, on my cheeks, on my own lips—so much like a dream, yet so vivid. "Somebody pushed me off a scaffolding."

"Jethro told me everything, Catherine," Zardos said. "Are you all right?"

"I think so," I said, making a circle with my wrist. It throbbed painfully. "I'll live," I said, knowing somebody out there wanted me dead. "It could have been worse." Jethro had stayed with me, standing guard in the living room all night. "I'm so glad Renaldo is awake."

"Yes," Zardos said. "I called his parents to let them know. They were so relieved. Now that he's out of the woods, I hope I can get a break on this thing,"

259

Zardos said. The codeine had worn off and I was feeling a bit hung over. I toyed with the cellophane and paper cigarette wrapper, and then crushed it in my good hand. "I would guess whoever pushed you last night is probably the same person who tried to kill Renaldo. Jethro and the State Police started interviewing people, asking questions. It was a pretty wild scene."

I murmured assent. Outside my windows I could hear the purple finches singing in the trees in Central Park. I sat up in bed, disturbing Blue. The Himalayan gave an insulted meow and leapt from his place among the lace pillows onto the floor, padding away like a jilted lover.

"I shouldn't have let you go to the Meadowlands," Zardos said. "But I'm beginning to learn it is not a good idea to tell you what to do. Or what not to do. See anyone suspicious?"

"An old pal of Hank Cramer, one of the production guys, was hanging around last night," I said slowly. "A guy named Bob Benhurst. You know him?"

"Benhurst is a friend of yours?" Zardos asked.

I said the mob lawyer was no friend.

Zardos paused, and then said, "I'd like you to come to the hospital with me this morning." He said Dr. March wanted him to question Renaldo after doctor's rounds at ten, and asked me to bring whatever pictures I had of my friends. He said he had received the message about Bella, and that he had interviewed Edward's business partners. They had told him that Bella's job was on the line because they suspected she was doing some extremely creative bookkeeping.

I took a deep breath and told Zardos that, according to Bella, Edward was having an affair with someone else. "I thought you should know that," I said, reluctantly. "You wanted to know if any of my friends' habits had changed recently."

Zardos's voice was sympathetic. "I'm sorry. This is all you need . . . I'm also interviewing Edward today. I want to check out his alibi."

"You don't really think he had anything to do with this, do you?" I said, upset. "I hope not."

"I have to interview everybody, Catherine," Zardos said. "Somebody is trying to kill you. I'll bring Benhurst in this afternoon; I'll find out why he was there last night." He paused. "Would Benhurst have any reason to hurt you?"

I had put the thought of a cigarette out of my mind since the package was empty. I chewed my lip instead, trying to think. I said no, I didn't know Benhurst except by sight and reputation.

Zardos went on. "I saw Wheeling late yesterday, by the way," he said. "He seems to think you ruined his business."

"Do you mean he's still *in* business?" I asked sarcastically, wondering if I were the only patient Wheeling raped.

"He has an alibi for the night Renaldo was attacked," Zardos told me. "He says he was with patients. He also says he knows Ellen Carney."

"That's strange. Ellen didn't tell me she knew Wheeling," I said.

"Right. Catherine, I'm trying to get at a motive here. Other than revenge, which I don't think makes any sense." Zardos paused, then went on. "I'm getting a warrant to search Ellen's office. Was she at the concert last night?"

"I didn't see her."

Zardos said he was going to talk to Bella and see Wheeling again.

"I know you must hate Wheeling after what happened," he said, sounding sympathetic.

"I don't hate him anymore. I got my money, he got his reputation. It was an even trade."

Zardos made a noise in his throat. "People often throw money at a problem but the wound is still there. Is that true with you?"

How does he know to ask this? I said to myself, petting the cat, who had jumped back onto the bed. I ran my fingers through Blue's silky fur.

"What do men know about wounds?" I asked, thinking of Edward, keeping my voice light.

"Some of us know a lot more than most women give us credit for, Catherine," he said.

"Well," I said to Zardos, "you are an unusual man."

"I'm not so unusual," he said lightly.

I could almost see his face, and then his voice turned serious once more. Blue made a friendly, humming noise. I asked Zardos if he had heard anything about Fred. I knew Max had asked Zardos to look for Fred.

"Not a thing," the detective said. "We're combing the city."

I hoped Fred was still alive. Poor Fred, I thought, and sat on the edge of the bed, cradling the telephone receiver with my shoulder.

Blue purred loudly, as though to console me.

"What's that noise?" Zardos asked.

"It's the cat. I think he hears your voice. You're apparently in good with him."

"I like Blue. I think we are bonding," Zardos said and laughed softly. It was a sexy laugh. "Bye, Catherine, see you at the hospital."

I put the receiver softly back on the telephone and headed to the kitchen for coffee. And wondered if Edward and I would ever see each other again, if we would ever sleep together again.

Somehow, in spite of everything, I felt a glimmer of hope. Renaldo was all right.

And Zardos made me feel hopeful.

*   *   *

Jethro was in the living room, reading the paper. I nodded to him on the way into the kitchen, where I cracked ice for a cold pack, smoothing it across the surface of a tea towel and wrapping it around my wrist. In one hand I held a mug of wonderful-smelling coffee, in the other a bagel on a flowered plate.

Thus pleasantly encumbered, I made my way into the office, where my desk was piled with work. The phone rang and I put on the speaker button. Shultz's voice boomed into the room.

"It's Stan." His voice was agitated. "How's the wrist?"

"It's much better," I said.

Stan asked me quickly if I had talked to Renaldo yet and I told him I was going to see him at the hospital later that morning. Stan was glad Renaldo was awake. He also asked if I was going to the AIDS research benefit at Sacred Heart that night. I said I doubted that Zardos would want me to go, especially after last night.

"In case you change your mind," he said, "it's Eighty Riverside Drive, at six. Kisses, darling," and he clicked off the phone.

I had an hour before I was to meet Zardos and realized I had to get to the bank to get cash and find out what Renaldo meant in his note about a problem.

At eight-thirty Jethro and I headed out for the bank, which was just three blocks from my door. An automated cash window was tucked under a shining arcade of polished marble, protected from the weather and the wandering homeless of Seventy-second Street by a sheet of glass a story high and a quarter of a block long.

"Please, miss, I gotta get some food," said a tattered-looking man outside the main door of the bank. "I promise I ain't using this money for any drugs.

Please." The man's shopping cart was stuffed with bottles and cans in plastic bags; his head was covered in a stocking cap. He wore a huge tartan plaid wool coat two sizes too big. He extended an empty paper cup.

My heart turned inside out, the knot of helplessness winding tight. This homeless man, probably mentally ill, dressed in rags, eating from garbage cans and what he could scoff off passersby, lean and haggard, was flimsily anchored outside the majestic wealth of the Chase Manhattan Bank. I scrambled in my bag and fished out a twenty-dollar bill.

"No drugs, hear?" I said, feeling guilty. I either gave nothing, gave a lot, said nothing, or said too much to these people whose lives were a shock and a reason for shame even for the most hardened New Yorker. Me.

"God bless you, miss!" The man looked astonished.

"God bless you," I said.

What else could God do but bless?

Inside the bank Jethro lingered by the window as I found my way to my personal banker's desk. We shook hands and he began talking immediately.

"About your accounts," Mr. Groden said. Usually crisp and detached, the banker seemed agitated today.

My mind still on the homeless man, I asked if I could cash a check, then fumbled in my purse for the checkbook, the pen. "My assistant told me there was some problem with an account," I said.

"There might be." Mr. Groden was dressed in a herringbone suit, a gray handkerchief in the pocket. "Your assistant—Mr. Pierce, is that his name?"

I nodded, starting to get worried.

"Some rather large withdrawals have been made from your main account in the past two weeks," the banker said. "I wanted to talk with you about them, but I couldn't reach you."

He had in fact called—twice—but I'd been so distracted with everything that was going on that I had only talked with his secretary to set up this appointment when I called him back.

"How large?" I said. "I don't remember making any large withdrawals."

The banker pulled the readouts from a folder on his desk. "The balance last week was just over five million dollars. Then there were these withdrawals: two hundred thousand, then another two hundred, then three hundred thousand, then two, till the day before yesterday, when there was another transfer of six hundred thousand. For a total of a million, five hundred thousand dollars." He looked up and said, "I assume this is all in order."

I was stunned. I sat down hard on the chair across from Mr. Groden. I had taken more codeine to ward off the pain, but the throbbing began again.

"Are you buying a house?" the banker added, looking up at me quizzically.

I shook my head. "Only Edward Valarian and his associate, Bella Windsor, have the ability to withdraw money for investments," I said, in shock. "And of course, me."

"The withdrawal slips bear your signature," the banker said in a careful tone. He pointed to a name at the bottom of the slips of paper, the same name repeated five times.

Indeed, I saw Mr. Groden was right. But when I looked more closely, I could see it wasn't my signature.

My name had been expertly forged.

I felt helpless, furious. Somebody had tried to kill me and my assistant, and now somebody had taken a great deal of my money. Blood and money, I thought. That sums it up. Whoever had tried to kill Renaldo had probably done so to prevent him from finding out what was going on at the bank. Who had forged my name?

Jethro had been hovering near me, watching my exchange with Groden, and now, seeing the concern on my face, he came to the desk to find out what was going on. I explained the situation to him.

My heart plunged. I tried to think what to do, then recovered my composure and continued the discussion calmly.

Jethro suggested I have the bank remove Edward and Bella as signers from my accounts, and invalidate any more withdrawal orders. The withdrawals had been made via telephone and confirmed with memos on my letterhead with the phony signatures. I asked Mr. Groden to freeze the account until further notice, and Jethro picked up the telephone on the banker's desk and tried Zardos's numbers but couldn't reach him.

Then Jethro called the precinct and talked to someone who handled forgery who asked if I would press charges. I said I would and I logged my name one more time that week into the files at the Twentieth Precinct, feeling like a regular.

The officer told Jethro he would get started right away on the problem. Trying to be helpful, he said to me that forgery is a felony.

Great, I thought.

I took the phone from Jethro, called Edward's number, got the voicemail and left him a message to call me. I did the same on Bella's voicemail.

Bella knew that Edward was having an affair. Maybe she knew who was forging my signature at the bank. Could it be Bella? I wondered. I had tried to keep the anger and fear out of my voice when I left the messages.

I cashed a check out of my business account. The

bank initialed and stamped the check I had written and put a thousand dollars in my hand, counting it in fifties, twenties, and tens. As I left, I told Mr. Groden we would speak again by the end of the day.

As Jethro and I made our way back to the car I glared at the marble and shining brass, the glass and the healthy, moist-looking plants.

The homeless man still stood in front of the plate-glass window, his paper cup outstretched in his hand, his shopping cart loaded with his treasures, collectibles from the street. He leaned over and opened the car door for me. I thanked him; he smiled a benign smile and waved his gloved hand. He gave me a smile worth a million, a dazzled, amazed smile, and turned to go somewhere.

Where could he be going? I thought. His look, as he turned, seemed to say that he would help me if he could.

48

*A dream from the night before rushes through my
head. I find myself tied to the posts of an antique,
elegant four-poster bed, lying on my back, naked.
My wrists and ankles are strapped tight to the
posts at the ornate carved head and foot of the bed.
Over me, like a white banner, is a velvet canopy,
and white velvet drapes fall in soft folds at the sides
of the bed, obscuring the room to my right and
left. Under my naked body are white silk sheets. My
legs are spread, my breasts bare, my hair falling
in curls around my face. The room is semi-dark as
I awake and immediately I begin to struggle,
fighting to free myself, and then I lie back and
breathe, trying to feel the silence of the room, trying to understand where I am. Beyond the foot of
the bed a fire burns in a marble fireplace, the
flames pricking patterns on the ceiling, the walls,
throughout the darkened room, so that I see at
last, floating into my view, the figure of a man at the
end of the bed, his legs parted, his back to the fireplace,
his face to me.*

*I see he is naked too, his flesh shining. Around
his figure dance the flamelike shadows; they lick
the darkened ceiling and the walls, throwing enough*

light to tell me that the man is tall and lean, and revealing the whip he holds in his hand.

I cannot see his face clearly, but the firelight on his cheeks shows them wet with perspiration. I struggle against the posts and begin to cry out again as the figure moves toward me, cracking the whip over my figure on the bed, sounding a terrible noise. The whip makes contact with my flesh, scoring my legs, then my arms; searing pain makes me call out as the man drops the whip and kneels over my body, caressing my breasts with his fingers, running both hands between my stinging legs, putting his fingers in me, the tingling of his touch arousing me in spite of my pain.

Then he runs his tongue from the nipples of my breasts to my neck, licking my throat where the whip caught me and cut the flesh, and then my chin, my lips. He pulls away and once more whips my skin, but gently this time, touching my stomach, my thighs, with the leather strip, as I writhe and moan and try to pull away to the other side of the bed, but softly he touches me and then hurls the whip across the room into the marble fireplace, feeling his way, sliding himself into my body. I strain against the bedposts even as I feel the pulse of the man's lips against my cheeks, his naked legs mounting my thighs, his body moving into mine, the stinging marks from the whip throbbing under his caress, his lips soothing the places he wounded, the places he hurt.

I awake in a frenzy of sexual desire—and fear for my life.

49

Back at my apartment I was in a daze. I still had an hour before I was due at Martindale Hospital. While Jethro waited for me, I tried Zardos again, and when I couldn't reach him, I took another codeine pill, swallowing it down with cold coffee.

Work, I thought. In all situations, work calmed me. There was the Cher series for *Mirabella,* and I still had a lot to do on the article on Julia's opening. I listened to the tapes of the interviews from Julia's opening at the Siren, transcribing them on the computer, trying to concentrate but failing.

I was just as agitated as before, and my wrist began throbbing again. Nothing was helping my frustration, my feeling of invasion. I couldn't concentrate.

I donned the heavy plastic apron I wore to keep the chemicals off my skin, thinking I might as well work in the darkroom. That usually took my mind off everything else that was going on. First I developed the negatives from the shoot at the Meadowlands. Grateful the film had survived my fall, I decided to make some prints and enlargements.

I wrapped a scarf around my head and got to work. Think about anything else, I said to myself, don't think about elephants. I repeated the phrase as though it were a mantra.

My first photography instructor at the New School had stressed being organized. I could trash a hotel room in a matter of minutes but my darkroom was always pristine. Everything was in order, ready to go, to print my black and white film. I sent color film out—it was too difficult a process to manage by myself—but I loved the control I got making my own black and white pictures.

A pungent, forever new smell infused the room from the chemicals I used in the development process as I immersed the prints in the bath. My eyes and hands moved in the dark, checking, tapping, tallying up the right time to the second.

Printing always soothed my nerves. I was tranquil; it was only the twinge in my stomach that told me something was wrong.

At first I couldn't be sure; they were almost too far off. But in the distance of a number of photographs, I saw two faces that looked rather familiar. I cropped in close, bringing the images closer, bigger. They dissolved into fragments, floating in a sea of dots, refusing to take shape.

Then, hazy and faint, but unmistakable among the wild hair, outrageous outfits, and kids with dreadlocks and rock-and-roll costumes, I could see the faces clearly.

In the crowd at the Meadowlands, slightly out of focus but emerging from behind the rock-and-roll groupies, were the faces of Ellen Carney and Dr. Ernest Wheeling.

50

I dream of an old man in a purple raincoat who comes to my door.

"Remember that time by the river, when you and Ben went on the camping trip?" he asks. I remember the cowboys, rednecks, rough types, wranglers, who saddled the horses and cooked the meals and went ahead to cut through a trail. They had too much to drink at the campfire after dinner and sneaked up to my sleeping bag and cut off a hunk of hair while I slept. I awoke swearing, screaming, for Ben, who beat the pants off the two of them and sent them packing in the middle of the night.

"I have a message for the wranglers," he says. His coat becomes transparent and the rain on the windows turns to tears that fall on my cheeks. He hands me a letter, but it is not from the wranglers, it is from my mother, and I read it as I ride in a helicopter over the mountains of sand where my ancestors are buried.

"My dear," she says, "your father will never forgive you." My cousin Marty, his hair wild, rides on top of the hood of a pickup truck with a guitar across his hips, his legs and arms thin. Suddenly my father and my mother's singing teacher, Mr. Christian, are in the dream. Buster has Christian

by the throat and is banging his head, over and over, against the side of the truck. My mother is singing a song about a dead child while I scream at my father, "Stop it, stop, Daddy, you're killing him, you're killing him, don't kill him, Daddy!"

"I will never forgive you, never forgive you, never forgive you," Mr. Christian sings like Bruce Springsteen. Dancers come out of the tumbleweed and the sandhills to cavort behind him in the road, doing an intricate step as in a music video, their arms and legs flying, their heads bobbing to the music, shadow dancing with the tumbleweed; the dancers are wearing nothing but tiny black strips of leather across their bare shoulders, breasts, thighs, buttocks.

I am crying and calling to my mother as the pickup speeds across the desert, leaving a trail of dust. The pickup with my cousin Marty and Ben on the hood disappears, the dancers become smaller and smaller. The old man walks toward me again, waving a letter in his hands, struggling, limping, trying to catch me. I turn, running for all I am worth, but I am drunk and stumble at the side of the road, weeping.

51

I blew up a pair of the fuzzy but unmistakable pictures of Dr. Wheeling and Ellen and put them in a manila envelope. I knew Zardos would want to see them. The man who had raped me and my lawyer's wife. Extraordinary.

Before I could leave for the hospital the phone rang.

"It's Bella, Catherine," the voice said. For a moment I was still so puzzled by the pictures of Ellen and Ernest Wheeling that I had forgotten the bank, and now I remembered and felt angry, hardly knowing what to ask her about first—the money, Wheeling, or Edward.

"Bella, you left so quickly yesterday," I said. "You were going to tell me who Edward is seeing." I clutched a paperclip in the palm of my hand like a worry bead.

Bella hesitated for a moment, and then she said, "I think it might be your friend Julia."

The point of the clip cut into my skin, making me wince. I stared at the big print of the nude portrait of Julia I had hung on the wall—her voluptuous body, fine skin, short dark hair, pouting lips, and beautiful breasts. I tried to imagine Edward running his fingers through that hair, running his hands over that body. Try as I may, I couldn't imagine Julia's body in the arms of my former lover. Julia, I was sure, wouldn't have time for Edward when she was having a mad, passionate affair with a twenty-two-year-old. I asked Bella if she had actually seen Julia with Edward and she said she hadn't.

"Well, I guess I'm not so sure," she said, backing down.

"Bella," I said. "The police are going to want to talk to you."

"The police?" Bella sounded suddenly nervous, a bit shaky. I thought again about her little silver pillbox.

"Somebody's been forging my signature at the bank, making withdrawals in my name."

"But," Bella said, sounding truly upset, "I just make the transfers Edward gives me!" She said she couldn't imagine how it had happened, but that she would call me if she thought of anything. I repeated that the police would be calling.

"Bella, there's something else," I said, keeping my voice calm, steeling myself. "Do you know Ernest Wheeling?"

"Of course," she replied, laughing nervously. "He's my therapist." I took a breath while Bella continued. "He's got me on the right medication now, and I'm feeling great." She sounded nervous as a cat.

I got off the phone quickly, shaken up. I knew Zardos would want to question Bella about the mysterious withdrawals from my account, and while he was at it, explore this link to Wheeling. My former shrink and my financial advisor were much too close for comfort.

I realized with a sickening clarity that Bella was throwing sand in my face about Julia to put me off the questions about the bank. I put my coat on and left for the hospital to meet Zardos.

*   *   *

A snowstorm seemed to be hovering behind dark clouds in the city. Intermittent shafts of sunlight scurried along the streets and climbed the sides of the buildings on Park Avenue as Jethro pulled the car up in front of the hospital. Zardos met us in the flickering sunlight. He was dressed in blue trousers, a white crisp shirt, a green tie with tiny blue flowers, and a blue blazer.

When I saw Zardos this time, something in my heart jumped like a thoroughbred at the starting gate at the Kentucky Derby, and for a moment I forgot every problem I had. Suddenly this man looked wonderful. The color rushed to my face as I tried to concentrate.

I scrambled out of the car as he held the door. Zardos's handsome face rendered me shy, reluctant to take the hand he offered.

"You look pale, Catherine," he said, taking my good hand. "Is the wrist all right?"

"Yes," I said, forcing myself to think of Zardos as just another detective and failing, wiggling my wrist in the elastic bandage to assure him I was out of danger. "But a lot has been going on. I tried to call." I told him about the forgeries at the bank.

Zardos nodded. "Jethro filled me in. We're trying to trace the handwriting, using the samples you gave me. I'm looking for a match in the computers, someone with a sheet, but I assume the forgery was done by someone you know."

"And look at these," I said, keeping my voice steady as I handed Zardos the pair of black-and-white prints. I kept a proper distance from his shoulder, conscious of his body, his salty, fresh scent. People fall in love from scent, I remembered hearing somewhere. His was like sage, like fresh rainwater, familiar as my own skin.

"The faces are pretty clear, in spite of the distance," Zardos said. "I was able to get a warrant today to search Ellen's office, so I'm not surprised to see these. There are canceled checks and entries in Ellen's date-book with Wheeling's name on them. Ellen is a patient of Dr. Wheeling's."

I let out a breath.

"I didn't know you even suspected Ellen," I said.

Zardos leaned back against the side of the hospital wall, looking at me with his beautiful blue-black eyes so that I had to steady my voice. "I suspect everyone, Catherine." He slid the pictures back into the envelope and tucked it under his arm. "I'll keep these," he said.

"Bella says *she's* a patient of Wheeling's too," I said.

He nodded. "I have a lot of questions for her, since she has been doing your banking for Edward."

I told him about my conversation with Bella, leaving out the part about Edward and Julia. I took a deep breath. "Why would Ellen and Wheeling go to the concert together?" I asked.

"From what you've told me," Zardos said, "Wheeling likes to maintain a certain closeness with his patients."

I wondered quietly whether Ellen was sleeping with Wheeling as well as going to concerts with him, whether she was cheating on Stan. Ellen, though not a beauty, was always alluring, always sexy. I remembered her once jokingly bragging to me that she was so connected that she had slept with the Chicago Seven, the Harrisburg Dozen, and the Hollywood Ten. And I remembered the vacation with Ellen so long ago, before she had gotten married . . . before therapy. Before Stan. Before Wheeling.

Before Edward.

Zardos took my arm and led me across the sidewalk through the shadows to the hospital entrance, leaving Jethro on guard on the sidewalk in a tan version of his usual raincoat, stains and all. The sudden warmth I felt from Zardos made my heart melt.

As we stepped off the elevator on the fifteenth floor of Martindale Hospital there was a scene of chaos. A loud bell was ringing and people with stretchers were moving at a run. It was five minutes after eleven and as Zardos and I walked past the row of semiprivate rooms, their doors open, the occupants' faces peering out curiously from beds, from chairs, hoping to catch sight of a friend, a savior—maybe even a doctor— shouts came from a room at the end of the hall.

A bewildered-looking hospital staff ran here and there, a circus of confusion. A thin man with a mop was working wet, foamy circles on the linoleum floor, but even as he mopped, he looked toward the commotion at the end of the hall.

Suddenly Dr. March burst out of a doorway, shouting.

"What's going on?" Zardos said.

"Oh, God, Zardos, you're too late," he said, "he's dead."

"What do you mean?" I asked in horror. "I thought he had regained consciousness."

"He had," March said. "I saw him no more than an hour ago. Since then, somebody has murdered him." He scowled. "Broken his neck, to be exact."

We stopped in front of a door with Renaldo's name on it. A breakfast tray sat on an aluminum rack outside Renaldo's room. The food looked untouched.

Dr. March went to the door and opened it onto a scene of mayhem.

"He fought hard, but he lost," he said. The bedclothes were strewn about the bed, glass was shattered on the floor, chairs were overturned. Renaldo's body lay askew on the bed. Half a dozen doctors and nurses stood about him, looking distraught, defeated. There was an unnatural silence. The head was turned far to one side. Much too far.

My heart sank.

"It's murder, then," Zardos said quietly. "Whoever tried before has succeeded this time."

March nodded and we left the room, closing the door quietly behind us.

I suddenly found myself in tears; sobs that came from my stomach found their way up to my lungs.

A nurse handed me some tissues and put her arm around my shoulders.

I buried my face in the tissues and continued to cry and blow my nose as Zardos went on with questions.

"Wasn't there security on the door?" Zardos asked, looking about the hallway.

"Of course," Dr. March said, looking from me to the detective sadly. "He's over there, having a panic attack." He pointed to a skinny man in the blue uniform of the security service who was sitting on a chair near the nurses' station with his head in his hands. "He went to the bathroom—he was gone all of three minutes. He's devastated."

Zardos stepped over to talk to the security officer, who looked up at him with pitifully sad eyes. I couldn't watch.

"Will you call the family?" Dr. March asked me. I nodded, my body feeling numb.

Zardos spoke into his two-way radio, and in a matter of moments Jethro stepped off the elevator. They talked in a huddle with members of the hospital security staff. More officers were arriving by then, looking into rooms, asking questions.

Renaldo's room was still as death.

In the next half-hour, police swarmed over the hospital. I called Renaldo's family in England with my cellular phone to tell them the terrible news. The conversation with Renaldo's parents was hard. They said they would be over on the next possible plane. I felt criminal, guilty, as though I had caused Renaldo's death.

The hospital was crawling with cops. Renaldo's body was taken to the morgue, and the man who was on security duty was sent home. Everyone on the floor was being questioned—for that matter, everyone in the hospital. The only thing anyone knew for sure was that flowers had been delivered to Renaldo's room by a man who said he was from the florist down the block. The flowers, pink tulips, lay in a bunch on the floor of Renaldo's room. Renaldo had indeed put up a struggle.

My mouth was dry.

I called Julia to tell her what happened. I considered telling her of Bella's accusation but didn't have the heart to talk about it. In a way, it didn't seem important anymore.

Then I called my mother in Kansas. She asked me if I wanted to come home, and I said no, that I was already home and nobody, not even a murderer, was going to chase me out of it.

An hour later, Zardos and I stepped into the elevator together, and although it was empty except for the two of us, I found myself standing very close to his tall, well-carved form. My shoulder touched his and I felt his warmth, almost as though we were lying together. Finally, Zardos put his arm delicately around my shoulders.

"I feel so awful," I said. "I feel somehow as though this is all my fault."

Zardos shook his head and looked into my eyes.

"It isn't your fault," he said.

I felt like a cigarette and then realized: *no cigarettes for almost twenty-four hours.* It was a pale accomplishment compared to the terrible thing that had happened, but I realized I wasn't going to smoke no matter what.

And then, from somewhere deep in my psyche, I got the glimmer, again, of the truth. I looked up at Zardos as the elevator pulled to a stop. It was as though everything came together, suddenly, in an instant, like a brew that has come to a boil, a hunch that has paid off, a tingling in the spine that leads you to the right place, at the right time. Paydirt.

The realization held me for a moment in a place of total silence that seemed to last forever. I knew it would completely change my life. I knew what I had to do.

The elevator door slid open and Zardos's voice called me back from the edge of memory, the beginning of a new life.

"I don't want you to go to the AIDS fund-raiser at Sacred Heart School tonight," I heard him say.

I said I didn't remember telling him about it.

"It's on your calendar," he said.

I told him I wanted to go. He argued, but I insisted. "I want to be there, Zardos," I said, "just like nothing was wrong. Announce my plans to everyone. Draw them out—whoever killed Renaldo and whoever pushed me last night, as well as the forger. They didn't succeed in stopping me, and I'm sure they'll try again."

He looked at me, thoughtful, quizzical. Calm.

"You want to be the bait?" he asked.

"Absolutely," I said. "I've been the bait all along. Why should that change now?"

"All right," he said reluctantly, "but you have to watch yourself. It could be dangerous. I don't necessarily like it, but you'll go no matter what I say anyway."

"You really are heartless," I said, trying to keep things light, attempting a smile of my own.

"Sure I am." He ran his hand over the ace bandage on my wrist. "So heartless I want not to worry about you anymore." He ran his fingers through his hair and looked at me. "At least not this way."

I looked up into his eyes, thinking of Edward. In spite of everything that had happened—in spite of Renaldo's death and the fact that somebody was trying to kill me, that somebody was robbing me—I felt somehow very alive.

"You're shameless," I said softly, thinking of the handsome detective with no clothes on, staring at him.

He nodded, but didn't answer directly. "I have a few hours more work at the station," he said. "Some calls to confirm my suspicions. But don't worry, Catherine, I won't steal your thunder. We'll take whoever is guilty down together." He held my look and I let my eyes drop to the floor.

"I've been having a lot of confusing feelings the last couple of days," I said. "It may be the fall, or finding out about Edward." I looked up at him. "But I don't feel confusion anymore. I feel sorrow about Renaldo, but also expectation."

Zardos looked deeply into my eyes. "Catherine, I'm not confused. But I don't want to push you." He smiled. "I live alone. In fact," he looked at his watch, "I'm not sure I have much time for a relationship anyway."

"Neither did Edward," I said so softly I was sure Zardos hadn't heard me.

"Sacred Heart School," Zardos said, "on Riverside Drive. At six. I'll be there."

"As though nothing were the matter," I said.

Zardos took my wrist softly in his long, beautiful fingers. "I'll be as close as your heartbeat. Is this hurting you?" he asked.

"I can work a camera, if that's what you're wondering." I smiled. He looked at me with more than a look of police protection. I was aware of gratitude I didn't smell like cigarette smoke.

Outside, snow was falling gently and the white flakes settled on Zardos's eyelashes as I looked at his face so close to mine. Spring, it seemed, was arriving, right on time.

"I can work a camera, if that's what you're looking for," I smiled. She looked at me with more than a look of polite profession. I was aware of perfume. I didn't smell the cigarette smoke.

Outside I saw — what I wished I had. As white faces called on Zacko's face, as I looked at her, less at ease to mine, as I watched, we arrived right on time.

52

A dream, a fragment from my early teenage years, when sex was a phantom, a promised view as yet unseen.

The moon is high, very white and mottled, layers of whiteness upon whiteness over her face in the black sky, as though she were wearing layers of silk across her mouth. She looks down at me from space, at my body—my arms, breasts, fingers, legs, lips. The moon's silver light fills the wheatfields and the long slope of hills to the mountain's edge. Her whiteness outlines the branches of the Russian olive tree in our small flower garden, so that a silhouette, like a web of lace, draws across my window and penetrates the dark room where I lie in my bed, naked, tossing, a girl no longer of the age of innocence.

My hands touch my naked body. Under the lace of the Russian olive tree is a square of white lawn, black lace on white snow. A fence runs along the garden's edge under the moonlight, twisting among the lacy shadows cast by the olive tree; the fence has picket points high and sharp enough to draw blood. The tips of the fence pierce the light of the moon, shedding white tears that become an

*ocean running over my body, wave after wave. I
struggle to catch the white waves, racing them
down the shore, over and over as they break in the
black and white garden, over and over as the
fence pierces the moon's ghostly surface, over and
over, white-liquid-silver foam pouring in waves
from the moon onto the Russian olive tree, onto my
nakedness, until at last I make the shore and vault
the fence, vault the moonlight, spring over the olive
tree and into the sky, my path unblocked, my
blood running free of the web, free of the snow, free
of the border, the fence, and the barrier, drowned
in an ocean of red moonlight.*

53

Jethro pulled the car away from the curb and we rode in silence into the fast-falling snow. I looked at the snowflakes as they loaded the bare branches of the trees in the park in gloves of white. I watched as fresh snow settled on the sidewalks and canopies along Central Park West, thinking of my lively young assistant, his body lying dead in Martindale Hospital.

I was terribly sad. And yet I felt light, almost euphoric—almost like that crazy giddiness I had often experienced as a child.

Jethro parked the car in the gathering whiteness of the gutter in front of my apartment building—illegally, of course. We made our way to the elevator, stamping the snow off our feet.

Jethro and I hardly spoke; I knew that he was upset. In my office, I sat down on the edge of a once-more cluttered desk, picked up the photograph of Edward, and carefully removed the silver clasps on the back. Whatever he was doing, with whomever, I wasn't going to look at his face anymore.

I wanted to take control of something, anything, and removed the picture from its velvet-backed frame, sliding it slowly, as though taking off my white silk lingerie, as I had so often done for Edward before we made love. I looked into those dark, sexy eyes for a moment and then tore the picture across Edward's mouth, right in half; then in four pieces, splitting the sexy eyes; I tore the portrait again and again—an eye here, the corner of a lip there, a section of hair in another fragment of the photograph. I dropped the pieces of Edward's face into a large pewter bowl I had received from the Photographers' International Pop Music Awards in Paris three years before. I took my green lighter, snapped it on, and put the flame to Edward's eyes; the fire spread slowly to every scrap of the photograph, illuminating the inscription that circled the inner lip of the bowl: *Catherine Saint, Pop Photographer of the Year.*

A photograph is difficult to burn, and wherever the fire had trouble igniting the pieces of Edward's portrait, I put the flame to his face again. It was an exorcism.

When black ashes were all that was left in the bowl, I had some answers: I knew I would never make love to Edward again. Perhaps I would never see him again. I knew I was not going to smoke. I knew I was going to Sacred Heart to see my adversary eye to eye. And I knew I wanted Zardos to kiss me.

The phone rang, startling me out of my reverie.

It was Edward. I had conjured him. His voice was smooth.

"I can't believe you have the chutzpah to call me, Edward," I said.

"I want to see you," he said.

"My assistant died this morning, Edward," I said. "He was murdered. Somebody broke his neck." There was a silence on the other end of the telephone. Either Edward knew nothing of Renaldo's death, or he was truly shocked.

"That's terrible, awful," he said after a moment. "Do they know who killed him?"

I only said the police were looking for suspects.

"And," I went on, fearlessly, "a lot of money is missing, Edward, from the account you were handling for me."

Edward's voice jumped on the end of my sentence. "I've got to see you," he said, "I've got to explain. Are you going to the fund-raiser?" The invitation that had come to me had been sent to Edward as well.

I admitted I was going to be at Sacred Heart. "Why on earth would you want to see me?" I asked, but felt a tug at my heart. "I don't care anymore, Edward. I don't have anything to say to you." I paused, not wanting to say too much. "But the police do."

"You don't know what's been going on," he said.

"You're right—at least I didn't know," I said, "but I do now. The police are convinced you forged my name on withdrawals at the bank, Edward." There was a silence on the other end of the telephone.

"I want to explain, Catherine." I thought I detected a frightened tone in his voice. "But I have to see you."

"Do what you want, Edward," I said, slamming the phone down.

At six o'clock Jethro and I pulled up in front of Sacred Heart School. Jethro parked in the NO PARKING zone, near the trucks from *ET,* NBC, ABC, and CBS crews that were lined up on the street. A pair of police cars was parked illegally on the far side of the street and a blue-and-white police van with barred windows sat near the corner. *NYPD Blue,* I thought, reaching into the back seat to get my camera bags. It seemed everyone knew that more would happen tonight than just a fund-raiser.

Black limousines disgorged well-dressed stars at the entrance and hovered along the side streets as Jethro and I made our way over the light dusting of snow on the pavement to the statue-encrusted building that was already jammed with the famous and the would-be famous.

"Please don't climb on anything tonight, Ms. Saint," Jethro said gently, helping me with my gear.

A dozen uniformed police joined the crowd at the door, and as they moved inside the entrance hall a chill wind fluttered, playing with the corners of the gold-embossed invitations laid out on a long table over which women dressed in Ungaro and Mary McFadden fashions presided. Their fashions covered just enough of their shoulders to keep them from freezing to death.

Snow-dappled wind blustered in through the door whenever it opened and rustled the women's hairdos as they chased invitations and lists with manicured fingers, turning expectant smiles toward high-profile guests clustered by the door, shedding their politically correct, faux fur coats.

Jethro and I had locked our coats in the car and now we stamped fresh snow off our feet and searched for Zardos among the crowd of men in black tie, women in couture dresses. I was warm enough, wearing a midnight-black crushed-velvet pantsuit. We moved through the big oak doors to the wood-paneled auditorium, where the party was already in full swing.

My cameras were loaded with film and I put one over each shoulder and began working the room as if I were there on assignment—which I was. I put aside my sadness for Renaldo and my anxiety for my own safety. Jethro kept with me, right at my side.

Sting had arrived, and stood in the big hall stamping snow from his manly feet. I shot a picture of the tall, intelligent singer as he talked energetically to Annie Leibovitz.

Just then, Zardos spoke my name and I turned to see his tall figure emerge from among the stars.

God, I thought, this man is getting better-looking every time I see him. I felt my heart beat faster.

"Here I am," Zardos said, coming up behind me and putting an arm around my shoulders. He hadn't worn an overcoat either and snow melted on the tops of his polished shoes and the shoulders of his dark blue jacket.

I gave Zardos a discreet cheek-to-cheek greeting, and felt a throb of electricity pass between us. We looked at each other briefly, then avoided each other's eyes. Whatever it was that was happening, I didn't want to rush it. Or lose it.

It felt strange, in the midst of my sorrow for Renaldo. But it felt wonderful too.

"Blue uniforms," I said. "I'm glad. The more the better. Edward called me to tell me he would be here," I said. "He says he wants to explain."

Zardos nodded. "Your boyfriend has a lot to explain, that's for sure," he said.

Zardos let his gaze roam over the crowd. The sound of the crowd faded as I looked up into his gorgeous eyes. "Keep on the lookout," he said. "Don't forget— you're the bait." He smiled, then let my fingers stay in his for a long moment. "Take pictures, like you always do." He put his arm through mine, guiding me across the room.

I was ready.

Max, Z-Train, Malinda, Denzel, Reed, Julia, and Sahid burst into Sacred Heart's main room, followed by more lights, cameras and television crews and the uniformed police floating among the crowd, keeping back, watching.

The Newborns must have heard of Renaldo's death from Julia. They all surrounded me, offering their comfort, their condolences.

"So it's murder," Reed said quietly, and put his arm

around me. Julia had told me she had told Reed about the threats on my life. "I'm so sorry."

Jethro pulled Zardos aside, but he spoke loudly enough that I could hear him. "We've had another I.D. from a witness, and the item they found checks out. You were right."

"God, Catherine, I'm so sorry about Renaldo," Julia said, embracing me tightly. She put her head on my shoulder and held me and I felt tears in my eyes again. "I've told everyone. I hope it was the right thing to do."

"Of course it was. Thanks, Julia." Julia couldn't betray me. How could she? I let her hold me and let the tears fall, reaching for the tissues in my pocket. I knew, after the shock had passed a bit, there would be time for many things—including the talk I knew I must have with my friend.

"Hello, Julia," Zardos said.

"Hello," she said. Her eyes flitted away from Zardos, avoiding contact, as he leveled his gaze at her. She was looking sensational and Zardos took in her beauty. She wore a jump suit of black silk covered with tiny points of light like diamonds, her perfect size four shining from head to toe.

"I'm surprised you're here," Julia said, looking at me with renewed concern. My friend looked at me for a long moment. Finally I summoned the courage to repeat Bella's accusation, softly. "Is there any truth to it, Julia?" I asked.

My friend's answer dispelled my fears as she threw her head back lustily and laughed loudly enough for the whole room to hear.

"That will be the day!" she said. "Me with Edward? God spare me."

"I didn't think it was true," I said quickly, relieved. "I didn't believe it for a minute. . . . Well, maybe for a second."

"Would I do that to you?" she asked, answering her own question. *"Never!"*

"Good," I said, truly relieved. Then I told Julia the details of Renaldo's murder and about the forgeries at the bank.

"God, how gruesome," she said. "But darling Catherine, don't worry about the money, it doesn't matter. I have enough money for both of us." Love had turned Julia into a flower child all over again. "Does Zardos know who the killer is?" she asked, looking at Zardos out of the corner of her eye. I didn't answer and looked past Julia toward the main entrance. Julia squeezed my hand in hers—whether in sympathy or congratulations or anxiety, I couldn't tell.

"It's not over till it's over," I said as Zardos turned his attention to Reed and smiled with the look of a hunter.

After Edward had called that afternoon, Zardos and I had spoken a number of times. I had made calls, played back tapes, gone through my calendar, and then had a hot bath, knowing I would need to be relaxed and ready. I called my mother and told her that I thought things were going to be solved in the next twenty-four hours. She was consoling, and said Ben and Buster sent their love. I felt better talking to her, and when I hung up, I was able to lie down and take a nap, knowing I needed a rest for what was coming that evening at Sacred Heart.

Zardos and I had agreed neither of us would make a move until the entire group of friends, lovers, and others were assembled.

Now, Reed put an arm around Julia, then called out to Malinda, who was talking to Robert De Niro. Malinda was dressed in a white leather miniskirt and a low-cut white velvet bodice with lacing up the back that revealed the delicious curves of her shoulder blades. She looked drawn and pale in spite of her makeup and the sexy outfit. Zardos eyed her cannily, then greeted her.

I felt a rush of jealousy, inappropriate and maddening.

And I wanted a cigarette.

The thought of Renaldo's body, dead and silent, came to me as though I had been with him when his soul had left his body. I felt I had met a new friend, only to lose him before I even really knew him.

Zardos gazed about the room, waiting, as I was. I wondered what more he had learned that afternoon after we had spoken. The detective turned to Reed and Malinda and spoke like an old rock-and-roller. "Will you still go to the Grammys without Fred, if he doesn't show up?" Zardos asked. "Fred has reappeared," Zardos continued. "So to speak. Not sober, but alive. He called Max last night in the middle of the night, to say he might come back. And he was spotted last night in the East Village with a buzz on and a half dozen twelve-year-old groupies hovering around him. Not in good shape. But, as I said, alive."

"We have to go on as though Fred were gone forever. Fred doesn't want any help, Max says." Malinda spoke softly, looking around the room. She gave a tug at her short leather skirt, trying to get it to cover her knees. Failing to do so, she shivered and put her head on my shoulder. "I just keep imagining Fred," she said, "lying in an alley somewhere, dead of an overdose."

Julia moved closer at Malinda's words, and I could have sworn her eyes misted over. She shot a glance at Zardos, which he returned, this time forceful and unmistakable.

Zardos and Julia knew something between them that neither of them wished me to know.

"Where is my dad?" Malinda said, interrupting my thoughts and scanning the room in vain for Edward.

I told her I had no idea. I shot pictures of Sting and Alec Baldwin, trying not to think of Edward.

"He has been very odd lately," Malinda said. "I mean more than usual." I eyed the blond singer sharply. "Tell me, Malinda," I said, "what is it about your father that upset you so much? You've never told me. Now I want to know."

"You deserve to know the truth, Catherine," she said, then smiled at Fran, the TV anchor who was leading a group of press photographers toward our group. Malinda smiled mysteriously as Gayle Burns, on assignment from *Style* magazine, asked if she could take some pictures. Malinda nodded.

Sahid and Z-Train moved into our circle, and I thought of the euphoria of the night before, the dream of their gentle hands moving over me. I blushed just thinking about it. Sahid gave me a kiss on the cheek. I thought I detected a territorial impulse in his movements, but he just smiled. In one hand he held a flute of champagne, and in the other what was left of a shrimp tail, red with cocktail sauce. He parked it on the outstretched palm of a stone cherub.

Suddenly a strange feeling came over me: it was as if all of us were caught in a time capsule. *Someone* was missing.

Just as suddenly the action in the room started up again, and the voices sounded once more.

"I told Julia that unless Fred gets himself together before the Grammy night," Reed said to Zardos, waving his champagne flute in the air, "Julia will have to join our band." He washed down a scoop of caviar on a toast point with the rest of his champagne. Julia made a face and gave Malinda a nudge.

"I know you'll get another Grammy, Julia," Malinda said to her. "For 'Melody.' "

Julia ignored Malinda's reference to another possible Grammy. It wasn't like my friend to turn a cold shoulder to the professional side of the business, even though she had retired from it.

Z-Train opened his arms out wide and embraced the air. "I am too. And I'm not angry at Fred anymore," he said, "but after I hug him and welcome him home, I'm definitely going to tear him to pieces." There was a silence and Z-Train looked suddenly defeated. Then he lifted his shoulders. "I think he'll get it together," he said, trying to sound convinced.

"Fred is just out sick for a while," Max said, "that's the way I'm looking at it." He squared his huge shoulders, as though to take on a tough job.

"Yes," Julia's voice chimed in. "Fred is just ill." She sounded young and innocent.

Reed joined the group again and I got a good shot of him and Julia together. I wanted to look like a photographer, not a sleuth.

Zardos stayed close to me, watching the crowd as I kept the cameras going. He was waiting as I was waiting. My eyes flitted from the door, where I expected I might see Edward, back to Zardos, and I got pictures of the Newborns with De Niro, Linda McCartney, George Harrison, and some of the members of the Harlem Boys' Choir.

"Canapé?" a young man said, balancing a tray of green celery smothered in eggplant and cream cheese. I watched distractedly as a dozen other college-age kids clad in black tie moved through the sculptured rooms, proposing rare sliced beef on endive, goose liver pâté on wheat thins, puff pastry filled with tiny hot dogs, moussaka, salmon caviar on toast, bacon over oysters, lamb and peppers on skewers, and celery stalks with yogurt dressing to the crowd of mostly anorexic stars, most of whom refused everything.

An announcer came on the little carved podium at the end of the hall to thank the members of the Harlem Boys' Choir, who had donated their time tonight. The thirty African-American boys, aged eight to sixteen, began to sing "Amazing Grace." The crowd was rapt in silence.

Searching the room, my eyes found Ellen Carney. As she made her way through the crowd toward us, Zardos pointed like a bird dog, watching and waiting as Ellen flew our way. Ellen shoved past another waiter carrying trays.

"Bingo," Zardos said softly. "Right on time."

"Hello, Ellen," I said. Ellen's voluptuous figure was clothed in heavy golden coyote fur and Zardos helped her out of the dozen or so animal skins that had gone into the construction of her coat. Under the fur Ellen's slim body was clothed in a chic black Gauthier cocktail dress that fit her like a glove. She wore long, black silk stockings that showed off her good legs. Her expensively highlighted blond hair was piled high on her head, her makeup and hair done to perfection. Ruby earrings dangled at her ears; her nails and lips were matching vermilion.

"You're here," Zardos said.

Ellen looked past Zardos to me.

The boys' choir finished their set and filed off the stage in their bright jackets, then moved through the enthusiastic crowd, followed by television crews and well-wishers.

"Shall we?" Zardos said, fixing his eyes on Ellen. "We can talk in here." Zardos led the way into a small chapel off the auditorium, away from the tumult of the auditorium.

I followed, cameras at rest on my shoulders. The time for taking pictures was over. The time for seeing the truth had begun.

Jethro stationed himself by the door.

We found ourselves in a small, oval-shaped prayer and meditation room. Above the altar was an intricately carved relief that depicted the saints praying, humbling themselves. The altar itself was laid out with gold-embossed white satin fabrics, and white lilies stood in tall, rectangular vases around the crucifix. A small, rosette stained-glass window twinkled near the ceiling above the altar; glints of blue and gold, amethyst and yellow glass flashed into the room. Candles burned in every nook and cranny and in the tall candle holders around the font. This, I thought, is where we will have Renaldo's memorial service, in this beautiful little chapel.

I put down my camera bag on one of the delicate wooden chairs.

"Ms. Carney," Zardos said, "I'd like you to begin. I want you to tell Catherine everything."

Ellen responded impatiently. "Can't I talk to Catherine privately, first?" She had crossed herself as she entered the chapel and bent her knee briefly in the short black dress, but she didn't look like a woman at peace.

"Nothing is private, not now," Zardos said. "Not since the first threat on Catherine's life."

Ellen looked at Zardos. "I guess you thought it necessary to break into my office," she said with unconcealed ill humor.

"I had a warrant, Ms. Carney. The clues were plentiful," Zardos said. "I want Catherine to hear this from you."

Ellen took a seat in the wooden pew and sighed in resignation. "First of all, Catherine, I don't feel guilty about any of this," Ellen said. "Stan and I haven't been getting along for years." She looked up at Zardos. "Stan's a bastard, you know. And not just because of what he's done to you, Catherine."

The glimmer of truth shone like a beacon. The one

who wasn't here tonight was Stan, my friend; Stan, my lawyer. Stan, Ellen's husband. Stan, the Newborns' agent.

"When I saw Bob Benhurst at the Meadowlands, I had a hunch," I said.

Ellen nodded. "I was suspicious of Stan and Edward phoning each other all the time," Ellen said, "and I started taping the calls at home and in the car. I learned that Stan needed money to get the Newborns the big promotion he felt they needed to collect their Grammys. He couldn't risk their not being played on the radio all the time. Vertigo Records said they wouldn't foot the bill for the promotion."

I nodded. The promotion for the group must have cost a fortune. As the picture became clearer and clearer, a lot of little things came together. Deals to get records played on the radio were often made—at great cost—by record companies.

"Payola, bribery, and it's all the same thing. All illegal," Zardos said.

"Stan made a deal with Benhurst," Ellen said. "Something like a million and a half dollars in radio time and promo favors." She paused, to make sure I was following.

"Stan figured he could get the money from Catherine," Zardos said.

Ellen nodded. "Stan stole some stationery on a visit to your office and then had Edward set up the procedure for the transfers." She gave me a hard smile. "Stan figured you would never miss it. He says you're a ditz when it comes to money."

I didn't respond.

"He blackmailed Edward," she continued. Ellen nodded. "Stan needed Edward to help him get money from your bank accounts." She concentrated on her fingernails. "Edward was in trouble: He was embezzling money from his partnership. Stan found out and threatened to tell Edward's partners."

"Yes," Zardos said, "and we know it's Edward's forgery of Catherine's signature at the bank. And I questioned Bob Benhurst today. He said he just happened to be at the Meadowlands last night, but I think Benhurst threatened to kill Stan if he didn't come up with the money."

"That's the kind of trouble my husband was in," Ellen said. "Desperate trouble. And you're lucky, Catherine. If I hadn't been having the affair with Edward, Stan might have gotten away with everything!"

"I'm not sure if that makes me feel any better," I said.

"Stan got Hank Cramer to write the threatening notes to Catherine," Zardos said. "He was blackmailing Hank, threatening to expose what he knew about Hank's illegal activities."

I nodded. It all made perfect, horrible sense.

Ellen sighed deeply. The well-dressed, cool woman must have been upset, yet except for the sigh, her poise was unruffled. Years of playing the game had steeled her to this kind of thing, I supposed. Not me. My hands were shaking and I felt my breath coming in short, agitated spurts.

"Stan and Edward have been plotting this for weeks," Ellen said.

I nodded, remembering that I had seen the two of them huddled together for too long a time at Julia's opening, in the few minutes Edward had deigned to appear. I realized he hadn't come to see me at all, but to see Stan.

I was shaken with what I was learning. It all seemed so unlikely. Stan in trouble? Nothing would have been further from my mind before this. Stan, my friend, secure and firm about his opinions and about your opinions. Stan, generous with his humor, with his jokes. In three days, everything had changed. Stan, I thought—my would-be killer.

"It took me a few hours to put it all together, but I think Hank messed with that rigging," I said. "He knows I always climb up there to get good pictures."

"That's right," Ellen said. "He did. I know because Wheeling and I saw him." She paused, then went on. "By the way, Catherine, Wheeling was always my shrink. Stan knew that." I frowned, amazed that Stan could keep this from me as well.

I shook my head. "Did you know he raped me?" I asked.

"You called it rape, Stan called it rape." She smiled. "Wheeling calls it therapy."

I asked Ellen about Bella.

"Bella is a good person. Even if she takes too many pills." She looked suddenly angry. "I've told Edward's firm everything. They were planning to fire Bella. Edward was going to let her take the fall for the trouble he's in at the firm. But I knew Bella didn't do it. I taped the phone calls between Stan and Edward. I had proof. And Wheeling *offered* to come to the Meadowlands with me. I wanted to stop Stan before he succeeded in killing someone and ruining my life and the lives of our children. I took my shrink with me for . . ." she hesitated, "let us say, for protection."

The man who had raped me would be able to testify against my attempted killer. I sank into a chair beneath the marble angels and felt frozen in time, like the stone figures.

But now, I wasn't dreaming. I could see with crystal clarity.

"I suppose you know everything else," Ellen said.

"Pretty much," he said. "Stan got nervous when Catherine hired Renaldo."

"He had to do something to stop me from finding

out about the bank withdrawals," I said. "So he attacked Renaldo."

"He just wanted to frighten Renaldo, I think," Ellen said, "to find out what Renaldo knew."

"But Renaldo wouldn't frighten," I said.

I shook my head, but I knew she was telling the truth.

Zardos looked gently at me. "I've suspected Stan all along," he said. "But I didn't get the proof I needed until I searched Ellen's office. Three witnesses have now identified Stan as the person who pushed Renaldo down the subway stairs."

"Did you know Renaldo died this afternoon?" I asked Ellen. "That someone broke his neck?"

Ellen shook her head and bowed it over the smart, black skirt that covered her lap. Still, she seemed strangely unmoved. "Oh, God," she said. "That means it's even worse for my husband than all the rest of it put together." She looked from me to Zardos. "It seems I was too late." She paused. "I'm sorry, Catherine. He was a lovely young man," she said almost inaudibly.

"Yes, he was," I said, exhausted and suddenly depressed, "and Stan was the only lawyer I ever trusted."

"Well, you know lawyers," Ellen said with a wicked smile. "You introduced me to Stan, so, in a way, you have yourself to blame."

"And I introduced you to Edward," I said. "I suppose I have myself to blame for that as well."

Ellen stood up to go. "I know I'll have to come down to the precinct and put this on the record," she said. Zardos nodded his head.

"I'd like you to do that tonight," he said. "Jethro will take you. I had Jethro put out an all-points warrant for Stan's arrest," Zardos said, putting his hand on my shoulder gently.

I sighed. I didn't want to face the Newborns. I cared for them. I didn't want them to get hurt. But of course, I thought, that's rock and roll. Just about everybody gets hurt. It's the rules of the game.

Poor Renaldo—wanting to get into the music business.

I stood up, looking around the room at the stone saints with their old, patient eyes. I felt weary, angry, and sorrowful all at the same time.

In the stillness of the chapel no one spoke for a few minutes. The din of the party in the auditorium reached us like the sound of waves crashing on a distant shore.

Zardos reached out and took my hand in his. "Jethro," Zardos said, "take Ellen to the precinct."

"So long, Catherine," Ellen said. She shrugged into her politically incorrect fur coat and extended the hand with the red nails.

I couldn't bring myself to shake it.

"Edward and I will continue to see one another," she said. "He's in love with me, you know." She put her hands into a pair of slim black leather gloves and wiggled her fingers around. "He didn't mean to do you any harm, Catherine, he just got in over his head." She paused, and looked at me again. "I always thought Edward was sexy—so sexy I couldn't resist."

"Somebody should have," I said. "I'm sorry it wasn't me." I looked around the tiny chapel at the burning candles and the saints. The saints, I thought, had seen it all.

Above us the sculpted Christ looked down on the miserable world, promising the impossible.

There was a scuffle at the door and Stan's big, tuxedo-clad figure emerged into the small, candle-lit space. Behind him were two uniformed policemen.

"Ellen, I've got to talk to you," Stan said in a loud

voice, ignoring the rest of us. Jethro moved to where Stan had appeared, just inside the door, and two uniformed policemen stood at the ready, just behind my old friend.

I could hear Malinda's voice in the outside room.

"Stan, Stan," Malinda called, "what's going on?"

"Here he is, Detective," the taller of the two uniformed men said to Zardos. "He just arrived." They reached out to cuff Stan, but he jerked his hands away.

"This is an outrage," Stan exclaimed, "I'm here to speak to my wife." He looked around the room, first at me, than at Zardos. "Ellen, we've got to talk."

"I have nothing to say to you, Stan," she said, moving toward the door in her fur, trying to slip around him.

"Mr. Shultz, you're under arrest," Zardos informed Stan. "You have the right to remain silent—"

"What are you talking about!" Stan shouted, his face red, his eyes bulging at Zardos. "What am I accused of?"

"Murder, Mr. Shultz," Zardos said calmly.

There was a short silence and then Zardos continued reading Stan his rights. Stan's shoulders, formerly arched and firm, began to sag.

"Murder," Stan said to himself. He looked at me, finally, and then at Ellen. "What did you tell them, Ellen?"

His wife remained near the door, prepared to fly at a moment's notice.

Malinda hovered near the door, a stunned look on her face.

"Your pen was found in Renaldo's hospital room, Mr. Shultz," Zardos said. "The pen with your initials on it."

I looked at my old friend with anger, disappointment, and pity. His face reflected no discernible emotion.

"I want my lawyer" was all he said.

54

*I dream I am in the sea, far from land, and it is
night, and the wind and the waves pound me, I
am so afraid I will drown. The water is deep and
the fish and whales are playing in the water, and
dawn comes after a night of thrashing about in the
ocean, staying afloat and above the jaws of the
moray eel who chases me. The waves wash over me
and I remember a friend whose father was in the
water seven days after the sinking of his ship and
his legs were chewed off by the sharks and he
nearly bled to death but he stayed afloat and he lived
to tell the story. I have my legs and my arms, and
I can move about in this salt water among the
schools of fish.*

*As the dawn breaks I am near the shore; I can
see the islands, the trees, the animals. A family of
elephants comes to the edge of the water, looking
out toward me. Lions sprawl in the sun by the
water and a black panther sits in a fig tree, looking
out at me, licking his fur, cleaning his face with
his paws. He looks mild and friendly, like Blue. I
tread water, looking for a wave that will throw
me up on the shore, a wave I can ride, a deep,
rounded horn of water that has an engine in it
and can hurl me to the shore, where the seabirds*

*nest in the big trees and the light of the sun warms
the sand, and the moray eels and the deep, dark,
tangled arms of the octopus are just memories;
where sharks are a memory.*

*I gulp water and ride the small waves that come
by, looking for the big one, and as I do I look
into the sky and see an airplane, so far overhead it
casts a shadow onto the clouds. A wave catches
me in its curl and carries me to the shore, throwing
me down on the sand, safe, with a rainbow in a
circle riding in the sky above. I have my arms and
my legs and I am panting and spitting sand out
of my mouth and the lions look at me and the elephants and the panther and the sharks are looking
into the sky, too, at the rainbow in a circle.*

55

I tried to concentrate my mind on prayer; I said the Lord's Prayer, trying to remember some of the things I might have done right in my life, remembering lots of the mistakes I knew I had made, thinking of Ben and my parents, of Marty. I thought of Renaldo and prayed for his soul. I thought of Zardos . . . all of this in the moments it took for everything to be revealed and Stan to be put under arrest.

Zardos led Stan out of the little chapel in handcuffs and the officers in uniforms took over, leading Stan through the crowded auditorium toward the exit. Malinda fought off the officers' restraining arms and grabbed Stan in a tight embrace, burying her head in his chest. She cried softly while her agent tried to console her, muttering, "It's all right, Malinda."

But it wasn't all right. Renaldo was dead, and Stan would probably spend the rest of his life in jail. There would be some repercussions in Malinda's life, and the group would no doubt have many problems to deal with since their agent was under arrest. Reed, Julia, Sahid, and Z-Train looked on in disbelief at the sight of Stan in handcuffs. Max stood speechless, filling most of one corner of the little chapel. Paraded through the big room, Stan said nothing to the rest of his clients, trying to muster for their benefit some semblance of a professional smile and failing.

Jethro led Ellen out and took her to the precinct. Zardos left with them and when they were gone I quickly filled Julia in on everything Ellen had told us. Malinda and the rest of the Newborns listened as well, looking paler with each successive revelation.

In the main auditorium, the buzz, the drinking, the laughter, went on uninterrupted. There were too many stars at this party to let the spectacle of a man in handcuffs disturb the festive atmosphere. One handsome young man with a piece of toast and smoked salmon in his hand stopped to ask me if somebody was making a movie.

But Fran got her scoop, and so did the other networks, complete with pictures of Zardos walking Stan to the police van. The news would be out in a matter of minutes that Catherine Saint's assistant had been murdered by the Newborns' agent, and that Stan Shultz was under arrest.

Having deposited Stan in the police car, Zardos came back to our deflated little group. By then I had told them everything.

"Edward Valarian will lose his job and probably be charged on some kind of fraud or conspiracy rap," Zardos said.

I was feeling completely exhausted, emotionally and physically. Zardos reached for my hand and led me out of the big oak doors to the street.

"Let's get out of here," he said.

Max herded the Newborns out the door, but Malinda hung behind to talk to Julia. They were deep in conversation as they retrieved their coats. I thought the younger singer looked older, but her blond hair was still lighting up the room.

"Catherine," Malinda said, drawing me off to the

side of the room, "I think I have to tell you this now. Maybe it will be easier for you."

"What is it?" I asked, not knowing if I was prepared for any more news at the moment.

"It's just that my father is a total narcissist. He always has to have another woman in his life," Malinda said. "That was what split my parents up, and I was so afraid for you, but I didn't want to tell you that I knew he was seeing someone else." She paused. "He always does, he's a sex addict."

"Did you know it was Ellen?" I asked.

The blond singer nodded.

"Why didn't you tell me about this, Malinda?" I asked. I was hurt.

"I just couldn't tell you. I didn't want to hurt you," she said. "But now you understand why I have problems with him."

I nodded, knowing Malinda would be all right. I hoped that I would too.

Outside Sacred Heart, the snow was melting softly on the television trucks as they moved slowly down the street, and big fat flakes fell on our shoulders and our heads.

Reed walked with Julia, Zardos, and me, while Malinda, Z-Train, Max, and Sahid headed for their limousine, which had just pulled up in front of the school.

"I have to go to the precinct, Catherine," Zardos said.

Julia and I looked around at the police cars and the crowd dispersing outside Sacred Heart.

"Why don't the three of us go together?" Julia said, looking in my direction. "Ride with us in my car, Zardos."

"I've got to go with the kids," Reed said. "We've got to figure out what we're going to do now." He gave Julia a kiss on the lips. Denzel had never left

Reed's side the entire evening. "Can you guys come over to the Plaza later?" Reed went on. "Sort of a wake"—his voice fell—"for Renaldo, and for Stan, I guess. And a wake-up call for Fred." He frowned. "We've got to find a new agent—and probably a new member of the band, I think. Fred's a mess."

Julia, Zardos, and I headed for Julia's limousine. I stashed my cameras in the trunk. The doors closed on the sleek Cadillac and I settled into the back seat of the car with Julia and Zardos.

Zardos and I sat discreetly apart, our shoulders not touching but a fire moving between us nonetheless. "I'm glad Stan's in custody," he said, adding, "and I like *some* of your friends a great deal," glancing over at Julia.

I sighed, sinking into the plush seats of the limousine and wrapping my velvet coat more tightly about my shoulders.

A nearly complete darkness had fallen in the mid-March evening air. Snowflakes melted in Zardos's hair, snow fell softly on the statues in Riverside Park as limousines pulled away from Sacred Heart with their baggage of stars; snow draped the old-fashioned lamps glowing in the soft evening light at the edge of the park like white lace.

We were headed for police headquarters, where, sometime in the next few hours, Ellen would be making her statement and witnesses would be coming to make formal I.D.s of Stan as Renaldo's murderer.

The driver made his way along the streets, moving as quickly as he could on the wet, slippery surface. I sneaked glances at Zardos's profile—handsome, concentrated, powerful—and felt a tug at my heart.

I shook my head, wondering how this had all come to pass in such a few short days, but mostly fretting about poor Renaldo.

Then I thought about Edward, Stan, and Wheeling.

I had put my faith in these men. I had expected, somehow, that each of them could make of me the woman I needed to be—secure, creative, sexual, and free. But I had become all of these things not because of these men, but in spite of them.

In spite of them all.

At the precinct, I formally pressed charges against Stan Shultz. It was a sad hour. The coffee machine in Zardos's office was still brewing terrible coffee; the sound and the noise and the furor were going on in the station as they had the first time I had visited the precinct, only days before. Stan had been locked up till his lawyer got there, and there was a warrant out for the arrest of Edward, who was wanted for complicity in forgery and embezzlement. He had probably skipped town.

I made some phone calls from the police station. I called my mother. When I heard her sweet voice I started to cry again. It all just poured out. She comforted me, telling me I had done everything I could and not to be so hard on myself.

After hanging up, I still felt teary. But at least now I knew what had happened, and although I felt a great sorrow for Renaldo and a certain sadness for Stan and for Edward, I felt lighter than I had in days.

After the formality of signing papers, Zardos took care of a few more details and we all climbed back in the car to go to the Plaza.

Julia, Zardos, and I were quiet, subdued after the events of the day. We drove without talking.

At Broadway and Fifty-ninth the driver turned left and the sound of sirens hit our ears. Ahead we could see red lights flashing in the street. It looked like a fire, the street filled with engines and ambulances.

The driver rolled the dividing window down. "Ms. Clearwater, ma'am, I can't get through," he said.

"There's some kind of emergency up there." Two blocks ahead of us the lights were flashing through the steamy clouds that poured out of the street. Fire trucks were lined two and three deep.

Zardos leaned forward in the seat and guided the limo driver through side streets until we stopped at the side entrance to the Plaza on Fifty-eighth. Zardos opened the door and an officer in uniform greeted us.

"What's up?" Zardos asked. Swirling lights trembled in red and white among the snowflakes. Red flares played on the crowd surrounding the gold statue in the park across from the hotel. All eyes searched the roof of the hotel and, tilting my head back, I saw what was attracting the crowd's attention. A figure, legs dangling, sat poised in an open window on a high floor.

The officer lowered his voice and spoke to us in the window, the snowflakes falling about his face.

"What's wrong?" I asked, feeling sick.

The officer blinked his eyes against the swirling snow and glanced up toward the roof before he turned to me and looked me straight in the eye. "He says he's going to jump."

56

*I had a dream that the place they met looked like a
fancy restaurant, one of the elegant places on
Madison Avenue or Park, with a bar in front and
in back a dozen or so small tables, each covered
with a linen tablecloth, each bearing a single rose in
a blue glass vase.*

*It is early evening. The place is nearly empty. They
sit at the bar, separately, checking themselves out
in the mirror behind the colored bottles of Pernod
and Courvoisier, Tanqueray gin and McCallan
scotch, crème de menthe and Poire William. They
become aware of each other's eyes first; each is
obviously waiting for someone, each is obviously
alone, each nurses a drink, uninterested in the
taste of alcohol; each is hungry for something, someone else.*

*He approaches her first; she accepts a Dunhill Red
cigarette although she doesn't usually smoke. He
compliments her on her perfume, buys her a drink
although she hasn't finished the one in front of
her. He runs his fingers down her arm with its soft
down that leads up her shoulder to the silk, soft
bodice of the dress she wears. Their eyes never leave
one another's, it is as though they have been
struck at once with a single plan. He takes her arm,*

*pays their bills, puts her in a cab, and takes her
twenty blocks north to his small hotel, where the
concierge nods and the elevator sighs to a stop
on a carpeted floor.*

*Julia takes off her heels at the door to the suite
and falls into his arms, as though the plan had
always been to do so.*

*It is hours before they make love. Instead, they lie
on the bed, fully clothed, looking into each other's
eyes, caressing each other's faces. It is as though they
never knew they had a twin, another, a soul the
same as theirs. Their lips touch each other's, their
eyes hold each other's, they hold each other's
hands. They seek, finally undressing each other, to
find each other's scars. They know they are the
same—one soul, two bodies; one mind, two hearts.
They are never strangers again.*

57

I looked up to the roof of the Plaza, where thick slabs of light from industrial spotlights, housed on the bed of a semi-trailer, illuminated hotel and sky. The officer buttoned his oilskin coat against the snow and continued to speak while looking up at the fragile figure on the ledge.

"He's been out there for an hour. They're trying to talk him down."

"Take us up," Zardos said. He got out of the car and extended his hand to help Julia and me onto the curb. I didn't want to think about how familiar the figure seemed. I thought of my cousin Marty, and the terrible death he had died. Not another, I thought. Not after Renaldo.

"Yes, sir." We stumbled over our feet to keep up with the big policeman as he bounded past the crowd that had gathered around the entrance to the hotel. We made our way past ropes and ladders and a layered section of foam on top of a large net placed directly under the drop line from the window.

"Watch it! Look out!" voices shouted as equipment was wheeled into place. Fire and police trucks were parked half a dozen deep. A cherry picker, its ladder stretched into the air, was positioned at the corner of the hotel, a fireman standing in the nest like a high-flying bird, his face turned toward the ragged-looked figure teetering on the edge. A gaping audience of two or three hundred onlookers were being kept behind a rope stretched across the sidewalk from the main entrance to the hotel. Each time there was movement up above an audible gasp went up from the crowd.

"Step aside, please," the officer said to reporters and television crews hanging around the elevators.

"Who is it?" a reporter asked Zardos and Julia.

"We don't have any information, sir," the officer said. His big arm blocked the entrance, barring the reporter from joining us. He pushed the number sixteen and we rose in the glass-paneled elevator. The door opened onto a scene of controlled panic.

"Who is it?" I asked, a knot of fear playing around my stomach.

"One of those rock-and-roll singers," came the reply.

"Oh my God, Catherine." It was Malinda, running down the hall in her white velvet outfit, "after everything else that's happened, Fred's out there and he says he's going to kill himself!"

Z-Train was in the hallway behind Malinda, his face fallen, his lights dimmed. "Fred's so stoned he doesn't know what he's doing," he said, taking my hand and leading me toward a door down the hall where a dozen people were crowded in a circle. "He's out of his mind."

Max rushed from the room and practically knocked me over. "Fred is back, we found him," he said. "And now, he's in there, suicidal, threatening to jump." I nodded and he paused, taking a deep breath as Reed materialized from the suite and grabbed Julia.

"Babe, I don't know what to do," he said. He put his arms around Julia, but she didn't return the embrace and said nothing. Reed put his head in his hands. "I don't know what to say, what to do."

We moved around the cluster of uniformed police inside the room and a slight, brown-haired woman introduced herself as a social worker. There was a medic in a green cotton suit standing guard next to a stretcher outside the room.

"We tried to get near enough to sedate him," Reed told Zardos. Come in, he gestured.

Denzel was inside, not far from the window ledge, trying to talk Fred down. I tiptoed behind Zardos, and could hear Denzel's voice, quiet and soothing, coming from the bedroom. Reed took Julia's hand and led her into the room. We all moved quietly to where we could see him.

"Fred, Fred," Denzel was saying, "you're wrong, it isn't hopeless." There was no response from the ledge. The wind poured in from the wide-open window, carrying dancing snowflakes into the room. Fred was perched like a cat on the ledge. His ragged rock-and-roll garb no longer looked chic but rather pathetic, like a homeless man's rags. His legs dangled dangerously out the window, and even from across the room I could see that he was shivering. More snowflakes spun in through the window, lit from behind by the spotlights, an occasional flake making its way across the room to settle on the stuffed pillows of the couch or the pink moiré silk wallpaper, melting in tiny droplets. I felt sick.

"I can't do it, I can't get straight again," Fred said, his lips looking blue.

Denzel had pulled his own jacket close about his neck and looked terribly uncomfortable. "You know you did it before, you can do it again," Denzel said. "It's just a matter of a day, not your whole life. It's a matter of an hour. You can stay straight for an hour, right?" The sound of sobbing came from the window, a wretched sound that tore at my heart.

"I don't know." Fred's voice was small and weak

and defeated between sobs. "I don't know, I can't seem to get it together, there's no way. I'd rather die than have to live like this."

"But that's great—you don't *have* to live like this." Denzel got up off his haunches, where he had been sitting about six feet from Fred. "Let it go, Fred. You're in no shape to decide this thing now. Why don't you get some rest, then we'll talk about it."

Fred was teetering again, his narrow, bony ass rocking on the edge of the window. All of us seemed to be holding our breath in the opulent hotel room— "the crème de la crème," Max had said. There was an ebony chifforobe, its rich surface etched with gold orchards and water birds. Drapes of satin embroidered in gold and silver hung around the window, and by the double, canopied bed, covered in white lace duvet and piled with tapestry-covered feather pillows, a glass table sparkled.

The suite Stan had arranged for the Newborns was meant for a honeymoon, not a suicide. Now Stan was in jail for murder and Fred was threatening to end it all.

Denzel tiptoed across the deep-piled, honey-colored carpet to where I stood with Zardos and Julia. "I'm doing my best," he said, sipping from a glass of water Zardos offered him, "but it doesn't seem to be enough." His place by the window had been taken by Z-Train, who started to talk quietly to Fred.

"I called security as soon as he climbed up on the windowsill, and pretty soon everybody else showed up as well," Denzel said. "He's still pretty wasted. I'm hoping he'll just give up and come in. I think at this point he's just being stubborn."

Z-Train crouched on the carpet near the window. "The show didn't sound that great without you last night, Fred," Z-Train said. Fred kept his head bowed.

"It sure didn't," Malinda said. "Sahid had to sing

your parts and I did the harmonies." Malinda had slipped into the room and sat down by Z-Train. Sahid came up behind them and squatted beside them, and Reed catwalked across the carpet and joined his partner.

"We really missed you, Fred," Reed said, "and that's no bullshit. The songs just don't sound the same without you."

"I told Reed not to say that," Max whispered. "He just couldn't resist."

Fred was muttering under his breath.

In this cocaine nightmare, never say never, I told myself.

Malinda and Z-Train started singing softly, and Reed and Sahid joined them.

"That beautiful hymn, Catherine," Julia said suddenly. "It's magic!"

It truly was magic as the lyrics to "Bright Morning Star" rose from the four band members huddled on the floor in front of the window.

> *Bright morning stars are rising,*
> *bright morning stars are rising,*
> *bright morning stars are rising,*
> *day is breaking in my soul.*

As they sang softly, Malinda stood up from where she was crouched, and with the voices carrying her, she tiptoed over to the window.

Julia had been looking with fixed concentration at Fred, not speaking, just watching. Her eyes seemed, once again, to be misty, and now she joined the melody, her lilting lyric soprano reaching Fred's ears.

Fred sat on the ledge, his eyes closed, tears sliding down his cheeks.

"Sing with us, Fred," Malinda said softly.

He opened his eyes, then his lips, looked at Edward's beautiful daughter and then at Z-Train, who was nodding his dreadlocks, and at Sahid, who was smiling his most beautiful smile.

Fred looked at Julia, and a moment passed between them as Julia's voice picked up the melody. She sang with more strength, the vibrancy of the tone filling the room, and then Fred's faltering voice lifted, as though hearing Julia's had given him courage. All were singing now; the melody filled the room and spilled out into the snowy night. Reed gently swayed his head back and forth.

"Day is breaking in my soul," Fred sang, then the tears streamed down and his face collapsed into his hands. Malinda touched him, he recoiled, and then he let her put her arms around him. The other singers rose, moving slowly to the window. *"Bright morning stars are rising,"* they sang again, and embraced Fred, surrounding his body, bringing him in from the ledge. The fireman rushed to the window, closing it firmly behind Fred. The medics moved in with the stretcher while Z-Train, Malinda, Sahid, and Reed gently rocked Fred and sang on as a medic poked a needle in Fred's arm.

"I'm sorry, Reed, Malinda," Fred said, as he was lifted onto the stretcher, "Sahid, I didn't mean to threaten the group. Z-Train, can you forgive me?"

The Newborns surrounded their wounded member, closing ranks and walking Fred to the elevator.

"It's all right, man," Z-Train said, "you're gonna be all right, Fred." He gave Fred a hug, leaning over the medic to get at the reeling figure of the slight, hundred-pound singer.

"I'm so sorry, everybody," he said. "I didn't mean to cause such a fuss."

"Of course you did!" Reed said, but he was smiling and hugging Julia, who was crying, tears streaming down her face. "He's all right, Julia, what's the matter?" Reed said.

Zardos stepped up to me so that he was between the door to the suite and Julia.

"Are you ready for this?" Zardos asked softly. Julia looked up at him, her wet eyes as big as saucers. As big as I had ever seen them.

She nodded.

"What do you mean, is she ready for this?" Malinda asked. "What has Julia got to do with this?"

Julia took a deep breath and spoke.

"Fred is my son."

58

THE NIGHT AFTER SHE HAD RECEIVED HER GRAMMYS
two years before, Julia had a bit to drink and became
sorrowful and nostalgic about the birth of Fred, nineteen years before. We sat in her living room, thick
with paintings and fine fabrics, Steuben glass, and
deep, velvet-covered couches. She drank wine out of
a crystal glass and described blood and tissue and
screams, thirty hours of pushing and cursing and fighting the stirrups, the nurse's attempts to get Julia up,
then down, walking in the corridor of a green-walled
hospital, filled with shame because the pain she was
feeling was not her own, not the pain of a baby who
would be coming home with her, but the pain of a
child she had promised to give up for adoption as soon
as he poked his head out of her body.

She told me of the agony not only physical but emotional, soul pain, searing her flesh as the dilation took
over her muscles, her heart, her mind, her spirit. Her
soul was dilating like her vagina.

The baby pushed into the world like a bar of soap
out into a world not his own, into a void where Julia
would not be able to find him again once they had

slapped breath into his body—once he had screamed and opened his eyes to the world, once he had held her finger and been bundled off in swaddling to another room where another mother waited, her arms open, her body and breasts, vagina and nipples, lips and mind and soul intact.

Julia told me the pain of her soul was bigger than her physical pain.

The next birth, when she was older, wiser, better, different, successful, matured, sensible, caring, knowing, guilty, thoughtful, and married, was painless and pure, she said. It was wanted and celebrated and sealed with a vow, a triumph of conventional wisdom, private schools, clothes from the Gap and Hannah Anderson, politically correct toys, trips to the Museum of Natural History, summer camps and dental appointments, sleep-over dates and pre-k, clay modeling and ballet lessons, down parkas and lunch boxes with Juicy Juice and chocolate bars for treats.

Julia told me that night, drunk on expensive champagne, that the first birth, the wrenching thirty-hour ordeal, the baby born big and beautiful with a look that nailed his mother to the wall in the instant they looked into each other's eyes, had taken a toll she had never known she would pay. Had she known, she said, she would have grabbed the baby from the arms of the doctor, his mouth curled in contempt, and run into the streets, into the traffic, down the corridors of her single, agonized, blessed life.

59

"You never told us your real mother was alive," Malinda said.

"I was trying to find my mother for a long time, because I felt she must be alive," Fred said, somewhat incoherently, holding onto Julia's hand, looking into her eyes. The long IV tube was in his arm, and his face was still very pale. "Then this letter came from my adoptive parents, telling me I was right. That my mother was alive." He looked up sheepishly. "I think it sort of pushed me over the edge. I mean, it was so emotional and all."

I embraced Julia and told her I was happy for her. "It must be such a relief," I said. "You've been looking for 'the kid' for years."

"Yes," Julia said. Fred, on the stretcher, couldn't take his eyes off Julia. "He can't want to take his own life," she said.

"How did you find me?" Fred kept saying, his voice shaking.

"The agency called two days ago. This woman helped me," Julia said, taking the hand of the middle-aged social worker who had quietly hovered near Julia since our arrival at the Plaza.

"I'm the investigator Julia hired to find her son,"

she said. "This one came out all right!" she said. "They don't all come out this way, believe me."

"Maybe this will be the answer I've been looking for," Reed said softly, holding Julia's hand as the elevator doors opened.

"I've told Jenny everything," Julia said. "You have a sister, Fred—well, a half-sister." She smiled at the shaken Newborn on the stretcher. "She is thrilled, of course, to have an older brother. And now that I have found you, I must say, I am terribly frightened." She looked at Fred intently. "Do you hate me?" She looked worried. "I mean, for abandoning you? Is that why you tried to kill yourself?"

Fred's only answer was the tears that fell down his cheeks. He reached up from the stretcher, embracing Julia tightly.

I excused myself, saying I had to get home. Zardos offered to take me home in a police car, and I told him that sounded appropriate after all that had happened.

We rode uptown through the park. It was late, there was no traffic. Ours were the rare tracks in the snow on the roadway. A deep blanket covered the trees and the merry-go-round, the lampposts with their old-fashioned lights cupped in lead, the white and iced surfaces of the ponds. The late-winter storm had eased and a few hesitant flakes made their way toward the layers of marshmallow-like topping that covered the park and the streets of New York. From every surface sparkled diamonds of light, glinting winter's promise under the lamplights of gold.

At my apartment Zardos and I shook the last snowflakes out of our hair. Blue bounded out of the kitchen into the foyer and rubbed up against our legs, responding to Zardos as though he had always known him and making both his joy at my return and his disdain at being abandoned clear in one loud meow. I clamped my teeth together, desperate for a cigarette. I knew it was hopeless to reach into my purse and fumble through it in search of Pall Malls. There were none.

No more smoking in tough times, or in good times; no more smoking, period.

But my heart is just warming up, I thought. I took off my coat and Zardos took off his jacket and we dropped them in a chair by the front door; then I led the way into the living room, lighting the stained-glass lamps as I went.

Zardos sat in a chair by the window, and I sat, a short distance away, on the couch under Julia's sexy, multicolored painting.

"I'm exhausted," he said. "It's hell being an older man."

"I think you look young," I said. I leaned my head back. "For a person with your experience." He smiled at me.

"Ditto," he said. "I am so sorry about Renaldo." He paused, then reached over to put his hand in mine. "We should get some sleep." I sank deeper into the cushioned folds of the couch. In the chair opposite me, his long muscular legs stretched out until our knees were practically touching. Blue rubbed against Zardos's legs, meowing at him as though he'd found a long-lost friend.

"You know," I said, "life isn't fair. Renaldo was so innocent and so young. Stan should hang for what he's done."

"No, but I think I can promise you that Stan will go away for a long time, Catherine," he said. "Nothing will make up for Renaldo's death, but then, you knew all along that life wasn't fair." He stood and stretched his long legs. "I have to be going," he said, and even as he spoke of leaving, lowered himself onto the couch beside me. Then he reached across me to turn the light down. I dropped my head back against his shoulder, and Blue, sensing a comfort zone, leapt up on Zardos's lap. Zardos leaned over to pet the purring cat and his dark hair brushed my forehead, then my nose, then the top of my lip, then my lips, until his mouth was on mine, and Blue was purring between us and I let my lips open.

My fingers found Zardos's fingers in the darkness, my breasts reached up to his chest; my face was touching his shirt, where I could hear his heart beating—a flawed heart, he had said. His skin was satiny smooth and his breath was sweet, and the feel of his palm running over the skin on my shoulder, his hand on the silk of my blouse as he held me near him was soft and ancient, new and supple in the right places, hard in the right places.

Zardos pulled away and stood up. The cat dropped onto the floor on all fours, and Zardos stood above me. I realized I was holding my breath.

"Your heart sounds perfect to me, Zardos," I whispered. He leaned over and kissed me again on the lips, tenderly, quickly, promisingly.

"It's all yours, Catherine, if you want it." He pulled away, straightened up, and smoothed his dark, shining hair.

"We've just met," I said, yet knowing I'd always known him.

"When this is over, we can do something about it," Zardos said, hesitating, that Sam Shepard sound in his voice. "Or not. It's up to you." He moved toward the living room door.

"You remind me of St. Augustine, Zardos. 'Oh lord, make me chaste, but not yet, not yet.' Good night," I said, almost whispering.

"Good night, Catherine," he said. "Sleep tight."

As the door closed and I locked it behind my detective, I knew my life would never be the same.

Now *I* was shameless.

60

"Breathe, Catherine, breathe, I have you. Breathe!"

Someone is struggling to bring me back from a long distance, and I am looking down into the room. I see him bending over me; my own body is lying unconscious on the floor. He seems familiar. There is glass everywhere on the floor, and further away, by the window, Edward Valarian, his arms tied up behind him, lies unconscious on the floor. I suddenly remember hands on my throat and a last choking off of air before I blacked out. Now the familiar stranger holds me in his arms, and his lips find mine once more.

"Catherine." Zardos's voice is calling me. "Come back to me! Breathe, please," he whispers, forcing breath into me over and over, in and out, until my own lungs and body respond, and I am breathing, in and out, in and out, until I am breathing on my own and his lips are on mine.

I gasp, catching my breath between the kisses.

"Catherine," Zardos's voice sings, "you're all right now. I have you now. We have each other now."

I put my arms around his neck and bury my face in his chest, breathing in and out, realizing it is a dream—and what a relief it is to come all this way and find that the dream has come true.

61

Stan was in jail awaiting trial on charges of murder, attempted murder, forgery, and bribery.

Edward was charged with bank fraud and would go to trial separately.

Hank was under arrest for his role as an accessory to attempted murder.

I organized a memorial service for Renaldo in the chapel at Sacred Heart School. It was attended by his parents and many of my friends. It was also attended by the man whose name on Renaldo's résumé had surprised me so, the man I suspected all along of being involved, the one who proved totally innocent, in this case. Wheeling came, accompanying Ellen. He and I didn't speak, though we did nod grimly to each other over the white roses.

The money Stan had stolen from me was being tracked down by the feds, who had been called in by my banker, Mr. Groden. In any case, my account was insured against fraud.

Ellen filed for divorce; the papers reached Stan in jail. She testified before the grand jury that Stan had forged my name on the bank slips, and that she had seen Hank rig the scaffolding at the Meadowlands.

Witnesses identified Stan as the man who pushed Renaldo; there were also witnesses at the hospital who identified Stan as the person who posed as the flower delivery man. The gold pen with Stan's initials on it had his prints all over it as well, and would help prove that he had murdered Renaldo.

Wheeling appeared with Ellen once more, this time to testify against Stan, to confirm that he had seen Stan shake the lighting rig in order to push me off the scaffolding. After the grand jury hearing, Wheeling approached me, sleazy but on his best behavior, wanting to talk. I chose not to speak to him.

Fred was in a rehab in Florida, getting sober. He and Julia had a tearful, happy reunion during his detox. According to the people at the treatment center, Julia's reunion with Fred was very important to his recovery. Julia and Jenny went to family week at the drug and alcohol center, and helped convince Fred's adoptive family to attend.

Jenny was thrilled to have a half-brother, especially a rock-and-roll star. She was quite sure that now that he had his birth family as well as his adopted family, Fred wouldn't have to take drugs anymore.

Though skeptical as always, I didn't rain on Jenny and Julia's parade. Things might, after all, work out just fine.

With my usual warped sense of humor, I said I thought that it might be a good idea for Julia and Reed to adopt Fred. Neither of them thought it was very funny.

Julia, in fact, feeling a bit reluctant and uncomfortable about having a son the same age as her lover, told Reed that although she thought she loved him, she wanted time to think the relationship over. Reed told her that was all right, he would wait for her. He wasn't going to go away.

I hired a new lawyer.

Zardos and I finally made love.

It was wonderful.

62
〜

Radio City Music Hall was jammed to capacity the night of the Grammys. I was celebrating the Newborns, I was celebrating my friends, I was celebrating being alive.

"You were born for black tie, Detective," Reed said, looking at a tuxedo-clad Zardos, the handsomest man in the star-studded hall.

"I was born to retire and become a groupie," Zardos said with lovely irony, laughing and looking over the crowd. "I'm sure that in this illustrious group I could easily find a way to ply my trades of music fan and expert sleuth."

"I think I'm giving up sleuthing for rock and roll," Jethro said. At the last minute I had been able to come up with an extra ticket for him. Somewhere he had managed to find a tuxedo imprinted with the same stains and wrinkles that were on every other piece of clothing he owned.

The Newborns minus Fred had already gone up to collect nine Grammys by the time the album-of-the-year nominees were announced.

The contenders for the best albums in jazz and New Age, the best singer-songwriter, and the best male and female pop writers were named. Sting was given a Grammy Lifetime Achievement Award. Leonard

Cohen and Glenn Frey were named best male performers, and Cher received an award for best song in a film.

Julia got her Grammy for the single "Melody," and when she sang it, the crowd gave her a five-minute standing ovation. She announced again that it was the last time she would perform. I said, "Sure, Julia," and took more pictures of my beautiful friend.

"And in the category of best rock-and-roll album of the year, the winner is . . ." There was a pause as Whitney Houston, dressed in a black sequined headband and skintight black silk running outfit, struggled with the envelope. Billy Crystal stood next to her, smiling at the audience with benign amusement as the tall beauty struggled. Finally, Crystal took the envelope gently from her hand.

"Here, darling," Crystal said, "let me. I know it must be hard to give this award away to somebody else after getting it yourself for so many years, but that's show business." He tore the envelope open and spoke immediately to the camera, so you knew he already knew the answer.

"The winner is the Newborns—for *Birth Canal.*"

Screams broke out in our aisles of the Radio City Music Hall's six-thousand-seat auditorium, and the rest of the glittering, star-studded audience went wild again for the newest and hottest band of the era.

Malinda was all in silver lamé that clung to each curve and bone in her thin, tall body, her blond curls glittering, reminding you of a beautiful silver angel. Silver glints danced on her face as she smiled and smiled, a star, a beauty, a healthy, lovely woman who richly deserved the awards she was getting. The visual contrast between Malinda and Z-Train was so striking that it took your breath away, she all silver and gold and gleaming and he all shining and smooth and beautifully black.

Z-Train wore diamond studs in his black dreadlocks, a wide smile on his face that showed all thirty-eight of his teeth. He was dressed in a long, flowing African robe laced with silver and gold hoops in great, long ropes; hanging on the silver hoops were clumps of turquoise, garnets, and amethysts, all shining together in a tapestry of color. Charms, cures, poems written on black ebony tablets the size of your thumb, prayers in tiny scrolls made of precious metals: Z-Train told me he had worn all the jewelry he owned, for good luck—for Fred and for the group.

It had worked.

"I can't believe it," Sahid said as he leaned over into my aisle and kissed me on the lips with his red mouth.

"Congratulations," Zardos said as the young artists moved down the aisle past our seats.

Julia watched the Newborns with a mixture of motherly and not-so-motherly love as they mounted the long staircase to the podium. Julia had immortalized Reed in oils—purple arms, blue legs, green hair, orange penis, and a bronze smile—but now that she had found her son, Fred, and Fred was in the group, there would be no more nude portraits of Reed.

The mixed image of Julia as mother, den mother, and object of sexual desire for Reed seemed perfectly natural to all concerned, yet Julia had been reluctant to go to the festivities until Reed promised her he wouldn't be romantic in public until they figured out what was really going on with them—love or lust.

People, Life, Spin, Rolling Stone, and *Newsweek* had asked me to shoot the evening, but I was here as a fan, not as a photographer. I had a good, small, long-distance lens and my Leica in a velvet evening bag with me. I slipped out of my seat, and crouching in front of the stage, I got shots of the boys and Malinda accepting their awards. These pictures were not for publication; they were a tribute to the kids whose careers had rocketed during the most terrible time of my life.

Fred had asked Denzel to read the note he had written. "I can't be in two places at once, so I'm going to stay here, where I'm supposed to be," the note read. "I'll be back, just you wait."

Next came Reed. "We want to thank Vertigo Records," he said into the microphone. "And we want to send our condolences to the family of Renaldo Pierce, who was a victim of greed." There was an audible sigh in the packed auditorium. "We also want to say something about our agent, Stan Shultz." A murmur ran through the crowd. The papers had been full of Stan's exploits—the murder charge and his attempts on my life. Reed paused. "We don't want to have anyone break the law in order for us to be a success. We want to succeed on our own merits."

The crowd cheered.

"I want to thank my father and my mother," Sahid said. "And Catherine for taking such beautiful pictures."

"I want to thank God," Malinda said, "for getting us out of the jam we were in when Fred got sick again; and everyone at GTO; and Catherine for nearly getting herself killed at our concert taking pictures of us." Malinda's eyes shone, as though she were crying. "I'd like to thank my father and my mother and tell them that I love them very much, in spite of everything. And," she went on, "I want to thank Julia Clearwater."

Heads turned in the audience to look at Julia in her pearls and low-cut purple silk dress. She looked twenty and took in the appreciation, smiling back at Malinda.

"I want to thank Fred," Malinda went on, "for returning from the dead and going into treatment. And

I want to congratulate Julia and Fred on being re-united." Malinda paused, taking in the silent expecta-tion of the crowd. Julia and Fred had agreed to Malinda's public announcement. "As mother and son."

This time the room went wild and reporters could be seen running for telephones or using their cellular phones if they were sitting in the middle of a row where they couldn't get out. I saw Fran from *ET* in the back of the auditorium, her back to the stage, talking into the camera. Fran, always there at the right time, had another scoop.

Grammy statues in hand, the four Newborns plus Denzel followed Whitney Houston and Billy Crystal offstage. After fifteen minutes or so, during which I knew the group was being photographed with their trophies, they rejoined us.

The ceremony was over and all of us got our coats and entered the swarm of stars and civilians pouring out onto the street from Radio City. A red carpet stretched along the sidewalk in front of the theater up Sixth Avenue, and New York City cops were out in all their glory, shepherding the Grammy crowd to the 21 Club, the Pierre, the Rainbow Room, the Hilton, La Côte Basque—all of which were hosting Grammy parties that night.

Detectives in plainclothes kept coming up to Zardos and saying hello, asking to be introduced to me, Julia, and the Newborns.

Zardos was good-natured about it all. We headed across the street into Rockefeller Center and up the crowded elevators to the Rainbow Room for the Ver-tigo Records reception.

The maître d' took us to the biggest table in the room on the mezzanine, signaling to waiters to serve us champagne and hors d'oeuvres.

Strobes flashed as the stars arrived in droves, making their way past the velvet cables and the bodyguards. Madonna, Linda Ronstadt, Elizabeth Taylor, Michael Bolton, Kevin Costner, Michelle Pfeiffer, Liza Minnelli—all came up and congratulated the Newborns.

Over glasses of Perrier, Julia and I talked about Edward. "I left myself open for it," I said. "If I had never asked Edward to invest my money, we might still be together."

"And that would be terrible!" my friend said. "It wasn't meant."

A crowd of A&R men in black tuxedos swooped down on Z-Train and Sahid and began talking loudly about new material for their next record. I love the music business, where all hours were business hours.

Julia and Reed sat together, not too close, but their eyes kept finding each other's. Good luck, I thought, pursuing a platonic friendship.

Sahid stretched his elegant hand across the table, proffering a fresh blue pack of Gauloises. "Cigarette, Catherine?" he said.

"I don't smoke anymore," I said. Sahid continued to puff energetically, his dark, sexy eyes wandering over my face and body just as if we were in a room alone together, just as if I weren't sitting with Zardos, practically in his lap. "I smoked with a vengeance, and I quit with a vengeance," I said. Or maybe the goddess had done for me what I couldn't do for myself.

It was late and I found myself yawning. The Newborns looked weary, stardom and life having taken their toll. The ballroom was beginning to clear out. I stood up to leave.

"You can't go," Z-Train said. "The night is young!"

"Watch me," I said and Reed pulled out something he had been carrying around all night—a narrow, mangled-looking package tied with a red ribbon.

"This is for you, Catherine." I tore the ribbon and wrapping off and held out a framed platinum CD inscribed: *To Catherine, Our Bright Morning Star.*

Truly touched by their affectionate gesture, I grinned and gave Reed a hug.

"I'll just hang that up in the office," I said. "It will look great on the wall next to the pictures of you guys at the Grammys tonight."

Zardos looked across at me, watching me put my silk shawl around my shoulders and wrapping the CD back in its tissue paper. I looked from his handsome face to the crowded dance floor, past the glitz, the paparazzi, the famous, and the near-famous.

After all the trouble, after the tragic loss of Renaldo, after all the storms of the past weeks, I was exhausted.

And I couldn't wait to get my handsome detective alone.

Julia gave me a wink from across the table, leaning over to whisper in my ear.

"You see," she said, giving me a smile and glancing over at the handsome detective, "even the devil works for God."

63

On a late September afternoon that year, Zardos and I took the narrow-gauge railway from Silver Plume to Durango, Colorado. The aspens were beginning to turn, the Sangre de Cristo Mountains across the valley were purple and jagged, their peaks dusted in white, their shadowed pockets filled with gold and draped at their sides like the saddlebags of long-dead miners, laden with treasure. The narrow-gauge clipped through the dense pines and threaded along the top sides of the steep canyon where, looking a mile into the deep ravine, you could see a silver wire at the bottom, the shining, narrow ribbon of water headed for its rendezvous with the Colorado River some thousand miles and three states downstream.

Watching the mountains go by from the windows of our miniature stateroom in the wheeled carriage behind the elegant, fierce engine, I would have said it was the altitude that was making me light-headed—but I had been feeling that way for months.

Zardos had taken a leave from the police department that was so long it looked like early retirement. Everyone congratulated him on his marriage, on getting away from the rat race, and on starting a sleuth-and-photography business. I promised to send Julia shots of the Grand Canyon. She had mentioned doing landscapes—or, I suspected, painting Reed, Fred, and the rest of the Newborns in western landscapes. Clothed.

I took one Leica and enough luggage for half a year. I told Edna to finish the work on the articles that were due and not to expect me back until the snow fell.

On the way west we stopped in Moline and I introduced Zardos to my brother, Ben. Ben was enjoying running the ranch and he was doing a great job of it. My mother consoled me about Renaldo's death. Buster was getting around pretty well by now, and he welcomed me and Zardos.

Then Mother took one good look at Zardos, smiled at me, and said, "What took you so long, honey?"

Over a late cup of coffee in the same kitchen I had fled to when I caught my father with Lou-Lou, I took Mother aside and asked her about Buster's affairs. Her soft face wrinkled in all the places that didn't wrinkle, and she said, "I knew all that, Catherine. But I am the prize in Buster Saint's life. He knows it and I know it."

I looked out the kitchen window across the prairies, where my father had ridden his horses and run his cattle. I thought about the bulls, the coyotes, the snake, the horse, and the power I had learned I owned.

Zardos and I traveled on to Wyoming and I took him to my old haunts; we visited Miss Carolyn's grave and went to the music school in Jackson Hole where we spoke to students of Mr. Christian who were in their seventies. In the Ford Explorer, with a thermos of good coffee and a dozen buttery homemade oatmeal-raisin cookies, we drove to the top of the Continental Divide and looked across the emerald, lake-studded green and golden landscape of pines and aspens. We wrapped ourselves in parkas against the freezing air that blew in with thunderheads towering above Grand Teton's shining summits.

Zardos knew the names of all the peaks and all the valleys. He had studied them in his youth in New York, waiting for that moment when he knew he would come west to find his heart.

64

I dreamed we hiked into Emerald Lake Canyon to
fish in a glade deep with ferns and green nettles,
where the river comes down like a splashing jewel
from the spruce and Douglas trees above. There
were a thousand shining trout, long and spangled;
we could see them through the mist that hung
above the water. Our hand-tied flies touched upon
the silver surface gently before the fish hit them,
open-mouthed, and we must have pulled out twenty
in an hour.

We lay back in the tall, dew-covered ferns after
we cleaned and hooked the dappled trout on the
branch points of a sapling half a yard long, and
cooked the amethyst- and rust-spotted fish over
the fire that burned in the last light of the afternoon,
talking of how they would taste as they sizzled in
the frying pan, bubbling gently in the butter we had
brought in, creamery butter bars squashed by the
fresh fruit in our packs, smelling faintly of honey.

In the remaining light of the day the fire shone
pale as though building its courage for the coming night.

I thought of living here forever, far from busy
streets and busy tongues, living in a simple manner, blackening trout in the heating pan upon the

flame, alongside the flowing water, in the fern-clad glade in the mystic mountains. My brother and my father, my mother and my lovers of the past gathered in the twilight, in the comfort of the silence. I recognized their faces, lighted by the pale twist of flame that glowed through the still lingering daylight.

Dusk came down from the peaks, softly closing over the aspens and the blue spruce. A single shining fish leapt out of the water in a rainbow arc, splashing diamonds and sapphires into the air.

As the moon came up between the ridge and the river, the trout's silver body disappeared back into the water like smoke, wispy and fine, back into the river as it moved down the mountain and curled off into the rose-hued twilight.